TO MARJORIE.
Love -
Samantha Green.

Samantha Green

JANUS PUBLISHING COMPANY
London, England

First published in Great Britain 1993
by Janus Publishing Company

Copyright © Samantha Green 1993

British Library Cataloguing-in-Publication Data.
A catalogue record for this book is available from the British Library.

ISBN 1 85756 023 X

All rights reserved. No part of this publication may be reproduced, stored in a retrieval system or transmitted in any form or by any means, electronic, mechanical, photocopying, recording or otherwise, without the prior permission of the publisher.

Cover design David Murphy

Printed & bound in England by
Antony Rowe Ltd, Chippenham, Wiltshire

The characters and situations in this book are entirely imaginary and bear no relation to any real person or actual happening.

Chapter 1

After Tina's christening, her grandmother Jennifer revealed the dream in which Nancy had appeared to her. In the dream, Nancy, her own grandmother, told Jennifer that Tina had inherited the unfortunate condition that ran in the family and would have a lot more problems than either she herself or Jennifer had had. The whole family had listened in amazement, feeling sad and worried; wondering what would happen to Tina, what Tina's life would be like. They had all promised to take care of her and love her, knowing how much support she would need. This is the story of Tina.

It was Christmas. They all enjoyed the festivities at the big house. Millie enjoyed looking after her new baby, Tina, and Jennifer loved helping her.

Tina proved to be a very difficult baby. She cried a lot and had tantrums, but Millie was very patient and so were the rest of the family, including Jennifer, her loving and loyal husband Derek and her mother, Dorothy – Tina's great-grandmother. Tina couldn't have wished for a better family to take care of her in that big house. She could want for nothing and love was showered around her. But, unlike Nancy and Jennifer, Tina could not respond to that love. Even when Tina was a baby, her mother Millie noticed it and felt very sad.

'You know she seems so distant,' said Millie one day to Derek.

'I know,' said her father, 'I've noticed that.' Derek, a clever and qualified psychologist working at Forest Dene Hospital, had noticed already that Tina just couldn't seem to respond or give love, even as a baby.

At two years old, Tina was getting more and more difficult. Life up at the big house wasn't as easy as the family had thought it would be when Tina was born. 'She is so difficult,' said Dorothy one evening to Derek and Millie. They were all sitting on the settee in that beautiful big lounge, looking out at those mystical woods that they always looked at when they had a family conference. Jennifer was sitting in the chair in the corner. Tina was now tucked up in bed, after a long hard struggle. She was always very difficult about going to bed, screaming and crying and having tantrums. Jennifer had had her problems at night, years before, but that had easily been resolved by her dog, Colonel. The dog had been a comforter to her and the problem was over. Jennifer as a child always went to sleep with him by her side, but no dog could console Tina. Jennifer tried that, hoping that Tina would be, like herself, comforted by the dog. She took her King Charles spaniel, Bill, into the room, and Trixie the corgi, but it made no difference.

'We'll have to take her to a doctor,' said Dorothy. 'Let's call Dr. Margaret and ask her to come over and have a talk.'

Dorothy went and phoned Dr. Margaret. 'Please come over. Tina's getting worse. We don't know what to do.'

'I've told you before,' said Dr. Margaret. 'She'll have to come into hospital and have some tests.'

'She's very young for that,' said Dorothy.

'I know,' said Dr. Margaret. 'But you can't go on like this. She's so very difficult.'

'Millie's going to have a breakdown if this goes on. She's a very sensitive girl.'

'That's what worries me,' said Dr. Margaret. 'We'll have to do something about Tina. Very well, I'll come over tomorrow night.'

And so the next evening a meeting was held in the lounge, as so many meetings had been held before: family meetings, with the psychiatrist present. Sandy, Dr. Margaret's friend and colleague, came with her and they talked and talked until halfway through the night.

'She must come into hospital,' said Dr. Margaret to Millie. 'You look tired out.'

'I am,' said Millie. 'In spite of help from the staff. I'm worn out.'

'Very well, we'll get her in tomorrow for some tests and then you'll have a little break.'

'Thank you,' said Millie. 'What worries me,' she said, with tears in her eyes, 'is the fact that she won't accept our love.'

'Don't worry,' said Dr. Margaret. 'We'll do something for her, I promise.'

The next day Tina was taken to the general hospital for some tests. They found nothing physically wrong with her and some brain tests were done. It was very early for Tina to have these tests but they had to be done in view of the situation. Dr. Margaret and Dr. Williams, the neurologist, discussed the results.

'She's got very irregular brain patterns,' said Dr. Williams. 'There's something wrong.'

'It looks to me like epilepsy,' said Dr. Margaret.

'She hasn't had any fits.'

'Well, we'll just have to wait and see as time goes on. But what are we going to do in the meantime?'

'I don't know,' said Dr. Williams. 'I just don't know.'

'The family are at their wits' end,' said Dr. Margaret. 'Perhaps she should go into a home. Just for a little while anyway.'

'Well, we'll talk to them about it.'

And so next day Dr. Williams and Dr. Margaret talked to Derek and Millie who had come to see them at the hospital about Tina. Dr. Williams explained about the irregular brain patterns.

'She's very young for her age. Mentally she's not too backward, just the same as Jennifer and Nancy, but she's got more problems and we don't know how it will develop. How would you feel if she went into a home where she could be looked after?'

'Oh, I couldn't bear that,' said Millie. 'I just couldn't.'

'I know,' said Dr. Margaret, 'but couldn't she come in for a little while, just to give you a break: three months, say. Then if she improves she could come home. You could even have her at weekends if you like.'

'Well, I am very tired,' said Millie, 'and I haven't been able to go back to my job, which I wanted to do. I couldn't leave her in the charge of the new housekeeper, Joan, who's been so good looking after her. I just couldn't.'

'I know,' said Dr. Margaret. 'It's very difficult. Would you agree then? She can be transferred straight from here.'

'Very well,' said Millie. 'I can't cope and I never thought I'd say that. I'm so sad but I'll go back to work and try and take my mind off it and have her at weekends.'

'Well,' said Dr. Williams, 'there's a nice little place called Greenacres, not too far from Forest Dene Hospital. It's for very difficult children and they are very happy there. Tina will be the youngest, you know.'

'It's very sad,' said Millie, with tears in her eyes. 'I never thought my little girl would come to this. Oh dear! She's far worse than Nancy and Jennifer!'

Dr. Margaret put her arm round her to comfort her. 'Don't worry. We'll win through, you'll see.'

Tina was admitted first of all to the general hospital for a routine assessment. It was a heart-breaking moment for all of them. Millie and Derek accompanied her, with Dr. Margaret, and Millie cried when they had to leave her. Tina screamed and sobbed but Dr. Margaret assured them that she would settle down, so Millie left her baby girl in the ward and went with Derek and Dr. Margaret to talk to the doctors.

After they had talked, Millie and Derek went up with Dr. Margaret to the little room where they had put Tina alone. Now she was quiet. The poor little child had been given tranquillisers at two years old and was now sleeping peacefully.

With tears in their eyes they bent over and kissed her. Tina did not wake.

'At least she's having some peace with the tablets,' said Millie 'and the doctors know what they're about.'

They went home and talked at some length; Dr. Margaret going with them. She had supper at the big house and then left them all very distressed, thinking about Tina in that hospital; knowing that the next day she was to be moved to a special home near Forest Dene Hospital. Dr. Margaret knew from her knowledge and experience, how difficult things were going to be for Tina.

The next day Derek, Jennifer, who insisted on coming, and Millie went along to the hospital and met Dr. Margaret. They all went quietly in the car with Tina, who was very quiet for she was sedated with a very small dose of an anti-convulsant to calm her down. She snuggled into Millie's arms as they drove to the hospital, and looked up with her big, pathetic, blue eyes. Millie looked down at that little face. 'How normal!' she reflected aloud. 'How normal she looks!'

'I know,' said Dr. Margaret. 'You wouldn't think she had anything wrong with her to look at her.'

'Her eyes go wild though at times,' said Millie, 'when she gets in those tantrums.'

So Tina was taken to Greenacres, the little home where she was to be for a short while. Tina settled in. It did not seem to worry her, being apart from her family, for she was just too distant to give out love to them. The family had her at home at weekends to start with but Tina was not going to be any easier. She didn't seem to want to come home. She was much quieter for she was on medication but it did not make her less difficult and she remained withdrawn, pulling herself away very violently if anybody kissed her or put their arms around her.

Tina did not come home after three months. She stayed at Greenacres. It was the only way, the doctors had said.

Chapter 2

Millie started back to work and two years passed. Tina was still at Greenacres. Millie was going out with a young man.

One night the family were sitting in the lounge talking. Millie was out with her new boyfriend, Raymond.

'I hope she'll marry him,' said Jennifer. 'It will make her so happy: like I'm happy with you, Derek.' Jennifer still sounded so childish and so loving.

Julian, Jennifer's cousin, and Georgina, his wife, spent a lot of time walking in the woods. They worked together at the riding stables. They were in their fifties and still very happily married but, living at the big house, they couldn't help being sad about Tina. It reflected upon them all.

When Tina was six Millie married Raymond but little Tina was not fit to come to her mother's wedding: she had to stay at Greenacres. The preparations were made for the wedding which was to be held by the Reverend Moss at the little village church. He was a very kind man, knew all about the problems of the big house and tried to console the family when he saw them.

'We always pray for Tina,' he said. 'We always will. I'm sure things will turn out right in the end.'

The night before the wedding Millie and Raymond went for a walk in the woods.

'Do you know,' said Millie. 'These woods have been so romantic, and meant such a lot to my family. I wonder if Tina will ever be well enough to fall in love and walk here?'

'I hope so,' said Raymond who was very kind and understanding, and who had promised faithfully he would be as a father to Tina and would adopt her as his own. He really adored Millie.

'You know, I'd like to have one more child, and take a chance on it, Raymond.'

'Of course you shall, for whatever the child is like we'll take care of him or her.'

'Yes,' said Millie, with tears in her eyes 'but I hope I could have a normal child.'

'I'm sure you will. It doesn't happen every time.'

'No, thank goodness,' said Millie. 'I'm sure it will be a normal child. I'm getting older now, Raymond. Can we try straight away as soon as we're married?'

'Of course,' said Raymond. 'It will do you good, that honeymoon we're taking.' They were going to Spain for two weeks and were looking forward to a real break.

Raymond had met Millie at the pathology laboratory where she worked in Guildford. He was also a pathologist, so they had much in common. They were to live at the big house and the family knew that Raymond would fit in there. Everyone liked him, including Jennifer. He seemed just right for Millie.

There was hustle and bustle everywhere. On the day of the wedding, a typical spring day in May, the flowers were in full bloom at the big house, in full bloom everywhere, and the woods looked verdant and beautiful. 'What a wonderful day for the wedding,' said Jennifer to Derek when they awoke. 'She's going to look beautiful in that white dress.' Jennifer was much more mature these days, but she still had the charm of a young girl and Derek loved her for it. Jennifer still liked to dress in a very youthful style, still had to take her little pills and tranquillisers and was rather on the plump side, but even in her mid-fifties she was still very graceful and looked much younger than she was. Derek adored his wife and Jennifer adored Derek.

They had both been adopted, many years before, by the same people and now had found their way back to the big house where they belonged; where their true families were. They had grown up together and, later on, fallen in love. It was a bizarre chain of events, but they were happier for it, with their shared childhood memories to bond them closer together.

Their close friends Georgina and Julian were also contented. Georgina had been Jennifer's best friend at school and had met Julian at the big house when on a visit with Jennifer. They had been happy for years.

Now the caterers were arriving to prepare the big spread for the wedding feast. The house was decorated, the band was to come and play music. There was to be a disco for the young ones. Everything was cleared away. Jennifer looked very pretty in her outfit; still liking to dress in a very young way. She wore a very pretty long blue skirt and matching top, more formal than her favourite jeans, and hoped that people wouldn't automatically label her as the bride's mother. Jennifer did not like people to think that, for she liked to feel that Millie was her sister. With her little gold earrings and her tousled dark hair which was now greying, cut short as always, she looked lovely.

Millie, though, was the centre of attention: stunning in her white flowing gown bedecked with frills and flounces, for she liked frills on the right occasion. This dress was lavish with lace and luxurious silk. She wore a matching veil and carried a bouquet of delicate jonquils. Looking at the little village girls dressed as her bridesmaids, she was only sad that her little girl Tina could not be there.

They all got into the cars and off they went to the village church. Many weddings had taken place from that big house, at that little village church, many christenings and many funerals, but now, on this sunny May day, it was Millie's wedding day. The church was full to the brim. People loved them in the village: everyone at the big house was loved, and pitied, especially now they knew about Tina. It was a very happy place indeed, that little village in Surrey, surrounded by beautiful countryside and trees. The little church was attractive – small and very old – and in the old-fashioned churchyard there were the gravestones of Tina's forebears from the big house.

Now this happy day had come. Millie walked up the aisle to meet Raymond, the one she loved and was to marry. The Reverend Moss conducted the wedding service. Millie looked at Raymond with love in her eyes which filled with tears as she thought back on the past. So many weddings had taken place here. She knew about them: Jennifer's wedding, Georgina's and even, many years before, Nancy's wedding to Gordon, where it had all begun; the romantic young ones at the big house. Now Millie was getting married and hoping that she would be able to have another child. This much she knew: she would never let her daughter Tina, her firstborn, down. If only she could have been here, she thought tearfully. She hoped Tina would be all right in the end.

Raymond sensed Millie's thoughts and squeezed her hand. 'Don't worry,' he whispered. 'I understand. All will be well.'

Millie smiled a watery smile at him. 'I love you,' she whispered. 'I love you too.'

The service was simple and extremely moving; there wasn't a dry eye in that church. All of them knew Millie and loved her and felt such pity for her because of Tina. Everyone was so happy that Millie was at last getting married. She would still be able to have another child by the man she loved, Raymond.

When the wedding was over, everyone came back to the big house in the cars; even the Rev. Moss, his wife and two sons. He was a young man and, with his wife and young family, was well liked in the village: they had always been kind to the young ones at the big house.

The reception was beautiful, with a magnificent buffet. People circulated, looking all over the big house, which was massive and breathtaking with the portraits hanging everywhere. In pride of place was the portrait of Nancy, the beautiful girl with the big blue eyes and long blonde hair, in the hall. Next to her was the portrait of her husband Gordon, who she had met in the woods and who was, like her, young for his age. Then there was a portrait of Hayley, Nancy's daughter, who had loved her child-mother so much she had been obsessed by her until death. There were portraits of the people who had lived at the big house before them. Bert and Mabel, Gordon's parents, Helen and Philip, Nancy's parents, and many more besides.

After the buffet and speeches were over people danced outside to the music. It was a very romantic affair indeed. Millie was blissfully happy. Everyone had drunk champagne and Millie had now forgotten her troubles for a while. All she was aware of was her love for Raymond. That night they were to travel to London, to the airport, and stay at a hotel before they flew on to Spain in the morning.

Millie went upstairs to get changed and came down the spiral staircase, all eyes upon her, looking very beautiful with her dark hair down to her shoulders, her dark eyes sparkling. She looked gorgeous in a new suit in dark blue and a little jacket in black with black shoes and handbag to match. She was such an attractive young woman and Raymond was very much in love with her. He was tall and dark with blue eyes and was very handsome. Millie knew it and often teased him. 'I'll have to keep an eye on you,' she would say.

They kissed everyone goodbye. Jennifer had tears in her big blue eyes.

'Oh, Millie, take care of yourself! And you, Raymond! I love you. I long for you to come back. We'll go and see Tina.'

'I know,' said Millie, her eyes suddenly full of tears. 'Take care of Tina, won't you?'

'We will,' said Jennifer.

Millie hugged her father. She was so close to him. Derek had adopted Millie when he had married Jennifer: he wasn't her real father. Millie's real father had gone back to Canada. The marriage had been annulled when Jennifer was very young, but Derek had come to the rescue. He had loved Jennifer so much and had adopted the child, taking care of them both. The family were very happy, except for the shadow of Tina hanging over them.

When the reception was over Raymond and Millie got into the car and everyone waved to them as they drove down the long drive of the big house. Everywhere was floodlit: it looked beautiful. Dancing went on long after they had gone to London to the airport hotel. People danced until halfway through the night.

Millie and Raymond went off to Spain the next morning. They had a very happy first night on their honeymoon and made love through the night, for they were deeply in love. They felt the thrills go through their bodies.

'Make a baby now, shall we, Raymond?' said Millie. 'A baby that will be perfect and normal.'

'We'll do it,' said Raymond and they made love and were very happy. The next morning they flew off to Spain.

Things settled down once more at the big house. Millie and Raymond came back from their honeymoon and went back to work. Tina came home at weekends: she was now six years old. Raymond knew he'd taken on a lot: he could see how difficult this child was. Tina was on tablets but still very withdrawn and finding it hard to give or receive love. Her cold retreat from them had been so unexpected.

Jennifer said, 'Tina, why won't you let me give you a kiss and a hug sometimes? I love you, you know.'

Tina was very attractive. She had fair curly hair, to her shoulders, and the big blue eyes of Nancy and Jennifer. The big blue eyes; the normal look that showed when they were born they were going to inherit the family condition.

Now Tina looked, with her big blue eyes, at Jennifer. 'I don't want to kiss and hug. I don't like it,' she said.

'You're a strange child. We love you.'

'I know you do and I like school: I get bored here.'

'You're very lucky,' said Jennifer. 'You've got everything here.'

'I know.' Tina ignored Jennifer, she just ran off. She would take the dogs in the woods when she felt like it. She was kind to animals and loved them. In fact, she gave all her love to animals. She couldn't relate to human beings. She would hug the dogs and kiss them. People would watch her very closely and Derek, especially, would notice that Tina would secretly go into the woods all alone, she was very reclusive, and would take Bill and Trixie and kiss, cuddle and love them.

Derek knew, as a psychologist, that Tina would have to be approached with great care. Any attempt to force her to be more demonstrative could lead to further withdrawal.

That evening Tina went in to the little video room that Jennifer, Georgina and Julian always occupied and they put on videos for Tina to watch. She would watch films but would get bored easily. She was never satisfied for long and would wander off on her own. She did not seem to want to relate to her family at all.

Sunday night came and Tina, quite happily, without any show of emotion, went back to school. She kissed her mother and Raymond as they saw her off through the gate.

'I can go in on my own,' said Tina.

'Very well,' said Millie. 'But kiss your mum.'

Tina kissed Millie on the cheek. 'All right. Bye, Mummy. See you at the weekend.' That's what Tina was like: very evasive, unable to show her love.

Chapter 3

It was to be a long, long time before Tina came right for she would have a lot of problems, as Nancy had prophesied in Jennifer's dream. Tina had inherited things from them, but she had a different personality and more brain problems. It seemed that the trouble was getting worse now, as the generations passed, or was it just a one-off? Derek hoped it was, for it would be awful if they had more children like Tina in the future. He hoped that it would never happen again and prayed so too.

Tina was very happy at Greenacres School. There were only thirty or forty children there. It was a pretty building, very modern and light-coloured to make it look cheerful: a very large house, set in tree-lined grounds, typical of Surrey. There were playgrounds and large lawns where the children could play. There was a tennis court, a football field – everything the children could want – and inside there were large playrooms downstairs as well as the classrooms. There were three, for different grades of children, all of whom were retarded or maladjusted. Upstairs were the dormitories and the rooms in which the staff slept. Tina shared a room with eleven other girls. At first she had to have a room on her own for she was very difficult, but now she was stabilised on her tablets, she was able to be with other children. Tina did not mix well, however, with the others. She kept herself to herself, even at school, and it worried the staff.

That night Tina walked in and up to the dormitory. Tina had made friends with a nice girl named Jane. 'Hello, Tina, have you had a nice weekend?' said Jane.

'Not too bad,' said Tina. 'Usual, you know. It's always the same at home.'

'You live in a lovely big house,' said Jane. 'I only live in a small house.'

'Well, you can come home with me one weekend,' said Tina. 'I'm sure Mummy wouldn't mind.'

'I'd really like that. Can we be best friends? I really like you, Tina.'

'Well, sort of, I suppose,' said Tina, 'but I don't like people to worry me.' Tina even kept her friends at arm's length. Still, she thought it would be fun if Jane could come to the big house.

'It would be great if you could come for the weekend, Jane.'

'All right, fix it up,' said Jane.

Greenacres was a caring school, for maladjusted children, catering for children from a very young age, children who had problems, children whose parents could not cope with them at home, children who were very difficult or retarded. At the school, Tina did not make friends easily but she did her best, for even though she was difficult, underneath it all, she had love in her heart; a heart of gold, as Nancy had had, as Jennifer had. Poor Tina, unlike Nancy and Jennifer, could not bring it out, could not show it so everyone thought she was a hard little girl and didn't know the true Tina deep within. She made friends, but never had a best friend; as yet she just made casual friends but was always picking quarrels and having rows.

Tina remained at the school for another four years. She was now ten years old, and at weekends she went back to the big house and saw Dr. Margaret regularly.

Dr. Margaret was very keen on helping Tina, for she had loved Jennifer so much and still did. Jennifer still consulted her and told her all her problems and now Tina was ten, still going home at weekends and at holidays, still taking the dogs for walks in the woods but Tina was very much to herself, very withdrawn indeed. The doctors had tried different tablets to bring her out of herself but as yet had not found the right one. She had to be on tranquillisers regularly as her unusual brain patterns were not epilepsy, but something very similar which caused her mind to be very confused. Tina was a very unhappy child for she did not know herself. At least Nancy and Jennifer, with the same condition, had known who they were and what they were but Tina did not feel she had an identity and the worst of it all was, she hated herself.

At the age of eleven, Tina was found to be very intelligent. If it hadn't been for her difficult nature she could have gone to a normal school, but had to remain at Greenacres because of her complex and unusual personality. Tina enjoyed games at school, she enjoyed her work, but most of all, she enjoyed art: she could paint beautifully. Along with her illness, Tina had inherited that gift from Nancy. She could draw skilfully and would go outside in the grounds on her own and draw trees and flowers. Her nature was beautiful deep within herself but Tina did not want people to think she was interested in anything. She was very rebellious indeed.

The headmaster and his wife who ran the school, Mr. and Mrs. Powell, were helpful to all the children and tried to encourage Tina in her art, but nobody could get Tina to talk about herself to anyone, either at home or at school.

However Tina did manage to talk to her friend Jane. It was the closest she could get to anyone: she really felt she was on Jane's wavelength. One day they were walking in the grounds and sat down in the sunshine, looking at the stream at the bottom of the large garden, and Tina said, 'Jane, are you happy at home?'

Jane was a retarded girl and not as intelligent as Tina, but very sweet-natured and felt she could lean on Tina. 'I like it at home. I have a brother and I'm very happy.'

'I wish I could come home for a weekend with you,' said Tina.

'Why? You've got a beautiful big house to live in and very loving parents. You've got everything you could want.'

'I know,' said Tina. 'I love Jennifer and my mother and I quite like my stepfather, but, Jane, I can't show it. I just feel bottled up all the time. You're the only one I can talk to. But promise me,' said Tina, looking intently at Jane, 'that you won't tell anyone. Swear on the Bible. Please Jane! Or I won't tell you any more.'

'You've got to have someone to talk to,' said Jane. 'Of course I'll swear on the Bible and you know you can trust me, Tina. Well now you're eleven and you've never had a best friend and I haven't found one. Couldn't we be best friends?'

'I don't know,' said Tina. 'I'm not close to anyone.'

'Well, you're as close to me as you could be to anyone. Please, Tina, let's be best friends,' said Jane.

'All right,' said Tina, her big blue eyes looking intently at Jane. Jane kissed Tina on the cheek but Tina withdrew. 'I'm sorry, Jane. I can't kiss you at the moment. I feel I can't.'

'I understand,' said Jane. 'You'll do it when you're ready – everything.'

'I'll shake hands with you, though,' said Tina, smiling. Tina looked very attractive when she smiled. She was now a very tall girl for her age and rather lanky. Her fair hair had grown dark but it was still rather curly; something like Jennifer's. She kept it short for she liked it that way. Her big blue eyes were slightly paler than Jennifer's and Nancy's had been and looked as though they could change, possibly, before she was fully grown. She had a pale complexion, very pale indeed, and always looked worried. Still, now she had found a best friend in Jane.

'Look, Jane, now we've made our vows about being best friends, I'd like to have a weekend with you.'

'I can't understand why,' said Jane, 'because you've got that lovely home, but if you want to I'll ask Mummy and Daddy this weekend.'

'Then you could come back to the big house with me. You see, Jane, it wouldn't be so bad if you were with me.'

'I can't understand you,' said Jane. 'Why you can't talk to them at home?'

'I just can't.'

At that moment Mrs. Powell, out for a stroll with one of her springer spaniels, was behind a tree close to the two girls and couldn't help overhearing the conversation between Tina and Jane. So Tina has got a heart. She does want love, it just won't come out, thought Mrs. Powell. I'll have to talk to her sometime, she thought. In fact I'll have to talk to all the girls in that class. We've to tell them the facts of life this term. Mrs. Powell went back to talk to her husband. 'You know, Henry, Tina has got a heart. It'll come out one day.'

'I don't think it will for years,' said Henry. 'Not really.'

Henry knew a lot about maladjusted girls and knew Tina had a hard, long struggle ahead of her.

'Well, I hope so,' said his wife. 'I really do. I'm going to try to help her.'

Tina seemed hard, but it was a façade; a front. In her heart she was tender but she had built up this front, this tomboyish way. She had to have this façade and could not show her feelings at all.

Only Dr. Margaret knew, or suspected, that Tina had deep feelings underneath that hard façade she was showing and hoped it would come out. She voiced this one day to Jennifer and Dorothy.

'I hope it's correct,' said Dorothy. 'I couldn't bear to think of anyone in our family being hard, because we just aren't.'

'I know,' said Millie, walking in. 'I overheard that. I think Tina's got a heart too. I've got some news for you, anyway. I'm going to have a baby.'

'Oh,' said Jennifer. 'I hope he or she will be all right.'

'We're so happy,' said Millie. 'I know it's been a long time, but I'm pregnant at last.' She was rather old to be pregnant again. But Millie didn't mind, she was happy.

'I wonder if Tina will be jealous,' said Dorothy.

'I don't think so,' said Millie.

Dr. Margaret, however, wasn't so sure. 'We'll just have to tell her at the weekend and see how it works out,' she said. 'We'll all tell her on Sunday at tea, before she goes back to school.'

That weekend Tina said goodbye to Jane. 'Always be my best friend,' said Tina, looking intently at Jane.

'I'll have you next weekend if Mummy and Daddy say it's all right,' said Jane.

Millie picked her up in the car and they went home.

'I may be going to Jane's next weekend,' said Tina in a curt manner, the voice she always put on for her family.

'If you'd like that, dear, that'll be fine,' said Millie.

'She's my best friend.'

'Oh, is she? I'm glad you have a best friend now, dear.'

'Well, I have now, yes. But if she lets me down I'll never have another best friend,' said Tina, fiercely.

'She won't let you down,' said Millie. 'Jane's a lovely girl.'

Jane was a very attractive little girl of eleven, smaller than Tina, with fair hair and greeny-coloured eyes, quite different in appearance to Tina. She had a very sweet nature. She lived in a nice home, the other side of Guildford, with her brother and her parents. Jane went home that night and talked to her mother.

'May I have Tina home next weekend? It would be company for me.' Her mother knew a little bit about Tina. 'She's very tomboyish, dear. Must it be Tina?'

'Please Mum!' said Jane. 'She'll be good. I'll make her be!'

'All right,' said her mother. 'You can have her next weekend, if it will make you happy.'

'Oh thanks!' said Jane and ran off to play with her little dog Toby.

Tina spent the weekend as usual, pottering around the big house, wondering what to do, watching videos, playing records and walking in the woods with Bill and Trixie. The weekend flew past and on Sunday they all sat down for tea in the lovely big lounge that overlooked the woods where Nancy and Gordon had met.

'We've something to tell you, Tina,' said Millie. Dr. Margaret had arrived with Sandy and was sitting there so that if there was any crisis they could help. They were part of the big house now, somehow.

'Tina, I'm going to have a baby,' said Millie.

'Oh, you are, are you?' said Tina. 'Well, I don't care!'

'It will be your half-brother or sister, though, and I'm sure it'll be fun for you, even though you're a lot older.'

'I said I don't care,' said Tina. She looked around.

'Don't be like that,' said Jennifer. 'Please, Tina, let's go for a walk.' Tina liked Jennifer. She was more like herself, and the only one she could really relate to at the big house.

'All right,' said Tina sulkily. She glared at her mother and the others and walked out. She and Jennifer took the dogs into the woods.

'Don't be like that,' said Jennifer, who could cope with Tina and understand her. 'Don't be jealous of the baby, will you, Tina? I can read your thoughts. I know how you feel.'

'How can you know how I feel, Jennifer? You're a softy-pot, you are!'

'I know,' Jennifer smiled 'and you are, deep within yourself.'

'I'm not,' retorted Tina. 'I'll never be called a softie. I'm a tomboy and a rebel.'

'You like to think you are,' said Jennifer, 'but try and be kind to Gran, please, and to your mum. Please be kind to them! Gran's very upset you don't show her any love for she's getting very old and you've disappointed her, Tina.'

'Well, I'll try,' said Tina. She felt the tears welling up in her eyes. Jennifer noticed it. Tina swallowed quickly and started to run around playing with the dogs. She wasn't going to show her emotions. No, not even to Jennifer.

They walked some more in the woods and sat under the big tree where Nancy and Gordon had sat, where Jennifer often sat with Derek, where the young ones had been lovers so many times over the many years that had passed. Would Tina ever sit there with a lover, wondered Jennifer. They walked back. Dr. Margaret said, 'Tina, do you feel better now about the baby? Have you talked to Jennifer?'

'I'm OK.' said Tina, smiling.

'That's better,' said Millie, smiling. 'Kiss me goodnight, it's time you went to bed. You've got to be back to school early in the morning.'

'All right,' said Tina. 'Gran, I'm coming over to say goodnight to you first,' said Tina, remembering what Jennifer had said. Suddenly Tina went over and hugged Dorothy and kissed her and then ran from the room and up to her bedroom.

'So she does love me,' said Dorothy. 'That's made my day.'

Tina went up to bed and lay, looking out at the trees in the distance, and thought of Dorothy and of her family. I do love them, but I can't show it. I'll try and be kind to Gran though, because she might die one day, thought Tina. Tina had a very sensible and normal mind, far more normal than even the doctors knew. It was just that Tina's personality was wrong. There was certainly a twisted nerve in her mind somewhere, that Nancy and Jennifer had passed down to her. But it had become worse, more twisted, in Tina.

I love my home, thought Tina. I love Jennifer. Why can't I show my love? Tina cried often, but never let anyone see her. That night Tina thought of the baby and felt a little jealous. She thought of her gran and then fell asleep, the tears pouring down her cheeks.

The next morning she got up, after having weird dreams through the night; just as Jennifer had done when she was upset. But Tina's dreams were worse; really nasty negative dreams. She woke up in a mood. Tina was always in a mood when she'd had nightmares and had been disturbed the day before. She got up quietly and got ready to back to her school.

Derek drove her back to school that day and Tina did not forget to say cheerio to Dorothy. 'Goodbye, Gran. I won't see you next weekend. I'll see you the weekend after. May I bring Jane home with me?'

'Of course you can, dear,' said Dorothy. 'I love you, Tina.'

'I know,' said Tina. I want to say I love you, Gran, thought Tina, but I can't. She hugged her and ran from the room.

Tina sat quietly in the car as Derek drove her back to school. I wish I could have said I love you back to Gran, she thought.

'Don't worry,' said Derek, as if he could read her mind. 'Don't worry. Everything will be all right in the end, Tina. You look so anxious this morning.'

'I'm all right,' said Tina. 'Don't worry about me, Grandad.'

Derek felt old being called Grandad. He was sixty now and

would be retiring in another five years. He was a wonderful psychologist, at Forest Dene Hospital, and still worked there helping people. He would work as long as he could. Derek got very tired of late, for he had had a very happy, but difficult, life helping Jennifer. He had noticed how tired he had been feeling lately. I must see a doctor, he thought. I hope I'm all right, for Jennifer's sake. I must live to be very old.

Derek got Tina to school and Jane was waiting for her at the door. 'Bye, Grandad,' said Tina kissed him on the cheek and ran. She always felt very embarrassed whenever she showed emotion of any kind, but she felt she had to kiss Derek that morning. She really did love her grandfather.

'You can come and stay with me,' cried Jane, as they watched Derek, waving to them, going down the drive. Jane and Tina waved back to him, as he rounded the corner in his car and drove off to work at Forest Dene Hospital.

'Oh, I'm so happy,' said Tina. 'It will be fantastic coming home with you. It'll be a change for me. Do you know, my Mum's having a baby, at her age!'

'Well, that's good. She wants to.'

'I hope she's not like me,' said Tina. 'I know I'm difficult.'

The two girls went back to class and spent a happy week at school. On the Friday Mrs. Powell sat them all down in the classroom and said, 'Now, I've told you girls that this term I was going to tell you the facts of life.' The children looked amazed at what Mrs. Powell had to tell them. When she had finished she said, 'Now, you can all ask me questions.'

Tina asked many questions, which amazed Mrs. Powell. She didn't expect it from Tina. She wanted to know everything there was to know about the facts of life. Then she said, 'May I be excused now, Mrs. Powell?'

'May I too?' said Jane.

'All right. All of you go off in twos and threes and talk about it if you wish. You can have an hour off this morning.'

Jane and Tina rushed up to their room.

'I'm interested,' said Tina.

'I suppose you are,' said Jane. 'I'm not really.'

Jane was less mature than Tina but Tina had understood every word and it had aroused her natural curiosity. She and Jane talked for ages about what they had heard; then, at the end of the day, they packed their things and Jane's father picked them up and drove them back to Jane's home.

Jane lived in a nice, ordinary house on the other side of Guildford. Tina looked around with interest. It seemed cosy to her. She had always felt that, although the big house was her home, unlike the others in the family, she had never felt truly at home, always felt unsettled. Tina somehow felt she'd like a cosy little home one day.

Tina looked at the pretty house. There was a small driveway which led up to the front door. It was a four-bedroomed house with a pretty front garden, tidily-kept lawns and flowers all around and a few trees, for Jane's father loved gardening. It was on the outskirts of the town and Tina liked the idea of that: the idea of being in the country all the time bored her. She hoped that when she was older she would be able to live in a town and see the bright lights.

Tina looked at the house. 'Come on, Jane, I want to look around.' They walked into the house and Jane's mother, smiling, came to greet them. They were just nice ordinary people. 'Hello, Tina! Welcome for the weekend.' Tina felt the warm smile and felt she could give out more to strangers, for somehow she did not feel trapped with them. At home she felt trapped with the people, though she loved them dearly. She felt safe with this kind lady, Jane's mother, Mrs. Simpson. 'It's nice to see you, Mrs. Simpson,' she said, smiling.

What a pretty girl she's going to be, thought Jane's mother. 'Now, I'll show you your room. You'll be next to Jane. Bill's away this weekend,' that was Jane's brother, 'staying with his friend, so you're to sleep next to Jane.'

'Thank you, that'll be fine,' said Tina.

Downstairs was a cosy lounge overlooking the front lawn; nice and roomy. Beyond it was a small dining room, looking on the back garden, very modernly furnished, so different to the big house with all its antiques. Tina looked around in delight. She had always hated the antiques, they depressed her so. She liked the modern furniture and felt an uplift straight away. 'I like it, Mrs. Simpson. Oh, Jane, you are lucky to live here!'

'But you live in that beautiful big house,' said Jane.

'I know,' said Tina, 'but I don't really like it. I've always wanted a home like this.'

Mrs. Simpson and her husband looked at one another, amazed. They couldn't believe what Tina had said.

She can't be happy, thought Mr. Simpson. Then he remembered that Tina was maladjusted and thought no more about it.

The girls went out into the hall again, and down the passage was a small room where Jane and her brother could watch videos and telly and play their music centre as much as they wanted to. It was their own den.

'Oh, it's fantastic in here,' said Tina. 'Will we be able to watch some videos, Jane?'

'Of course we will. We've got loads,' said Jane 'and look, Tina, tomorrow let's go into town and hire a film.'

'I'd like that,' said Tina. 'We can't do that in the village. There isn't anywhere.'

'I know,' said Jane. 'That's the trouble with villages.'

Hm, thought Tina, I like it here.

The kitchen was very spacious and looked out on to the back garden. It was bright and cheerful. Everything in it was modern, Tina noted approvingly.

They had a little cairn terrier dog called Sam, who was very friendly. Tina liked dogs and bent down and stroked him and he licked her face. The girls went upstairs with Mrs. Simpson behind them. When they got upstairs Jane showed Tina the room she was to be in. It was modern and had a portable television in it: Tina approved at once. It had a modern little single bed and was decorated in blue. A very pretty room, thought Tina. I like it.

'I'll be next door,' said Jane. 'Come and see my room.'

It was a lovely spacious room with everything a young girl could want. Tina loved it. 'It's so modern. I like it!' She looked out of the window and could see the cars going up and down the road.

'I like it here, Mrs. Simpson. Thank you for having me. Will I be able to come again?' said Tina eagerly.

'Of course you will,' said Mrs. Simpson 'and thank you for saying that Jane can come and stay with you next weekend.'

'It'll be nice,' said Tina. 'I get so fed up in the big house.'

'I'm sorry,' said Mrs. Simpson, 'but your family do love you.'

'I know,' said Tina, 'but it's nice being here.'

'Come down to tea when you're settled in.'

The two girls settled in, chatting eagerly. Tina had a fine time and enjoyed her tea that evening and then she and Jane watched videos until bedtime. They had started to watch love films quite early. Tina was nearly twelve and was quite interested in love.

The next day they went into town and hired two films. Tina chose one thriller and one love film.

'That'll do nicely,' said Jane. 'A nice combination.'

They looked round the shops and Tina, who was never short

of money for her family were well-off, bought some little things for the two of them. They bought sweets and cassette tapes and Tina bought some new socks that she fancied in a shop. She had a very generous heart and knew that Jane wasn't as well off as she was, so she bought some for her as well. Jane was thrilled. Tina then bought a small box of chocolates for Mrs. Simpson. When they got back Mrs. Simpson was pleased. They had another happy evening watching videos. The two films were enjoyed by both girls.

The next day was Sunday and the family all went to church. Tina was used to going to church in the village and quite enjoyed the service. She liked spiritual things but couldn't quite make out her life, for her mind was so very confused, but she had always believed in God, had been brought up to do so, and loved Him.

After lunch the two girls went into town again and chose the video that Mr. Simpson had promised them.

'You choose, Tina,' said Jane. 'We're going back tomorrow.'

'I know,' said Tina. 'Isn't it awful?' She chose another love film. It seemed to have brought the love out in Tina, this weekend in Jane's little happy home with her parents and her brother. They were all so happy together. Tina sighed and wished she had just a small family like this but Tina's life was very different, living in the big house with a large family; Julian and Georgina, middle-aged people, and yet so young for their age with their problems, and Jennifer, and Derek a psychologist; and there was always so much talking and Dr. Margaret there and they entertained quite a lot at times. Tina wanted a quiet life.

The next day the two girls were driven back to school by Mr. Simpson. Tina felt very tearful when she said goodbye to Mrs. Simpson.

The car arrived back at school and the two girls got out and said goodbye to Mr. Simpson.

'See you the weekend after next, Jane. And you can come again, Tina. Take care of Jane when she comes to your house next weekend.'

'We'll take care of her and we'll phone you,' said Tina.

'Very considerate of you.' She's very sensible, thought Mr. Simpson, as he drove down the drive. Somehow, she's more intelligent than the others, more grown-up mentally but emotionally she's a child, he thought. What a complex girl! But he couldn't help liking her. She's going to be pretty, too, he thought smiling.

The two girls settled back at the school and did their work. The following weekend Tina took Jane home to the big house. Tina felt very tense that weekend but it was easier having Jane there. They all talked about Millie's new baby so much that Tina got bored and fed up and so they went off on their bicycles and took the dogs for walks in the woods – luckily it was good weather – and spent the evenings watching videos. The family only saw them at mealtimes. Except for Jennifer, that was, who loved to come in and watch the videos with the girls. She had been and hired some for them when Derek had driven her into Guildford shopping that week. Jennifer thought of the girls and knew they'd want some films and she loved films herself.

Tina loved Jennifer. Deep in her heart she loved her more than anyone. She felt she was a little more like herself and never minded having her with them when they were watching a film. Jennifer would laugh at the comments they'd make about the films and quite enjoyed it. She enjoyed the weekend with them.

The weekend flew by all too fast and the girls went back to school, driven by Derek.

'Be good, Tina. You've been very happy this weekend and I know you loved it at Jane's.'

'I liked the small house,' said Tina.

The girls went on enjoying school and weekends together at home, and Tina and Jane got closer and closer together, which was doing Tina a lot of good. They really were best friends now. Life ran very smoothly at the big house and at Greenacres School.

Another year passed. Tina was now twelve and a half years old. Millie's baby was a few months old now and she had had rather a difficult birth. Tina had found it very difficult to face the christening and had been very upset for a few weeks over the holidays so she had stayed with Jane and been very happy there. Tina was not jealous of the baby but felt she could not cope with the crowds and the fuss. Millie had a baby boy they named Robert. He was a normal baby and they could see he was going to be all right. Millie and her husband doted on the baby, who responded to them in a way that Tina never had. Millie gave more and more love to Robert. Tina noticed this and was a little hurt, but realised it was partly her own fault.

But Tina had a lot more to think about at that time than Robert and her mother, or anyone at the big house, a great deal more. For Tina's body was changing.

She was one of the young ones, emotionally immature, but mentally and physically she wasn't. That was the difference between her and Jennifer and Nancy: they had been slower in growing up. Their physical changes had been slower, though they were mentally fairly alert but Tina was even more alert, although emotionally she was as a child. And now her body was changing. She was nearly thirteen years old, still at Greenacres School, and she was experiencing things she just couldn't talk to anyone about, not even to Jane, who was physically less mature.

Chapter 4

One night Tina was in bed at school. She started to read a book for a little while and then turned the light out. The other girls in the dormitory, including Jane, were fast asleep and Tina lay down and looked out of the window as she always did just as she was going to sleep. Suddenly, she felt an irritation and she started to feel her body. As she felt herself, with no warning, she had this ecstatic feeling that went right through her body. Tina couldn't believe it and wondered what it was. It felt so beautiful, she thought. What was it? This happened night after night and at home at weekends also, and Tina began to start feeling herself and getting very excited about it but it also upset her, for she did not know what it meant. All she could remember was what Mrs. Powell had told them at school. But Tina had not been told enough. They had not told her about the masturbation of young girls and boys. Mrs. Powell must have forgotten or thought it not necessary, and now Tina was very confused.

A few weeks later, to Tina's dismay, her periods started. She had been told about those and went rushing to Mrs. Powell. It was at school, during midweek, and she told Mrs. Powell that she had started bleeding.

'Right, I have everything ready. Don't be afraid, Tina. All you have to do is wear some tampons or some stick-on pads, whichever you wish, and in a few days time it will go away. You might get a tummy ache . . .'

'I've had a tummy ache,' said Tina. 'For a whole day. And now it's started to bleed and I'm frightened.'

'Don't be frightened. All girls get this. I did explain to you. And if you want to talk to me about anything else, you may.'

Tina coloured up and looked up at Mrs. Powell pathetically. 'There's nothing I have to say, Mrs. Powell,' she said and rushed away with the tampons and the pads which she had been told about. She went into the toilet and put them on.

She mooned around for a couple of days. It worried her, the period, and gave her tummy ache. She had to get used to it and accept it, like all girls have to. Tina did tell Jane that she had started her periods. Jane had as yet not started.

'It'll be my turn next. Don't worry, Tina,' said Jane laughing. Jane did not worry about many things. Tina worried a lot.

A few weeks went past. Tina went on getting those ecstatic feelings and masturbating herself, as most young girls do and then one day she felt she couldn't keep it to herself any longer. What does this mean? she thought. I don't understand it and the holidays are coming up and I wouldn't tell anyone at home. I must tell someone.

'Jane, may I talk to you? The holidays are coming. I know you're coming to stay with me for a few days, and I'm coming to stay with you, but I must tell you this before we go.'

'All right,' said Jane. 'Let's go for a walk.'

The two girls walked round the school grounds. There was a little shed, with some chairs in it, where a lot of the youngsters sat in the summer and talked, or went to be quiet and alone there.

'Jane, I must explain things to you,' said Tina. 'I shall burst if I don't.'

'What is it?' said Jane.

'Well,' said Tina. 'I . . . um . . . get these . . . er . . . feelings. I mean, down here.'

'Oh, is that it?' said Jane. 'I get that.'

'Do you touch yourself?' said Tina.

'Well, yes,' said Jane.

'But you haven't started your periods yet, have you?'

'No, but I expect I will soon,' said Jane 'and I know the other girls do it as well. One told me, Christine. She told one of the older girls and she told Mrs. Powell; they had a talk apparently, and she explained that it was quite natural and that boys do it too.'

The two girls started to giggle.

'Gosh!' said Tina. 'The boys do it, do they?'

'Yes,' said Jane. The two girls went on giggling and talking. A few days later, the Christmas holidays came. Tina and Jane kissed each other goodbye.

'We'll keep our secret,' they said to one another.

'You're coming to stay with me after Christmas, aren't you, Jane?'

'Yes, that's right, Tina. See you then.'

Millie had come to pick up Tina in the car.

'Hello, Mummy. I'm glad to see you,' said Tina.

'You have changed lately. I know I've seen you weekends, but you look so different today, Tina. You look like you're growing up.'

'Oh, I am, Mummy,' said Tina and smiled at her.

They drove back, Tina telling her mother all about school. Back to the big house, where all the Christmas festivities were being prepared. As always the big tree in the hall with the beautiful lights was already up, and all the presents were being prepared. There was to be a large party, as there always was just before Christmas. Tina had to settle in and join in with things, but still stuck to Jennifer. She took very little interest in baby Robert.

Just before Christmas Jennifer and Tina went for a walk in the woods. It was a cold, crisp day.

Jennifer said, 'Tina, you're growing up, aren't you?'

'I am,' said Tina. 'Aren't these the woods where Nancy and Gordon made love?'

'You know a lot, don't you, for your age,' said Jennifer, laughing.

'Quite a bit,' said Tina.

'You're going to be a little devil by the sound of it.'

'I don't care,' said Tina. She could put on a façade but in her heart she felt sad. She would have liked to have burst into tears and run into Jennifer's arms and tell her everything. Her eyes suddenly filled with tears. 'Oh Jennifer!'

'What's wrong, dear?'

'I . . . um, I'm so confused. I'm getting to know things about growing up.'

'You're quite young to do that,' said Jennifer 'but you're not all that young for your age.'

'I am, emotionally. Mrs. Powell said so,' said Tina. She liked to let everyone know about that.

'And I've noticed you've started to put on a little lipstick,' said Jennifer. 'I didn't do that till I was much older than you.'

'Oh well, they're different, the girls now,' said Tina.

'I suppose so,' said Jennifer. 'Is there anything you'd like to tell me, Tina?'

'Not really. If I want to we'll talk again, Jennifer.'

They took the dogs and walked back to the big house where Derek was sitting in the lounge, looking out at the woods.

'Hello, Derek,' said Jennifer, kissing him, loving him as much as ever. Derek was getting very tired lately. He didn't seem to be too well.

Christmas came and went. It was a very happy time for them all. Tina had gone into Guildford shopping and met Jane. Millie had driven them and Jennifer had come too. They had all had a very happy day and gone out to lunch. Tina bought all the presents for the family that she wanted, and something for Jane and her parents. She was a very generous girl and liked to give. She had bought Jane a video she wanted and Jane had bought her one. They were both very happy indeed.

'Don't forget, Jane, you're coming two days after Christmas. I can't wait,' said Tina. 'I have lots more to tell you. I've got a love film. We must watch it. Jennifer bought it for me. I haven't seen it yet, it's a present for Christmas.'

'Brilliant!' said Jane. 'We'll watch that together.'

'All right,' said Tina, grinning.

She looked round at Jane, who said, 'See you soon then,' and off they went, back to the big house.

Two days later a large party was given for the village people and the friends they had around them at the very big house. The band came and played music and there was music for the young ones in the big lounge. How Tina enjoyed dancing. Two or three friends came over at the last minute. She'd managed to persuade Millie to let Jane and her brother come, which was very exciting for them. Tina enjoyed dancing with Jane's brother. She was certainly growing up physically. As the music played Tina started thinking about love and romance. I'm so confused, she thought. I get these feelings. I love music. I want someone to love and cuddle. A boy. It was the only way she could show her feelings.

Jennifer noticed that Tina was worried and kept a watchful eye on her. Derek and Dr. Margaret did likewise on the quiet. Dr. Margaret had often tried to talk to Tina and had failed badly. Tina just couldn't relate to anyone who was connected to the big house. She was still very withdrawn from the family. The closest she had got to anyone was Jennifer.

The party over, everyone settled down again and a few days

later they all had a very happy Christmas. Gifts were handed round and they all sat around the tree, which was traditional at the big house, but all Tina could think of was seeing that new film, which Jennifer had given her, with Jane in two days' time. She went off into the video room and was very tempted to watch the film but she had promised Jane she wouldn't and Tina always kept a promise. Still, she had other films. Derek had given her some and so had the rest of the family for they knew how much Tina loved films; she did very well that Christmas. She had also been given some new jeans, which she loved, a new skirt which she would wear when she was in the right mood, two sweaters and three sweatshirts.

Tina knew that she was beginning to look attractive and felt conscious of it and now she wore a little lipstick and it was noticed by her family. But she had to grow up and they knew it. They were worried though, for they knew that Tina was emotionally not ready.

After Christmas Dr. Margaret had a long talk with Derek.

'You know Tina's growing up far too quickly physically and mentally, and her emotions are still childlike.'

'I know,' sighed Derek. 'We've all tried to talk to her, but it's no good.'

'Look, I'll tell you what,' said Dr. Margaret. 'I'll talk to Mrs. Powell next term and see if she feels Tina needs any help. If so, she could go to Forest Dene Hospital. There's a Dr. Phillips there, and I believe he's the son of Jeremy Phillips.'

Jeremy Phillips, who had looked after Jennifer, was now dead and so was his wife, but his son, who was now middle aged, had taken his place at Forest Dene Hospital.

'He'd be just the person,' said Derek. 'He's a wonderful man. His name's Tom, I believe. I'll come and talk to Mrs. Powell with you after Christmas when they're back at school.'

'That's settled then,' said Dr. Margaret.

The holidays flew past. Tina went on having her ecstatic feelings. She went to Jane's for a week's holiday and they had a great time watching films together. Jane came to stay with Tina and they saw the new love film and enjoyed it. Jennifer watched it with them and observed Tina's feelings. She was excitable and romantic. Yes, thought Jennifer, she's growing up far quicker than I did, and Nancy from what I've heard, and yet, emotionally she's like a child. Poor Tina, she thought. Nancy was right when she predicted that Tina would have a lot of problems.

Tina had a wonderful time for she was happy now enjoying her new 'love-life' as she called it. She had romantic dreams and posters all over her room of rock stars and singers and film stars that she loved. Men and women, Derek had observed.

Physically, Tina was well-covered and well-proportioned. She had a nice figure and it was beginning to show: Tina felt it and noticed it. She looked very nice when she was dressed and made up. Derek began to think that Tina was going to be quite a girl, and felt rather worried about it. He would indeed have to talk to Mrs. Powell next term.

At last the holidays were over. Tina and Jane had a lovely time visiting one another and now they were to go back to Greenacres School once more.

'Back to the grindstone,' groaned Tina, as she was being driven back by her mother and Derek and Jennifer. She had been worried, before she left home. She had been to see her gran, Dorothy.

'I'm not very well, Tina,' she had said. 'I'm getting very old now. You're going to have a lot of problems, I feel. Perhaps more than Jennifer and Nancy, for you know about them.'

'I do, Gran,' said Tina. Tina felt she could talk to her gran, now that she was an old lady. When she was younger Tina hadn't been able to relate to her at all, but now she loved the old lady and felt sorry for her. For Tina knew that Granny wouldn't be there for much longer. She had been told by her mother. Tina felt sad, but knew she had to face it, for her gran was old. Her mother had told her that she might not see her granny any more. So Tina and Dorothy had a long talk the day before she went back to school.

'Tina, I've noticed you're getting quite a grown up girl and you look very attractive with your make-up. Do you like the boys?'

'Well, I'm getting a bit interested,' said Tina. 'I've not had a boyfriend yet, but I might.' She grinned and her eyes shone and sparkled.

She is going to be quite a girl, thought Dorothy. She sighed. 'Be careful, Tina, for me, won't you?'

'Oh Gran, don't worry about me,' said Tina. 'I'm all right at school. When I grow up I want to get married and I want a little house, like Jane's. I've told you about it, Gran.'

'No, you've never really liked the big house, have you?'

'Well, not really. I like small, cosy places.'

'Well, you're the only one who hasn't loved the big house,' said Dorothy. 'I'm sorry, my dear.'

'Oh, it's not your fault, Gran. It's a beautiful house, don't get me wrong.'

'I feel that one day you'll be happy here,' said Dorothy.

'Perhaps when I'm older, but first of all, when I grow up I want to get married and have a little house, like Jane's.'

'Well I hope you'll be very happy. You take care of yourself, Tina.'

'Oh Gran, I'll take care of myself for you. I love you very much.' It was out. Tina had at last, after all these years, managed to tell her great-grandmother that she loved her. Suddenly Tina rushed over to Dorothy and hugged her and kissed her.

'Oh Tina, you've made me so happy. You've shown me that you love me.'

'I'm finding it easier now, Gran. I couldn't before. I'm still finding it hard with the others though.'

'I know, but I predict that it will come in time. But not just yet. You're a bit reserved, Tina, but we'll keep it our secret. You always give me a nice big hug and kiss and I'll be very happy.'

'I'm glad I've made you happy, Gran. I do love you,' said Tina. Suddenly Tina felt the tears welling up in her eyes and she had this strange feeling that she wouldn't see her granny very much more.

Tina was right, for two weeks later Dorothy passed away. One Wednesday morning she had a heart attack. She was well on in her eighties. She had talked to Derek and Jennifer before she died.

'Please, please, Jennifer, look after Tina. She's going to need it. She's very different from you, you know.'

'I realise that,' said Jennifer quietly.

'Don't worry,' said Derek. 'Don't worry, Dorothy. We're going to get her to see another psychiatrist. We know she can't relate to Dr. Margaret and she understands. She's going to be all right.'

'But not for a long, long time,' said Dorothy. 'The future is going to be hard for her. She's going to be very different from you, Jennifer.'

'That I realise,' said Jennifer again.

Dorothy had a heart attack and passed away peacefully one Wednesday morning in her sleep. The doctor had been called early but she had died peacefully. She was happy that Tina had managed to show her, before she died, that she loved her deeply.

Tina was told by Derek who came to the school to explain about Dorothy's death.

'Do you want to come to the funeral, Tina?'

'I'd like to,' said Tina, 'and I think Jane would because she loved Gran.'

'You'll be given time off. It's the day after tomorrow. I'll come over and fetch you.'

'All right,' Tina couldn't cry in front of Derek but she fled down to the shed. Jane noticed from the schoolroom window and guessing something was wrong she rushed down to join her. Tina wept in her arms.

'I loved my gran. I wish I could have shown it before. I feel so guilty,' said Tina.

'Don't worry,' said Jane. 'At least you did it a few times. And that's all that matters. Your gran must have died very happy.'

'I'm glad I've got you to talk to, Jane,' said Tina through her tears. Jane looked at Tina's blue eyes. They looked so sincere and so sad at this moment.

'Oh, I love you, Tina!' said Jane. And don't worry about your gran, she's happy now. She's gone to join the other ones that you told me about. The lady – you know – Nancy, the one who fell in love in the woods.'

'Oh yes. Yes, her. She was my great, great – or something – grandmother. She was beautiful. You've seen her portrait.'

'I know.'

'I wish I could be beautiful like that one day,' said Tina.

'You probably will.'

'No, I will never be beautiful like Nancy, but I'd like to be attractive.'

'Well, you're that already,' said Jane.

'So are you.'

They embraced a lot more and Tina cried many more tears for her gran. Unable to do it at home, or in front of the other girls at school, it all had to come out in the shed, with Jane.

Mrs. Powell knew about it, for she watched the girls and boys carefully, and Derek had told her. 'I'll go and see to her, don't worry,' she said as Derek left. She walked towards the shed, knowing that Tina would have gone there. When she saw the two girls talking and embracing and the tears being shed she knew she could do no more. She depends on Jane. She can relate to her. I'm so glad she can relate to someone, thought Mrs. Powell, she would have gone mad otherwise. She went and told her husband. 'You know, Tina is relating well to Jane.'

'I'm so glad,' said Mr. Powell. 'I thought she'd never relate to anyone.'

'She's better since she's reached puberty, you know.'

'I know. She must be getting feelings now.'

They discussed Tina and Jane. 'I think they'll always be best friends. I'm glad,' said Mrs. Powell.

'So am I,' said her husband, 'but I think Tina's going to have a lot more problems than Jane when she grows up.'

Two days later, a very sad Tina and Jane were fetched by Derek and taken to the little village church, near the big house, in which all the family services had been held – baptisms, weddings and funerals. Reverend Moss gave a very moving talk about Dorothy. Everybody in the church shed tears, but they knew Dorothy was an old lady and was happy now. She was laid to rest among her family in that beautiful village churchyard surrounded by trees. When the service was over the whole family, and many in the village, including the vicar and his wife, went back to the big house, to the reception, to talk about Dorothy. Tina and Jane went too. Tina had huddled into Jane and shed many tears for her gran, hidden from the family. It was the first death that Tina had experienced in the family. 'I shall miss her,' she whispered to Jane.

Derek noticed that Tina's eyes were moist from crying and was glad. It's coming out, even if she can't show it to us, he thought. He voiced this to Dr. Margaret. 'She can talk to Jane, you know.'

'I know,' said Dr. Margaret. 'We really must go and see Mrs. Powell when all this is over.'

The funeral over, Jane and Tina went back to school. Tina soon settled down. She was young and resilient.

Chapter 5

At thirteen, Tina was maturing fast physically and mentally – although emotionally she was still as a young child. She continued having her sexual feelings and relieving herself of them and giggling in the shed with Jane. Now they had started to put make-up on and cast a hopeful eye towards the boys at school. There were plenty of opportunities to meet now, at the school disco. Tina loved the music and the dancing, but, like Jennifer, she hated flashing lights, which always gave her headaches and made her feel dizzy, so she would stand outside and listen to the music. Everybody knew that Tina could not bear the lights and often one of the boys would come out and dance with her outside. It fascinated her, for her mind was full of romance, and one night, at such a disco, Tina danced outside with Jerry. He was fifteen and she felt very happy and very romantic. It was that night that she had her first kiss with Jerry. They both felt desire well up inside them.

'I want you, Tina,' said Jerry urgently.

'I want you,' said Tina, 'but we're a bit young, aren't we?'

'I know,' said Jerry, 'but let's kiss for a while, and then see.'

'All right. I want you just as much as you want me.'

After that night, Tina saw Jerry a lot, and continued to enjoy life at school.

Back at the big house Derek and Dr. Margaret discussed at great length whether they should see Mrs. Powell about getting Tina to see a psychiatrist.

'We must go soon.' said Dr. Margaret. 'It's been delayed because of Dorothy's death, but we must go now things have settled down again. I'll phone up now.'

'Come tomorrow at eleven and then you can see Tina before you go back,' invited Mrs. Powell, when Margaret had explained.

'That'll be fine,' said Dr. Margaret. 'We'll talk to you then.'

The next day Derek and Dr. Margaret drove to Greenacres School and at eleven o'clock were shown into Mr. and Mrs. Powell's study. 'I want to talk to you about Tina,' said Derek.

They knew who Dr. Margaret was, and Derek, and had learned quite a lot about them. 'How is Tina doing at school?' inquired Margaret.

'She's doing very well,' said Mrs. Powell, 'but I think you'll have to watch her with the boys.'

'What do you mean?' said Derek.

'What I say,' said Mrs. Powell. 'I think she's going to be a bit oversexed. She's already interested in boys and seeing one. His name is Jerry and he's fifteen.'

'Oh, I hope they're not doing anything yet,' said Dr. Margaret.

'We'll keep an eye on those things,' said Mr. Powell. 'Don't worry, nothing's happened. Only a kiss.'

'She's started to wear a lot of make-up. I've noticed that at home,' said Derek. 'She's so different to Jennifer and Nancy, so much more forward. We thought she was going to be worse.'

'She is really,' said Mrs. Powell, who had heard about Jennifer and Nancy, and how Tina had inherited from them. 'Mentally she is practically up to standard and physically she's over-mature, but her emotions are those of a seven-year-old. That's what makes it harder for Tina.'

'Look,' interjected Dr. Margaret. 'What we've come about is this. She can't relate to us well at home.'

'I know,' said Mrs. Powell. 'She has told me. She'd like to live in a house like Jane's and . . . well, some people can't handle big houses, they feel lost in them. They want something cosy and more secure. You see, Tina's very insecure.'

'I realise that,' said Dr. Margaret, 'and I feel it's time she saw a psychiatrist.'

'But you're a psychiatrist, Dr. Margaret,' said Mr. Powell.

'She won't talk to me, or my friend, or my son. It's useless. She just can't relate to anyone close to home.'

'What do you suggest then?'

'Well,' said Derek, 'We'd like to arrange for Dr. Jeremy Phillips' son, Tom, who's now at Forest Dene Hospital, to see her there and see what he can work out.'

'What a marvellous idea,' said Mr. Powell. 'She does need a little help and guidance.'

'We'll make the arrangements,' said Dr. Margaret, 'and we'll try and make the appointment, say for Monday morning, before she comes back to school. Will you tell her please, Mrs. Powell, that she's to see the psychiatrist?'

'I'll do that,' said Mrs. Powell. 'It's been very nice to see you. It's break time now so she can talk to you for a while.'

'We'll break the ice,' said Dr. Margaret, 'and explain that we've been talking to you.'

'All right, but she'll ask questions,' said Mr. Powell.

'We'll answer them truthfully,' said Derek. 'It's the only way with Tina. She's so suspicious.'

They all shook hands and Derek and Dr. Margaret went outside in the grounds, where the youngsters were having their break. Tina saw them and came running over, with Jane beside her.

'Hello, Derek; hello, Dr. Margaret,' she said smiling. 'Why are you here?'

'We came to see Mr. and Mrs. Powell about you, Tina. We'll be honest with you,' said Dr. Margaret. 'You can't relate to me or Sandy and we feel that you need to see a psychiatrist, like Jennifer used to, and Nancy. You've got problems.'

'I'm not like them.'

'No, not exactly,' said Dr. Margaret, 'but you aren't well otherwise you wouldn't be in this school.'

'I realise that. I'm young for my age, aren't I?'

'You are emotionally,' said Dr. Margaret, 'but you can't seem to talk to me. I wish you could.'

'I'm sorry,' said Tina. 'I hope it hasn't hurt you.'

'Well,' said Dr. Margaret, smiling. 'We feel that you ought to see somebody on the outside, somebody independent. You like to be independent, Tina.' Dr. Margaret was a clever psychiatrist and knew exactly what to say.

'Well, who do you want me to see?' said Tina.

'We want you to see Dr. Tom Phillips at Forest Dene Hospital. He's a very nice doctor.'

'On Monday morning, if we can arrange it, before you come back to school,' said Derek.

'Why have I got to see him?' demanded Tina sulkily.

'There's nothing to worry about,' said Dr. Margaret. 'Anyway, Mrs. Powell will explain things to you.'

'All right,' muttered Tina.

'We've got to go now,' said Derek. 'I've got to get back to work.'

'Take care of yourself, Tina, and you, Jane,' said Dr. Margaret.

'Bye,' they said and ran off with the others, but Tina was worried. She went off with Jane to the shed.

'They want me to see a psychiatrist. I suppose it's because I like Jerry and I'm young for my age. It's all mixed up,' said Tina. It upset her so that she bottled it up in her mind. 'I'll have to see him, I suppose. Perhaps I'll be able to talk to him.'

'Don't worry,' said Jane. 'I know you're worried because you're quiet, Tina.'

'I'm all right,' said Tina. 'I'll get it over with. I'll see the shrink. I'm not worried anyway,' she continued. 'I'm more interested in tonight. I'm seeing Jerry again.'

'Yes, and I'm seeing Leonard,' said Jane.

Tina wasn't pretty like Jane. She was more what you might call good-looking or attractive and she was certainly attractive to the opposite sex; she made sure of that. She spent a lot of time, at night, thinking about boys, thinking about getting married one day, but her young emotions wondered if she could cope with it. Tina knew that she wouldn't be able to. But another part of her wanted to and she was in constant turmoil.

Just before Tina went home for the weekend Mrs. Powell called her into the study. 'You know you're going to see Dr. Phillips, don't you, on Monday? The appointment's been arranged, I had a phone call from Dr. Margaret.'

'I know,' said Tina. 'It's because I can't talk to the others, isn't it?'

'Yes,' said Mrs. Powell. 'You must tell him how you feel, he'll help you.'

'I'll try,' said Tina.

'And, Tina, you're a very pretty girl, you know, and you're becoming very attractive to boys. Be careful, please. Don't do anything that you shouldn't, not now. We don't want you getting pregnant.'

'I don't want to,' said Tina. 'I promise not to do anything. But it's very hard.'

'You're very oversexed, Tina,' said Mrs. Powell, 'and the doctor wants to help you and talk to you.'

'All right,' said Tina, blushing. She felt rather embarrassed about

Mrs. Powell telling her she was oversexed but she knew it was true. Perhaps she could be helped a little but Tina was quite happy the way she was at the moment. It had given her something different. She had been very unhappy as a small child, had been a tomboy and very rebellious, but her hormones were changing now and she was softening and felt romantic and happier. She didn't feel so hardened towards people. Things were even easier at home, which pleased Tina, yet still she felt different to them. She knew the way she was and she knew they wouldn't understand, or at least she thought they wouldn't.

Millie was very busy with baby Robert, and her marriage wasn't as good as it might have been at the beginning. Married for some years now, Millie had found out that her husband had been seeing somebody else at the hospital they worked in and it had upset her very much; they were thinking of separating. Tina knew her mother was upset and felt sorry for her, yet she couldn't get close to her and tell her so. 'I'll try and tell everything to the doctor,' said Tina, coming out of her reverie.

'You were far away then, Tina.'

'I was thinking of Mummy. I can't talk to her, but I'm sorry for her at the moment.'

'I know you are. It's a shame you can't relate to her and tell her.'

'I just can't,' said Tina.

'I know how you feel. You feel a bit trapped and smothered, don't you, at home?'

'Well, they fuss over me – they've always smothered me and tried to protect me too much and I don't like it. I mean, they say Nancy liked it, and Jennifer. But I'm not them, I'm me.'

'I know you are,' said Mrs. Powell. 'Now, don't worry, Tina. You've told me and now you're beginning to talk to me quite a lot. You couldn't when you first came here. You were awful. And so rebellious!'

'I'm doing well, aren't I?'

'You are, and as I've said, you're a very pretty girl.'

'Thank you,' said Tina, feeling very flattered. It was the first real compliment she'd ever been paid and she was very happy when she left the room that day. So happy, she didn't even mind the prospect of seeing the doctor at Forest Dene Hospital on the following Monday.

That night she had a long talk with Jerry. They had a long walk in the grounds and kissed at length. They were very worked up.

'It can't go on like this,' said Jerry. 'I've got to make love to you.'

'I want to, too,' said Tina. 'Look, I'll talk to the doctor and see what we can do.'

'Like, possibly, getting hold of the pill or something?'

'Well,' said Tina again. 'I'll see what I can do.'

'All right, I'll try and be patient,' said Jerry. They kissed for a long time and then Tina went back in, feeling very frustrated.

That weekend Tina spent a lot of time walking the dogs in the woods and sitting alone in the room where they watched the video. She had a lot to think about. She wondered if she'd be able to talk to this Dr. Phillips. Jennifer saw her quite a lot and walked with her once or twice.

'I do understand you, whatever you think, Tina. I know you're worried about seeing the doctor. But he'll help you, I'm sure.'

'I'll try and tell you about it afterwards, but this weekend I need to be quiet. And I've got a boyfriend, Jennifer.'

'So I understand,' said Jennifer. 'You have started young.'

'I know,' said Tina, 'but I like boys.'

'Yes, I know, but be careful, won't you, Tina? I wasn't very careful, else you wouldn't be here. For I had your mother.'

'I know. Jennifer, I want him so much!'

'You're very young to be feeling like that.' Jennifer was surprised, remembering her own experiences.

'I'm afraid I've started a lot younger than you, Jennifer.'

'But you're young emotionally,' said Jennifer. 'I understand you.'

'Yes, but my body's developed quicker than yours. Mrs. Powell explained it to me.'

'Oh, I see,' said Jennifer. 'Oh Tina, I'm sorry. Is it hard for you?'

'It's hard for me to handle, yes,' said Tina 'I try but I do need love. I need my boyfriend and I want to marry young. I need to be with someone.'

'I think I understand,' said Jennifer, 'but try and talk to the doctor about it, won't you?'

'All right,' said Tina. 'Come on, Jennifer. Let's go in and see a film after supper.'

Tina was very quiet at supper. Everybody looked at her sitting there at the table, thinking deeply. They knew what she was thinking about – partly about Jerry, in her mixed up little mind, and partly about her interview on Monday morning. Tina looked very pretty sitting at the table, Millie thought, with her dark hair hanging down wavy on her shoulders. She was curling it a lot more now and it looked thick and bushy on her shoulders, a little piece falling over her eye, giving her a very seductive look.

They all had their thoughts about Tina that night, sitting there with her hair over one eye, her make-up on her face, in a tight jumper and tight jeans. She certainly looked very womanly. And very sexy.

Derek thought, that girl is going to get into a lot of trouble one day, if we don't watch her. She's going to need a lot of help. If she does go out into the world on her own, as I fear she may do, she's going to be in trouble. Her young emotions won't take this. Nancy and Jennifer were contented to stay at home but Tina's not going to be.

Derek wasn't well. He hadn't been for a long time; feeling constantly exhausted. With retirement still a little way ahead, he was worried that he might be forced into it for health reasons. He still hadn't been to see a doctor but knew he'd have to go; he kept feeling so very tired.

I must go next week, thought Derek, but he was very interested in Tina's changes. She had been very rebellious as a baby, crying all the time. And then as a little girl, so tomboyish. Until this sudden change at puberty. Her physical body had grown up very quickly and she was very mature in that way, but her emotions were not. She was as a child of seven. He could see she might have a bad time.

The weekend flew past. Tina still remained quiet and watched her videos or walked the dogs. She had little to say to Derek and Millie that weekend, or even to Jennifer. On Monday morning Dr. Margaret came to the big house where Tina had dolled herself up to the nines to see Dr. Tom Phillips. She had done her hair the night before, and made it look very attractive and curly. She had on a very pretty blue jumper, which was rather tight and showed off her well-rounded figure, and quite a long skirt. Tina did not favour short skirts for she was rather conscious of her puffy knees, and she hated them to show. She preferred to show off the best of herself – her blue eyes, which were paler now but very pretty, and her dark eyebrows which she'd accentuated with black pencil. She had a beauty spot painted on her face, which she always did herself, for she had a small mole that she liked to make the best of. That day her lips and nails were painted a dark dramatic colour.

What a shock Jennifer and Derek got when she came down to breakfast on Monday morning. Jennifer's first thought was how glad she was that Dorothy couldn't see her – it would have broken her heart. She looked terrible, but strangely attractive.

'You've really overdressed yourself to see Dr. Phillips. I don't know what he's going to think of you.'

'Well, I want to look my best for the doctor,' said Tina in a cheeky voice.

'I know,' said Derek. 'But you'd better wipe some of that muck of your face.'

'I'm not going to,' said Tina. 'Stop interfering, please, Grandad. You're old-fashioned.'

'You shouldn't wear all that make-up,' said Millie. 'I'm your mother. I've a right to tell you and so has your grandfather. Don't be rude to him, Tina.'

Tina's eyes filled with tears. Here we go again, she thought. She stamped her foot and flew up the stairs in a tantrum. She still had tantrums when she couldn't get her own way, or if anyone told her off, for she was very sensitive under her tough exterior.

'Oh dear, this is awful,' said Millie. 'I'd better go up to her.'

'I'll go,' said Jennifer. 'Leave her to me.'

Jennifer went up the stairs. 'Listen, Tina, just take a little bit of that lipstick off, please. And some of that colour on your face, please, just a little. You really do look a bit cheap, actually.'

'I just want to look sexy for the doctor,' said Tina.

Jennifer couldn't help laughing. But it was very sad really, in a thirteen-year-old.

'All right, just to please you, Jennifer. You don't boss me and demand and fuss the way they do. You ask me in a nice way.'

'I understand you better than they do, even Derek. Now hurry up. You'll be late. Do you want me to come?'

'No, it's all right,' said Tina. 'I'll be fine.'

Tina got into the car. Dr. Margaret had just arrived and had been appalled at the sight of her. Even though she had wiped some of the make up off she still looked like a Lolita. Margaret and Derek exchanged glances, both of them worried and concerned.

They got into the car quietly and drove to the hospital. Tina had forgotten the place. She had been there before and looked interestedly around the grounds, remembering them. She also recalled how Jennifer had been there for years, when she was younger, and thought how awful it must have been for her. She wondered briefly if she would end up there herself, for she knew she had problems. The thought of being shut in or trapped terrified her.

They went inside, into the waiting room. 'Now tell him all you can,' urged Dr. Margaret.

Tina got out her compact and looked in the mirror. 'You look all right,' said Dr. Margaret. 'You don't need to worry, you're pretty enough to see Dr. Tom Phillips anyway. He's married.'

Tina laughed. 'I know. I just like to look nice when I'm seeing a doctor.' She smiled at Derek, very sweetly. He wondered why, for it wasn't often she did that. Then the nurse came and said, 'Come on, Tina. It's time for you to go in and see Dr. Phillips.'

Tina walked into the consulting room and looked at Dr. Phillips who was sitting the other side of the desk.

'Sit down, Tina,' said Dr Phillips. He was in his fifties, a very clever psychiatrist, a slim, good-looking man with dark, greying hair, nice pale blue eyes and a very kind smile, suggesting a sense of humour lurking. He knew all about Tina from the letters he had received from the school and her own doctor. Also Dr. Margaret and Derek had been along and had a long talk with him so he knew that Tina had great problems. He knew of the cases of Jennifer and Nancy from his father, who had been quite interested by the family, and had loved Jennifer when he'd looked after her years before.

So Dr. Tom Phillips immediately took a liking to Tina, knowing it was all in the family, but he also liked the look of her. She's attractive. Doesn't look very immature to me. But of course, it's her emotions. Physically, she's very attractive, he thought, looking approvingly at her full, provocative breasts and her curvaceous hips, for the long, straight skirt was figure-hugging and alluring.

'You look very nice, Tina,' said Dr. Phillips. He knew what she was thinking.

Tina gave a knowing grin. 'Thank you,' she replied confidently.

Dr. Phillips knew at once that this was Tina's only weapon. Sex. Her sexual attraction. She had no other weapon, for Tina was a frightened child inside; he knew that from her records. But also, with his knowledge and his brains, he could see that underneath it all was just a frightened little emotional child. This was all a façade. He also knew, from her records and from Mrs. Powell, that Tina was oversexed, for she had learned that she could use her sexual charms: but what would Tina use when she was no longer attractive to men, when she was older? She would have nothing left. Unless of course she found something else, something better in the future, than this. Oh, I hope so, he thought, for she's going to have so many problems.

Tina grinned at him again, wondering what he was thinking about. 'Thinking about my case, I suppose,' said Tina smiling.

'Well, yes,' said Dr. Phillips. 'Now, let's get down to talking, shall we, Tina?'

'All right,' said Tina, looking approvingly at the kind smile. She liked what she saw, a fatherly friend. Knowing that she was going to have to talk with someone for her own sake, she was glad she could relate to him. 'I'm going to talk to you, Dr. Phillips. I feel I can.'

'That's good, Tina. Now would you like to lie on the couch or sit in the chair? There's an armchair over there.'

'I think I'll sit in the armchair,' said Tina.

'All right, you go and sit in the armchair and I'll sit here and we'll have a long talk. As this is your first interview I've spared you an hour.'

'Thank you,' said Tina. 'How do we start?'

'Well,' said the doctor. 'We'll start by me asking you some questions.'

'All right.'

'Now tell me about your home and family.'

Tina found herself, for the first time in her life, pouring her troubles out to an adult. 'You see, Dr. Phillips, I've always felt trapped at home. They smother me. I know they love me and I love them but they fuss over me all the time. They've done it ever since I can remember and it upsets me. I know they say I'm young for my age like Jennifer, but I'm different to her. They try and make me seem like Nancy, like Jennifer, but I'm not them. I'm me.'

'You're very different to them, Tina. But you're still emotionally very immature. In fact, far more than they were at your age.'

'Am I?' said Tina. 'Could you explain that to me, Dr. Phillips?'

'Of course I will. You've grown up physically, Tina, that is, your body's grown up. You've grown up sexually, or at least you're growing up.'

'I know.'

'Mentally, you're good at your work at school. You're only slightly behind your grade. It's not that,' said Dr. Phillips, 'but emotionally, you feel you want to cry sometimes, like a little child, if something upsets you. You're over-sensitive and you still love your toys deep down, and your dogs. You know, you sort of hide, deep down, if you can't cope. You can't cope with stress.'

'How do you know all that?' said Tina in amazement. 'I didn't even have to tell you that.'

'It's my job to know.'

'I think you're wonderful!' said Tina. 'You understand me.' She went on pouring out her troubles. For an hour she talked solidly, as she'd never talked before.

Dr. Tom was a very good listener. When Tina had finished he sat back and said, 'Well, Tina, you've told me everything now. It sounds as if you've never talked to anyone before, not really, apart from your friend Jane. Now I must tell you a few things, Tina, to help you and I want to see you regularly, every two weeks, for the time being. I think as well that you should go back on some tablets.'

'But why?' objected Tina. 'I don't like tablets.'

'I think you should take one a day,' said Dr. Tom. 'You see, you're rather oversexed, Tina. You know that, don't you.'

'I like being like that,' said Tina.

'Yes, that's your façade,' said Dr. Phillips. 'I know you inside out for you're very much like someone I used to know, with similar problems, and she ended up very badly. I don't want that to happen to you, Tina.'

'I want to get married very young,' said Tina. 'And have a nice little house.'

'If you get married young, it would be unwise, for you're emotionally young and you'd never be able to cope with a husband, let alone a child, until you're more mature. And you must be sterilised. You must never have a child. If you ever want sex before you're married, you'll have to take the pill. In fact, I think you should be sterilised early, Tina.'

'I don't want to be sterilised now. I want a child one day.'

'You mustn't feel like that. I know it's the mother instinct in you but you would not be able to look after a child,' said Dr. Phillips, 'but we'll talk about that later on, Tina. You're very young yet. Now remember, no more than kissing with that boyfriend at school. It wouldn't do. You mustn't get yourself into trouble. Do you promise me that, Tina?'

'I promise,' said Tina. 'I promise if ever it has to be, that I'll tell you first.'

'That's a fair deal,' said Dr. Tom. 'I'm very pleased with you today, Tina. And I want to see you regularly for a while. On a Monday morning every two weeks on your way back to school.'

'Very well,' said Tina.

'And do try and get on a little at home. Be nice to Jennifer, she's very good to you.'

'I like Jennifer,' said Tina.

'Yes. She's more like you than the others. But you're one on your own, you know,' said Dr. Tom.

'I know,' said Tina. 'Thank you, Dr. Phillips, for a wonderful talk, and I'll be along to see you again soon.' Suddenly she turned round and smiled a sweet smile at him, her blue eyes flashing.

She is attractive, he thought, and very forward. He smiled. 'Get on with you! See you in a fortnight, Tina.'

'All right,' said Tina. 'See you soon then. Goodbye.' Tina walked out happily, rather tired after her interview. Never had she talked like that before.

Tina said very little on the way back to school. She was thinking of her interview with Dr. Phillips.

Dr. Tom Phillips was thinking of his interview with Tina also. He realised that she would need a lot of support. She was emotionally like a young child, yet over-developed physically. Oversexed. Mentally she was pretty well normal. He could see there might be difficulties, and hope she would co-operate by taking the medication he had prescribed. Musing about her, he could see that she was rather attractive: he was a man after all. Tina had made sure she looked very seductive for that interview, he guessed that. He smiled to himself.

When Tina got back to school she kissed Derek on the cheek.

'Take care of yourself, Grandad.'

'That's nice,' said Derek. 'I think that interview with Dr. Tom has done you good. See you at the weekend, Tina.'

'All right, Grandad. Bye.'

Tina was worried about Derek. She'd heard that he wasn't well; he looked pale and she could see it. In her heart she adored her grandad. It upset her as well to see her mother unhappy. She had told this to Dr. Phillips; how Raymond, having been so much in love with Millie when they got married, had disappointed the family by going off with someone else, seeing other women behind Millie's back, and now she was to have a divorce. Raymond had gone off with another girl.

Derek drove back to Forest Dene Hospital and went to see Dr. Tom, who told him how pleased he was, how Tina had opened up to him. 'You know, Derek, she is fond of you, deep down, and worried about you. So am I. Please see a doctor. You look so thin and pale.'

'I know I'm not well,' said Derek. 'I'm overworked. I may have to retire early.'

'We'd be sorry to lose you, but your health comes first, Derek, and Jennifer matters.'

'She matters more than anything else in the world. That's why I'm so worried,' said Derek.

'Go and see a doctor.'

'I will, I promise. This week,' said Derek. 'Now tell me about Tina.'

'Right,' said Dr. Phillips and he told the interested Derek about Tina's condition. So different to Nancy and Jennifer, and yet similar in many ways. She was oversexed which they had not been; they were normal in that respect. She had developed earlier. Emotionally she was younger than they were, but mentally older.

'She's very mixed up because of this and she must take those pills, they'll help her not to be worried by sexual desires quite so much.'

'Ah, I'll see she takes them when she's at home,' said Derek.

'And Mrs. Powell's going to see she takes them at school,' said Dr. Tom.

'Thanks for all you've done,' said Derek. 'I'll look forward to the next report in a fortnight.'

'Mind you see that doctor.'

'I will,' said Derek. He left the room and went into his office, feeling fatigued and rang his doctor for an appointment.

Back at Greenacres School Tina got Jane into a corner and told her all about Dr. Phillips. She always talked to her friend now and explained everything to her. 'But you must tell no one, Jane. Swear?'

'I swear,' said Jane. 'We'll always keep our secrets, won't we, Tina?'

'Yes,' said Tina.

'By the way,' said Jane, 'we've got a new mistress starting today. She's ever so pretty. Her name's Miss Higman.'

'Sounds nice,' said Tina. 'But I bet she's a bit of a battleaxe, they all are.'

'She's not,' said Jane, 'she's kind and she going to teach us dancing. I mean the old-fashioned dancing.'

'That'll be interesting,' said Tina. 'Let's go and see what she's like.'

'OK,' said Jane.

They ran back into the school and there, standing in the hall, talking to Mrs. Powell, was Miss Higman. Tina was breathtaken by her. She was very pretty indeed.

'This is Tina and Jane,' said Mrs. Powell. 'Shake hands with Miss Higman, girls.'

She was warm and kind, Tina picked it up at once. I like her, she thought, she's lovely.

The two girls giggled and ran off. 'I really like her,' said Tina. For the next week Tina did everything she could to please Miss Higman. By the end of the week Jane started teasing her. 'You've got a crush on her.'

'I haven't,' said Tina, blushing.

'But you have,' said Jane. 'It's your first crush.'

'Well, I'll tell you a secret, Jane. I love her. I do love her.'

'It's a crush,' said Jane.

'You won't tell anyone, will you?' said Tina. 'I'll hit you if you do!' She was quite vicious about it.

'Of course I won't,' said Jane. 'We'll keep that secret to ourselves.'

Tina went on trying to please Miss Higman and she thoroughly enjoyed the dancing lessons, trying her hardest to get a dance with Miss Higman, who knew at once that Tina had a crush on her and did everything she could to discourage her. She was used to this sort of thing. She'll get over it, thought Miss Higman.

The girls spent a very happy weekend at Jane's. Tina was teased a lot by Bill but she could take it and could give him as good as he gave her. Tina still loved this happy family and the small house that went with it.

'Oh Jane!' she said, on the Saturday morning when they went off shopping. 'If only I could live with you. I'd be much happier.'

'Well, that's not possible,' said Jane. 'It would upset your family dreadfully.'

'Mum's got Robert now,' said Tina, 'and he's getting older and pottering about and he'll soon be at school anyway. He has children to play with him and I get fed up. There are always so many people there: Dr. Margaret, Sandy, Joe and Vicky – it's hopeless!'

'I know,' said Jane, 'but you're not there a lot, you're at school. What are you going to do when you leave school, Tina?'

'I do want to talk to Dr. Phillips about that. I don't really know,' said Tina. 'But between you and me . . . can you keep a real secret, Jane? Do you swear?'

'I swear,' said Jane, holding her hand up as always. They took hands and Jane swore she'd keep another secret for Tina.

'When I leave school, and when I'm old enough legally, I'm going to run away,' said Tina. 'I'm going to go and live in a town and one day I'll find a husband and have a small house – just like you, Jane.'

'Oh Tina, you won't be able to cope alone like that.'

'I will,' said Tina stubbornly. 'I'll find someone.'

'Well, don't let's talk about it till you do leave school. It's not for a long time yet.' Jane felt very worried about Tina. 'Look, Tina, let's stick together in everything, shall we? At least let's try.'

'We'll try,' said Tina. 'We're best friends and we'll have lots of fun, but I don't like boys my own age like you do.'

Jane had got very friendly with boys her own age and she was now seeing Jerry at school, but Tina kept out of the way of the boys: she found them immature and boring.

The two girls watched videos at the weekend, love films mostly now, and thrillers. 'I do like older men,' said Tina to Jane.

'I know,' said Jane. 'Perhaps you'll marry one day. Someone who can take care of you and understand you.'

'Maybe,' said Tina. 'We'll see. But I'm going to have lots of fun first.'

'I bet you will,' said Jane laughing. 'Knowing you!'

They both laughed and enjoyed the films. On Sunday they went to church as always and Tina still enjoyed the service, for deep in her heart she was very curious about spiritual things and she loved God. She just wondered why she got weird thoughts and felt the way she did.

Jane went home with Tina the following weekend and they thoroughly enjoyed themselves at the big house. Jane played with little Robert; she liked babies but Tina was bored with them.

'Jane will make a good mother,' Millie said. 'Just the type of girl who would. Simple, but able to cope and Robert loves her.'

Raymond had now left home altogether and Millie had got a divorce on the grounds of adultery. Raymond was allowed to see his son one weekend every month. That had been arranged between themselves. They were to be friends, but that was all. Millie was very bitter about Raymond.

Tina was now trying to show love to Derek though, her grandfather, for Derek wasn't well at all. He had arranged to go and see the doctor the following week; he had put it off two or three times but this time he knew he must go. Jennifer knew her husband wasn't well and was very worried.

The weekend flew by quickly. The girls had enjoyed walking in the woods with the dogs, watching videos and talking about love, looking at clothes and wearing make-up.

On Monday morning Derek and Millie drove them to the hospital, where Jane was to wait while Tina saw Dr. Phillips. 'How are you getting on, Tina?' said Dr. Tom.

'I'm all right,' said Tina, 'but I'm in love. I don't like young boys, they bore me.'

'Well, who are you in love with?' said Dr. Tom.

'I'm in love with Miss Higman at school. She is one of my teachers and she's awfully pretty. I really love her and I do all I can for her.'

'Oh, that's a schoolgirl crush.' Dr. Phillips tried to explain crushes in schools, even in normal schools, but Tina was very stubborn about it.

'It's not a crush! I really love her, Dr. Tom.'

'You'll get over it.'

'I'll never get over it,' insisted Tina.

'Well, we'll see. Now are you taking your pills, Tina? Do you feel better?'

'Yes,' said Tina. 'I do really, and it's made me quieten down a bit. I know what you mean, Dr. Phillips, but it hasn't stopped me altogether.'

'It wasn't intended to. It was just to help you a bit.'

'I still get feelings,' said Tina.

'Of course you will. That's quite normal.'

Tina opened up her heart to Dr. Tom once more and they had a long, long talk. Tina would only talk to him and he knew it. She would never talk to Dr. Margaret. Dr. Tom hoped that one day she might be able to, or perhaps to her son, Joe, but at present Tina needed an outsider to talk to and as she was willing to talk to Dr. Tom, he was quite willing for her to do so. 'I'm worried about Grandad,' said Tina. 'He's not very well.'

'Have you noticed it?' said Dr. Tom.

'Yes,' said Tina. 'Is he going to die? Because it would upset Jennifer very much and I do love her, you know.'

'I know you do,' said Dr. Tom, 'and I hope he won't die, but he must go to the doctor's.'

'He's promised to go tomorrow,' said Tina. 'I heard him telling my mum.'

'I'm glad to hear it,' said Dr. Tom. 'Don't worry, Tina, I'm sure your grandfather will be all right.'

'I hope so,' said Tina with a sigh, 'for Jennifer would be very upset. They're happy, you know.'

'I know they are,' said Dr. Tom. 'Now our hour has passed. Come again in a fortnight, Tina, and if you go on doing well as this, it'll be once a month.'

So Tina left Dr. Phillips' office, having had a long session with him. He was very pleased with her. She was taking her tablets regularly and looked much better for them. He was amused about the crush on Miss Higman, but knew that would pass in time.

Tina and Jane were driven back to school by Millie and Derek.

'Take care of yourself, Grandad,' said Tina, as they got out of the car. 'Go to the doctor tomorrow, won't you.' She gave him a kiss on the cheek and then pecked her mother and ran, colouring up as she ran through the door with Jane. Derek could see that Tina did love him, and how shy she was still. When they were driving back Millie said, 'Dad, please go to the doctor tomorrow. Don't cancel it again.'

'I won't this time. I'm dreadfully tired.'

'I'm worried about you,' said Millie. 'What happens to Jennifer if . . .'

'I know what you're thinking, Millie. I hope it won't be for a long time.'

'I'm sure it won't, but please go to the doctor!'

'I will,' said Derek.

The girls settled in at Greenacres School once more. Tina went on enjoying being with Miss Higman. She had started doing a lot more painting now, for Miss Higman also taught art and Tina set out to please her in every way. This resulted in the production of some beautiful paintings which amazed everyone in the school; including the Powells, who were absolutely thrilled with the work.

'She's got a real gift,' said Mr. Powell one evening.

'I know she has,' said Mrs. Powell, 'and honestly, I wish she'd take it up, even as a hobby, when she's older.'

Chapter 6

The next day Derek went to see the doctor in Guildford, having recently changed from the family doctor in the village. It was time to seek a younger and fresher opinion, he had decided.

'Dr. Jones, I've been feeling terribly tired lately. I want you to find out what's wrong with me. I've got a great deal to worry about with my work at Forest Dene Hospital and my wife at home, and Tina.'

'Yes, I've read all your records,' said Dr. Jones. 'You've got quite a lot on your plate. Come on, old boy, let's examine you.' The doctor examined Derek and then they went and sat down. 'I want you to see a specialist, Derek,' said Dr. Jones.

'Why?'

'It's just that I want you to have a cardiograph and one or two tests. I don't think there's anything wrong with your blood – I've taken some this morning, as you know – but your heart is tired. It's not quite right. I want you to see a specialist next week. I'll arrange it. You'll be sent an appointment. Now listen, Derek,' said Dr. Jones. 'You must be careful. And I want you to take some time off work. Two or three days a week, say.'

'All right,' said Derek. 'I'll arrange it.'

Derek felt depressed as he drove home. He was sure it was his heart. He had felt very tired and weak somehow, and had to lie down a lot. It just wasn't like him, who'd always been so lively. He was only just over sixty, after all.

Derek went into work and explained to Dr. Tom, 'I'll have to have two or three days off a week. It's doctor's orders. It's my heart, you know.'

'I thought it might be,' said Dr. Tom. 'Derek, for years you've had so much stress and worry and you've coped with it. All these years. Even in your childhood you had Jennifer to worry about. You've never had a bit of peace of your own. Or a proper holiday. Nothing. Even your honeymoon was spent taking care of Jennifer's wishes, thinking of her.'

'I know,' said Derek. 'I like being kind to other people.'

'Now you've got the worry of Tina, but let it be my worry from now on,' said Dr. Tom.

'I will,' said Derek. 'I'll take it easy.'

'Don't come in tomorrow, come in the next day, and go home today, Derek. You look so white.'

'I think I will go home, if you don't mind. The doctor has given me a few tablets.'

Derek went home and lay down: he did feel very tired. Jennifer was very concerned. 'Oh Derek, if anything happened to you, what would I do?'

'Jennifer,' said Derek. 'I've taught you how. You're older now and you can cope, if anything did happen to me,' said Derek.

'I don't want anything to happen to you yet, Derek. Try and stay for me.'

'I'll try and oblige,' said Derek, 'but take care of me, Jennifer. Don't give me any worry, will you?'

'Do I ever?' said Jennifer.

'Huh! You've given me a lot of worry in your life but I've wanted to do it. I've always loved you.'

'I'll take care of you,' said Jennifer.

Years before she could never have done that but now she was able to do so. Knowing that Rene, the housekeeper, was there she didn't feel she would have to have the full responsibility of things and so she could cope. Had she been alone she would have run away, terrified, but there was always someone there to take full responsibility, so Jennifer was able to handle the situation.

The following week Derek went to see the specialist in Guildford. He had some heart tests and was told that he had a bad heart. 'How long have I got?' said Derek. 'Be honest with me, Dr. Wilcox.'

'I will. You're a sensible man, Derek. You can work two days a week at the hospital, but light duties, please. You must take the medication and I insist you rest a lot and have no stress at all. I say you'll make it for another five years. If you're lucky, a bit longer. But you must be careful. If you're not, you won't have a year.'

'All right,' said Derek, feeling very depressed.

'I know it depresses you. You're an active man, Derek. I'm so sorry I can't do any more for you,' said Dr. Wilcox.

'I understand,' said Derek. He was to see the specialist and have a checkup once a month and knew he'd have to do as he was told.

Derek had to retire after three months. He was given a wonderful send-off and a beautiful gift by the patients and staff who had loved him all those years. They had given him a beautiful gold watch, the very best money could buy. Derek said he would treasure it always.

'I've been happy here,' he said. 'I shall miss everybody, and I'm sure a new psychologist will take my place.'

'He had met the young man who was to take his place, who seemed very sympathetic and competent, and he had dropped him a few hints. 'I think Philip will do very well at his job.'

So Derek left Forest Dene Hospital for good and went home to take it easy in the house he loved so much, the big house. Jennifer and Georgina would look after him and love him. That was all he wanted now.

He spent a lot of time in his room. He was allowed to go downstairs, but only once a day. He was quite an invalid really.

Even Tina loved him at weekends. She really loved her grandfather and now she knew he was so sick she managed to show more love towards him. 'I love you, Grandad,' she said one weekend. 'Don't die on me, will you?'

'I'll try not to for a long time. You and Jennifer, you're dreadful!'

'We're not, we just love you,' said Tina.

Derek never thought he'd hear Tina say that. 'And I love you, Tina.'

She hugged her grandfather and went out of the room. She went into her own room and cried her eyes out. Jane was with her and comforted her. 'Oh Tina, you'll have to face it in the end.'

'I do love my grandfather. I wish I could have shown it before,' said Tina.

'You couldn't,' said Jane. 'He understands, but do it now; you've got him now. Better late than never.'

So life settled down once more at the big house, with Derek taking it easy and having a lot of love and help. Tina went on happily at school, seeing Dr. Tom regularly now and taking the tranquillisers he had given her to help her. Tina went on loving Miss Higman for a little while longer and then Miss Higman had to leave the school and go and live in Cornwall, for she had met a young man there and they were to be married. That had broken Tina's heart. She cried the day Miss Higman left. 'Oh, Miss Higman, I've always loved you. I'll send you paintings,' said Tina.

'I'll always remember you, Tina. I was your first crush. I understand these things,' said Miss Higman. She had grown to love the young girl with the big blue eyes. There was something about her, she thought. 'We'll write to one another if you like,' said Miss Higman kindly.

'I hope your wedding's wonderful, and I'm ever so jealous of your husband.'

'You mustn't be like that. Because one day you'll have one of your own, I'm sure.'

'I hope so,' said Tina forlornly.

Chapter 7

Tina was now sixteen years old. It was just before Christmas. They had just broken up from school. Jane had been asked to stay with her for the Christmas holidays and to spend her birthday with her. Tina was now a young woman, although emotionally still as retarded as ever. Mentally she was quite normal, though complex, and physically very advanced. Tina was now tall, with a good figure, well-covered, still taking her tranquillisers, still seeing Dr. Phillips once a month. Tina was not interested in boys at school. She was interested in older men, but had not, as yet, had a relationship. She was not ready for that, but Tina had fantasies of what she wanted in the future. She always dressed nicely. Tina liked casual clothes as Jennifer had done. She liked her jeans. But she liked to wear clothes which were more revealing. Tina liked to show her body off to men. She felt it was all she had and Tina liked to wear make-up on her face, and lipstick. Her appearance was what she felt was her weapon.

Now she was home at the big house for the Christmas holidays. Derek, her grandfather, was still alive and keeping as well as could be expected. He had long since retired now, but was still having to rest a lot. His heart had grown a little stronger with all the rest he'd had and the love, so the doctor hoped he might live for a little while yet.

The day before Tina's birthday, she talked to Jane. 'Oh, Jane, I wonder what they're going to give me.'

'I know you want that hi-fi unit. I wonder if you'll get it.'

'And all those tapes I've written down on the list,' said Tina.

'I've got you something but I'm not going to tell you what it is,' said Jane.

'I know Mum's going to try and buy me some clothes. We're going into town this afternoon,' said Tina. 'Would you like to come as well, Jane?'

'I'd rather go in the woods for a walk with Georgina and the dogs. I've got a bit of a headache today,' said Jane.

'Go on then, I expect Jennifer will go too.'

'Oh, she will,' said Jane.

'I'm looking forward to going into town with Mummy.'

'Robert can come with us,' said Jane. 'If he likes.'

Robert was now over five years old. He had started at the village school and was totally normal and very intelligent, much to Millie's joy, and that of the rest of the family. Robert adored Tina, his older half-sister. He was an attractive young boy, with dark hair and pale blue eyes and such a lovely nature. He loved everyone at the big house and fitted in beautifully, and Robert had friends. Margaret's grandson often came to play, and there were friends from the village school who would come over to play in the big house.

Now, after lunch Tina was excited as her birthday grew closer. 'Come on,' said Millie. 'Or we're going to be late getting into town.'

Tina flew upstairs and tidied herself up and put on her make-up. She was to have her hair done that afternoon as a treat for her birthday. They drove into town quietly. Tina never had too much to say to Millie. In Guildford they parked the car and went straight to the hairdresser's. Tina's hair was beautiful when it was finished and she was very pleased with it. It was wavy and cut short and she looked very attractive indeed, and Millie knew it. She's a real sexpot, she thought. She could see that men were going to love her. It was a worry, especially as Tina was leaving school soon.

They went into several boutiques. At last Tina found what she wanted from her mother. She chose a longish skirt, and a very pretty jumper in blue, with leaves embroidered on the front. It was a tight-fitting jumper, Millie noticed. Then she bought some underwear, two nightshirts, and a new bra with panties to match. She also bought a pair of jeans and another sweater, in black, with money that Derek had given her. To go with them, a denim jacket. That was to be from Robert.

When they'd finished the shopping, Millie said, 'Let's get a cup of tea, Tina.'

'I'd like that,' said Tina, feeling friendly towards her mother that afternoon. She still felt distant from her, but was enjoying the little outing. It was very rarely that they did this. Millie felt the strain too, but loved her daughter, realising how hard it was for her to express affection.

They had a cup of tea and Tina had some cakes. Two men at the next table stared at her quite openly. Millie noticed that. So did Tina, turning round to grin at them. 'You shouldn't do that. It's very bad manners,' admonished her mother.

'I don't care,' said Tina. 'I like to be admired.'

'I know but you shouldn't do it,' said Millie.

'I don't care, I do what I want, Mummy.'

'You're a very naughty girl, Tina.'

'Tina went sulky and quiet. They walked silently back to the car. Suddenly, Tina saw a tiny shop. In the window was a jumper she really liked. Better than what she'd bought in fact. It was white and had a cowboy like fringe round it in a grey colour.

'Oh, that would go with my boots, Mum. I wish I'd seen this one before, and it's a big size. It would fit me. Oh, Mum. It would go with my jeans. Oh, please, Mum'

'Look, Tina, I'm not going to spoil you. You've had enough.'

'I want the jumper. Oh please,' said Tina, tears streaming down her face, like the young child she still was emotionally.

'Well, I'll tell you what I'll do. I'm not going to spoil you,' said Millie. 'Christmas is coming up soon. You may have it for your Christmas present.'

'But I want it for my birthday,' raged Tina. 'I want it now!'

'I will buy you the jumper, but you'll have it for Christmas. Or,' said her mother, 'you will not have the new skirt and the other two jumpers till Christmas. Now which is it to be?'

'I'll wait for the other skirt and two jumpers till Christmas. I want this one for my birthday. I want to wear it for my party.'

'All right,' said Millie, 'but you will not get the other items until Christmas.'

That did not worry Tina. She had seen this jumper. She adored jumpers. She had any amount of them, more than anything else. This one fitted her well, showing up her rounded bust.

'This will go very well with a pair of my best jeans.'

Tina now felt tired. She sat in the car relaxing, almost falling asleep, and was glad to get home.

She took the clothes upstairs and put them on her mother's bed. She wasn't allowed to have the skirt and two jumpers till Christmas, she knew that. She knew her mother would pack the other jumper for her birthday tomorrow.

Tina went into her bedroom to lie down and immediately fell asleep. It was all too much. Any display of emotion upset her.

At teatime Jennifer came up with a cup of tea for her. So many times before in the past Tina had taken Jennifer tea up. And now Jennifer was helping Tina, knowing that Tina was going through many things that she had.

'Oh, thank you, Jennifer,' said Tina, looking a bit tearful, waking up the same way as Jennifer did, depressed and upset. 'I did feel tired. I still do.'

'You're like I was, still am,' said Jennifer, 'but take it easy tonight, Tina. Tell you what, it's your birthday tomorrow, you mustn't do too much. Let's watch a video together tonight. Jane would like that. We'll show one to Robert before he goes to bed, shall we? And then we'll watch one of your love films.'

'Oh yes,' said Tina. 'I'd like that, Jennifer. You're an angel! Thank you for helping me.'

'I understand you, and so does Grandad,' said Jennifer.

'Grandad's sick, isn't he?'

'He's a lot better than he was, but nobody must worry him.'

'I know that,' said Tina. 'I won't anyway. I love him.'

Tina put on her jeans and an old sweater as she always did when she got tired. She didn't even bother to look at her new hairstyle, or spend time re-doing her face; she was too tired. Millie liked the look of her. She looked more casual and much fresher, less cheap without the make-up on.

'Your hair does look nice,' said Derek. 'You'll look beautiful for your birthday.'

After tea Jennifer took Tina and Robert into the little video room. Later on Georgina and Julian joined them. They watched a little child's film, which Tina enjoyed for she was still so very young for her age, and then Millie came to take Robert to bed.

'Goodnight, Tina,' said Robert.

'Goodnight, Robert.' Tina was quite fond of him now.

Robert said, 'I've got a present for you, Tina, tomorrow. It's your birthday.'

'Thank you,' said Tina. 'I'm looking forward to that.'

Millie took Robert up to bed. She was very close to the little boy and showered all her love upon him. She read him a story and tucked him up and hugged him.

'Goodnight, Mummy. I love you.'

'Say your prayers,' said Millie.

Robert said his prayers with his mother and hugged and kissed her, which made her so happy. They would be very close in the future, Millie knew that.

Jennifer and Tina, Georgina and Jane watched a love film. Jennifer watched very carefully, so Tina wouldn't notice, for Tina was so shy about these things, and saw, as the story went on, a few tears trickle down Tina's cheeks. Poor thing, thought Jennifer. She can't show it to us. Suddenly Tina saw Jennifer looking at her and quickly brushed the tears away with her hand.

'Don't be ashamed of your tears, Tina,' said Jennifer.

'It's nothing,' said Tina. 'My eyes are just watering. You know they get sore and red when I strain them, and I've been straining them.' She looked back at Jennifer. 'I wasn't crying, you know.'

'You were crying,' said Jennifer. 'You were crying at the love film.'

Tina's lip quivered. 'And so what if I was, Jennifer?' Suddenly she burst into tears. Jennifer took her into her arms, and held her for ten minutes while she sobbed. Jane and Georgina disappeared from the room, knowing that Tina would be embarrassed.

'There' said Jennifer. 'Is that better, dear?'

She wiped Tina's eyes. Her own eyes were full of tears.

'Oh,' said Tina. 'I've made you cry, Jennifer.'

'Yes,' said Jennifer, who was never ashamed of her tears.

'Promise not to tell Mum,' said Tina.

'What would it matter if I did?' said Jennifer.

'I don't want her to know. I'm tough.' said Tina.

'You're no more tough than I am,' said Jennifer.

'Do you swear to God it's a secret?' said Tina. 'Please!'

'All right,' said Jennifer. 'Until you want me to, I won't tell her you're a softy-pot over love films. It's your age, Tina. You like love.'

'I know,' said Tina. 'Can we see the end of the film?'

'What, and cry a bit more?' said Jennifer. 'All right, let's cry together.' They both got on to the settee and Jennifer held Tina in her arms tightly and they watched the end of the film. Neither one cared about their tears then. They both shed some together and then at the end of the film, sat back and roared with laughter at themselves.

'Keep our secret,' said Tina. She hugged Jennifer as she'd never hugged her before and kissed her.

'That's a wonderful hug for your birthday tomorrow, but I'll want another one tomorrow morning,' said Jennifer.

'I'll come up with you, if you like.'

They both went up the spiral staircase and went and said goodnight to Millie, who was in her room, reading.

'Goodnight, Mum,' said Tina.

Millie noticed the red eyes, and knew that Tina had been crying. 'Goodnight, Tina. Happy birthday tomorrow,' she said, wishing that she could get close to her daughter. She was just glad that Tina could be herself with someone, and decided not to comment on her tear-stained face. Tina kissed her mother on the cheek and fled from the room. She suddenly felt she wanted to cry again, for she did love her mother, but fled into her bedroom before that could happen, where Jane was sitting up in bed reading a book.

'I'm sorry I left you,' said Jane.

'It's all right,' said Tina. 'You were very kind.'

'You had a good cry, then, over that film. How did it end?'

'Oh, it was OK at the end. He got back with her and she forgave him about the other woman.'

'Good,' said Jane. 'You'll have plenty of films to watch tomorrow.'

'I won't,' said Tina. 'I've seen them all before.'

'I'm not going to tell you my secret,' said Jane.

'They both laughed. Tina guessed she might get some films for her birthday.

Tina had a lovely bedroom in the big house which faced out on to the woods and the great lawns with the beautiful trees and flowers around. The room had two single beds in, one for Tina and one for her friend. It had been arranged when Jane started coming home for the holidays. Jane's bed was always in the room now, and there were bookshelves and a small portable television. There was a cassette player in the corner and a very old record player, but Jane knew that tomorrow Tina was to have a music centre; her own music centre. It was a surprise but Jane wasn't going to tell her.

Jane put her book down and looked around, contemplating Tina and the big house. She was more settled than she was, it was true. Jane couldn't understand why Tina hated it so much. She, Jane, wouldn't have minded being there all the time.

Tina had bad dreams that night, very weird and disturbed

dreams, as she always did when she was in an emotional turmoil. She awoke to a crisp, sunny day and looked around her, still feeling rather depressed. Jane was still sleeping. It was early, seven o'clock. It's my birthday, thought Tina, but I don't feel cheerful as I should. Perhaps I will when I've had my tea and my pill. She lay and looked about the room. I've got to watch it, she thought. I'm showing my emotions too much. I mustn't. Or perhaps I must.

With that, the door opened and in came Millie, with a cup of tea and her tablet. 'Good morning, Tina. A happy birthday, darling! A happy sixteenth birthday.'

'Thank you, Mummy, said Tina and kissed her on the cheek.

'You'll have your presents at breakfast. Now have your tea quietly, and your tablet, and come down to breakfast.'

'All right, Mummy. Thank you.'

Millie put a cup of tea beside Jane's bed. 'Good morning, Jane.'

'Good morning Millie,' said Jane, at once waking up with no trouble at all. 'It's a lovely day for Tina's birthday.'

Millie left the room and left the two girls talking.

As Tina's pill began to work she and Jane began chattering. Tina felt better. It was her birthday, she had better cheer up. I'm getting too soppy, thought Tina. She voiced this to Jane.

'But you're sixteen, and all sixteen-year-old girls are soppy. I was sixteen last month, remember, and I'm just the same over boys.'

'I like older men,' said Tina, 'like the one in the film last night. That's what made me cry.'

They both laughed and then got up and had a shower.

'I'm dying to open my presents,' said Tina, putting on some old jeans and a sweater, knowing that later on in the day she would be wearing some new clothes. I'm going to enjoy my birthday, she thought.

'Come on, Jane. Let's get down to breakfast and see what I've got for my birthday.'

They ran down the spiral staircase and into the large dining room where everyone was sitting down to breakfast. They all looked up as Tina came in.

'Good morning, Tina. Happy birthday to you.'

Tina curled up. She always felt embarrassed with any emotion. She just smiled a watery smile and felt the tears welling up. Oh dear, I am getting silly, she thought. She swallowed very hard and said, 'Thank you, everybody,' sat down with Jane and drank her juice.

Tina smoked. She had started smoking at school. Some of the boys and girls did the same. Jane did not smoke. They knew it was bad for their health, but Tina felt a great comfort in smoking cigarettes and had smoked since she was about thirteen. They had found out at home about the smoking and had told her she was not to do it. But every morning, when Tina got up, she had a cigarette in her room. She felt at this moment, drinking her orange, with all the eyes at the table watching her, that she would love to have a cigarette. She looked up, her grey blue eyes looking straight at her grandfather, Derek, sitting there looking very tired and pale, but happy.

'Grandad, it's my birthday and you're a psychologist, let me have a cigarette with my juice before I eat. Please, Grandad.'

They all roared with laughter, even little Robert. It sounded so funny.

'I'm not a psychologist for nothing,' said Derek, roaring with laughter. It did him good and cheered him up. 'Of course you can have one. It's your birthday, Tina.' He knew he could have said nothing else for Tina would have been very upset. She lit a cigarette and sat there and enjoyed it with her juice.

Millie felt rather cross. She did not want Tina to smoke or be encouraged but Derek knew no one would ever stop Tina doing what she wanted and if a cigarette comforted her, he and Dr. Tom Phillips realised it was better to let her do it. Millie had not agreed with them but there were some things Millie was wrong about and this was one of them.

The family quietly finished their breakfast, then Tina opened her presents while the others sat around watching. Little Robert got very excited as he watched his older sister opening her presents. 'Isn't there one for me?' he chanted in his little voice.

Jane, who was very good with small children, went over to him and said, 'Oh Robert, but it's not your birthday, it's Tina's. On your birthday, you'll have presents but today, only Tina has presents.'

'I've got a surprise for you,' said Millie.

'What's that, Mummy?' said Robert.

'I haven't forgotten you. Because you're such a little boy I've bought you one present, to mark Tina's birthday.'

Robert jumped up and down in excitement as his mother gave him a little parcel. He opened it and was very pleased with it. It was two little video films. 'Oh, I shall watch them tonight, after the party,' he said, and ran off to play happily.

Tina thoroughly enjoyed opening her presents. She was thrilled with the clothes that she and her mother had bought the day before. Millie kept to her word and kept back the skirt and two sweaters for Christmas but the rest of the clothes Tina was given. She was very pleased with the undies and the nightshirts and with the beautiful jumper she had seen in the window on the way back to the car. 'Thank you, Mummy. I shall wear it to my party this afternoon,' said Tina.

'I'm glad you like it,' said Millie smiling.

Tina went over and pecked her mother on the cheek, for that was all she could do with Millie at the moment.

'Come and open my present now,' said Jennifer.

Tina opened some nice presents, from Derek and Jennifer. There were five video films: three thrillers and two love stories. She was thrilled to bits and couldn't have wanted anything more. She was short of films and so pleased. There were also some cassette tapes of some music she wanted. Tina didn't like the modern music too much. She hated the heavy stuff of the modern day and liked the old love songs that could still be bought in the shops, of the fifties, sixties and seventies. Jennifer and Derek had carefully chosen three or four cassette tapes for her, as well as the videos. She was delighted.

'Oh, thank you, Grandad! Thank you, Jennifer,' Tina said, feeling a lump in her throat again and swallowing it, as she went on opening the other presents. Millie had bought Tina two more cassette tapes from Robert. Tina went over and kissed her little brother. She was very pleased and very fond of him, deep down. Then Jane said, 'Open my present, Tina.'

Tina happily opened three more video films. 'Hooray!' she said. 'More films! You couldn't have bought me anything I would have wanted more.'

Millie went and fetched the present that Dr. Margaret had brought in for her daughter. There were two beautiful blue nightshirts and one more video tape. How lucky Tina was! This was a blank tape she could tape films on. She was very pleased. 'They know my favourite colour', said Tina.

'They know you,' said her grandfather, laughing.

'I suppose so.' Even though she couldn't relate to Dr. Margaret and Sandy, she was very fond of them, and they were coming to her party that afternoon, bringing the family with them.

'Now for the family present – the big present from everybody,' announced Jennifer. 'Come into the lounge, Tina.'

They all went into the lounge and there, standing in the window, was a beautiful music centre, the one Tina had coveted for so long and had pointed out to her mother and Jennifer in a shop in Guildford.

'Oh, it's wonderful!' shrieked Tina. 'Where can I have it? Can I have it in my room, Mummy?'

'You can have it in your room or in the video room. It's up to you, Tina.'

'I'd like this one in my room, to play my own personal music on.' There were headphones so Tina would be able to listen to things that she didn't want others to hear. They knew she got embarrassed about music; the love songs of the fifties and sixties that she loved so much.

'This is from all of us,' said Derek.

'Oh Grandad, Jennifer, Mummy – thank you so much!' She went and hugged everybody. Tina felt the tears welling up again and ran over to Jennifer and hugged and kissed her. 'Jennifer, can we go for a walk in the woods, on our own? Just for a while. I feel very . . . you know . . .'

'Tina and I would like to go for a walk on our own,' said Jennifer, winking at Derek.

'That's fine,' said Millie. 'We've got a lot to do to get ready for the party. Rene's getting the other staff to help. We've got to get everything laid out nicely.'

'Thanks,' said Tina and flew out of the French windows, Jennifer behind her, the dogs following. They went to the big tree where all the romances had taken place.

'I wonder,' said Tina. 'if I'll ever have a lover here. As Nancy and Gordon were, as you and Grandad were. Oh Jennifer! I'm getting all soppy, aren't I?'

'You are, you're sixteen now; and so you should be, Tina.'

'But I can't show it to the others. I don't want to.'

'You don't have to,' said Jennifer. 'You don't have to, dear. Let's keep it our secret.'

'Well, Jane knows. She's my best friend.'

'Georgina has always been my best friend. She's at work now,' said Jennifer. 'She and Julian have got something for you. Tina, there is something I must tell you today. Julian and Georgina are leaving the big house in a month's time, to go and live by the seaside, in Exmouth, Devon. They've always loved the sea and wanted to be close to it so they feel they'd like to retire there. We're going down to help them buy a little house. They've been down once and seen somewhere they'd like, but they want to go and Georgina, whose parents are now dead, as you know, has a cousin living there. She's very fond of him and he will be able to help them with little things they can't cope with. They really want to go. They love the big house but they feel they really want to go there and be quiet and alone for the rest of their lives.'

'I shall be sad to see them go but they're very quiet and withdrawn, a bit like me,' said Tina. 'Always on their own.'

'I know,' said Jennifer, 'but you do understand? You're not too upset?'

'Of course not,' said Tina. 'I don't like too many crowds myself.'

'I thought you'd say that,' said Jennifer. 'The house is getting much thinner now with less people.'

'There'll always be someone in it, I'm sure,' said Tina.

'I hope so,' said Jennifer. 'In the future. I really hope so. Well we'd better be getting back.'

Tina gave Jennifer another cuddle.

'I love you,' said Tina. 'Jennifer, you understand me. You're more like me.'

'Come on, cheer up! You are all funny today. It's your birthday. Be happy today.' Jennifer sighed and they walked back to the big house with the dogs behind them and got ready for the party in the afternoon.

After lunch Julian and Georgina came in and gave Tina their present. 'I know you're going away,' said Tina. 'Jennifer told me this morning. I do understand and I hope you'll be ever so happy in Exmouth. You'll like the sea, won't you?'

'I've always wanted to live by the sea,' said Julian.'

'So have I,' said Georgina. 'We've loved it here and always been happy. We'll always be grateful to the family for having us, but we want to be by the sea now.'

'Well, you love swimming, don't you,' said Tina. 'I'll be able to come and stay with you sometimes.'

'Of course,' said Georgina. 'We're all going down to the new house next week and we're moving in a month.'

'I know you'll be happy,' said Tina.

Tina then opened Julian and Georgina's present, a pair of trainers for walking, an LP that Tina had wanted for a long time, and two blank cassette tapes. 'Thanks, Julian and Georgina,' said Tina.

'It's just what I wanted. Thanks!' She hugged and kissed them both, realising that she would miss them a lot.

After lunch Millie insisted that Tina rested. She could see that she was very emotional and that it was one of her bad days, that she was edgy. 'You must take a rest, and you, Jennifer. You look tired today,' said Millie. After dealing with Tina, Jennifer felt very emotional that day and was glad to go and have a rest. Derek was already lying there, resting, as he had to do a lot of that these days.

'You seem upset today, Jennifer,' he said.

'I know,' said Jennifer. 'It's Tina. She seems very fragile these days and I can't make it out.'

'It's her age,' said Derek. 'I could see it coming. She's trying to hide it from the rest of us but she's letting you know about it, Jennifer. You should feel very honoured.'

'I understand her. I'm like her and she knows that,' said Jennifer. 'People respond. Like attracts like.'

'The clever psychologist!' laughed Derek.

'Oh, you tease!' Jennifer kissed him.

Millie called them all at four o'clock.

Both girls got up and ready for the party, Tina in her new jumper with the cowboy fringes. They ran downstairs to the big lounge where everybody was now gathered. Dr. Margaret had brought her son and his wife Vicky. Joe was now a qualified psychiatrist and had started to work at Forest Dene Hospital.

'We've got some presents for you,' said Joe.

In a tiny parcel was a pair of gold earrings. 'It's with mine and Joe's love,' said Vicky. Then she handed Tina a little parcel from their son, Richard, containing another video tape, a love film.

'Hooray!' said Tina. 'Another film. Thank you, Richard. Thank you all for the lovely presents.'

The big tea party went off well, with everybody sitting at the table while Tina had to get up, as was the tradition, make three wishes and cut the cake. In the middle of the hubbub, Derek complained of pains in his chest. Jennifer helped him to bed, very worried. Tina went up to see him, crying.

'Grandad, please don't be ill. I love you.'

'It's only I'm a bit tired today,' said Derek. He took a tablet and lay back against the pillows, grey with exhaustion.

For the rest of the evening they played records and danced. Jane's parents came over with Bill and brought her more presents. She danced with Bill, in the old-fashioned, smoochy way and that suited Bill fine. 'I wish you'd be my girlfriend, Tina. You're very attractive today. And I'm eighteen. We're just the right age for one another.'

'I've told you before, Bill,' said Tina, 'I really like you. But I prefer older men.'

'Pooh,' said Bill. 'You won't like them for long. They're hopeless.'

'They're not,' said Tina. 'I'm going to marry someone older than me.'

'Please yourself,' said Bill. 'But the offer's there. Don't keep me waiting long else I shall see somebody else. There are plenty of girls in Guildford.'

He did not succeed in making Tina jealous. She liked Bill, as a brother, but certainly didn't want him as a boyfriend. She went off, laughing, enjoying the rest of the evening, dancing, chattering.

Dr. Margaret went up and saw Derek before she left, and found him looking very poorly. 'If you don't feel better in the morning, Derek, you must have a doctor.'

As Dr. Margaret and Sandy left, Tina ran out into the driveway and touched Dr. Margaret's arm. 'What is it, Tina?' said Dr. Margaret, looking surprised. It was very rare for Tina to approach her.

'It's just that I'm very worried about Grandad. Why did he have to get sick on my birthday?'

'Oh, my dear, he's been sick for years. You know that, Tina. But he's very tired. He's been better for a while. I'm sure he'll be all right, Tina. Don't worry.'

'Oh, Dr. Margaret, I don't want him to die.'

'He'll be all right. But you'll have to face the fact that your grandfather's going to die sometime.'

'But it's Jennifer I'm worried about,' said Tina. 'It'll break her heart.'

'She couldn't face these things years ago,' said Dr. Margaret. 'But she's got me and she's got you now. You're close to her, Tina.'

Tina suddenly felt a warmth towards Dr. Margaret. She liked the lady doctor. Later on she felt she might even be able to talk to her. 'Thanks Dr. Margaret,' she said, the tears welling up in her eyes. She ran back into the house, tired out after all the excitement of the day, and up to her room, after going to see Derek.

'Goodnight, Jennifer. Goodnight, Grandad. Get well, please, Grandad.'

'I'll try, for your sake and for Jennifer's.'

Jennifer and Tina looked at one another, both of them with eyes full of tears, sensing that Derek was very sick indeed.

When Tina had gone to bed, Derek said, 'You know, Jennifer, when I'm gone you'll always have Tina. You'll be close to her. Take care of her for me, won't you?'

'Oh, don't talk like that, Derek. I can't let you go, ever.'

'You've got to,' said Derek, 'as you had to let Dr. Rosemary go in the end. You're old enough now to face it. You've got to, my darling.'

'Don't let's talk about it tonight. I'm too upset.'

'All right,' said Derek. 'I'm too tired anyway.'

After Derek was asleep Jennifer lay and thought about it. She knew he was very sick. Dr. Margaret had been talking to her each week about it and preparing her for it, giving her confidence that she could face the crisis.

Everyone felt a bit flat the next day but Derek seemed to rally, much to everyone's relief. The rest had done him good and he had taken the pills prescribed for him.

'Be careful, Derek,' warned Dr. Simpson. 'Be very careful. You know you have to be, don't you?'

'I will,' said Derek.

Christmas was drawing near and the whole family were engaged in preparing for the big day. There was to be the traditional big party at the big house two days before Christmas as well. It wasn't as big as the parties that had taken place when Nancy was alive and when Jennifer was younger. There weren't enough people now and a lot of people had gone away, but they wanted this party to mark Christmas and also as a farewell party for Julian and Georgina. There was to be a band for dancing and a big buffet and plenty of champagne flowing.

At last the day arrived and everything had been prepared. Once more the driveway was floodlit, showing the splendour of the building. Inside, in the hall, the big tree with the lights, standing high, was a welcoming sight. As always the crystal chandelier was the centrepiece of the decorations.

Tina looked beautiful in a new, blue, long dress. Jane wore a shorter dress in green and they both looked very glamorous. Since her birthday Tina had retreated behind her tough façade again, and dressed to kill, as she always did when she felt vulnerable.

Millie was not impressed. 'You look very cheap, Tina. I won't have it.'

'I will dress how I want,' retorted Tina.

'You won't while I'm your mother.'

When Millie was like that she had to be obeyed, but even with some of the make-up removed, Tina still looked very glamorous and sexy, with her tight blue dress on.

There were three boys, with their parents from the village, who were very interested in Tina that night, as was Bill. She flirted with them unmercifully and danced with them, but she didn't want them, preferring to dance with their fathers, much to the dismay of their wives.

Julian danced with Tina that night too, and she smooched with him. Georgina laughed and remembered the good old days when they used to do it. She understood Tina and wasn't at all jealous.

'You look beautiful tonight,' said Julian. 'If I was younger . . .'

'I know, I've always liked you, Julian.

'You flirt,' said Julian. 'You know I love Georgina and I shall love her always. I shall miss you when we go. You're so full of life, Tina but I think you're going to be quite a girl.'

'I guess so,' said Tina.

For the rest of the evening she danced with Julian, having taken a fancy to him. Even though he was one of the young ones at the big house and was devoted to his wife, he had always liked the girls and Tina looking so glamorous that night made Julian want to dance with her. Georgina wasn't worried about it. She knew Julian. She knew he'd always love her and they were going away soon, to live in Exmouth. She danced with other people, quite happy, an easy-going woman and not jealous. She trusted her husband.

'Julian,' said Tina as they were dancing late into the night, in that beautiful hall with the chandelier suspended above them, and now the dim lights, with the music playing, so romantic. 'Could I come and stay with you when you're settled in at Exmouth? I mean, when I'm seventeen I'll be able to do what I like, even if Mummy says I can't go.'

'Well, she wouldn't mind,' said Julian, 'not if you came to stay with us.'

'Thanks,' said Tina. 'I really like you, Julian.'

'And I like you, Tina, but remember; I love Georgina.'

'I'll remember that,' said Tina, but she fancied Julian, because he was older and it made Tina more serious in her quest for someone older. When I've left school, she thought. When I'm seventeen I'll try and meet an older man who can help me because I'm immature.

That night Tina was quite brazen and by the end of the evening was dancing in a very provocative way. Breaking away from Julian, she went into another room and sneaked a little champagne. She wasn't supposed to drink with her pills and her mother was very cross. 'Stop showing off, Tina! I'm fed up. You've been like it all evening.'

All the guests looked round at Tina. The boys had been looking at her with admiration but the rest of them didn't like it at all.

'Stop showing off or you'll go to bed.'

Tina looked around. Suddenly she could take no more. Her mother was at her again, picking on her. She doesn't understand me. Tina was tired, it was late at night. The tears filled her eyes. She stood there dumb for a moment, and then shouted, 'I hate you! I hate you all!' Then she ran up the spiral staircase into her room, jumped on to the bed and cried into her pillow; cried and cried for about half an hour. When I'm seventeen, she thought angrily through her tears, I'll leave home. I can't stand Mummy, she doesn't understand me! Everything's horrid, thought Tina. I'm leaving school and I've got to live here. Well, I won't when I'm seventeen. I shall go, she thought.

Julian and Georgina were talking in bed.

'Really, you were pretty interested in Tina tonight,' said Georgina. 'Good thing I'm not jealous.'

'Well, you've no need to be,' said Julian. 'Can't you see she's unhappy? I only did it to please her.'

'I know,' said Georgina.

'Remember the romantic woods? It'll always be you.'

'I love you, Julian,' said Georgina.

They held each other and made love as they had done all those years ago when they were young.

Jennifer went to Tina and comforted her. She was still sobbing bitterly.

'Stop crying, dear. At least your tears come out now. But you were a bit "sexy", you know.'

'I know, I felt it. I'm sixteen! I want to enjoy my life.'

'Well, you must never behave like that in front of your mother. Really, Tina, we don't want you to look cheap. We want you to be a lady.'

'I'll never be one of those,' said Tina defiantly.

'Well casual then, like me,' said Jennifer. 'I'm not a lady. You know what I'm like.'

'I reckon I will be one day,' said Tina, 'but I'm young and at the moment I want to be the way I am.'

'Well, try to tone it down in front of your mother,' said Jennifer. 'I think it'll do you good, later on, to go and stay with Julian and Georgina and have a break from her. Look, she's very unhappy. She still misses Raymond. She did love him, you know.'

'I do realise that,' said Tina. 'She hasn't even looked for anyone else.'

'She won't,' said Jennifer. 'Deep inside she still hopes he'll come back to her.'

'Perhaps he will,' said Tina. 'Then perhaps she might be more human again.'

'I know,' said Jennifer. 'Let's hope so.'

Jennifer comforted Tina and Jane came to bed, tired out. She had enjoyed the party, in her easy-going way. 'I'll be with her now,' said Jane. 'You look tired, Jennifer.'

'I am. And Derek had to go to bed. I must go to him. Goodnight, Tina,' said Jennifer, hugging her. Tina clung to Jennifer and then lay back exhausted. Jane talked to her for a while and then they went to sleep, worn out.

Christmas morning was bedlam, for Robert opened his presents, his stocking. Millie loved being with him, although his happiness only underlined Raymond's absence. Millie still loved Raymond and missed him very much that day, but kept it to herself. Robert was having the time of his life.

After breakfast the family went to church. Tina enjoyed the service. She loved the Christmas carols. They always brought tears to her eyes. She believed in God and loved spiritual things, but she was a teenager and had pushed it rather to one side. Love seemed to come first but, of course, spiritual things were love too. Tina realised it that day and felt very emotional when she heard the Reverend Moss preach the Christmas sermon. She heard the Christmas carols and looked at her mother and thought how sad she looked, for she was missing Raymond. If only he'd come back, thought Tina. And in her childish way, she prayed for Raymond's return and her mother's happiness.

Back at the big house, Tina enjoyed her presents. She had been shopping with Jane before Christmas and had bought nice gifts for the family which they were very pleased with, including Jennifer. Tina had very carefully chosen a sweater to match

Jennifer's big blue eyes and she was thrilled with it, and she had bought her grandfather a book he wanted, a spiritual book, as she knew he was preparing for spiritual things. Christmas lunch was a noisy and happy affair, everyone pulling crackers and laughing, feasting with relish on the big turkey and the drinks.

After lunch, Dr. Margaret arrived with Sandy, Joe and Vicky and their little boy, Richard. Richard enjoyed playing with Robert. They had a fine time showing each other their toys.

In the evening they all sat round in that beautiful big lounge that faced on to the mystical woods, the big fire burning in the grate, the big old-fashioned fire that they always lit at Christmas. It grew late and Tina and Jane ran upstairs, Bill behind them.

'It's nice to be staying the night, Tina. I wish I was sleeping . . .'

'Oh, don't be so cheeky. I know what you're going to say,' said Tina. 'Well, you can't! I like older men, I've told you that.'

'Well, just give me a kiss goodnight. It's Christmas Night.'

'All right,' said Tina.

Bill kissed her passionately outside the door of her room. He felt the desire well up inside him. He wanted this cheeky girl but she did not feel anything for him. She enjoyed the kiss but knew she was saving herself for someone else.

Julian and Georgina came up the stairs.

'Can I kiss you goodnight under the mistletoe?' said Tina to Julian.

'Very well,' said Julian. 'Is that all right, Georgina?'

'Yes, all right,' said Georgina. 'I'll kiss Bill.'

Bill laughed and kissed Georgina.

Julian gave Tina a kiss under the mistletoe. Tina melted. It was an older man she wanted. She didn't feel this for Bill, hadn't felt it for Jerry. She felt it for Julian but knew she must never say anything. She would never be disloyal to Georgina.

Tina lay in bed, and, as often, felt the thrills go through her as she thought of her kiss with Julian. I shall want an older man, she thought, as she felt her body all over.

Jane went straight to sleep, tired and happy. But Tina did not feel sleepy that night. She felt full of ecstasy, full of love for Julian. I mustn't love him, she thought. I think I've got a crush on him. I must wait until I meet someone else. I'll wait until I'm seventeen and have left school. I'll go and stay at Julian's and perhaps meet an older man. And with that she relieved her frustrated feelings and then fell asleep, exhausted.

On Boxing Day, everyone felt rather tired after their exciting

Christmas. Tina felt tired and a bit crotchety so she went for a walk in the woods with Jennifer. 'You do look tired today, Tina. What have you been up to?'

Tina coloured up. 'Oh nothing,' she said. 'But I've got a bit of a crush on Julian.'

'You mustn't do that,' said Jennifer. 'It would break Georgina's heart. She's my best friend from school, you know.'

'I promise I never will,' said Tina, 'but Jennifer, when I'm seventeen I want to meet an older man.'

'You will. Don't forget to tell Dr. Tom when you see him after Christmas.'

'I'll tell him,' said Tina.

Christmas over, life went on in the usual routine at the big house. Tina continued to spend time with her grandfather, for she knew he wasn't at all well. Playing her records, she spent many a long hour dreaming of her future. She had had a lot of music for her birthday and Christmas. Her new music centre had everything on it that she needed. She was also thrilled as Jennifer had found an old record in the record library at the house, called 'The Story of Tina,' a song of the fifties.

'It's your record. You must have it, Tina. I used to love that one,' said Jennifer. 'It's yours.'

Tina played it over and over and recorded it on a cassette tape. That's my favourite song, thought Tina. Perhaps I'll have a story one day. I hope so. And I hope it's as romantic as the record.

At last the holidays were over. Tina went to see Derek, who was in bed.

'Grandad,' she said. 'I'm going back to school.'

'Thank you,' said Derek, 'for coming in to see me and looking after me. We've grown close, Tina. But in case anything happens to me, may we have a little talk?'

Tina's eyes filled with tears. 'You're not going yet, Grandad.'

'It won't be long, Tina. I must be honest with you. I've already told Jennifer. Promise me, Tina, that when I've gone, you'll take care of Jennifer, for she'll miss me terribly. She depended on me. Now Tina, your life's not going to be easy, and I feel you'll go away when you're older. You'll need to. And Georgina and Julian will be gone. They'll be going to Exmouth soon. The big house will be very quiet but, Tina, do your best for Jennifer, and for the young ones of the future. For Robert and you could have children – though I advise you not to, Tina. If you did – by any mistake – please see that the big house is kept on, if you can. Find someone to love, if you want an older man. Make sure he's the right one for you but you'll find it hard to give out love, Tina. You're the kind of girl who won't want to feel trapped,' said Derek. 'Do your painting, Tina. I know it bores you now. But when you're older, try, please.'

'I'll do all you say, Grandad.' She burst into tears, it was all too much for her, knowing that she might never see Derek again.

Her mother came in then and said, 'You must go now, Tina. And don't upset your grandad, he's very ill.'

'I'm sorry,' said Tina. 'Grandad, I love you.'

'I'll always love you,' said her grandfather. 'Now, Tina, remember what I told you.'

'I'll always remember,' said Tina, giving her grandfather one more kiss. 'I'll always remember and I promise to do my best.'

Millie drove them to school. They were both very quiet, sitting in the back of the car, while Robert sat in front, chattering to his mother. Tina was sad, knowing that her grandfather was not going to last long.

Millie said goodbye to the two girls and went back to the house to take care of her father.

Tina and Jane settled back at school. Both girls would be leaving at the end of the term, and they both hoped that they would be able to get a job at a shop in Guildford. Tina thought, just till I'm seventeen and then I'll be able to go and stay at Julian's.

A few weeks passed. Tina went home every weekend to see her grandfather.

A few weeks later Derek had a heart attack and the doctor was sent for. Derek told Jennifer breathlessly how much he had always loved her. Jennifer was crying bitterly, leaning on Millie for support.

'Take care of Tina, Jennifer. Be strong. I love you.'

It was too much for Jennifer. She ran from the room.

'Millie, take care of Jennifer,' said Derek. He was now exhausted and he lay back as the doctor examined him. Lying there, he thought of William, how he had had heart trouble. Almost as if I'd been his real son, thought Derek. He thought of his real mother, Olive. She had died a few years previously. Theirs had been a long-distance love for Olive had lived in Canada. He thought of his childhood with Jennifer, his adopted sister, of Mildred, his mother, how Jennifer had been so adrift from her, just like Tina with Millie. His life flashed in front of him and his eyes closed, as he sent up a prayer for Tina and Jennifer. Derek realised soon he would be joining Gordon and Nancy, and Hayley, and all those who'd gone, whom he'd loved: Mildred and William, his adopted parents, Olive his mother.

A few hours later Derek died peacefully in his sleep.

Chapter 8

Jennifer was devastated after Derek died. She cried inconsolably, and Millie and Dr. Margaret took care of her. Tina was allowed to come home and see Jennifer but they upset each other so much that Tina was sent back to school, and it was decided that she should not attend the funeral. 'It's better not,' Dr. Margaret said kindly. 'You're too upset, Tina. Go back to school, there's a dear.'

Tina had grown to like Dr. Margaret and felt that she could talk to her better now. 'I did love Grandad,' she said.

'I know, and I'm glad you got so much closer to him before he died but remember, he's with the ones he loved now, and he's at peace. Jennifer will be all right. I'll look after her.'

Another funeral service was taken by the Reverend Moss at the little church in the village. The church was overflowing with family and friends from the village and colleagues from Forest Dene Hospital, who had all loved and respected Derek so much. Jennifer had to be taken out, she got so upset, and Dr. Margaret took her home.

The funeral service over, there was a gathering at the big house. Millie was very upset indeed, but Jennifer was devastated. Georgina and Julian, who'd been due to go that week, postponed their leaving so they could be a comfort to the family.

Things were very gloomy at the big house for a while after Derek had gone, but Jennifer realised that she could face it this time, and with Dr. Margaret's help she did. Tina came home at weekends and they went for walks in the woods and cried together.

A few weeks after Derek died, Julian and Georgina left to live in Exmouth. Everyone cried.

'Come and stay with us, Tina,' said Georgina, 'as soon as you want to. We've arranged it with your mother.'

'It'll be a change for you,' said Millie. 'You've been through a lot, Tina.' After they had gone, the big house seemed so empty. Tina went to bed that night, thinking about how quiet it would be – and then she had a brainwave. She decided to suggest to Jennifer that Dr. Margaret, her whole family and Sandy should move into the big house. She went to sleep happier that night, thinking of her idea.

The next morning at breakfast Tina said, 'Jennifer, let's go for a walk in the woods. I've had a fantastic brainwave.' The house certainly seemed empty: so many empty places at the breakfast table.

They walked in the woods with the dogs and sat down by the big tree, the romantic tree. Jennifer thought back to the time when she and Derek had kissed. They were young lovers then, just about to be married. 'Now, Tina,' said Jennifer, breaking away from her reminiscences. 'What is it? What's your idea? I could do with some cheering up.'

'I've had a brilliant idea,' said Tina. 'You know, Jennifer, the house is very empty now.'

'I know. But there's nothing we can do about that.'

'Oh, but there is,' said Tina. 'You know Dr. Margaret and Sandy and Vicky and Joe and Richard – they could come and live at the big house, and sell theirs; there'd be a family again, and you'd be happy, Jennifer. You'd have Dr. Margaret there. She's retiring soon.'

'Gosh!' Jennifer was stunned. 'I don't expect they'd do it, but it's a fantastic idea, Tina. Sometimes you have some hair-raising ideas, but this one's good. I'll talk to Millie.'

When they got back to the big house Jennifer went to look for Millie. To her surprise, Millie was in a very sunny mood indeed.

'I've got something to tell you,' said Millie.

'Well, I've got something to tell you,' said Jennifer.

'May I tell you first?' said Millie.

'All right.'

'Well, I've just had a phone call.' Tears filled Millie's eyes. 'You'll never guess who it was from.'

'I can,' said Jennifer. 'Was it Raymond?'

'Raymond's girlfriend ran off and left him. They didn't marry after all and now he wants to come back. He's really sorry. He said he was going through a silly crisis – a silly, forty-year-old crisis or something daft, he said. He said he's always really loved me,' said Millie. 'He's terribly sad about Daddy and he's coming back.'

'When?'

'Tonight,' said Millie.

'Oh, that's wonderful!' said Jennifer. 'One more person in the big house. I've always liked Raymond. I thought it was just something stupid like that. But can you forgive him, Millie?'

'I'd forgive him anything. He's my true love,' said Millie. 'I wish there could be some more people here, though,' she added. 'It's so quiet.'

'There could be,' said Jennifer. 'Tina's had a brainwave.'

Jennifer told Millie the whole story of Tina's idea.

'You know, that idea's not a bad one,' said Millie. 'I doubt they'd do it but the only one who's going to get round Dr. Margaret is you, Jennifer.' Jennifer had perked up. This was a great idea. 'But you've got to ask her, Jennifer.'

Tina and Jennifer schemed for the rest of the day and talked of how they would get round Dr. Margaret to sell her home and come and live at the big house with her family. It would be a difficult decision to make, a lot involved, but Jennifer and Tina knew they had to pull it off for the sake of the big house which was now so empty.

After supper they walked down to Dr. Margaret's. As they walked down the long driveway, the wintry trees looked very beautiful, with the moon shining down, imparting a mystical glow. They strolled along the village street, laughing a lot of the way and felt cheerful and light-headed. Somehow, both Jennifer and Tina knew they were going to succeed.

Vicky answered the door. 'Hello, you two! You didn't phone. Do you want to see Mum?'

'Yes, please,' said Tina. 'We've got something very important to ask her.'

'Come in,' said Vicky. 'I'll send Dr. Margaret into the lounge.'

Tina and Jennifer went into the lounge and sat by the fire. It was nice to get warm, after their walk in the cold, wintry night.

'Dr. Margaret came in on her own. 'I expect this is private,' she said. 'I've told the others to wait in the other room.'

'It's very private,' said Jennifer. 'We've got a great big favour to ask you, Dr. Margaret.'

'Now what is it you're scheming, you two? I can see by your eyes you're scheming something.'

'Well,' said Tina. 'It's like this you see . . .'

'Yes,' said Jennifer. 'It is like this . . . well, Dr. Margaret . . . well . . . er . . .'

'Now come on, said Dr. Margaret. 'Spit it all out both of you. What is it you two have got on your minds tonight? You wouldn't have come here if it wasn't something very important indeed.'

They speedily babbled the whole story out to an amazed Dr. Margaret, who was speechless for a moment.

'Well! What a thing to ask me. I'll have to think it over,' she said. 'You can see, Jennifer and Tina, that there are many pros and cons to this. It's not a decision one can make suddenly, giving up one's home. Remember it was my mother's home, Rosemary's home, and my grandfather's home. There's also Sandy to consult, and Joe, Vicky and Richard. Remember we've got dogs; two springers.'

'I know,' said Jennifer. 'I know all that. You can all come.'

'Oh, you two!' said Dr. Margaret, laughing. 'You're so unpredictable, so very impulsive. You feel that we'll fill up the big house.'

'But you would,' said Jennifer. 'You know you would and I know that Dr. Rosemary would have liked it. She wouldn't want to see the big house empty. She loved that big house and I know,' said Jennifer with tears in her eyes, fearing that Margaret would say no, 'that Dr. Rosemary would have come, if we'd asked her. I know she would.'

Dr. Margaret softened a little, thinking of her mother, and realising that Jennifer was probably right.

'Oh please, Dr. Margaret,' said Tina. 'Please. You've got to give us an answer tonight.'

'That's not possible,' said Dr. Margaret firmly, 'and you know it. I must talk to the family myself. You two must go now. I promise to give you an answer in two or three days.'

'We can't wait for that length of time,' said Tina. 'It's impossible!'

'It's not,' said Dr. Margaret. 'You're both very immature and impatient and I love you both for it. Thank you for the most welcome offer. We'll really talk it over, I promise.'

'Please say yes,' said Tina.

'Yes,' said Jennifer. 'It's so sad now at the big house.'

'I know that,' said Dr. Margaret, 'and I will consider it, I promise. Now run along home. I've got a lot to think about. Would you like me to drive you? It's freezing.'

'We wouldn't mind,' said Tina.

'I'll tell you what, Joe will drive you home. I'll start talking to Sandy and Vicky about it.'

Margaret called Joe and he willingly drove Jennifer and Tina home. They said nothing in front of him at all and were both very quiet, sitting huddled up in the back seat of the car. Joe knew they hadn't come round there for nothing. He knew there was something up, but they weren't telling.

'I say, Raymond's car's outside. He must be back. I bet Mum's upstairs with him.'

'You would think that,' said Jennifer laughing. 'Anyway, I can hear them talking. They're in the lounge. Let's go and see him.'

'All right,' said Tina.

She walked in, and there, sitting in the big lounge, looking out at the beautiful mystical woods in the wintry moonlight, were Millie and Raymond. Jennifer and Tina could see at once they were properly reconciled.

'Hi!' said Raymond. 'I'm sorry about what happened, you two. Your mother's forgiven me. Will you too? I promise never to leave again. I'm going to look after you all. And I'm so sorry about Derek, Jennifer.' Jennifer's eyes misted and so did Tina's. 'I'll take care of things now. I'll help.'

'Thanks,' said Jennifer.

'Well, we'll leave you to it,' said Tina cheekily. She flashed her eyes at Raymond and ran from the room.

Dr. Margaret spent the evening talking to the family about moving. 'It is a good idea,' said Dr. Margaret.

'Well, actually,' said Sandy. 'It is. But I won't be coming.'

'Why ever not?' said Dr. Margaret. 'I'd miss you, Sandy.'

'Well, there is a reason,' said Sandy. 'I was going to tell you anyway.'

'What is it?' said Margaret.

'Well,' said Sandy. 'I know I'm old now – well, nearly retiring – but I've met a man after all these years. He's called Gerald. He's a G.P. in Guildford. I met him through my work at Forest Dene Hospital. He's a widower and we've sort of fallen in love. It's companionship really,' explained Sandy, 'but we're going to be married next week and I'm going to be living in Guildford with him. He has a lovely home. I was going to tell you tonight anyway. So that counts me out,' said Sandy.

'Congratulations!' said Margaret. 'Oh Sandy, I do hope you'll be happy with him. I must meet him.'

'You shall,' said Sandy. 'Of course you shall.'

'That's a turn-up for the books!' said Joe, 'and that leaves just four of us in this house. It is rather stupid, isn't it? We'll really think it over, I don't dislike the idea. It's a beautiful house.'

'What about Sally, our new housekeeper?' said Dr. Margaret.

'Well, she could come if she wants,' said Joe, 'they can always use more help at the big house, but if she doesn't, she can go home.'

'It seems practically settled,' said Dr. Margaret. 'There'll be an awful lot to do. We'll have to sell up and I shall be sad to leave this house. But I think Mum would have liked it, especially as we're so badly needed.'

'You know,' said Joe. 'It may not happen yet. It may be in many years' time, but I think that one day the big house could be turned into a home for young ones. You know, like Jennifer, Nancy, Tina, Julian and Georgina. You know, people who are young for their age, who need help.'

'I think that's a wonderful idea for the future, but not yet,' said Dr. Margaret.

'I don't mean yet,' said Joe, 'but it's an idea for the future, isn't it?'

'Well, it seems like you've settled on it. It's meant, I think,' said Dr. Margaret. 'When are we going to tell them?'

'Tomorrow,' said Joe. 'Jennifer and Tina will have a sleepless night tonight if I know them. They'll be worrying their heads off. Let's tell them tomorrow.'

So the next evening Dr. Margaret went to the big house, taking Joe, Vicky and Richard with her.

'Is it "yes"?' said Tina, rushing to the door.

'Yes,' said Dr. Margaret. 'It is yes, but I must talk to your mother about it, Tina.'

The evening was spent discussing plans for the future.

Within a few months Margaret sold her house and began to move in to the big house. Tina was now back at school and very pleased with the outcome of things; when she went back home there were lots of people.

Chapter 9

A few months passed and Tina had to leave Greenacres School. They had allowed her to stay on one more term, the summer term. She and Jane were to leave at the same time and they were both very upset indeed. Tina decided to go and stay with Jane and look for a job after they left school. Millie had agreed to this for it was necessary for them both to do something. They weren't able to pass exams like other young people, so they just had to get what jobs they could.

Tina wanted to work in a shop. She had hoped to work in a boutique, if somebody would take her, and Jane decided she would like to work in some dog kennels outside Guildford. Jane was more of a country girl at heart – she just wanted to be in the countryside peace and quiet and help with the dogs. Her father had arranged for her to have a job there as soon as she left school.

The day came for them to leave Greenacres School. Both girls cried many tears, for they loved the children and the staff, especially Mr. and Mrs. Powell. Even Mrs. Powell shed a few tears that day. After all, Tina had been there since she was two years old, the youngest child that had ever been there, for she had been so very difficult, and Jane had been there since she was five. It was a long time.

Now they were both sixteen and waiting to start their new lives in the outside world. The two girls packed up. It was the last day of term. 'Goodbye, Mrs. Powell. Goodbye, Mr. Powell,' cried Tina. She suddenly rushed up and hugged Mrs. Powell and kissed her husband on the cheek.

The girls were collected by their respective parents. Tina was to go over the following week and stay at Jane's to look for a job. Both girls cried when they looked round at Greenacres School as they were driven down that long driveway, the children and staff waving to them. 'I was happy there,' said Tina on the way home. 'I was, Mummy.'

'I know you were,' said Millie, 'but you'll be all right. You're much more settled now, Tina. I'm very pleased with you.'

'I'm happier at the big house now, Mummy, because Dr. Margaret's there and I can talk to her more now.'

'I'm glad about that.'

Tina went to stay at Jane's the following week, and looked for a job in Guildford. Jane's father found her a vacancy in a little clothes shop, selling clothes for young people, which suited Tina well. She was to stay at Jane's for the first two weeks until she got settled, and then she was to be driven in every day by Millie, but Tina swore that when she was seventeen she would leave that job and go and stay with Julian and Georgina. She wanted to learn to drive but she was keeping that to herself. Leaving school had made her more restless now and Jennifer noticed it with concern. So did Dr. Phillips.

Tina did not find it easy to settle in at the shop. She didn't like the discipline and was restless, but having made her plans to stay there until she was seventeen, she tried her best.

On Tina's seventeenth birthday she thought, now I can do what I want. I'm going to learn to drive, I'm going to leave the shop. I'm going on holiday, on my own, to Julian and Georgina's. She secretly wrote a letter to Julian and asked if she could come and stay for a month.

Tina said nothing to the family at all, not even to Dr. Phillips. Since she had left school she had become reserved again, more cagey, but she was still very sexy, still dressed up to the nines to attract the opposite sex. A lot of men had asked her out. She had been out with one or two, but Millie had tried to discourage her. Dr. Tom wanted her to be sterilised but Tina had refused point blank. He felt, later on, he would have to make it compulsory if Tina went on this way. They were so afraid she might get into trouble. Julian replied and to Tina's joy, said she was welcome to come the following week. Tina left work on the Friday night. She had given a week's notice and came home. She walked in and said, 'Jennifer, I'm going to stay with Julian and Georgina. I'm going for a month. It's all fixed.'

'All fixed?' said Jennifer. 'You haven't mentioned it. What about your work?'

'I've left,' said Tina.

'What, just like that?'

'Yes,' said Tina. 'I've left.' She had a very strong mind and did what she liked. Tina never did what she was told.

'You know, your mother's going to be pretty angry about this, and Raymond.'

'It's nothing to do with them.'

That night Jennifer had to tell Dr. Margaret and Millie for she knew that if she didn't Tina would just run away. Dr. Margaret and Millie were very upset when they heard the news. 'She's just left the shop?' said Dr. Margaret. 'I don't believe it.'

'She has and she says she's going to Julian's on Monday.'

'Well, how's she getting there?' demanded Millie.

'She says she's going by coach. It's all fixed.'

'The little devil!' said Millie. 'Oh, she can't go by coach on her own. She's never travelled anywhere on her own.'

'I reckon she's quite capable of it,' said Dr. Margaret, 'if we put her on the coach at Guildford.'

'You mean, you think she should go, Dr. Margaret?'

'I do,' said Dr. Margaret, 'because if she doesn't go with our blessing she's going to run away and you won't see her. I warn you, Millie.'

That night Millie went to talk to Tina in her room. 'You know, you might have told us you were leaving the job, and that you'd written to Julian asking to stay. You're very devious, Tina.'

'Oh, shut up, Mummy! I should run away if you tried to stop me anyway.'

'You're devious. You got Jennifer to ask us. You didn't even tell us yourself. I'm very cross with you and disappointed.'

Tina stamped her foot. 'I hate you, Mum! I hate you! You're always at me.' She flew out of the room and ran down the stairs into the lounge where Jennifer and Dr. Margaret were sitting.

'I hate her!' Tina cried.

'What is it?' said Dr. Margaret. 'What's the matter, Tina?'

'My mother's getting at me because she says I'm devious.'

'Well, you are,' said Dr. Margaret, 'but it's no good her going on at you. It won't make any difference.'

Margaret knew, as a psychiatrist, that Tina needed kindness. It was the only way things would work out for her. Any strict talk or harsh voices would upset her. Tina couldn't bear to hear rows, couldn't bear anything like that. It upset her young emotions, for even now, she was so young for her age, like a child of eight years old.

'You must come back after the month is up, Tina. We'll need to talk to you.'

'Of course I will,' said Tina. 'Then I'll decide what I'm going to do with my life.'

Tina kept out of Millie's way that weekend and packed her things to go off to Devon and stay with Julian and Georgina.

On Monday morning she was dressed to kill, ready to go. She'd had her hair cut shorter and it suited her elfin face. Her pale blue eyes, now turning rather greyish, looked very pretty. She had make-up on and looked very attractive.

'I'm worried,' said Raymond. 'The men'll be after her.'

'That's what she wants,' said Millie bitterly.

'Don't be so bitter towards her. She's your daughter.'

'You wouldn't think so,' said Millie.

'Look,' said Raymond. 'Tina's herself. She has to have an identity. And she's got problems. You don't allow for that, Millie.'

'I'm sorry,' said Millie. 'I never did understand her. I understand Robert.'

'Yes, of course you do. He's easy to take care of. He's normal.'

Jennifer took Tina to see her off on the coach. Dr. Margaret had offered to drive them. It wasn't any good Millie going. She and Tina were very bad friends at the moment. They drove quietly to the coach station, Tina suddenly feeling very sad as she looked back at the big house and realised what a big step she was taking. Suddenly the child within her came out and she huddled into Jennifer and shed a few tears.

'You can change your mind,' said Jennifer.

'I can't,' said Tina. 'I've got to go. At least for this month. I may settle after that.'

'Don't be frightened.' Dr. Margaret could see the fear in Tina's eyes. 'You've made your own decision and you want to go.'

'I do,' said Tina.

'See you in a month then.'

She hugged Jennifer and kissed Dr. Margaret on the cheek, then jumped into the coach quickly and sat down. 'You take care of yourself, Tina.'

'I will.'

Jennifer missed Tina dreadfully. Life seemed empty without her. She looked forward to the evenings when Margaret would come home and she would talk to her. She was missing Derek more than ever, now Tina was gone.

Tina enjoyed the coach trip down to Devon. It was interesting and she was a friendly girl and got talking to a middle-aged woman who was sitting beside her. Tina loved to babble to strangers and found it easy to talk to them for she never felt trapped with them.

She looked out at the countryside and was interested. She had only been to Devon on holidays before, to Torquay, and also to Cornwall when she was younger, but hadn't enjoyed them due to her rebellious nature as a child. She had only been able to go away two or three times, as she had been at Greenacres School, except for the few holidays she'd been allowed. But now, I'm seventeen, she thought, I'm going to see the world.

When the coach arrived in Exmouth, there was a smiling Julian and Georgina to meet her. 'Oh Tina, it's great to see you,' said Georgina. 'I'm so glad you've come.'

'I've come for a month,' said Tina. 'I'm looking forward to it.'

'What will you do with yourself all the time?' said Julian. 'We lead a very simple life, you know.'

'Well, you can meet my cousin,' Georgina said. 'We'll go round there tomorrow.'

'All right,' said Tina, 'and I want to see the town and the sea and have a good time.'

'All right,' said Georgina, 'but you must be very tired. Come home and have a meal.'

Their home faced the sea; Julian and Georgina were very happy there and looking forward to staying there for the rest of their lives, just the two of them. They were glad to have Tina for that month, though. Tina looked at their house with interest. It was an end-terraced house that looked out over the town, with views of the sea in the distance. It was a pretty little house, a small garden in the front with a few flowers and a little lawn, and inside was a small hallway, so cosy, so beautifully furnished with modern furniture. Julian and Georgina liked modern things and had bought all their own things for their new home. There was a little lounge in the front and behind it was a little living- and dining-room and a very convenient kitchen at the back, which led out on to a backyard and a back entrance. Upstairs there were three nice bedrooms. One was for Tina. It looked out over the front and you could see the sea in the distance.

'It's a lovely little room,' said Tina. 'I'm going to like it here.'

She was beginning to feel less insecure and more at home. It is a dear little house, thought Tina, just what I want when I get married. She unpacked and then went down to supper with Julian and Georgina. Tina spent the evening telling them the news at the big house. Suddenly Tina felt very tired. She had been emotional, she had travelled, and she was mentally exhausted.

'You look so tired, Tina. Go up to bed now.'

Georgina tucked her in and then she felt secure.

The next morning she awoke and remembered to take her tablet. Georgina brought her in some tea. Then she got up and bathed and dressed in her jeans and a tight sweater and made herself look very attractive, much to Julian's delight when she came down to breakfast. Her figure was very rounded and her large bust showed well. Julian looked with approval. Georgina grinned.

'You look very attractive this morning, Tina.'

'You've got on too much make-up,' said Georgina.

'Oh, don't you start,' said Tina, 'but I'm free with you. You don't mind, do you?'

'Of course not. What would you like to do on your first day?'

'Well, some days I want to go off on my own and look around,' said Tina, 'but today I want to be with you. Could we go and look at the sea?'

'Yes,' said Julian, 'then we're to go to lunch with Georgina's cousin and his wife.'

So the morning was spent walking around Exmouth. They looked in the shops; Tina enjoyed that. She had her eye on two sweaters and thought she might buy them while she was there.

She looked at the sea, sparkling in the springtime sun. It wasn't too crowded but there were enough people to make an interesting scene.

After looking around Exmouth and at the sea they went to Georgina's cousins' for lunch. Georgina did the introductions and they sat down to lunch. Tina was very quiet and shy, for she was tired after the day before and a bit emotional. Secretly she felt a little bit homesick, but that would wear off, she told herself resolutely.

'You know, you won't know what to do with yourself,' said Gordon.

'Oh, I'll find something to do,' said Tina. 'There may be one or two discos. Though I don't like the lights, I can go and look in at night.'

'Well, you can't go out on your own.'

'I can!' said Tina. 'I want to!' She was always very snappy when she was threatened in any way.

'There are some people I'd like you to meet,' said Gordon. 'I think that they might be helpful to you. They're a husband and wife who live with his parents. They've never had any children of their own and they always like to help people. He's a sort of psychologist.'

'Oh, I don't want to meet any of those,' said Tina. 'I have enough of them at home.'

'Well, he's different somehow. He's ever so nice. I really want you to meet them. Would you?'

'Oh, all right. Who'll take me, then?'

'I'll tell you what, we'll give you a few days to settle in. Come to lunch, in a week's time and I'll take you up there,' said Mary.

Tina had taken to the simple and happy couple. Another small house, with three bedrooms and modern furniture. Tina felt so cosy there. She had begun to like it. She was looking forward to meeting this gentleman, this 'sort of psychologist'.

'By the way,' said Tina. 'What are their names?'

'They're called Ronald and Beryl,' said Mary.

'I see. How old are they?' said Tina.

'In their forties,' said Mary. 'Really, you'll like Ronald and you'll love talking to him.'

'I hope so,' said Tina, 'and I shall dress up for him: he's an older man.'

They all roared with laughter at her.

The next day Tina decided to branch out. After another early night she felt rested, and was beginning to get bored with the older couple. She wanted to get out and have a look around on her own. 'Well, don't be late back,' said Georgina. 'We shall worry about you.'

'I won't.'

Tina went off into Exmouth, feeling a bit lost and lonely and frightened at first, like a small child, but she found the shop with the jumpers in it and bought one of them. Then she went for a milkshake and a sandwich in a café. After wandering around a bit more she found an amusement arcade. It didn't interest her a lot but she liked seeing the people there.

Then Tina noticed a man looking at her, staring at her. She felt frightened suddenly, wanting to flirt with him and yet, when it came to it, feeling scared and threatened. He came over to her.

'Hello, out on your own then?' he said.

'Yes,' said Tina. 'I am.'

'How about coming out with me?'

'Can't,' said Tina, 'but I'll meet you tonight.' It was a way of escape. Tina wanted to, and yet she didn't. She had to have time to think. 'I'll meet you at seven here.'

'All right, but turn up, won't you? My name's John.'

'Mine's Tina.'

'See you tonight then.'

John was about twenty-six and Tina liked the look of him, but she still felt fearful of meeting him. Would he try and have sex with her? She knew she mustn't take chances. And so Tina, after walking about for the rest of the day, felt she'd better go back at the right time.

The next day Tina began to feel a bit more brazen and off she went again into the town alone. This time, she did bump into John at the arcade again and stayed with him. She felt better, more rested, but she had made up her mind she wasn't going to have anything to do with him. 'I'd like to go to a dance,' she said.

'We'll find somewhere.'

'I don't like flashing lights.'

'You're a funny girl, Tina.'

'Well they give me headaches, and I'm young for my age.'

'You don't look it,' said John. He didn't realise, he wasn't an understanding man, just an ordinary type of man who wanted a girl to pick up.

They went to a dance that evening, where there were no flashing lights. It was an old-fashioned dance and Tina enjoyed it. John tried to make her drink, but she refused, remembering feeling woozy that time she had done. After the dance John said, 'Can I take you home?'

She agreed.

John had a car and drove Tina a little way.

'This is not the way home.'

'Well we're gonna stop for a kiss, aren't we?'

'I don't want to,' said Tina. Yet she did. She suddenly felt she wanted some love. Her curiosity got the better of her. She found it difficult to say no to strangers and she felt a little nervous of John.

He wasn't a good-looking man, he had dark curly hair and brown eyes and was slim and rather coarse-looking, but Tina felt she must have this experience. Curiosity was really getting hold of her right now.

'I don't think I could make love,' she hedged, 'I've never done it before, and we were warned at school about AIDS and about having a baby.'

'I'll take care of you,' said John. 'I'll use something, don't worry, and I'll be gentle with you, Tina.'

'I'm not sure that I want to.'

John thought he'd better play it very cautiously or he wouldn't get his own way. He was very crafty and said, 'Tina, let's leave it tonight, Meet me again tomorrow. We'll go to the cinema or the arcade, or out to a dance, or even out to dinner if you'd like, and perhaps you'd like to come to my little flat and we'll discuss it again.'

'That's very kind of you, John. Thank you.'

John dropped her outside Julian's house and soon whizzed away in his car, not wanting to be seen by them. He meant to keep well out of their way. Tina went in.

'You're very late,' said Georgina.

'I know,' said Tina. 'I met someone. A man.'

'What man?' cried Georgina, thoroughly alarmed.

'He's twenty-six and he's called John and he's quite nice. I've never had a real boyfriend before, but I've got one now.'

'Now you be careful,' said Julian. 'You know the warnings you've had about AIDS and about getting pregnant. You've not been sterilised yet, Tina. You're not to go out with him.'

'We won't do anything.'

'Do you promise?' said Julian. 'I think we ought to meet this man if you go out with him tomorrow night.'

'All right,' said Tina. 'I'll get him to come in when he brings me back tomorrow.'

'Now, no hanky-panky,' said Julian. 'Promise?'

'All right.'

Tina went up to bed thinking about John and wondering if she liked him. Suddenly she felt, I might be in love with him. Her young emotions had taken over and she wondered if she was. She felt the desires running through her body as she thought of him and that night relieved herself and felt the ecstatic thrills going through her once more.

The next day Tina stayed at home. She felt tired as she always did after any excitement, so she took it easy and stayed in the house with Julian and Georgina, but in the evening she dressed herself up provocatively.

'My God!' said Julian. 'You've got a tight enough skirt on, and look at that sweater! You're asking for trouble.'

'Yes,' said Georgina, 'and all that make-up! Take some of it off.'

'I won't,' said Tina. 'He'll be all right, and I'll be good.'

'You'd better!' said Julian, 'and you'd better bring that John home for us to meet tonight. And don't be late!'

Tina ran all the way down to the arcade and met John at seven o'clock and they decided to go to a cinema. Tina didn't like the film much. It was a horror film and those sort of things frightened her, so John took her out early. He thought, she's a bit of a ninny, this girl. She is rather young for her age, but I'll get what I want from her. John was not an honourable man and certainly had not got Tina's interests at heart.

'Tonight I want you to meet the friends I'm staying with,' said Tina.

'All right,' said John, knowing full well he wasn't going to, but he wanted to play it safe and try and get Tina to agree to make love. He liked the attractive girl and fancied her, the way she wore her make-up, her pretty hair, her tight clothes – they made him want her very much indeed. John hadn't had a girlfriend for a long time. No one wanted him really. He was just a layabout.

But poor naive Tina didn't know that, and John took her back to his flat, after having had a coffee and sandwiches at a little café on the way. When they got back to the flat, which wasn't very clean, Tina noticed, John put on some music.

'I'll be gentle with you, Tina.'

They started kissing. Suddenly Tina felt true desire well up in her. She really felt she wanted to make love. John took Tina's clothes off and then his own and they got into his bed. He had made sure that the bed was clean that morning, which was very rare for him, for he had every intention of having Tina that night.

They got into bed and John started kissing Tina all over. He certainly knew how to make love properly and Tina was absolutely full of desire by this time and felt the ecstatic thrills going through her.

'Oh John, I do want you! If it's like this, it's gorgeous,' said Tina. 'Oh John, do it please.'

'I'll be gentle with you, Tina, as it's your first time. You're a virgin, that turns me on.'

It hurt Tina and she cried out, but he had got so worked up he didn't care and Tina bled a little. He explained to her she was a virgin and that it often happened the first time.

'But I liked what you did before.'

Tina wasn't sure whether to meet John again or not, but she had enjoyed being with him and he had said it wouldn't hurt the next time. So John took her back to Julian's and agreed to go in and meet them. They didn't really like him, but being naive and young for their age they didn't see through him. He was very cunning and very polite to them. They allowed Tina to go out for the next three nights with John.

For those three nights Tina let John make love to her, and she liked it more and more, but the actual sexual intercourse she did not enjoy, like other girls do. Tina did not know why. She felt the desire, but afterwards she felt she wanted to cry and run away. The physical body was ready but her young emotions weren't. Poor Tina felt she was deeply in love.

When Tina went to meet John on the fourth night, he did not turn up. He had tired of her. Having seen her for four nights and got what he wanted, he had taken off for another town. Tina went round to his flat to look for him, but they told her he had left that morning. Tina was terribly upset. He didn't want me after all. What a fool I was! Then she remembered. I wonder if he used anything? He said he would. I didn't notice, she thought.

Tina put it all to the back of her mind and thought no more of it. But I'll be more careful next time, that I'm not used like that. She went back and told Julian and Georgina that he had gone.

'Did he make love to you?' said Julian.

'No,' lied Tina. 'We just kissed,' but Tina was nursing a secret and deep in her heart she was a very worried girl indeed. She wondered if she wasn't attractive enough, why John had taken off. With her lack of experience, she didn't know that many men were like that.

But the next day Tina had other things to think about.

Georgina's cousin Mary came and took Tina to meet Mr. and Mrs. Willis, Ronald and Beryl, the man who was supposed to help Tina while she was there. They caught the bus, it wasn't too far, to a nice part on the outskirts of the town, and they walked up a little hill from where they could see the sea. It was a very attractive street and you could see that the people who lived in it were comfortably-off.

Mary rang the bell and a man answered the door. Tina looked at him. He was bespectacled, about forty-two or -three, of average height, with wavy grey hair, grey eyes and sallow skin. He was quite good-looking. He looked at Tina with interest. She had dolled herself up as usual, with a lot of make-up and figure-hugging clothes.

'You must be Tina,' he said, smiling.

What a nice smile he's got, she thought, and he seemed so cheerful.

'Do come in and meet Beryl. I'm Ronald. Ronald Willis. What would you like to call me, Tina?'

'I think I would like to call you Mr. Willis.'

'All right, Mr. Willis it shall be for the time being. And this is Mrs. Willis.'

A nice lady came over. She was slim with dark hair and brown eyes and very nervous and shy. Shaking hands with Tina she said, 'Go into the lounge with Mr. Willis. He'll talk to you and then I'll bring tea in later, Tina.' Mary went home. The Willises had arranged for a taxi to pick Tina up and take her back to Georgina's in the evening, after tea.

Tina felt quite at home there and enjoyed talking to Mr. Willis. Suddenly she felt warm towards him. He was nicer than John, she thought, more sincere, but she noticed he talked about spiritual things, about religion and God. Tina had always loved God and spiritual things, but at this stage in her life she only wanted one thing; love and romance. It was not really the right time to talk to Tina about spiritual things, but Mr. Willis knew about Tina's problems, for he had been told by Georgina's cousin, and felt he must do this. Tina sat and listened and then she got bored and began to take a fancy to Mr. Willis and started to flirt with him.

He smiled at her. 'You mustn't do that, Tina. I'm married.'

'I've got a boyfriend anyway,' lied Tina. 'He's called John.'

She wasn't going to let it be known that she had been abandoned. She was far too proud. Her appearance, her sex-appeal, was all she had.

For the next three weeks Tina saw Mr. Willis on a regular basis, three times a week, really enjoying his company. Then she announced to him one afternoon that she was going back home the following day. Her month was up. 'I've enjoyed talking to you,' said Tina.

'Would you like to write to me, and for me to write to you,' said Mr. Willis, 'and when you're down here again, please come and see us.'

'Why don't you and your wife come and visit us?' suggested Tina. 'We've got a big house.'

'I can't.' Mr. Willis sadly shook his head. 'I've got a mother and father to look after.'

'I never see them,' said Tina.

'They keep themselves to themselves but they live here and we have to look after them.'

'Well, can I come and stay with you next time?' said Tina innocently.

'I'm sorry,' said Mr. Willis 'but they won't allow us to have guests. It's my mother actually. She doesn't like anyone to come.'

'I'd hate it if Mummy was like that,' said Tina. 'She loves guests.'

'I know,' said Mr. Willis, 'but one day perhaps.'

'All right,' said Tina. 'Let's write to one another then.' She gave him her address and when she left she suddenly went over to him and kissed him full on the lips.

Mr. Willis was very tempted. He was very attracted to her, and he kissed her back, whispering, 'It's wrong, you know.'

'I know,' said Tina, 'but I like you.'

'Thank you,' said Mr. Willis.

'I'll come and see you one day,' said Tina, 'when I come and stay with Julian again.'

'Please, Tina, be careful. Don't get into trouble,' said Mr. Willis. His wife Beryl came and said goodbye to Tina and they promised to write to one another.

Tina left the house and went back to Julian's that night thinking of Mr. Willis. She had felt desire when she had kissed him, far more than when she had made love to John. I like him, but he's married, she thought, I'll never get him. Oh well, I'll see him someday. She remembered the things he'd told her, or tried to tell her, and they stayed in the back of her mind.

That night in bed Tina realised that she was glad she was going home. She thought of the big house and then she thought of Jane, and wondered what she was going to do with her life. She wanted to see Dr. Tom. She wanted to get another job and stay at home for a while. She just hadn't made up her mind what she was going to do yet. But Tina felt desire as she thought of Mr. Willis, the attractive middle-aged man she had seen so many times these last three weeks. Once again Tina felt her body and felt the ecstatic thrills go through her as she imagined him making love to her, instead of John who wasn't nice and wasn't all that clean. She had realised she hadn't liked him at all, it was just sex. But she fancied Mr. Willis, who looked clean and wholesome, he was a different type. Tina thought of him as she felt the thrills go through her that night.

The next day Georgina and Julian saw Tina off on the coach. They all shed a few tears.

'I shall miss you, Tina,' said Georgina, 'you brought life to the house, and my cousin liked you.'

'So did Mr. Willis,' said Tina.

'So I gather,' said Julian. 'We'll phone him up and tell him how you are.'

'I shall phone him up from the big house,' said Tina.

So Tina was seen off on the coach back to Surrey, back to her home. She sat in the coach thinking of her holiday, thinking of John, who had made love to her, hoping he had used something, of Mr. Willis. Again she felt thrills go through her. I really did fancy him, she thought. Perhaps one day I'll meet someone else, who's not married.

Tina arrived home and Millie met her off the coach with Jennifer. It was lovely to see Jennifer again. Tina ran into her arms. She kissed her mother on the cheek, but as always, could not embrace her.

Everything was running smoothly at the big house. It was working well with Dr. Margaret and her family there, and Vicky, Joe and Richard were happy. Robert and Richard were thrilled to have one another's company and it was bedlam to hear them run around the garden, but it had brought life to the big house once more.

'What are you going to do?' said Dr. Margaret after supper.

'I don't know,' Tina replied, 'but I think I'd like to work with Jane for a while at the kennels. Do you think it's possible? Do you think there might be a vacancy?'

'Well, I don't see why not,' said Dr. Margaret. 'You could go. I'll ring up and see.'

Dr. Margaret rang the kennels and luckily there was a vacancy for Tina. Dr. Margaret wondered if she'd like the job, getting dirty, looking after dogs, but at least Tina could try it.

'You're to start Monday,' said Dr. Margaret. 'It's all arranged.'

'Oh great!' said Tina. 'I'll be with Jane again.' She was dying to tell Jane about John and Mr. Willis. The rest of the week flew by and Tina got settled in at home once more. She thought of Mr. Willis many times, as she relieved her feelings and felt the thrills go through her at night.

Tina wrote to Mr. Willis and told him how much she liked him, and merely hinted about her sexual feelings towards him. She was a good writer. John she forgot about very quickly.

Tina started work at the kennels outside Guildford. She met Jane there, and to Margaret's amazement, she liked the work in the fresh air. She liked wearing her jeans and casual sweater and being free with Jane, feeding the dogs and cleaning their kennels out.

Jane had a boyfriend who worked there and they were going out together regularly. Tina was most interested but David was only interested in Jane. Tina always liked to try and tempt men away from people, even her best friend, but David was in love with Jane and did not want her.

Chapter 10

Three months after Tina's return from Exmouth, she suddenly realised she hadn't seen her periods and she started being sick every morning. She knew she'd have to tell Dr. Tom about it when she saw him next.

Tina told Dr. Phillips the whole story of her trip to Exmouth, of Mr. Willis, of how she wrote to him and he wrote back, and then she told him the whole story of John and how he'd ditched her; how he'd made love to her.

'I don't know if he used anything. But I haven't seen a period for three months and I remember Mrs. Powell telling us the facts of life and I'm worried,' said Tina. 'Also, I keep being sick.'

'Oh my God!' said Dr. Tom. 'Why didn't you tell me before? Is it really three months ago? I think you must be pregnant, Tina. Oh you are a fool. I did warn you. You must be sterilised first or take the pill.'

'I'm sorry.'

'That's you all over,' said Dr. Tom. 'Now we'll have to try and get you out of this mess. You'll have to have the baby terminated and be sterilised.'

'I don't want to,' cried Tina. 'I don't want to! I want to have a baby. I want to get married.'

'I can't make you,' said Dr. Tom. 'You're legally old enough now to do what you want in that respect, but I really must insist.'

'I don't want to,' said Tina crying.

Suddenly Dr. Tom realised that it might be very difficult to stop Tina having the baby, but he was worried and now the child could inherit Tina's condition. What were they to do?

Dr. Tom told the family, as Tina asked him to. Millie gave Tina a good telling off; she was furious. Tina had row after row with her. Tina refused to have the operation but promised to be sterilised when the baby was born. Millie did not object too much to this. She and Raymond had not been able to have another child of their own, and she was rather happy at the idea of looking after the baby, for they knew that Tina would not be able to look after it herself.

'But there must never be another one,' said Millie. 'Never. Do you understand that? Stop being so promiscuous and learn to say no to the men.'

One day Tina met a man at the kennels. He had come to buy a puppy because he was lonely. He was thirty-eight years old, a widower for two years, with no children.

Tina attracted him. He gazed at her and liked what he saw. They struck up a conversation and Tina was drawn to his friendly, cheerful manner. She asked him where he lived.

'I live in Guildford, in a little house. Come and see it one day. No strings,' he said.

'Well, it's awkward,' said Tina. 'I'm pregnant. I'm young for my age and I got into trouble in Exmouth. John ran away and left me.'

'Oh dear,' said Henry. 'He shouldn't have run away from an attractive girl like you.'

'I know,' said Tina, 'but he did.'

'Come and help me choose a dog, Tina.'

Henry chose a pretty King Charles spaniel. It was a girl dog and Tina helped him choose a name for her. They decided to call her Gemma.

'She's gorgeous,' said Tina. 'You're going to love her. She's got a jolly good pedigree.'

Henry took the dog home but not before he had made a date for the next evening to meet Tina. He was to pick her up after work in his car. He had told Tina she could change at his house.

Tina wondered what Millie would say, but she had no intention of breaking that date so she made a tale up when she got home, about seeing Jane, and Jane had promised to be her alibi. She was too busy to see much of Tina now. She was going steady with the boy from the kennels. They were thinking of getting married. Jane had now been sterilised and wanted to be married. The boy was slightly backward and wasn't worried about having children. It would make a perfect match.

The next evening Henry picked up Tina from work. They drove straight back to the little house right in the centre of Guildford, on an estate. It was his own little house with two bedrooms. There were a lot of houses exactly the same in the road and no country views around there, only town, more and more houses. But Tina found it interesting, it was something different. The front garden was beautifully kept, for Henry liked gardening, and out at the back he had a little allotment as he loved to grow vegetables.

Inside the house there was a small kitchen-cum-living-room and a front room. That was all. A staircase led up to two good sized bedrooms and a bathroom and toilet. It was a lovely cosy little house, thought Tina. She felt suddenly warm towards Henry. He was very lonely, but despite that, cheerful and smiling. He liked the girl and was physically attracted to her. He knew that she was young for her age but didn't know the deep problems she had.

Tina did not make love with Henry for a week, and then one night he asked her and Tina allowed him to make love to her.

'I'm quite safe,' he said, 'I haven't got AIDS or anything, and you're pregnant so you're all right.'

Tina felt the thrills go through her as Henry gently made love to her. He was good at making love and she was happy with him. Tina enjoyed it thoroughly.

A week later Henry said, 'I'm lonely, Tina. Shall we get married?'

'Oh, they wouldn't let me do that,' said Tina. 'Remember, I'm having a baby, Henry.'

'Well, I'd give it a name,' said Henry. 'I'd adopt it.'

'You can't do that,' said Tina. 'Mummy's doing that.'

'Well, we could just be together, on our own. You're to be sterilised after the baby's born, and I don't care if we don't have any children. I just want to be with you, Tina, I'm lonely.'

He wanted this girl, he desired her. A sexy man, he felt a certain amount of love and compassion towards Tina, who was so young and so fresh.

'You'd better come home and meet my family on Sunday, Henry.'

At the big house, none of the family approved of Henry at all. He was a very ordinary man and rather coarse, though very friendly and kind.

'I'd look after Tina if you'd let us get engaged,' said Henry, 'and we could marry later on.'

'I can't approve of it,' said Millie.

'Nor can I,' said Dr. Margaret. 'Tina's far too young to get married.'

'I can do what I like when I'm eighteen,' said Tina.

'Well, you'll have to wait till then. I do not give my consent.'

Henry left with a flea in his ear. He did not like the big house or the snooty family and went off home, rather cross. The experience made him doubt his feelings for Tina, but she went on seeing him and Henry went on using her for sex, until she was too far on in her pregnancy to do any more. He promised to phone her, for her time was drawing near, but he did not. He found someone else at work and decided to marry her instead.

Poor Tina was very upset when she received the letter. Two rejections, she thought. I can't be that attractive to men. Well, after the baby's born I'll find a husband.

Tina was very upset and insecure. The pregnancy was making her worse. What would the child be like? Would it inherit from Nancy and Jennifer?

Tina was very upset about Henry letting her down and wrote more and more letters to Mr. Willis. He always wrote back and never let her down. If only I could have married him, she thought, he would have looked after me, but poor Tina wasn't really fit to marry anyone. She was far too insecure for that and far too immature.

At last the time came for the baby to be born. Tina's waters broke one evening while they were sitting in the lounge. It was two weeks before she was due and she was taken to the hospital in Guildford. Jennifer went with her, as she begged her to.

Tina had a terrible time giving birth to that child. It was a long hard labour and she screamed continuously. She had had no idea what was involved, having refused to go to any classes before the birth to help her prepare for the labour.

At last, after twelve hours, she gave birth to a baby girl. She was exhausted and fell fast asleep.

Her new-born daughter had dark hair and eyes and looked completely normal, but of course they wouldn't be able to tell yet what she was to be like. Tina did not take to it. Remembering John, she turned on her daughter, becoming aggressive and distraught.

After the birth, she had post-natal depression and a mental breakdown. It had all been too much for her. Tina, like Jennifer and Nancy, couldn't cope and practically switched off. All she did was cry. She had gone into a very deep depression.

Dr. Tom Phillips came to see her at the hospital and told her she would have to be sterilised at once. When she was over the birth she had the small operation, but her depression got worse. They could not keep her at that hospital and poor Tina was transferred to Forest Dene Hospital as a patient; the thing she had dreaded most of all.

Everyone at the big house was heartbroken about Tina. What a shock it was. They knew it would have been right for her to have been sterilised long ago and wished they hadn't allowed her to have the baby. Dr. Tom had warned them, so had Dr. Margaret, but they had given in to her.

Millie was rather selfish about it really. She had not thought of Tina, only of the child, the second child she could not have herself, and would like to have, knowing it would be a blood relation. It was a chance Millie was willing to take.

Now the baby was born and everyone in the big house was upset. On the day Millie went to collect her new granddaughter, Tina was being transferred to Forest Dene Hospital with post-natal depression and a severe breakdown.

Tina was in no state to name the baby, but Millie and Raymond had decided to call her Megan Jennifer. They loved Jennifer and wanted to give the second name after her, and they had always liked the name Megan.

Dr. Margaret, Jennifer, Millie and Raymond went to the hospital to pick up little Megan. Jennifer and Dr. Margaret were to escort Tina to Forest Dene Hospital, while Millie and Raymond took the baby home.

First of all Millie called in to see Tina, but it was no use. Tina just cried. She didn't want to know her mother.

'Don't you want to know about the baby?' said Millie.

'No,' said Tina. 'Oh Mummy, I'm glad you're having her. I'm glad you've named her Megan, but I don't want her myself. I can't cope.'

'I suppose I shouldn't have let you have her,' said Millie.

'But you wanted her, Mummy.'

'Yes,' said Millie. 'I'll take on the responsibility. When you're better, Tina, you can come home and look upon her as your little sister, just as Jennifer looked on me as a sister.'

'All right,' said Tina. She cheered up very slightly at that thought. She thought when she was better she might start all over again.

Jennifer and Dr. Margaret took Tina sobbing to Forest Dene

Hospital. She really was very depressed indeed and none of the anti-depressants she had been prescribed had helped her.

When they got there she was settled into a small four-bed dormitory, but she didn't want to see the others, she didn't want to know. She was so depressed she just wanted to lie down and go to sleep. Jennifer helped her get into bed, and then Dr. Phillips arrived to see her.

'Oh, Tina, you are in a mess,' he said. 'You should never have had that child. I wish I hadn't allowed you to, and now you've been sterilised and you're so run-down and depressed. We'll get you better, we will, Tina.' Tina didn't want to wash or do her hair, or even make up her face. She looked dreadful.

Back at the big house baby Megan was settling in well. She was not a crying baby as Tina had been, but was very contented and happy. Millie hoped she was going to be normal. It seemed that way at the moment, but of course she was very young yet. She had pretty dark hair and dark eyes. She must be a bit like the father, thought Millie. I wonder what he was like.

They arranged for the baby to be christened in the little village church. Once more a christening took place, of a baby who had been born by mistake. It was the third time it had happened. First Nancy had conceived, then Jennifer and now Tina. It had all been an accident but it seemed fated. There had to be a reason for it.

That evening the family gathered in the big lounge, and discussed Tina's future.

'When Tina comes out of hospital,' said Dr. Margaret, 'she'll have to have something to do. She can't go back to those kennels. She'll have to come home for a while of course, to convalesce, but then perhaps she could be encouraged to do her painting again. She'll never be able to hold down a proper job. She's too unstable ever to like a job for long. It wouldn't work.'

'I liked it at the riding stables though. So did Georgina when she was young,' said Jennifer.

'She might come to that later,' said Dr. Margaret, 'but she seems to want to see a bit of life first. At least now she won't have any children.'

Chapter 11

Jennifer visited Tina daily and so did Dr. Margaret. Millie went when she could but she was very busy, with the help of Rene, looking after little Megan. Millie had now given up her job for a while, she wanted to be with the baby.

Tina was unhappy at the hospital. She didn't want to talk to the other girls in the dormitory. She just kept herself to herself, feeling shy and embarrassed. Taking the pills had caused her to gain weight and, hoping to keep it down, she stopped eating, but it didn't work and she felt peculiar. The staff told her that if she didn't eat she wouldn't get well so Tina did eat and the tablets made her hungry in the end.

Gradually Tina's depression started to lift. She looked better although she had put on weight and lost some of her pretty figure. Tina began to get over the post-natal depression. She did occupational therapy and started to do a little painting, but most of all she looked forward to her visits with Tom Phillips in his consulting room. Tina opened up to him and talked to him. One day he had her in and said, 'Now look, Tina, you won't be in the hospital for long. We don't want to see you in these places too much, you know.'

'How long will I be here?' said Tina. 'I don't feel right to go home yet.'

'You can go home the weekend after next, Tina, if you go on the way you are but you must eat you know.'

'All right,' said Tina. 'I'll try and eat.'

She began to come out of herself and amuse the others with the antics she'd been up to. She was more happy and relaxed now.

She loved seeing Jennifer daily and was happy to cuddle into her arms and tell her all her troubles. Jennifer and Tina were now very close indeed.

Jane came in to see her, to Tina's delight.

'Have you still got your boyfriend, Jane?'

'Yes,' said Jane, 'but we're not getting married for a couple of years – if at all. I . . . er . . . honestly, I'm a bit fed up with him,' she said. She was unstable like Tina, but did not worry like her friend and was not so adventurous, content just to live at home with her parents, rather fearing the outside world, as Nancy and Jennifer had done.

'You can come and stay with me when I get out of here,' said Tina.

'I'd like that,' said Jane.

Tina started to go home at weekends. For three or four weekends she went home. She kept peeking at her baby Megan, but looked on her as a sister, just as Jennifer had done with Millie. Raymond and Millie were adopting Megan legally as their own child. Tina was relieved and thought no more of it.

At last, it was time for Tina to leave the hospital and come home. 'You look well now, Tina,' said Dr. Tom as she left. 'You're all made-up again, I see, and dressed up but you've certainly put on a bit of weight, haven't you?'

'Yes, and I'm cross about it,' said Tina. 'I don't want to be big.'

'Well you must take some tablets for a while,' said Dr. Tom, 'but in about a month's time I may be able to reduce the dose.'

'All right,' said Tina. 'I'll see you in two weeks then.'

'I want to see you every two weeks for the next six months,' said Dr. Tom. 'And no gallivanting off. I mean that.'

'I'll try not to but I still write to that Mr. Willis, you know.'

'And no hanky-panky with him,' said Dr. Tom.

'There's nothing like that possible,' said Tina. 'He's just a sort of father and what-not.'

'Oh, get on with you!' said Dr. Tom. 'Now go home, Tina, and don't come back here again as a patient. You've been here three months. We don't want you back here again.'

Once she got home, Tina's feelings started to come back. She went for walks in the woods with Jennifer and once again started to talk of romance and love. She had now got over the birth, the sterilisation operation and the depression. Except for being a bit fatter Tina looked the same, dolled up and pretty. She had started to grow her hair.

Tina was now practically eighteen. Christmas was coming and she was looking forward to having a party at the big house to mark her eighteenth birthday, combined with the usual family Christmas party. She wondered what she'd be given for her birthday. 'You know, Jennifer, I must learn to drive,' she said one day.

'I think you will be able to soon,' said Jennifer, her eyes sparkling.

Unknown to Tina, the family had planned to give her a little mini car for her eighteenth birthday and she would have driving lessons with a very sensible man in the village.

The night before her birthday Tina went to bed all excited, thinking about her birthday, when she would at last feel grown-up. She felt the thrills go through her as she hugged and squeezed herself that night. Her sexual feelings had certainly come back now. She was back to normal and thinking about men again. She had thoughts of men she liked, such as Dr. Tom and Mr. Willis. She knew she couldn't have them but her frustrated feelings came out as she thought of them in bed at night. At last she fell asleep. When she woke she looked out on to a sharp, clear day. Jennifer brought her in a cup of tea.

'Happy birthday, Tina. I've brought your pills and your tea.'

'All right,' said Tina. 'I wish I didn't have to take the pills today, I'd love to have a drink for my birthday.'

'I'm sorry,' said Jennifer. 'Dr. Margaret says that's just not on. You must take them.'

Tina dressed, showered and flew down to breakfast to open her cards from the family. A big card had arrived from Mr. and Mrs. Willis and inside was some money to buy a special pair of gold earrings she had admired. Tina felt thrilled and hugged the card. I'll keep that in my room, she thought, it'll make me think of him.

There was a card and some money from Julian and Georgina, video tapes, records, tokens and clothes that the family had given her.

From Margaret, Joe and Vicky there was a gold necklace and bracelet to match but the big present from everyone at the house was outside.

'Come,' said Jennifer, 'we've got something to show you.'

'Yes,' said Dr. Margaret. 'Come outside. I've got the day off today. We're going to spend it together, Tina.'

'Oh?'

They opened the front door and pushed her outside, handing Tina an envelope. Tina's hand was shaking as she opened it.

Inside was a set of keys and she looked up and saw a little blue mini car sitting in the driveway.

'Oh, my God!' she gasped, looking round. 'Is it from you all?'

The family were all standing there, smiling.

She dropped the keys, fled indoors, up the stairs and into her room, flung herself on the bed and cried and cried, quite overcome, as she realised how much her family loved her.

Dr. Margaret knew it was her time to be with Tina now and went into her bedroom and said, 'Tina. You can't cry and run away when we give you keys to your new car.'

'It's too much for me,' said Tina. 'Oh, Dr. Margaret, I love you all but what a gift to give me! I don't deserve it. I got into trouble. I had a baby. I had a breakdown.'

'It wasn't your fault,' said Dr. Margaret. 'You're ill. Well, not ill exactly – you're physically very well – but you know you're young for your age, Tina.'

'I'm happy,' said Tina. The tears gradually disappeared as Dr. Margaret explained to Tina that it was wonderful to be loved. 'And we hope that one day, dear, you'll settle here and be happy. Try not to get into any trouble. Promise?'

'I promise,' said Tina. 'I'm so pleased with the car, but who's going to teach me to drive?' she said, cheering up.

'You will be going to the school in the village, that man we told you about, Mr. Walters, and you'll be learning to drive. Your first lesson is this weekend.'

'Oh, that's wonderful,' said Tina. 'And I'll be learning in my own car, won't I?'

'Of course you will.'

'I'm looking forward to it,' said Tina, 'but thanks, I'm going to go and sit in it now. Come with me, Dr. Margaret, please.'

They went outside and sat in the car, and to Dr. Margaret's surprise Tina spent the whole morning telling her all about herself and her problems; her dreams of the future, her romantic dreams, how she felt when she dressed up and felt sexy. How she felt at night when she had her fantasy sexy dreams, when she thought of Mr. Willis and Dr. Tom. All her thoughts came out that morning. She talked to Margaret as she'd never talked to Dr. Tom. At last she sat back, exhausted.

'My God!' said Dr. Margaret. 'You're a complex girl, Tina. But at last you've talked to me.'

'I think now,' said Tina, 'that I want you to take care of me. I'll still see Dr. Tom sometimes but I want you to be my psychiatrist now.'

Dr. Margaret's eyes filled with tears and they started to trickle down her cheeks. This had been her hope and dream for eighteen years, since the child was born, that she would want to be helped by her, as Jennifer had been helped by Dr. Rosemary her mother, as Nancy had been helped by Joe Greaves, her grandfather, and now Tina was asking her, on her eighteenth birthday, to love and help her. She took Tina into her arms. Tina melted. All the tension dissolved.

'That's settled. I'm your psychiatrist,' said Dr. Margaret. 'Let's go and tell the others the good news.'

They all sat down to lunch, Tina and Margaret eating very little, for they both felt very emotional, but they were all laughing and happy and light. Jennifer was thrilled with the news.

'For ever and ever,' said Tina. 'I love you.' It had come out, even at the table in front of her mother.

'Oh, Tina, I'm pleased for you,' said Millie.

'I feel romantic today. I'm eighteen, I've got a car, I'm going to learn to drive it and I love Dr. Margaret. Yes, I love Dr. Margaret.'

Suddenly Tina said, 'Excuse me, but I want to go into the woods with the two dogs.'

There were always corgis and King Charles spaniels at the big house; as one died another would take its place and there was Trixie and Tina, always Trixie and Tina. So there were two Tinas at the big house and there was a Trixie too.

Tina took the three dogs into the woods and sat down by the big tree where Gordon and Nancy had sat so many years ago.

It's my eighteenth birthday, she thought. She looked up at the trees, they were beautiful. It was a cold crisp winter's day and Tina had on jeans, a heavy sweater and an anorak. The watery sun was shining through the trees and the woods looked mystical and romantic. They must have felt like me today. I somehow feel I'm in love. I've fallen in love today. Tina had a new crush. Her young emotional mind could take no more of men for the moment and she had given her love and heart to Dr. Margaret. I love her, she thought. She may be over sixty and old, but she's got a lovely face and I love her. I'm in love. Tina squeezed herself and felt the thrills go through her. She sighed, wondering what she could do to please the object of her affections.

She heard a rustle and looked round. It was Jane. Jane had

arrived and run off to find her. She knew where she'd find Tina on such a lovely day.

'Oh happy birthday, Tina,' said Jane. 'I've brought some things for you. They're at home.'

'Oh, I'm so glad you're staying. Let's go back and play some records in my room. I've got something to tell you, Jane.'

She wanted to tell the world, on this eighteenth birthday, that she was in love.

'You must swear, as we've always sworn our secrets,' said Tina. 'Swear, Jane, you'll never tell.'

'I swear,' said Jane. 'What is it, Tina?'

'I'm in love again. With Dr. Margaret.'

'Wow!' said Jane. 'She's old!'

'I don't care. I'm in love with her. As Jennifer was in love with Dr. Rosemary.'

'It's a crush,' said Jane. 'You're not gay.'

'Perhaps I am.'

'You're not!' said Jane. 'You'll never be gay. It's just a crush.'

'No, it's not,' said Tina. 'I must be gay. I am in love!'

But Tina was only trying out another game in the way she could be. She had her feelings whoever she loved, whether it was a man or a woman, for she was so emotionally immature, and now Dr. Margaret was the right one for her to feel a love for.

Jane realised that and said, 'Come on, Tina, the party will be on soon. You must get ready.'

'I've put my clothes out,' said Tina. 'I've got a very nice dress in blue, dark blue. Mummy bought it for my birthday. It's plain, as you know I like plain things. It's got a more flared skirt because tight skirts look awful on me now I'm fatter, but it shows my bust up well and I'm going to put on lots of make-up and do my hair for Dr. Margaret. I do love her!'

'Oh Tina, you're really funny,' said Jane. 'Come on!'

They flew into the big house and went upstairs like tornadoes.

'My God!' said Dr. Margaret. 'What was that?'

'It's the two girls,' said Jennifer. 'They're crazy. It's like Tina was in love again. They're behaving like that.'

'I wonder who it is now,' said Dr. Margaret.

'Don't know,' said Jennifer.

Dr. Margaret thought, I wonder if it's me? Jennifer fell in love with my mother all those years ago. Of course it was just a crush. But it was more than that. It was deep, sincere and beautiful. Nothing bad about it somehow. In Tina's case it was more intense.

Jennifer had given her whole heart to Rosemary but Tina was much more intense in a different way, more physical about the whole thing. The spiritual side would come later as she got older. Margaret dismissed her suspicions along with her reminiscences. Later on the two girls made their entrance. Jane was wearing a dark green dress her mother had bought her for the occasion and Tina looked beautiful in the dark blue, flared dress with flat shoes. She had paid a great deal of attention to her hair and make-up.

'Tina, you look beautiful,' said Dr. Margaret.

Tina coloured up. 'Oh, Dr. Margaret, do I?' she said.

'You do,' said Dr. Margaret, blushing as she realised with a jolt that Tina only had eyes for her.

'Dr. Margaret, thanks for everything,' said Tina. 'We'll talk again tomorrow and every day. I love you.' She kissed her on the cheek and ran giggling into the lounge.

Dr. Margaret resolved that Tina's love would be safe with her and she would love Tina as Rosemary loved Jennifer.

Jennifer was amused at the new-found love and went in and teased Tina. Jennifer, Tina and Jane did nothing but giggle for the next half hour and they all enjoyed themselves immensely.

The rest of the people arrived for the party. Jane's parents arrived with Bill, Sandy with her new husband, and two or three of Tina's old school friends arrived from Guildford, accompanied by their parents.

It was a lovely party. There was a sumptuous high tea and there was to be dancing in the evening. Tina's favourite old-fashioned music was played for her by a small band which Raymond had ordered as a special surprise.

After the big tea and the drinks and the speeches, though Tina was only allowed to drink lemonade, she was happy. She kept looking at Dr. Margaret and blushing and giggling, which amused them all very much, for they understood Tina.

Tina had the happiest birthday she had ever had. For this birthday she had her new found love and she felt well again. She was over her breakdown. That evening Tina danced with Dr. Margaret and every one roared with laughter at the way she danced with her.

'It tickles me pink,' said Raymond. 'She really is amusing. She loves men and women I think.'

'She'll find a man one day,' said Millie. 'She's normal. My daughter's normal, in that respect.'

'OK,' said Raymond, 'but it is amusing.'

Tina was amusing that night. She danced around happily and clung to Dr. Margaret, having got bored with Bill after two dances with him. Everyone was happy, everyone enjoyed the occasion.

The next day Tina was tired but enjoyed talking to Dr. Margaret and giggling with Jane and clearing things up with the rest of the family.

Tina and Jane went to Guildford a few days later to do some Christmas shopping, Tina very excited about choosing a present for Dr. Margaret.

'What about a pretty necklace or something?' suggested Jane.

'She doesn't wear necklaces. I know! There's a bracelet, it's real silver, I saw it in the jeweller's the other day. Dr. Margaret wears bracelets, I've seen them. I could have her name put on it. Oh, Jane, do you think she'd like it?'

'Of course,' said Jane.

They went to the jeweller's and looked at the bracelet.

'Would this be all right for an older lady?' asked Tina shyly. She and Jane started laughing. The jeweller thought they were quite mad but Tina bought the bracelet and had it wrapped up especially for Christmas. They went around and bought presents for the whole family then they went their separate ways to choose something for each other. Tina bought Jane a lovely green sweater in lambswool, and Jane chose for Tina a little denim waistcoat.

When they had finished, they met for a cup of tea.

'And by the way, Jane,' said Tina. 'I've got something for Mr. and Mrs. Willis. Mr. Willis is a laugh you know. I wish they'd come down but his mother's a bit cranky or something and won't let him go anywhere. It's horrible! I'm glad Mummy's not like that.'

'I wouldn't let my mother rule me like that either,' said Jane. 'If I was a man especially; but she must be a bit odd.'

'One day,' said Tina, 'I might go and see them again, and Julian and Georgina. They're fine. I'm sending them a box of chocolates.'

'That's nice,' said Jane. 'Oh well, we'd better get back now.'

They caught the bus to the village from Guildford and got off and walked back to the big house through the narrow village lanes. The Christmas atmosphere was everywhere. It was just getting dark when they walked up the driveway, admiring the trees, floodlit now, as was the custom.

With all their presents they went straight upstairs, and weren't seen again that evening. They even took their tea upstairs for they insisted on wrapping all the presents and writing all their cards together. At last they went downstairs to say goodnight.

'Dr. Margaret, we've wrapped all our presents and I've wrapped yours,' said Tina. 'May I kiss you goodnight?'

Tina blushed and kissed Dr. Margaret and the two girls flew up the spiral staircase giggling their heads off. They went to bed happy that night. Their presents were all wrapped, their cards were all ready, some to post and some for the people at home, and they went to bed happy, Tina thinking of Dr. Margaret and Jane with her own romantic dreams.

On Christmas morning, after Richard and Robert had had the time of their lives opening their Christmas stockings, they all went to church. As always Tina enjoyed the service and tears welled up in her eyes as she heard the Christmas carols. Spiritual things touched her heart and so did romantic music. Sitting next to Dr. Margaret she looked up at her with love in her eyes. Dr. Margaret saw the tears and squeezed her hand. That made Tina's Christmas perfect.

After church they all went back to the big house and had a wonderful Christmas dinner and then, as was the custom, they sat round the tree in the hall, roaring with laughter, happy, opening the presents, giving to one another. It was a true Christmas for them all. When Tina handed Dr. Margaret her Christmas present she shrieked with laughter and ran into the video room with Jane behind her. She was too shy to watch her open it. A few minutes later Dr. Margaret walked in.

'Tina, you shouldn't have! It must have cost you a lot, it's real silver! Very thick. And with my name on it. Oh Tina, I shall treasure it always.'

Tina flew into Dr. Margaret's arms and they embraced. Kissing Dr. Margaret she declared, 'I love you, Dr. Margaret,' and then ran out of the video room, giggling again.

Christmas day came to an end and very late that night they all went to bed. The two girls talked until they couldn't keep their eyes open any more, Tina jabbering about Dr. Margaret.

'It was wonderful, her cuddling me. Oh, I love her.'

'You'll get over that,' said Jane. 'Wait and see, Tina.'

'I never will,' said Tina. 'I never will.'

With that the two girls fell asleep exhausted.

In the spring Dr. Margaret decided that it was about time Tina thought about some work. Tina did not want to know. She was happy at home, waiting for Dr. Margaret to come home from work, and waiting also for the time when her dear friend would be retiring.

'Would you like to work at the riding stables?' said Dr. Margaret one day.

'Well, I'd rather work there than anywhere else at the moment.'

'Yes. Well, I think they're willing to have you there. You could work there five days a week and have weekends at home.'

'Yes, with you, Dr. Margaret,' said Tina.

'I've retired and I need rest,' said Dr. Margaret, 'but I've always time to talk to you, Tina, you know that.'

Dr. Margaret took Tina over to the riding stables to see the owner, Mr. Holder. He was very glad to take Tina on. He was short-staffed after Julian and Georgina had left.

Tina settled in at the riding stables and liked grooming the horses. She learned to ride and thoroughly enjoyed country life.

Margaret often wondered how long this little idyll would last.

Chapter 12

Tina was now twenty-three years old. Robert was eleven and was going to school in Guildford with Richard. He was growing up into a very nice boy. Millie could see he was going to be quite academic. Baby Megan had grown into a lovely child. At five, she didn't yet know that Tina was her real mother. She just thought that Millie was her mother and Raymond was her father. It was established by tests that she had not inherited Tina's condition; she had just started at the village school and was very happy there indeed. She was cheerful and bright and loved everyone at the big house. She was an attractive little girl, with very dark hair, like her father's.

Jennifer was getting on now, towards seventy, and so was Dr. Margaret, but they were both still quite lively. Jennifer got tired more easily, for she'd had a hard life with her young emotions, but she was well and happy, still on her tranquillisers, and still taking a great interest in Tina's life. Tina, now twenty-three years old, was just slightly more mature, still very romantic, but her crush on Dr. Margaret was subsiding, having grown now into a deep admiration and love.

Dr. Margaret was pleased. She had been worried for Tina had seemed to be too much in love with her. She was glad that Tina was turning her attention to men once more.

Tina was thinking a lot these days. She wasn't settled at the riding stables any more. The crush had subsided. She was contented at the big house but she knew she must find something more before she settled for ever. Perhaps she would when she was older. She loved the big house now and still saw Jane. Jane had not yet married but had a new boyfriend called Ernest with whom she was going steady. Tina knew they might get married at any time. She had been jealous at first and upset but now accepted that Jane would not come and see her so often but Tina missed her dreadfully and things did not seem the same. She had started to get bored and thought she might like to go for a holiday.

'I think, Dr. Margaret,' she said one evening, 'I'll go and stay at Julian's in Exmouth.'

'All right,' said Dr. Margaret. 'I think you should go away, but don't get into trouble.'

'I can't now,' said Tina. 'I'm sterilised.'

'I don't mean that. You know you could get AIDS or something. You must not do it unless you're really in love and know the man.'

'I promise,' said Tina. I'll be careful.'

Georgina and Julian were phoned and were glad to have Tina for she had refused so many times in the last five years. Tina, who could now drive her blue mini car, begged the family to let her drive down alone but Dr. Margaret wouldn't hear of it. She was frightfully worried.

'Look, Tina, you mustn't drive alone, you'll get too tired. You've only driven around here and as far as Guildford.'

Joe came to the rescue by offering to go with her, sharing the driving, and come back by train, after staying the night.

On the way Joe talked to Tina.

'You love Mum, don't you?'

'Yes,' said Tina, 'but I've got over the sort of crush thing.'

'I know,' said Joe. He was a very good psychiatrist and very interested in Tina's case. He liked her very much indeed. He hoped he'd be able to help her later on, when his mother was gone.

Tina talked to him quite frankly on the journey and he learned a lot about her. It was the first time she had really talked to him. Tina was quite personable now, at twenty-three. She still wore her hair short and was very attractive indeed, but she was more moderate with things for she had matured slightly.

Everything was the same at Julian's and they put Joe up for the night. They spent a happy evening talking, enjoying reminiscing. Julian and Georgina loved talking to Joe.

'We're getting old now,' said Julian. 'And we can't cope here. Georgina's cousin's old too. We're going into a home soon.'

'Are you?' said Joe.

'Yes,' said Julian. 'It's near here. We feel we'd be looked after. We can't cope any more and we're selling everything.'

'Oh,' said Tina. 'How awful! I shan't be able to come and stay any more.'

'No,' said Georgina. 'This will be the last time. The house is already sold and we move in two months but I'll give you the address of the home and you can come and see us.'

'I shan't be able to stay at Mr. Willis's either,' said Tina. 'He's got a cranky mother who won't allow any visitors.'

'What a shame,' said Joe. 'Make the best of the holiday and enjoy it for it will be the last time you'll spend in this house.'

It was a good idea for Georgina and Julian to go into the home. It was a nice little old people's home in Exmouth. It was near the sea and they would really enjoy it. They had met the people there who had liked the couple, so young for their age and so sweet-natured. They knew they would be happy there and they'd have company too which they needed badly now in their old age. They were rather young to be going in a home but they needed to be looked after and they were very happy about it.

Tina enjoyed the next day with Julian and Georgina pottering around. They went round the shops and out for lunch. But Julian and Georgina were rather boring now, Tina found. They had very little to say; they were just happy, wrapped up in themselves but Tina wanted to do other things. She wanted to see Mr. Willis. She had phoned and arranged to see him the next day. She would see quite a lot of him, she hoped, for she was staying with Julian and Georgina for three weeks this time, but she intended to do other things as well. Tina intended to drive off and look around the town and meet people. She wanted to meet an older man. She still had an idea about getting married. She had forgotten the idea about the little house. That did not worry her so much now. She had got used to her own home and loved it but she still felt that she wanted someone.

Tina had brought some nice clothes with her, for she wanted to look attractive when she went out. The next day she drove over to Mr. Willis's, proud of herself in her little blue mini car, and stopped outside the door. Mr. Willis was standing at the door grinning at her. Tina grinned cheekily back at him. 'It's years since I've seen you, Mr. Willis. Oh, it's great to see you.' Suddenly Tina felt the devil rise up within her. She wanted to flirt with him.

She went into his study and talked to him, told him all her

troubles. He listened but he talked to her a lot about spiritual things. Tina listened more this time. She was that much older.

'I do believe in it all, Mr. Willis. But I want to have fun and I want to get married.'

'Please be careful, Tina,' he said.

'I wish it was you,' said Tina.

'Well, it can't be, I'm married.'

Tina asked him for a kiss but he pushed her away and said it was wrong. She felt very rejected.

'If you're nasty to me I shan't come and see you again, Mr. Willis.'

'Oh, do come again before you go back.'

'I'll see you again, Mr. Willis,' she said, grinning at him as she left, but she didn't feel so happy as when she had arrived. She certainly had felt rejected that day. As she drove back to Julian's, she realised that she was wrong to pursue Mr. Willis.

The next day she decided to go off in the car and look around the town and see what was going on. She dressed up and told Julian and Georgina she was going into town on her own.

'Now you take care,' said Georgina.

'I will,' said Tina smiling and drove off into Exmouth and parked her little car. She wandered around for a little while and suddenly felt lost and wondered if she would ever meet the right person. Perhaps she would later on, she told herself.

Tina soon got bored looking round the shops and round the arcades and then she went into a pub for the first time on her own. She knew she couldn't drink but she could hear music and felt she wanted some excitement. Sitting in a corner with a glass of lemonade, she felt, in spite of her confident appearance, nervous and shy. A lot of men looked at her for she looked very attractive in her skirt and sweater, fitting closely to her figure. And she had on all her make-up that day. She had meant to look attractive.

Somebody came and sat beside her. Looking up, to her surprise she found an elderly woman looking at her, somewhat the worse for drink. Tina edged away. She wasn't sure she liked the look of the woman at all. Then the woman said, 'What are you doing here on your own?'

'Same as you,' said Tina grinning. She was a very friendly girl and after all the woman seemed quite friendly and harmless and it was someone to talk to.

'I live in Surrey,' Tina explained. 'I'm staying with some friends in Exmouth. I thought I'd just come in here and have some lemonade. I can't drink, you see, I'm on tablets.'

'I thought you might be,' said the woman, knowingly.

'Why?' said Tina.

'Well, I'm a trained nurse.'

'Oh, are you?' said Tina.

'Yes. I live in Torquay actually. I'm just here for the day.'

'How did you get up here?'

'I came up on the bus,' said the woman. 'My name's Madge.'

'My name's Tina. Are you going back to Torquay tonight then?'

'Yes I am,' said Madge. 'I live in a flat there. You know, I get ever so lonely. I'm afraid I drink too much at times. I work part-time now. I'm not quite old enough to retire. I'm fifty-five.'

'I'm twenty-three,' said Tina.

'Yes, you're young,' said Madge. 'You look very young too, and very attractive, may I say. Have you got a boyfriend?'

'No,' said Tina.

'You ought to come to Torquay,' said Madge. 'Why don't you come sometime and see my flat. Come and have a meal with me.'

Poor Tina fell for it.

'I'd like that very much. When could it be?'

'Tell you what,' said Madge. 'You'd better go and ask the people you're staying with if you could come away for the day. If you've got a car I could come up tomorrow and you could drive me back. We could spend the day there.'

'Oh thanks,' said Tina. 'I would like that very much indeed.'

'We'll meet here tomorrow morning at ten o'clock, when they open.'

'Very well,' said Tina. 'That'll be fine. Well, I'd better go now. I don't think I want to talk to any of the men and they keep looking at me.'

'You shouldn't be so attractive,' said Madge.

'I think I'll meet the right person someday.'

'You'll meet more people in Torquay. It's a big place, a big holiday resort.'

'I've never been there,' said Tina, 'although Julian and Georgina have and they liked it. It gets a bit crowded, they said.'

'It does,' said Madge, 'but where I live it's not too bad at all.'

Tina started thinking about the bright lights and getting excited. Torquay sounded good. She wanted to go with Madge.

Tina went back to Julian's for tea and told them all about Madge.

'I don't think you should go,' said Georgina. 'You say she'd had a lot to drink.'

'I want to. I felt sorry for the old girl. Oh, please let me go. It's only for the day.'

'Well I can't stop you,' said Georgina, 'but please come back in the evening, won't you?'

'I promise,' said Tina. 'Remember, I've got my own car.'

That evening they had supper and watched a video, the three of them. Tina had hired one on the way back that she thought they would like. It was a nice love story and they all enjoyed it. Tina had tears in her eyes once more as she thought of the man of her dreams that she had not yet met, and hoped to meet in Torquay where the bright lights were. It sounded good. Tina had a lot to learn yet.

After the film Tina went to bed and lay there thinking about Madge and wondering if she could possibly stay there sometime. Tina was crafty. If she wanted to get round something she always worked it somehow. She was getting bored at Julian and Georgina's. She had got bored with Mr. Willis going on about his mother and not letting her stay there. She wanted to get out of Exmouth – it was a dead place.

The next morning it was a nice day and Tina awoke and showered and dressed very well in anticipation of her day in Torquay. She had on a pretty dark blue skirt which fitted her well and showed off her figure, a nice shirt in pale blue, her boots that she loved so much and her leather jacket that her grandfather had bought her before he died. She spent a lot of time on her hair and face and then went down to breakfast.

'Now,' said Julian. 'Not too late tonight. Promise?'

'I promise,' said Tina.

After breakfast she left, having had her tablets, leaving behind her two worried people. She drove to the little pub where she had met Madge and there she was standing outside.

'Don't let's waste any time,' said Madge. 'We won't go in. I'll get into the car and we'll go straight back to Torquay. I didn't go back last night. I stayed in a bed and breakfast here.'

Tina was a good, confident driver. Madge gave her directions and they made good time to Torquay.

Tina looked around. It was a big crowded place and she felt an excitement well up inside her. Madge took her straight back to her flat where they sat down and had something to eat.

'Now, this afternoon,' said Madge, 'why don't you wander

about the town? Then this evening we could go out together if you'd like.'

'All right,' said Tina. 'I'll come back for you at tea-time.'

'Don't get lost,' said Madge. 'You don't know the place.'

'I can always ask someone,' said Tina. She seemed very confident. 'You see, I haven't got too long because I've got to get back.'

'You could stay the night,' said Madge.

'We'll see,' said Tina, secretly wondering if she dared to ring Julian and ask if she could stay at Madge's for the night.

Madge had a nice little flat, just outside the town of Torquay. One couldn't see the sea from there. She had a lot of friends, friends who drank with her. Madge took drugs, had been addicted, and had been sacked from her work for doing so, and Madge drank when she couldn't get any drugs. Sometimes young people came to Madge's flat and they would take drugs together and have parties.

Madge needed a bit of company at the moment. She could see, from her experience as a trained nurse, that Tina had mental problems, that Tina was immature, an easy touch. She was so right.

Tina drove around Torquay and was amazed by the large place. It half frightened her and half thrilled her. She went to look at the sea. It was a beautiful summer's day and the sea was a perfect blue. Watching the people on the beach she longed to go in the water, but she did not want to be alone. She wanted company of her own age. She wanted to meet her dream lover, as she called him in her immature mind.

Tina walked around the shops for a while, went into the amusement arcades and got thoroughly tired as she usually did in hot weather. She went back to the car and drove back to Madge's, earlier than expected.

'What's wrong?' said Madge. 'You look all in.'

'I'm tired,' said Tina, 'and I've got to drive all the way back. I haven't had any excitement here.'

'Well you won't unless you meet people,' said Madge.

'I know.'

'Would you like to stay the night?' said Madge. 'I've got some friends coming round later.'

'What sort of friends?' said Tina.

'Oh, some young people. You'd like them. They're a bit older than you though, in their thirties.'

'Well, I wouldn't mind meeting them. I'm a bit shy though,' said Tina.

'You'll be all right with me.'

'Well, look, I'll ring Julian and ask him but please, Madge, will you speak to him?'

'I'll get it over for you. I'll tell him you're tired after looking round the shops, you want to stay the night and that you'll go back tomorrow morning.'

'Thanks.' Tina nervously rang Julian.

'But you must come back tonight,' said Julian. 'I don't know what your mother would say if she knew where you were. I'm really worried.' Tina handed the phone to Madge.

'She'll be all right with me, said Madge confidently. 'Perfectly all right. I'm a trained nurse. She'll be fine.' She loved to tell everyone about that.

'Oh, all right,' said Julian. He thought that Madge sounded perfectly competent and felt very relieved.

Tina fell asleep in the scruffy little room that Madge had put her in. She was tired and wasn't sure she liked the flat, it was a bit sniffy, but Tina was so tired she just fell asleep. She just wanted to stay the night at Madge's and meet the friends. She just wanted to meet somebody. Poor Tina was very hungry for love.

That night four friends of Madge's came around. They were all in their thirties, except for Tony who was forty-two and divorced. He was a very good-looking man with dark hair, but had gone downhill since he had started taking drugs. Then there were Elizabeth and Kevin, who lived together, and Kevin's friend, Jack. They all took drugs and if they couldn't get them, like Madge, they drank, but tonight Tony had managed to get some and they were all going to have an orgy, taking drugs that night.

Tina came into the room where they were chattering. Madge had warned them that Tina knew nothing of these things. But Tony saw Tina walk in looking very glamorous, dressed up in a skirt and a tight jumper, her hair done beautifully and her make-up on.

'This is Tina,' said Madge.

Tony got up. 'I'm Tony.' He immediately felt an attraction towards Tina and she felt likewise.

'How do you do, Tony.' She was introduced to the others but did not take much interest in them.

Tony sat down and asked Tina to sit with him.

'I hoped you'd make friends,' said Madge. 'Tony gets very

lonely, Tina.' Madge made some coffee and they all sat round drinking it. Then Tony got out some tablets. They were not hard drugs but they were very addictive. Tony handed them round.

Tina said, 'What have you got there?'

Tony explained that they made you feel good.

'Oh,' said Tina, 'but I take tranquillisers.'

'What are they?' said Tony.

Tina took them out of her bag and showed them to him.

'Oh, they're just mild. They're nothing. They don't make you feel good. Try one of these, Tina.'

'Oh no! Mummy said, and Dr. Margaret, that I must never, never take drugs.'

'Try one,' Tony insisted.

'No,' said Tina. 'I don't want to.' She flatly refused. When she saw how the others were affected though she grew curious and decided to try one. 'I will try one, Tony. I feel a bit miserable.'

A few minutes later Tina started feeling marvellous, a feeling she had never had before. Tina had never been drunk, she had never been allowed to drink, but this felt marvellous. She felt so relaxed and happy.

'Let's talk in your room,' said Tony.

'Oh yes,' said. Tina. She started giggling and Tony took Tina into her room. They talked and laughed and messed about and finally they ended up making love. Tina couldn't enjoy making love, the drug had got a real hold on her but she enjoyed messing around and Tony managed to have sexual intercourse with her. Tina got nothing out of it though: she just felt swoony and stupid and hardly noticed what had happened. Then poor Tina passed out and fell asleep.

The next morning Tina woke up feeling terrible. The others had all gone and Madge was still asleep in her room. Tina felt so bad, remembering the night before. She could only recall bits of it and knew that Tony had made love to her. Oh, what a fool she had been! But she remembered how wonderful she'd felt taking the pills. She got up feeling dreadful.

'Oh, Madge,' she moaned, 'I feel awful,' when they were drinking some coffee in the kitchen. Tina couldn't eat any breakfast at all.

'Would you like another pill, Tina?' said Madge. 'It would make you feel better.'

'Yes, I would,' said Tina, 'but I won't take any more after that.'

'I'm very short of money,' said Madge slyly.

'Are you?' said Tina. 'I've got plenty on me.' Tina always had money on her, thanks to a generous allowance from Millie.

'If you give me some money,' said Madge craftily, 'I'll give you some tablets, a lot of them.'

'How much do you want?' said Tina.

'Well, quite a lot,' said Madge. 'I'm very short and the tablets cost a lot of money but I'll give you a hundred tablets if you give me a hundred pounds.'

'I haven't got that much on me,' said Tina, 'but I could give you a cheque.'

'I'd be worried about cashing it,' said Madge.

'You needn't worry. They'll cash it at your bank.'

'I don't have a bank account any more,' said Madge. 'Tina, take me to your bank. Any branch will cash it and I'll give you the pills then.'

'Yes, and then I'll go back.' Suddenly Tina started feeling wonderful again, after taking her tablet. She didn't care how much she gave Madge. 'You will give me the tablets, won't you Madge?'

'Yes.'

They went in the car to the bank. Tina felt very woozy on the pill, but happy, and she was able to drive the car. She cashed a cheque at the bank and gave the hundred pounds to Madge. Madge gave her the bottle of a hundred tablets.

'I must get back now,' said Tina. 'I promised Julian.'

'Well actually I've got to go to work,' said Madge.

'Got to work?' said Tina. 'I thought you said you'd retired early.'

'Well,' lied Madge, 'I do specialling you know.' Madge did nothing of the sort. She'd been sacked from nursing long ago for her drug-taking and alcoholism.

'Can you find your way back?' She was getting impatient and Tina sensed it, as it dawned on her that Madge had only wanted her money.

'Well,' said Tina. 'I can find my way back if you'll just show me the road to the motorway.'

They got into the car and Tina and Madge drove to the road that led on to the motorway. Madge directed Tina and got out of the car and caught a bus back to Torquay. She couldn't wait to get back to her friends. She had forgotten Tina before she was out of sight.

Tina drove slowly along the road. She was beginning to feel heady. She hadn't taken her usual tranquillisers. Her head was thumping. She felt awful. All she could think of was getting back to Exmouth but she felt so bad on the way she stopped and had a cup of coffee at a little café and smoked a cigarette.

Tina got back to Exmouth. She nearly lost her way twice but at last managed to get back to Julian's. When she got into the house Julian said, 'Oh Tina, you don't look well. Whatever's happened?'

'Nothing,' said Tina. 'I got fed up with Madge and decided to come back anyway.' She didn't tell Julian the truth about the money, the tablets, the party the night before.

'Well, what did you do?' said Georgina.

'Oh, she just had some friends in and we talked and had coffee. It was quite nice,' said Tina.

'Any nice young men?' said Georgina.

'Well, yes, there was a chap called Tony, but I didn't like him much.' She could hardly remember Tony now. She had been so fuzzy with those tablets and now she had them in her handbag.

Tina could hardly eat any lunch, she felt sick after taking that pill and went to bed and slept all the afternoon. That night she came down and had supper and watched a video but she didn't feel at all well. Tina wasn't enjoying herself. She wanted to go home. She didn't know what to do.

Tina did stay at Julian's and went down into Exmouth and wandered about during the day but all the time she was popping those tablets into her and Julian and Georgina wondered why she looked so white, why she was so high one minute and low the next. Little did they suspect, in their innocent, immature minds, what Tina had done.

Tina did not want to go and see Mr. Willis. She knew he might guess what was going on but she did ring him up a couple of times and make an excuse.

'I'll write to you when I get back, Mr. Willis. And thank you for your help.'

Tina had not found the love she had hoped to find but she went out with one or two boys in Exmouth. She was high on those pills and she had sex with them. They just used her as a one night stand.

Tina, realising how she'd been used, was beginning to feel bitter. Both men had met her and used her for sex, taken her back to their flats in the evenings and had sex with her, and arranged to meet her the next day and not turned up.

It's about four or five men who've done the dirty on me, thought Tina. If I was attractive like Nancy was they wouldn't do that. She thought it was the way she looked, not understanding that she had met the wrong type of men, nor recalling that Nancy didn't wander about like that but waited for love to come to her. Instead she started feeling embittered and discontented with herself. In the end Julian couldn't do anything with her and couldn't understand what was wrong with her.

'You've got to go home. We can't manage you and we're going into the home soon. You'll have to go back to Surrey.'

'I can't drive back alone,' said Tina. 'I'm nervous. I can manage the car but I just want someone with me.' Lonely now and unhappy, she just wanted to get back to the big house. Julian agreed to drive back with her.

Tina left Exmouth five days before she should have done and Georgina rang up after they'd left and said to Dr. Margaret, who answered the phone, 'Julian's bringing Tina back. She'll have to do all the driving, but she'll be all right as long as he's with her.'

'What's wrong?' asked Dr. Margaret. 'Why are they coming back so early? Why does she want to come home?'

'She's been ever so peculiar, very up and down in her moods and acting strangely – and she looks like a ghost. She's not eating.'

'Good heavens!' said Dr. Margaret. 'What's she been up to?'

Georgina was afraid to tell Dr. Margaret about Tina's trip to Torquay. She wondered if Madge had anything to do with what had happened but Georgina didn't have the sense to realise what it could have been.

'Oh, I don't know what it is,' said Georgina.

'Don't worry. You've done your best, Georgina. Take care. We'll keep Julian for the night and see him off back home by train in the morning.'

'Thanks. Goodbye, Dr. Margaret.'

Tina drove back slowly. She felt slowed down. The drugs were taking a hold on her, she kept taking them. She didn't know what to do. She didn't know how she would get some more when her supply ran out. She knew the name of the tablets and thought she would get some from a doctor in Guildford, or try her own doctor, but she knew she had to be careful. She wondered if they could be obtained from a doctor. All she could think of was that she must have them. Tina was already addicted to those tablets and wasn't taking her prescribed tablets. She was deteriorating.

They arrived before supper at the big house and were greeted by Dr. Margaret.

'Hello, Julian. You'll be in your old room for tonight.'

Julian was tired and went up to rest before supper.

'Well, Tina,' said Dr. Margaret. 'Come in here.' They went into the lounge. 'Oh Tina, you do look ill. What have you been doing?'

'Nothing,' said Tina. 'I've been ever so good but I got bored at Exmouth and I wanted to come back.' She did not tell Dr. Margaret about Madge and the escapade at Torquay.

'Are you taking your tablets?' said Dr. Margaret.

Tina hesitated before declaring that she had been.

Dr. Margaret felt suspicious. She didn't like the look of Tina's eyes which seemed smaller.

'Have you taken any other tablets? Has anyone given you anything?'

'No,' lied Tina.

But Dr. Margaret thought otherwise and was very suspicious indeed. She decided to let Tina rest and talk to her again the next day. Tina went up into her room and fell asleep immediately.

Julian and Tina came down to supper, both looking miserable. It was very quiet. Julian felt guilty and knew he must talk to Dr. Margaret. Tina excused herself after supper. She just wanted to go upstairs and play music and take a pill and be alone, and feel wonderful, as she called it. It was her secret.

Chapter 13

Julian went into the lounge with Dr. Margaret.

'I must talk to you,' he said.

'What is it?' said Dr. Margaret.

'Well,' said Julian, 'I think Tina has been up to something. You see, she wasn't well when she came back from Torquay.'

'Torquay?' exclaimed Dr. Margaret. 'What do you mean?'

Julian suddenly flushed and blurted out the whole story about Madge, about meeting her in Exmouth, about the flat in Torquay she'd stayed at for the night and come back looking scruffy and dirty.

'Thank you for telling me, Julian. I'll wait until you've gone back. I'll have to handle this myself.'

Tina lived in a world of her own for the next few days. She hid the tablets very carefully; she was getting more and more addicted, and she hid her chequebook. She didn't want anyone to see that she had written a cheque in Torquay and cashed it for Madge. Tina was worried where she would get some more tablets from and she went off by herself for the next few days, not wanting to mix with Jennifer or anyone. They all knew something was wrong and Dr. Margaret was out of her mind with worry.

She went to Forest Dene Hospital and told her fears to Dr. Tom Phillips.

'Now, Tom, I'm certain she's taking drugs and I'll be honest, I've looked through her things but I haven't found anything.'

'I'll see her next Monday. Make sure she comes, won't you? I'll soon be able to tell. I'll make her tell me somehow.'

'All right,' said Dr. Margaret. 'Shall I say anything to her in the meantime?'

'No,' said Dr. Tom. 'She might be on her guard and run away or something and that would never do.'

'Very well,' said Dr. Margaret. 'I'll bring her on Monday at ten.'

'Right. See you then,' said Dr. Phillips. He sat back feeling worried. If Tina was taking drugs, it would be the worst thing for her, for it could cause brain damage, with the condition she had already, if she took them for too long.

Meanwhile Tina went to see Jane in Guildford. Jane was now married to the boy she had met at the kennels and they were living in a very small house, near to where her parents lived so they could keep a watchful eye on her.

Tina could have gone to the wedding but she didn't want to. It had happened while she was away. Tina felt jealous and upset. Jane had found the right man and she hadn't. Men had let her down and she was bitter. That's why she was taking drugs. She felt ugly and unwanted, neglecting her appearance, just wearing old jeans and a sweater.

Tina went to see Jane while her husband was at work. Jane stayed at home now and was a good little housekeeper and cook.

'Oh Tina, you look dreadful!' said Jane. 'What is wrong?'

Tina was very down that morning. She hadn't take a pill as yet that day, she felt she ought to cut it down, but every time she did she felt dreadful. She knew she must have one soon.

'Well,' said Tina. 'I've been away and I feel horrible and rejected and ugly. I wish I looked like Nancy in the portrait in the hall, my great-great-grandmother. She was so beautiful. Men have let me down. I've not been wanted. No one's ever really wanted to marry me, not like you, Jane; and Nancy was loved by Gordon, Jennifer by Derek. I'm not really like them. I'm a horrible person and I hate myself.'

'You shouldn't do that,' said Jane. 'Oh Tina, you look ill. What have you been doing?'

Tina started crying. She felt very down indeed.

'Swear it's a secret, Jane, if I tell you,' said Tina.

'I swear,' said Jane.

Tina told her the whole story about Madge and Torquay and how she'd been used by Tony. It seemed to her that all men just used her and then cast her aside. It hurt her to the core.

'Oh, please tell Dr. Phillips or Dr. Margaret! Oh, please,' begged

Jane. 'You'll destroy yourself with those drugs. We've been warned about them. We were at school.'

'I know,' said Tina. 'But I don't care.'

Jane was worried. She had sworn not to tell but she felt it was her duty to do so. Tina read her mind.

'If you tell anyone, Jane, I'll never want to see you again.'

'I won't.' Jane feared Tina in this mood.

She had a cup of coffee with her and then Tina left, after having first gone in the toilet and taken a pill. She couldn't go on like this. She felt restless and was coming to the end of the pills. I must get some more, she thought.

After she left Jane, Tina walked around Guildford and went into a chemist's shop. She knew the name of the tablets and asked if she could buy some.

'Oh no. You have to get a doctor's prescription for those,' said the chemist.

'All right,' said Tina. She wondered what to do. She knew there was a doctor in Guildford that her grandfather had seen and she thought she'd try and get the tablets that way. Tina was desperate now as the supply of pills was running out. She hung around until surgery time and then went in and said, 'I'm on holiday. I'd like to see the doctor please.'

'You'll have to wait. There are quite a few people before you,' said the receptionist, 'but I think I can fit you in as a temporary.'

They didn't think anything of it. Tina had made her face up to look as normal as she could and had drunk some coffee. She had eaten nothing. She did not want to eat anything since she'd started taking these pills. They were badly affecting her nervous system, her brain, with the damage she was born with.

At last it was time to go into the doctor. Tina felt nervous. I mustn't show it, she thought. I must try and get the pills. Tina could be very clever and crafty at times and could act well.

'Oh doctor, I'm on holiday.'

'Where do you live?' asked the doctor.

'Exmouth,' lied Tina. She gave Georgina's name and address as her own and said, 'I'm on these tablets and I've gone and forgotten to bring them with me. I've run out.'

'Well, this is an addictive drug. Are you sure you're on them?'

'Of course.'

'Very well,' said the doctor. 'What's the name of your doctor at home?'

Tina quickly remembered the name of Georgina's doctor and gave that. The doctor gave her a prescription.

'Thank you,' said Tina and left.

She flew to the chemist and got the prescription. The doctor wondered if this was a genuine case. He rang the doctor in Exmouth.

'I have a patient by that name,' he said, 'but she would never take those tablets. She lives here, you know.'

'Describe her,' said the doctor.

'She's a woman of sixty-odd.'

'Oh, this was a girl of about twenty-something.' said Dr. Jones. 'I'm afraid she's given a false name. I'll have to try and find out who she is.'

He rang off and saw some more patients. After the surgery he began to think, wondering who she could be. There was something familiar about her; she must live locally in Guildford. Something began to ring a faint bell in his mind as he remembered Derek, the psychologist he had treated. Of course, the big house! He remembered seeing Tina there. Knowing that Dr. Margaret Greaves lived there now, he decided to ring her. Dr. Margaret answered.

'Hello, Dr. Jones, can I help you?'

'I had a young girl in today who gave a phony name and address.' He told the whole story to Dr. Margaret.

'Ah,' said Dr. Margaret. 'That's what I've been waiting for. It is Tina. Thank you so much, Dr. Jones, for helping us. Now we can get her sorted out.'

Tina wasn't back. She had gone off to a café in Guildford and taken a tablet. She wandered about, wondering whether to go back to Jane's. No, her husband would be back. How alone she felt. Tina started to sob, oblivious of the stares of the people in the street, then she got on the bus and went back towards the big house.

Tina got off the bus in the village and went away from the house to the woods. She felt so lost and alone. She began to feel the pill working and felt elated for a moment. But they weren't lasting so long now. As she was getting more and more addicted to the pills she needed more of them.

Reaching the woods she went and sat at the big tree. The pill affected her brain. It affected her in many ways and she had been seeing hallucinations since she'd been taking them. Perhaps some people call them hallucinations: others say they open the psychic centres and that the patient might even see visions. Perhaps this afternoon, this late afternoon in the summer, when the sun was shining through the trees, as Tina sat at the big tree, forlorn and lost, under the influence of this drug that was so wrong for her, perhaps what she saw was because her psychic centres had been opened up by the tablets.

Tina sat by the big tree and started to sob. Gordon and Nancy were here, Jennifer and Derek were here, Julian and Georgina were here. Jane was now married. They'd all had true love but not Tina. She felt useless and ugly, unwanted. What was she to do? She knew she couldn't stop taking the pills.

'Oh, dear God, show me what to do,' Tina cried out in desperation. She had been brought up to believe in God and love Him, and when desperate she prayed but this evening she prayed in earnest for help.

Then she laid her head back against the tree trunk. She was half asleep and half awake and suddenly she saw a beautiful lady with long blonde hair and blue eyes looking sadly at her. It was Nancy. She had appeared to Jennifer many times in her life, but as yet had never appeared to Tina.

Tina looked in amazement at the beautiful face. So young, for Nancy always appeared young and beautiful. Tina would have given heaven and earth to look like her. She stared in amazement at the beauty of Nancy.

'I've come,' said Nancy, 'to help you, Tina. I prophesied that you would have more problems than I did, or Jennifer. Well, let's say different problems. Oh Tina! You seek someone to love. You need someone to love, once in your life. You deserve this, Tina, but you won't achieve it by going on as you are. Go home, Tina, and tell Dr. Margaret that you want to get off the pills before your brain is damaged. Oh Tina, please do this for me,' said Nancy. 'I love you. You prayed to God for help and I've come. Tina, do it, and I promise and predict that if you do this thing you will meet someone soon afterwards.'

'Oh Nancy,' said Tina. 'I'm glad I've seen you. If only I could look like you, I would be loved.'

'You look attractive as you are. You are you, Tina, not me. We must all be satisfied and remember, beauty is in the eye of the beholder. I was beautiful to someone; you'll be beautiful to someone, but only if you do as I say, Tina. If you go on as you are you'll never be beautiful. You'll be ugly and old in no time. Go to

Dr. Margaret and get help now and I promise faithfully that you will meet someone who will love you.'

'Oh thank you, Nancy. You've given me hope.'

Suddenly the beautiful face and long blonde hair and blue eyes vanished. Tina slept on after that and awoke with a start. It was pitch dark. Suddenly she looked around, she was hazy and she saw torches everywhere. The people at the big house had wondered where she was, had wondered if she'd come back here. Margaret had thought of ringing the police and looking round Guildford, after ringing Jane and finding she wasn't there, but they thought they would look in the woods first, knowing Tina would come there if she was unhappy, as Jennifer and Nancy had always done.

Jennifer found Tina.

'Oh Jennifer, I've something to tell you. But I must see Dr. Margaret first,' said Tina.

'Come, child,' said Jennifer. 'You're all in.'

They helped Tina, who was very unsteady, to the big house, took her straight up into her room and popped her into bed.

'Jennifer, come back later,' said Dr. Margaret. 'I must talk to Tina now.'

'Dr. Margaret,' said Tina. 'I must talk to you first.'

Tina burst into tears and poured out the story of her prayer, of her vision, of the awful experiences in Torquay, of everything.

'Oh, please help me, Dr. Margaret,' pleaded Tina, 'and do you know, if I get off the pills, Nancy promised me that I wasn't ugly, like I think, and somebody would love me.'

The pills had upset Tina. They made her regress. She was like a little child, just as Jennifer and Nancy had been when they had a breakdown.

'I'm glad,' said Dr. Margaret, 'but you must get well first. Of course you'll meet someone. If Nancy said so, it'll happen but get yourself well. The only way to do it is to go to Forest Dene Hospital and get off those pills. You won't be able to stop them just like that. You've been on them a little while now, not too long, but they may have upset you a little bit.'

'All right,' said Tina.

'Now, if you promise to do as I say with the tablets, give them to me,' said Dr. Margaret. 'I will dole them out to you, until we go to the hospital, so that you get enough, but you won't be able to take what you want, as you've been doing. You must do as I say.'

'All right,' said Tina. 'I'll try.'

'You must,' said Dr. Margaret. 'Now where are the tablets?'

Suddenly Tina felt panic-stricken at the thought of being without the pills. She was weak. What was she to do?

'I'll go and get them. They're in the bathroom.'

She was not telling the truth, they were in the pocket of her jeans, but she undressed in her little en-suite bathroom and took the pills out of her jeans, took some of them out of the bottle and put it back into her pocket. She took the bottle in to Dr. Margaret.

'Aren't some of them missing?' Dr. Margaret challenged her.

'No,' lied Tina. 'That's all the doctor gave me.'

Dr. Margaret said, 'Now listen, Tina. You don't want any more tonight. You must go to sleep and we've got to get you gradually weaned back on to your ordinary tablets.'

She kissed Tina goodnight and Millie and Jennifer came in. Tina was not interested. Her brain and her body were hypersensitive. A little bit of something affected Tina whereas another person wouldn't be affected at all. She was a very unusual case and Tina had been taking high doses of the drugs she had become addicted to. On her normal tablets she had small doses because the doctors knew she was hypersensitive to medicine. They had found out when she was young that she responded badly to normal doses of medication. She fell asleep exhausted, feeling very ill indeed.

The next day Tina slipped a tablet into her mouth. She had a few left in her pocket. She was weak. She wanted that wonderful feeling. She should have listened to Nancy, but she couldn't help herself. I'll have a birthday this weekend, she thought. I'll take Dr. Margaret's and the ones I've got and then on Monday I'll be willing to take the treatment, as I promised Nancy. It was a wonderful vision she had seen and she knew it. She knew she was doing wrong. For the next three days Tina popped pills into her mouth regularly. Dr. Margaret wondered why she was so woozy. She should only be taking the two a day that she was giving her, as well as her normal pills. Little did Margaret know that Tina was having four or five more of the addictive drugs and that the two sorts of medication on such a big scale would not mix; a cocktail that was bound to clash.

It was on the Sunday afternoon that Tina popped one of the pills into her mouth. It was half an hour after Dr. Margaret had given her an ordinary tablet. That morning Tina had been having a birthday, as she called it. She knew that she was to go to the hospital the next day to see Dr. Tom about getting cured.

Suddenly Tina had a strange, unpleasant feeling in the head, which frightened her. This wasn't the wonderful feeling she expected. The whole world was going round, the whole of her body was shaking and her heart was going bang bang bang. She went into a state of terror, of anxiety, of fear and lay on the floor shaking. She was terrified. She thought she was going to die, her heart was beating so fast. The world seemed to be going away from her. She yelled out, 'Help me! Help me!'

She was in the little video lounge on her own, where she used to watch films in the happier days with Jane. Her mother was out with Robert and Raymond, leaving Dr. Margaret and Jennifer at home. Jennifer heard the sounds and went running.

'Dr. Margaret, come!' she called. 'Tina's on the floor having a fit or something.'

'She's not having a fit. She's having some kind of a drug reaction,' said Dr. Margaret. 'Quick, Jennifer. Ring the ambulance at once.'

Jennifer was shaking as she dialled for the ambulance.

Dr. Margaret got hold of Tina.

'I'm frightened. I think I'm going to die,' said Tina. 'What am I going to do? I'm terrified. Oh, Dr. Margaret.'

'You've been doing something, Tina, you must tell me at once.'

'I can't breathe,' she said. 'Oh, help me! My heart! I'm going to die. The world's going away. I took more, Dr. Margaret, I didn't know. They've done something to me. Oh, take me to hospital, I'm so afraid I'm going to die.'

It was a severe anxiety attack that Tina was having, caused by the drug cocktail. Dr. Margaret was worried. This could cause brain damage, could cause Tina to have a permanent anxiety state. Normally this would happen to a person after being on the drugs for some time, perhaps a year or two, if drugs didn't mix, but in Tina's case, being hypersensitive to drugs, it had happened within a few weeks.

Dr. Margaret was absolutely out of her mind with worry. Jennifer was crying.

'Don't cry, Jennifer. There's no one at home except Rene. Do you want to come with me?'

'Oh please,' said Jennifer. 'I must stay with her. I'm frightened, Dr. Margaret, but I must face it.'

The ambulance arrived. Jennifer opened the door.

Tina was in a state of terror. 'Please don't let me die. Oh help me! Help me!'

They got her to hospital in Guildford, the General. The doctors saw Tina and realised what was wrong with her.

'She is having a drug reaction. I'll give her some largactyl at once. That'll calm her down for the time being, but this could be a permanent thing, Dr. Greaves, do you know that?'

'Yes,' said Dr. Margaret. 'That's what I'm worried about.'

She explained how Tina was hypersensitive to drugs and how this had happened so quickly.

'Oh,' Tina was saying. 'If only I'd known. I'd never have taken them. Oh, help me, please help me. I'm so frightened.'

The largactyl worked instantly and Tina went into a state of numbness which was almost as bad as the panic attack. She couldn't sleep, she was so tense and was taken into a big ward with a lot of people in it. The doctor felt she should be with others for she was so frightened of being alone at the moment.

Dr. Margaret and Jennifer sat with Tina for a while. Then she did fall into a very restless sleep, thanks to the largactyl.

For the next week Tina was in the general hospital at Guildford, with anxiety attack after attack. She never took any more of those drugs. They didn't need to wean her off them but they had to give her something because of the panic attacks. They gave Tina Valium and then took her for her some brain tests. The Valium helped to calm her but she was still getting attacks. That was what Dr. Margaret feared.

Dr. Phillips had been in to see her. He knew at once that this could be a permanent thing. Her brainwaves were abnormal as before, but they couldn't tell if she had brain damage. It was quite impossible. The only way they could tell was to wait, and Tina physically now was fit and the hospital said she must leave as they needed beds.

'We must take Tina to Forest Dene Hospital,' said Dr. Tom Phillips. 'She can't go home, she's in a dreadful state, and she must be stabilised on the Valium. Then if there's no permanent damage she will be able to go home in a month, I would say, Margaret. Now, Tina,' he said 'you must come into Forest Dene Hospital.'

'I don't mind,' said Tina. 'I'm so afraid I'm going to die.'

The anxiety attacks continued unabated, even with the Valium. More and more was prescribed; nothing else at all. Everything else had been withdrawn.

Tina spent months in the hospital, having attacks of shaking, being terrified all the time, looking round like a hunted animal saying, 'I'm afraid I'm going to die, I've got something wrong with me. My heart keeps bumping. My heart keeps racing.'

She wouldn't go out of the room, she was petrified. The Valium was alleviating her symptoms only slightly. It was all they could give her.

After three months the doctors realised that Tina was not going to get over the anxiety state; she had permanent brain damage. The drugs had been too much for Tina on top of the damage that she had been born with. Now Tina would never be a boisterous, adventurous daredevil girl again. She would never be able to go off on her own as she had done, perhaps get into trouble, and do all the things that she had done. Tina would always want to lead a sheltered life and would need medication of a different kind, much stronger tranquillisers than she'd been on at school, and for the rest of her life she would need to lead a quiet life with people who cared for her and loved her. She would be in and out of hospital for a long time but she would live at home and want nothing more.

Tina had prayed in the woods. She had received help. She had seen a vision, or a hallucination, whatever one would like to call it, of Nancy, who had appeared to Jennifer many times; but Tina had not done what Nancy said.

Tina would never want to be adventurous again. She could perhaps be controlled by a drug such as Valium but she would never be as she had been before.

One day Tina had a very bad panic attack at the hospital and had to be kept in a room on her own, she was so frightened, and Dr. Margaret and Jennifer came to see her. Tranquillised with Valium, she just stared with her haunted eyes out of the window. Jennifer cried when she saw her. They stayed with her all the afternoon. Tina was very rigid, unable to laugh or cry. She was just in a state of tension and anxiety.

Dr. Phillips who had seen her that day, was most concerned and had arranged for some therapy for her. He felt that to occupy her mind would be the best thing but poor Tina was so afraid of having a heart attack or something, she couldn't move, she was rigid, as if she'd seen a burglar on the stairs. This was what the drugs had done to her brain.

Dr. Margaret and Jennifer went back to the big house and after tea Joe came home from an afternoon out with Vicky and Richard. Millie, Raymond and the children had gone with them. They had been worried about Tina and needed a day out. Their picnic in the country had done them a world of good and they came back happy but of course there was the shadow of Tina hanging over them.

After tea Millie was attending to the children and Dr. Margaret said, 'Joe, may I have a talk with you, please?'

Before they got started, Margaret suggested to Jennifer that she took the dogs for a walk. Jennifer went obediently and Margaret and her son went into the big lounge and sat on the large settee on which Hayley had once sat when there was any problem that had to be discussed. They looked out of the big French windows that faced the mystical woods, where so much had happened.

'Now,' said Dr. Margaret. 'I'm getting old as you know, and I'm getting tired lately.'

'You're not that old,' said Joe. 'Just turning seventy.'

'I know, but I'm like my mother, I've had a busy life, and, remember, it's a great strain looking after Jennifer and Tina and everybody I've had to look after at the hospital.'

'I know.'

'I want you to take over Tina's case, Joe. You see, Tom Phillips may be leaving the hospital.'

'Why?'

'He's retiring early. They want to move and take a private practice down in Devon somewhere.'

'Oh, I didn't know that,' said Joe. 'Who'll be taking his place?'

'It's possible that you might be asked, Joe. And I want you to learn about Tina in the meantime. Dr. Tom Phillips won't be leaving for six months.'

'Oh, I would be glad to look after Tina,' said Joe. 'It's so sad. It's an awful condition. I've met a few patients like it before, but she's in a really bad way.'

'I know,' said Dr. Margaret. 'We'll talk about her for a little while and I'll explain certain things to you, at least what you don't already know. And I want you to go to the hospital and read all her records this week. I want you to study her case, Joe. For one day you will be her doctor. I won't be here.'

'Don't talk like that, Mum.'

'But I won't always be here. I'm getting older,' insisted Dr. Margaret. 'I want you to know Tina for she's going to need someone in the future.'

'I realise that,' said Joe. 'I will be taking over one day. And I know all about Jennifer. She seems to be able to relate well to me now. Not that she's that much younger than you, Mum.'

'I know,' said Dr. Margaret, 'but Jennifer's settled now and very strong. She could live to be a ripe old age.'

'And so could you, Mum, so don't talk rubbish.'

'All right, so could I.'

'You'd better live to be as old as Dr. Rosemary, my grandmother. I'd like that,' said Joe.

'I'm sure you would and I'll do my best,' said Dr. Margaret laughing. 'Oh well, anyway, will you do that for me, Joe?'

'Yes, of course I will, Mum. Don't worry about it. I'd better get back to Vicky now. We've got to see to Richard and we want to watch a film tonight as I've got to work tomorrow and I like to relax on a Sunday evening.'

'Of course,' said Dr. Margaret, 'but I know you're the right person to take Tina's case over.'

'Right.'

'To think, Joe started with Nancy. It was Dr. Joe Greaves, and now you, Joe Greaves, are going to take over her great-great-great-granddaughter.'

'It's amazing, isn't it,' said Joe, 'when you think of it. Oh Mum, it is amazing!'

'Yes,' said Dr. Margaret. 'Now run along, Joe. That's fine. That's all I've got to say for now. Oh, by the way, Joe, a doctor's coming to see Tina tomorrow, a physician. They just want to check her heart rhythms and everything. She keeps complaining about her heart racing.'

'I'm sure it's nothing more than anxiety, Mum,' said Joe. 'Her heart is not affected.'

'Well, they want to be absolutely sure. He's coming from Guildford at eleven o'clock if you'd like to be present. I'll be there,' said Dr. Margaret.

'All right, I'll be there,' said Joe.

Dr. Margaret then went and had a rest. She needed it. And then she talked to Millie about Tina, explained everything to her. 'Be as kind as you can, won't you?'

'Oh, I will,' said Millie.

'And I think that you'll be closer now that she's like this. I'm sorry it had to happen this way, Millie.'

'I understand,' said Millie, 'and I'll do all I can for her.'

'Megan's doing very well, isn't she?'

'She is,' said Millie. 'She's fine.'

'Yes. I'm glad she didn't inherit. I expect it will be her child or their child. It seems to be jumping a generation or two.'

Jennifer, out in the woods with the dogs, was drawn like a magnet to the tree where so many amazing moments had occurred. She sat down to rest, closed her eyes, and as always when she was disturbed, began dreaming – such strange dreams. Suddenly she saw her lady, Nancy, appear to her in her dream. Her beautiful lady with the big blue eyes and long blonde hair.

'Hello, Jennifer,' said Nancy.

'I'm so upset about Tina,' said Jennifer.

'That's why I've come, Jennifer,' said Nancy. 'I know it's disturbed you. Now, Jennifer, Tina didn't do what I said and that's why she's suffering now. For people bring suffering upon themselves. It's cause and effect, you know.'

'I know.'

'I'm afraid,' said Nancy, 'when she was born I told you she would have to go through far more than you or I ever did. She will come home eventually, from the hospital, but she will have these attacks of anxiety. She will not be the girl she was, the daredevil girl. It may be for the best in the end,' said Nancy, 'for this illness will make her settle at home. But, Jennifer, please, do one thing for me.'

'I will if I can,' said Jennifer. 'You know that.'

'When Tina's better and able to cope more, love her as much as you can and look after her and encourage her to do her painting. For in years she hasn't done it. I wasted my talent when I was alive but she has great talent, even more than I had. Try and get her to paint, try and get her on to it, perhaps even at the hospital. She will meet someone later, but it will not be a long-lasting thing. I cannot tell you more about this now,' said Nancy, 'but help Tina, please, all you can and keep an eye on your own health. Do not get too upset. For I promise you that all will be well in the end, as it was for you, Jennifer. I predict this and promise you this.'

'Thank you, Nancy,' said Jennifer. 'I'll do all you say and I won't make myself ill. I feel much happier now. Thank you, Nancy.'

With that, Nancy disappeared into the mist. Jennifer awoke and felt refreshed and better. She had seen her lady in those beautiful romantic woods. She had seen her many, many times before when she was younger, and when she was a little girl, but never had she seen her in the woods.

Jennifer was happy and almost sang as she went back to the big house. Millie was sitting in the window as Jennifer walked in through the French windows.

'You look happier, Jennifer,' she said.

'I feel it,' said Jennifer. 'I've seen my lady.'

'Oh, how wonderful,' said Millie.

'You've what?' said a voice coming through the door. It was Dr. Margaret, she had come down once more, feeling rested.

'I've seen my lady again,' said Jennifer.

'That's wonderful!' said Dr. Margaret. 'Oh, she's been busy lately, hasn't she? Appearing to both you and Tina in the woods.'

'Yes, she seems to be appearing in the woods at the moment.'

'Well, perhaps it's necessary,' said Dr. Margaret. 'What did she say? Did she speak this time?'

Nancy had only spoken a couple of times to Jennifer in her visions. This was the third time and Jennifer was very happy. She recounted what Nancy had said to her.

Chapter 14

Forest Dene Hospital was much the same as it always had been. It had a beautiful long driveway. Typical of Surrey it was surrounded by trees, and there were big lawns in the front where the patients could sit and round the back there was a playing field for the young men who were well enough to play games – football or anything like that. There was a swimming pool indoors at the hospital, which was very therapeutic for some of the patients. It was always kept warm enough for them to go into. There was a large clinic there which had been opened since the days Jennifer had been there, and that was where Tina would be when she was a bit better. It had its own large dance hall where they had dances and discos. There were plenty of occupational therapy rooms in the hospital, for it was a very large place. There were little rooms for group therapy, quiet rooms for people to sit in, games rooms, rooms where one could play the music centre, television rooms and a huge lounge in the main hospital, the part that Tina was in. It was an enormous building with corridor after corridor.

Tina was not yet in the clinic which was at the side of the hospital. She was still in the main block and was in a ward downstairs by the main doors. It was a big ward with a large sitting room with chairs all around it and big windows that looked out on to the front lawns. It was as bright and cheerful as a hospital of that type could be. There were four-bedded dormitories and single rooms for people who were especially unwell. There was a kitchen where you could make your own tea or coffee, or toast if you wanted a snack. It made the patients feel more independent and they were provided with everything they needed there. There was a phone booth at the end of the ward, so if they wanted to ring home they could.

Tina had everything that was necessary there. There was a doctors' room, a nurses' room – each ward was individual – but these days they were not locked unless the patients were severely disturbed, and if they were, mainly they were on drugs and there was no need to lock anything up. The patients were encouraged to go out into the world more and live in hostels and in lodgings, or even had flats of their own, but there were patients who still needed hospitalisation. So Forest Dene Hospital was still well equipped for those people.

Tina was now far from fit to be out of hospital. Tina was back in the four-bedded dormitory. She needed to be there, the doctors thought, with others for company, for Tina was living in a state of horror. Her imagination was greater than ever and things were very twisted up in that mind. Emotionally she had regressed and was like a child of about six. She had a long way to go.

Oh, if only I hadn't taken those terrible tablets, she kept thinking. Oh, if only I hadn't! I wouldn't be suffering this way. But Tina knew she had done it herself and had to suffer for it and every day she prayed that she would get better and not be frightened any more.

The next day, Monday, Dr. Tom Phillips came in with the physician from Guildford who was to see Tina and examine her heart. She was to have a thorough examination and blood tests and an ECG.

'Hello, Tina,' said Dr. Tom, 'how are you today?'

'Oh, Dr. Tom, I'm so afraid,' said Tina. 'I think I've got something wrong. Who is this you've brought with you?'

'This is Dr. Taylor.'

Tina looked at him and her eyes opened wider and wider as she looked at the doctor in fear and terror. 'Whatever's wrong?' said Dr. Tom.

'He looks like . . . I don't want to see him . . . He looks like that horror film actor on the films. I've seen him,' said Tina.

'Who?'

'Peter Cushing. I don't want to see Cushing,' she said. 'Get him out of here! He does funny things on the films.'

'Oh, is that all?' said Dr. Tom. 'Yes, he does look like Peter Cushing, he knows that himself.'

The doctor smiled a watery smile at Tina. He was rather a strict, self-opinionated and cynical man, with a taciturn manner. He had been told many times he looked like Peter Cushing and was not amused by Tina's outburst. 'Perhaps I'd better go.'

'No,' said Dr. Phillips. 'I've told you before, Tina's very sick. She must be examined.'

'Very well.'

'He's even got a voice like Cushing,' shouted Tina frantically. 'Get him away from me!'

'No,' said Dr. Tom. 'You've got to have this examination. I'll be here all the time. Don't worry, Tina.'

Dr. Phillips was chuckling to himself. Taylor really did look like Cushing. He never smiled, it was a wonder his patients could bear him at all, but he was the only one he could get hold of to examine Tina that day.

'Now don't worry about Dr. Taylor. He'll examine you and I'll be here.'

All Tina, who was yelling, could say was 'He's Cushing! Get him away from me!'

Dr. Taylor was quite cross about it and said, 'Stop it, Tina!'

That frightened Tina all the more. She screamed, 'You are Cushing!'

Dr. Tom and the nurse roared with laughter and had to go out of the room which frightened Tina all the more. Dr. Taylor managed to complete his examination and found that her heart was racing, the fear had brought on an attack of tachycardia, but the test itself was normal. It was only the fear that had made her heart race. Relieved that he had finished the tests he made a hurried departure from the room.

Dr. Tom Phillips talked to Dr. Taylor. 'I am sorry about that business, you know. Though I must admit you do look like Cushing.'

'I know,' said Dr. Taylor. 'So I've been told before. Don't remind me, Dr. Phillips, but your patient is really in a state, isn't she. There is nothing at all physically wrong with her. She brings on her own anxiety. It's obviously the brain damage, but you found that on the EEG which I looked at.'

'That's correct,' said Dr. Tom, 'but she is all right?'

'The blood tests will have to be sent to the lab but the results will be back in a couple of days. I will see they're sent to you, Dr. Phillips.'

'Very well.'

Tina went on about it all day to the amusement of the other

patients and staff, but it did not amuse Tina. She was so afraid that he would come back and pounce on her.

Dr. Tom went to see Tina with Dr. Margaret.

'Cushing's gone, don't worry!' he said.

Tina smiled a watery smile.

'Do you know, Tina,' said Dr. Margaret, 'that's the first time you've smiled since your breakdown. We're winning through. The Valium are helping you. Gradually they are.'

'Oh, I still get those things. I've got something wrong. My heart . . . you know.'

'There is nothing wrong with your heart,' said Dr. Tom firmly. 'You've had examinations, you've had an EEG. You've had an ECG. Your EEG was not totally normal, it's still got spikes on it, and you know you've got slight brain damage but it will improve with time. I'm being honest with you, Tina, it's only fair. You know you'll never be quite the same again, but you will improve and you'll be able to live a life again. However, you'll have to live a more tranquil life. I don't say that Valium will be a suitable drug for you permanently, but you will always have to take something of that nature.'

'What about my old pills?' said Tina.

'No, you'll never take those again. They wouldn't suit you now. Tina, you're very different now. A different personality, a different person. Totally different. Now we've got to get you better and feed you up and get you well enough to go home. Tina, please co-operate with us, won't you?'

'I'll try,' said Tina, 'but I'm so frightened.'

'It will improve. It won't be perfect but it will improve,' said Dr. Margaret. 'I promise.'

Dr. Phillips went on his way, he was a busy man, and Dr. Margaret told Tina that she was to see Dr. Joe quite a lot in the future, as Dr. Phillips was moving away and retiring later on.

'It won't be while you're in hospital. You'll still see him, but from now on you'll be seeing Dr. Joe once a day.'

'I do like him,' said Tina. She hadn't liked him actually, before she was ill, but she had changed, and now she felt she could like him. It was only that she hadn't tried to like him, hadn't tried to know him. She had been so full of herself before, but she was different now and was glad to know anyone who would help her out of this terrible nightmare.

Dr. Margaret sat with her a little longer and suddenly, exhausted with her anxiety and drugged up to the hilt with her Valium, Tina fell into a disturbed sleep. Dr. Margaret stroked her head and then kissed it and said, 'My darling Tina, I do love you, as my mother loved Jennifer. I'll always take care of you, as long as I can. Please God, let her be better.' The nurse came in and said, 'Dr. Margaret, you're so tired. Go home. She'll be all right tonight. We'll take care of her.'

With that Dr. Margaret wearily drove back to the big house. It had been a lot for her to go through. She couldn't even eat any supper that night and went straight to bed, lying there thinking of the past, of her mother, of Jennifer and now of Tina with her problem. She was going to be disabled with this neurosis. She would have to be loved and looked after at the big house.

The next day it was all hustle and bustle at the big house, Millie getting the children off to school, Vicky getting Richard off to school and Joe and Margaret going off to Forest Dene Hospital. Dr. Margaret only went there to see Tina now she had retired, but felt refreshed after her night's sleep, and better, and Jennifer had said she would come along in the afternoon to see Tina.

Forest Dene Hospital was also a hive of activity that day. Joe went with Dr. Margaret to Dr. Tom's office and they all had a long talk about Tina's condition. Joe read all her records.

'I think I'd like to see Nancy's records, if they're anywhere around.'

'I've got those,' said Dr. Margaret. 'I've kept them on my files, from my grandfather, you know. I've also got Jennifer's.'

'I've seen those,' said Joe, 'but I'd like to study them more, if I'm to help Tina.'

'Well, they won't help this condition,' said Dr. Tom.

'One never can tell,' said Joe. He spent the whole morning discussing Tina's case with Dr. Phillips and Dr. Margaret. Then Dr. Margaret went to see Tina, Dr. Tom went about his duties.

Joe went on studying records, starting with Nancy's, which took him a long time to go through, then Jennifer's. He went on studying most of the day, writing notes, preparing himself to start with Tina's case the next morning. Dr. Joe realised that Tina's case was different from Nancy's and Jennifer's. Tina had got herself into this mess with drugs and had caused more brain damage on top of what she was born with. He knew that her case would be very much more difficult and that she was going to have a hard time of it. She would have to live with this anxiety neurosis, probably for the rest of her life. It could be curbed by drugs, he thought. It would have to be the right medication. At the moment she was being treated by Valium, large doses, or at least as large as Tina could take, for her system, for some unknown reason, would only take small doses of any chemicals. Tina was a very unusual case indeed.

He walked into the lounge where Tina was sitting. She had had a bad day again. She'd had a shaking attack, a panic attack, and had been given extra Valium, but now she was more calm and was sitting half asleep in a chair, with Dr. Margaret sitting beside her. Dr. Joe guessed that she would be doing this. For Dr. Margaret was as devoted to Tina now as Dr. Rosemary had been to Jennifer. Tina needed Dr. Margaret perhaps more than Jennifer had needed her mother.

'Hello, Mum,' said Dr. Joe. 'How is she?'

'She's had a very bad day,' said Dr. Margaret. 'She had the most terrible panic attack. It's going to be very difficult to get it right but of course it's early days yet.'

'Hello, Tina,' said Dr. Joe. 'Now listen, I'm coming to help you tomorrow. We're going to start work on getting you well.'

'Oh, Dr. Joe,' said Tina, 'I'm so afraid. I'm so afraid I'm going to die, have a heart attack or something. Can't you give me something that takes the fear away. I've never had this fear in my life.'

'No,' said Dr. Joe. 'It's very sad. You were very brazen before. I'm afraid you won't be like that again. You will have to take medication but I promise you that in the future, in a few months' time, you will be stabilised and on some medication that will help this problem.'

'You mean as long as that?'

'Well, you'll feel better long before that. Let's start talking tomorrow, shall we? Mum's tired now, do you mind if we go?'

'No,' said Tina. 'I must have a sleep now.'

'Good. We want you to have sleep, as much as you can get, Tina, and do try and eat something.'

Tina had been finding it difficult to eat as she was in such a state of tension and anxiety she felt she couldn't swallow. She could swallow fluids all right and they had been giving her glucose and milk and now Dr. Phillips had prescribed vitamin B injections to see if that would help her appetite.

'See you tomorrow, darling,' said Dr. Margaret. 'I promise. Don't be afraid. We'll help you to get better and God will help you too.'

'Will He really?' said Tina, doubtfully.

'Of course He will,' Dr. Margaret assured her.

They left the lounge where the patients were sitting round, some of them looking into space, some of them reading. Tina was sitting in a corner alone. She wanted to talk to no one. She felt drowsy now and was withdrawn from the others.

Dr. Joe started work with Tina the next morning. He talked to her for over an hour and she told him of her terrors and fears. He explained to her about the brain damage. He felt that she was intelligent enough to know and that it was right that she should know.

'You must try hard, Tina,' he said. 'Work on the fact that you have nothing physically wrong with you. It's all a mental problem. You'll feel better on the B injections and the Valium in time but try and mix a little bit with the others, please. Try and eat something. Sit at the table. Don't be afraid to walk about.' For Tina feared moving in case something happened to her. 'You must do it, Tina, if you want to get well. Do you want to get well?'

'I do,' said Tina. 'I do. I'm so afraid.'

Tina gradually, on the drug therapy, started to slightly improve. She started to go to occupational therapy and painted some nice pictures. Everybody was amazed by her talent, and some of her paintings were put up in the children's ward, they were so beautiful, of little horses, dogs and cats.

The people at the big house visited Tina regularly. Millie came and when Tina improved brought Megan and Robert to see her and Vicky came with Richard one day. Dr. Margaret went on helping Tina, visiting her for an hour each afternoon.

But Dr. Joe worked hardest with Tina.

Three months later, Tina was still in hospital but was not doing badly at all. She had even ventured to one or two of the dances, making sure that they weren't the discos with the flashing lights, for she feared them even more now, but Tina still wouldn't get up and dance. She still feared having a heart attack. But she would paint a bit for she sat down doing that and felt safer and she had got to know one or two of the girls in the ward.

Jane visited Tina three or four times, but it upset her very much, seeing the different Tina, her new and saddened personality. Her mother felt that she shouldn't go until Tina was completely well and home again.

Tina continued to do well and Dr. Joe helped her through panic attacks. She went to dances with the boys but would never allow them to go near her. She was far too fearful for that. Tina had no sexual feelings since the breakdown, since the brain damage. Now she just liked to be friends with people and valued true friendship far more than she had ever done before. She even valued spiritual things and the Reverend Moss had been to see her from the vicarage in the village. He visited her two or three times, praying with her and giving her Holy Communion.

That was the first time that Tina really felt deeply spiritual and felt perhaps that God would help her and she prayed for this to happen, and for the first time during the breakdown her eyes filled with tears.

At last, thought the Reverend Moss, she's going to come out of this when she can cry and get rid of the terrible tension. It pleased him and he went away feeling much happier about her but he knew that she would never be the same again. He prayed that Tina would be given the strength to cope with this new personality, full of fear and anxiety, the condition called anxiety neurosis, and he prayed that she would be able to lead as happy a life as possible at the big house in the future.

Tina was gradually able to cry. Often now as she talked to Dr. Joe the tears would flow.

'Come on, cry it out, Tina,' he said. 'This is what we want you to do but we want to see you laugh as well. You've been on Valium five months now and the tension should be lifting.'

It was indeed lifting and Tina, within another month, had laughed at some of the silly idiotic things that happened.

One day she was sitting at the meal table, she hadn't laughed at all, and she suddenly looked over and saw a funny man who'd been admitted, with glasses on. She turned round and for some unknown reason the man amused her. She let out a shriek of laughter which set the whole dining room off. They ended up laughing until the tears rolled down their faces and Tina laughed and laughed.

Weren't the staff pleased about that!

'At last,' they said, 'she's laughed and cried.'

Tina had another panic attack and was afraid for a while to laugh again in case she had a heart attack. She really believed there was something wrong with her heart and no one could convince her otherwise.

But time went on and she did some more of her art. She was made to go and do these things for often she would lie on the bed saying, 'I've got heart trouble. I'm afraid. I mustn't do anything.'

'Oh, but you must,' the nurses said. 'You have nothing physically wrong with you, Tina. It's your nerves.'

Tina gradually realised that it must be true and she had consultations with Dr. Tom Phillips, who was leaving soon, and with Joe, whom she'd come to love dearly, and of course with Dr. Margaret. She enjoyed the dances more and more and went on going to them. She would dance with different men. But she would not kiss one or have anything to do with them. Dr. Joe explained that it would be a long time before she got her sexual feelings back, probably long after she got home.

Then Tina started to walk around the grounds again and even asked Jennifer, who visited her regularly, to bring one of the dogs with her, one of the little corgis, Trixie.

'I'd like to see her. I miss the dogs at home. I haven't been able to go even for a weekend because I'm too afraid, Jennifer. Can I have one of the dogs one afternoon? Bring her.'

Jennifer brought Trixie in and Tina adored the little dog. She had always loved dogs, but somehow, this change in her personality made her appreciate nature more and animals more. Deep things, spiritual things.

Jennifer walked round the grounds. It was a sunny day. Tina's twenty-fourth birthday had passed. It was springtime; sunny but chilly. Tina walked round in her jeans and thick sweater with Jennifer and little Trixie. After a little while Tina got panicky and couldn't walk any further. 'I'm afraid! My heart's jumping. I must go back.'

'You've done well,' said Jennifer. 'I'll take you back.'

They went into the lounge and the nurse brought Tina a cup of tea and Jennifer too.

Tina cried. 'Oh Jennifer! I get so frightened. I can't do anything, you know. I've got heart trouble.'

'Darling, you haven't got heart trouble. It's an anxiety neurosis. You know, an anxiety state. Dr. Margaret's explained it all to me. Your mother will understand you more now too.'

Millie did realise that Tina was very sick and knew she had to try and help her when she got home.

Jennifer and Tina talked into the evening and Tina got out of her anxiety attack, after being given her medication, and released her feelings more. They were very close indeed now. This illness of Tina's had brought them closer.

'Do you know, Tina, I had a terrible breakdown once. It was different from yours. I went into a world of my own. They called it a catatonic state. It was because I had a shock.'

'What happened?'

'Well,' said Jennifer. 'It was before I knew who I really was. You know I was adopted.'

'That's right.'

'Well I saw the portrait in the hall of beautiful Nancy, with the big blue eyes and long blonde hair and do you know, I'd seen her in visions like you have now, Tina. Well, when I saw the portrait in the hall the shock was so great it must have tipped me over the edge. I wasn't too well anyway, but I had a terrible breakdown. I was in this hospital for months, in fact, I think it was over a year. Then, after Dr. Rosemary died, it happened again, but it wasn't for very long, but now I'm older I've grown to face these things. Nancy had a breakdown too, you know, when she was on the change, when Gordon went away to Canada and left her for a while.'

'Yes, I heard about that,' said Tina, 'but those breakdowns you and Nancy had were very different from mine, and I'm very young, aren't I, to have one?'

'Oh, you are, Tina! And it is very different. We didn't have the fear that you have.'

'I've got to face it for the rest of my life,' said Tina, her eyes brimming over.

'I know, darling,' said Jennifer, 'but remember, we're beside you and we'll take care of you.'

Trixie leapt up and licked Tina's nose. She felt that Tina wanted some love at the moment. Jennifer picked the little dog up and put her on Tina's knee and Tina cuddled the little dog and felt comforted by her. It was very therapeutic and Tina asked Jennifer to bring Trixie in every day.

'It's funny you should say that,' Jennifer said. 'I remember, when my memory was coming back after that catatonic thing, I asked Derek to bring my dog in every day, and I got better. So you'll get better, soon.'

'I think I will,' said Tina. 'I know I won't be the same. But I'll be all right, won't I?'

'You will, as long as you take your tablets, and remember, Tina, never take those wrong tablets again.'

'Don't worry about that,' said Tina. 'I'll never take anything unless I know it's not going to hurt me. In fact, Jennifer, I'm terrified of pills. I told Dr. Joe I'll only take the Valium, and the vitamins they give me, but nothing else. I'm frightened of them.'

'Well, in a way that's good,' said Jennifer. 'You'll only take what you're told then.'

'It's taught me a lesson,' said Tina. 'Really, Jennifer, it has.'

'Good,' said Jennifer. 'Well, I must be getting back now, I'm tired.'

Dr. Joe came in as Jennifer left with Trixie, and gave Tina a session, which helped her. 'You know, Tina, you can come home for a weekend any time you like now. You've got me there if you have a panic attack, and Dr. Margaret. You're very lucky. None of the other patients have a psychiatrist on the premises, so to speak.'

That made Tina laugh. 'I know I'm lucky, Dr. Joe. I'd like to come home this weekend.'

'And then, if it works out, you may be able to come home altogether in three months' time.'

'Will it be as long as that?' said Tina.

'I think so,' said Dr. Joe. 'You're still very unwell.'

Tina knew she was and was prepared to accept it but it would be nice to go back to the big house again, for it was many months since she had seen her home. Tina could only remember that terrible attack she'd had on the floor but gradually the pills were making her relax and the memory of it was not so vivid.

Tina started going for weekends at the big house and Jennifer took her for walks in the woods with Trixie the little dog, and Bill the King Charles, into the mystical woods where the romance had taken place of so many young ones at the big house. Tina couldn't think of romance at the moment. She was far too anxious. She was fidgety and unable to relax. But Joe and Dr. Margaret helped her, and Jennifer too.

Chapter 15

At first, she would not wash her hair or even keep herself clean. She had to be seen to in every way, but now she was bathing again and washing her hair every week with the help of the nurses. Her mother did it for her at home. Her hair had grown a lot. It had been very short and styled but Tina suddenly felt she wanted to be casual, she wanted her hair to grow. She had a completely new personality. Her hair had now grown down to her shoulders. The vitamin tablets had helped her hair to grow as she got stronger physically and her dark hair grew, wavy, to her shoulders but her white, tense face did not look too attractive just then. She wore no make-up and always wore denim jeans, a sweater and trainers; she could not be bothered to dress up to look glamorous any more.

The family were not sorry she had stopped using all that make-up, that daub, as they called it. They preferred to see Tina looking natural. She looked more like the young ones at the big house looked previously – Georgina, Jennifer, Nancy. They hoped that perhaps, when Tina was better, she might dress if necessary to go anywhere, and perhaps wear a little lipstick, but Dr. Joe knew that was all she'd ever be able to do, if that. So Tina went on coming home at weekends, in her denims and sweater, her hair now growing quite long, her panic attacks still going on, still taking Valium and vitamins, still fighting. For Tina did fight to get better. But Dr. Joe and Dr. Margaret knew that she would always get some attacks, would never be restored to her former self.

A month later, Dr. Tom Phillips retired from Forest Dene Hospital. He was to go down to Devon with his family and work part-time. He would miss Forest Dene, where his father had worked before him, and he would miss a lot of his patients that he had grown to love and help, especially Tina.

He went and said goodbye to Tina on the day he was leaving.

'Tina,' he said, 'I've loved you and helped you all I can and I'm terribly sorry about what happened. I felt it was my fault, not to warn you more about drugs.'

'But you did warn me. I remember,' said Tina in her gaspy nervous voice that she'd had ever since the breakdown.

'You'll get much better, Tina. We know, and I'm being honest with you, that you won't be perfect, but with the tablets you'll struggle through.'

'I know, Dr. Phillips, and thank you for all you've done for me.' The tears welled up in Tina's eyes and trickled down her cheeks. Her old pal was going. She had loved him as a father. He really had been good to her.

'Take care of yourself.'

'I will,' said Tina. 'Write to me occasionally, and I'll try and write back.'

'Of course I will. I'll drop you a line now and again.' Tina hugged Dr. Phillips suddenly and kissed him on the cheek as a father. All her feelings of affection now were totally sincere, totally childlike, with true spiritual love behind them.

'Goodbye, Tina. Take care and remember, I'll pray for you, you know.'

'Thank you,' said Tina. 'I hope they work.'

'Of course they will! You'll get on all right.'

Dr. Tom left the room, his own eyes filled with tears. He didn't want Tina to see that, it would upset her more. He waved and ran back to his room.

Tina cried after he left and later that evening had another terrible attack. It was the upset of him going. Dr. Margaret and Jennifer were there beside Tina, to comfort her and help her through it.

Jennifer and Dr. Margaret went home. They also bade a sad goodbye to Dr. Tom. Dr. Margaret had worked alongside him for years and she would miss her colleague but things had to change – Dr. Margaret knew that.

Tina went on going home for weekends and did better and better on her Valium. At last Dr. Joe, after many sessions with Tina, said that she would be able to come home out of hospital a fortnight later, for good. She would be able to go home to the big house and try to get back to leading as normal a life as she could.

Tina went on doing her art, trying to eat, talking to other patients, going to the dances when she felt she could, going for walks in the grounds with Jennifer and Trixie; having panic attacks now and again, for those were inevitable. But she was now looking forward to going home. She had that much more confidence. She would never be the same again, but she would be better.

At last the day came for Tina to go back to the big house, feeling very nervous indeed. Dr. Margaret, loyal Dr. Margaret, arrived with Jennifer and Millie to fetch Tina home. Dr. Joe, who was at work, came in to the room.

'Well, Tina, you're to come home for good today. Don't be nervous. Go home, and take it easy. You'll be helped. You've got Jennifer, Dr. Margaret and your mother. Just rest today. You've been given extra Valium today as you're bound to be nervous, it's completely different at home. You've been in hospital for many months, but I feel that you're as ready as you ever can be, to start at home and build up your confidence. We'll help you, Tina.'

'Thank you,' said Tina. 'I am nervous, Dr. Joe.' She had a lot of confidence in him now and was very close to him.

Tina was packed now and Dr. Joe left the room. Dr. Margaret and Jennifer took Tina by the arms and Millie followed behind with her suitcase. They said goodbye to the other patients for Tina had grown to like quite a few of them, especially one middle-aged lady. Tina was always drawn to mother figures because she couldn't get close to her own mother.

'Cheerio, Beryl. We'll keep in touch,' said Tina.

'Of course,' said Beryl. 'I'm going home next week.'

Tina said goodbye to the staff, the nurses and the psychologist who'd been seeing her, Robert.

'Come and see me occasionally,' said Robert, 'if you need me, but you've got plenty of help at home. And try and do those breathing exercises I told you about. They'll help the panic attacks.'

'All right,' said Tina. 'I'll try.' She was wearing blue jeans as usual and a scruffy old sweater. She had no interest in her clothes any more. Perhaps she would a little later on but Tina would never be the same girl again.

She had regrets but had come to accept this new self she was, knowing she'd have to put up with it and make the best of it. She would try and get well. For truthfully, Tina had a fairly strong willpower at the back of all this. She really wanted to get better, for the sake of the ones she loved, the ones who had stood by her through this terrible nightmare. Now she appreciated her home, the big house. She wanted to go back to it. She had been in hospital a long time, too afraid to leave, but she was ready now.

They waved to the staff and the patients and walked along the corridor and out of the front door. One or two of the patients came and waved to them as they drove down the driveway. Tina looked around as she was leaving and sighed, 'Oh well, they've helped me here. I did have to come here for a long time, just as Jennifer did, as Nancy did in another hospital, but it's a very different illness I had to come here for, a self-induced illness.' She voiced this to Dr. Margaret. 'I'll never really be well, I know. I've been told honestly,' said Tina.

'You must accept it,' said Dr. Margaret, 'but you will be a lot better, I promise you.'

So they drove back to the big house. The children were at school. It was a good time to go home. Raymond was at work at the hospital in Guildford.

They settled Tina back into her room. She looked around her room and saw the music centre she had loved so much. Perhaps she would play it later on. The television, the bookshelves with all the books she loved. The illness had affected her brain and her eyesight. Tina had to see an optician at the hospital and now had to wear glasses for reading.

Tina's looks were not quite the same. She was not unattractive. She would be attractive when she got better and could just put on a little make-up. Her hair had grown to her shoulders. It was dry, for she had been very ill, but would get better later on, with vitamin tablets to help it, but Tina wasn't even worried about her looks at the moment.

She unpacked her things and lay down to have a rest. Twice that day she had a panic attack and had to be helped by Dr. Margaret and Jennifer and was given extra Valium. Dr. Margaret advised her to go to bed and rest for the rest of the day.

That evening when Dr. Joe came in to see her, she was reading quietly. She told him about the panic attacks, and he reassured her that it was only to be expected, and that in time they would get less. She felt better then and settled down to sleep. Jennifer and Dr. Margaret came to say goodnight. Tina asked for Trixie the dog to sleep in her room that night, a comforting presence. She fell asleep with the dog in the crook of her knees.

Tina settled back at home at the big house, although she did not have an easy time; shaking attacks, anxiety attacks meant that she needed a large amount of Valium, and she had to rest a great deal. Although she realised that she would never be the same again, never be the girl that she was, she tried hard to get as completely well as she could. It was to be a long process.

Chapter 16

During the long months of recovery that followed, Tina periodically had to go into hospital for a few days, if her panic attacks became severe. It was a long hard struggle, and she was grateful for all the help and support she had at home.

During this time, Georgina and Julian had moved into the old people's home in Exmouth and started to make a very happy life for themselves there. Still, they could not forget that it was while she had been in their care that Tina had got involved with drugs.

One afternoon as they were taking their usual walk along the seafront at Exmouth they saw Georgina's cousin Mary and she invited them to her home for tea. Over tea, they caught up on all the news, and Mary told them that Mr. Willis knew about Tina. She had met him recently and told him all about it.

'He was really worried,' she told them.

'Well, tell him to ring Dr. Margaret at the big house if he wants news of her now,' said Georgina.

Mary drove them home; they all agreed they should meet more often.

That evening Mary rang Mr. Willis and told him all about Tina. She gave him the telephone number of the big house. 'Why don't you give Dr. Margaret a ring?'

'All right.'

He phoned the big house and spoke to Dr. Margaret. They spoke for a long time. Dr. Margaret explained the whole story of Tina's illness and her slow recovery, not complete yet, even after being out of hospital for all these months.

'It's terrible,' said Mr. Willis. 'When she does feel fit enough, could you ask her to phone me? I've been praying for her.'

'It's a pity you can't come down,' said Dr. Margaret.

'I'm sorry. I can't leave my mother.'

'You should break away from her a bit, you know.'

'I never have done.'

'Well I think it's a bit ridiculous.'

'I've never left her.'

'Oh well, it's not my business,' said Margaret, feeling irritated that he was such a mummy's boy. 'I'll get her to ring you sometime, Mr. Willis, and why don't you drop her a line?'

He did start writing to Tina regularly and she eventually replied. On the phone, she begged him to come down, but he never did. Gradually they drifted apart again. Over the months they stopped writing – he was wrapped up in his mother's condition and it was obvious he didn't intend to visit her, so it fizzled out.

The Reverend Moss retired around that time. His place was taken by a young family man, Eric Brown. He was a dynamic young man and introduced a lot of changes in the village church, but people liked and accepted him and so they accepted the changes. He was especially interested in spiritual healing. Curious about the rumours he had heard about the big house, he was anxious to find out all about the history of the family and what had gone on. He visited regularly at the big house and spent time with Tina. He was convinced of the power of prayer to heal people and prayed a great deal for Tina to be healed. She was interested but reticent, feeling that she wasn't quite ready for this kind of involvement.

'You must try yourself though, Tina,' he explained.

'I will. God can make me better, can't He?' she said innocently.

'Of course, and we'll help you all we can.'

Tina started to look forward to his weekly visits, but she wasn't ready yet to go to church or to take part in the healing services that Eric conducted. She was still frightened of everything and kept herself in the security of her home.

Chapter 17

After three years, Tina was still unable to lead a normal life. She was hardly better at all.

'I'm really disappointed,' said Margaret to Joe one day. 'She hasn't made the progress I had hoped for.'

'I know, but I think I should take over from you a bit more with Tina; you're doing far too much.'

Although Dr. Margaret wasn't seeing any other patients now that she was well past retiring age, she was, at eighty, getting too frail to be solely responsible for Tina.

'I was wondering whether some different medication might be the answer.'

'I don't know, Mum, the Valium does seem to suit her; but I'll have a think about it.'

One day, Tina was out for a walk in the woods, and sat down by the big tree. It was not one of her good days. She felt nervous and panicky, though as she closed her eyes and her loyal little dog sat down beside her, she felt soothed as she stroked the animal's silky fur. They dozed off together in the sunshine, and Nancy appeared to her again. As beautiful as ever, with her long blonde hair and big blue eyes, she chastised Tina for not having done what she had told her.

'I'm sorry, Nancy,' said Tina. 'I let you down.'

'Well, you will be better than you are now, but your life will be a long, hard struggle. I promised you that you would meet someone who would love you and help. It's the right time now, but you must make the effort with yourself. Take care of your appearance more. Wear some lipstick and brush your hair. Try harder.'

'I will.'

Nancy disappeared into the mist and Tina woke up, Nancy's words fresh in her mind. She felt much better, and decided she would start to make more of an effort with herself. Starting with eating properly, for she had grown thin and her face looked ravaged.

Tina returned to the big house deep in thought that afternoon. She had her tea and kept her thoughts to herself. Her illness had made her more reserved. She started to attend to her physical appearance, as Nancy had asked her to, washing her hair regularly, which was now quite long, curling down to her shoulders. Eating better had also improved the appearance of her hair, which was returning to its natural shiny condition. Occasional use of lipstick brought some colour to her face, and the family noticed that she was looking much better.

Chapter 18

Many years ago, when Nancy was alive, her real father Bill, an American, had two sons and a daughter. Their daughter lived in New York, but eventually moved to Canada to join the rest of the family who had gone there some years before. A descendant of that daughter, David, still living in Canada, still kept in touch with the family at the big house by letter and the occasional visit, although the two families hadn't seen each other for many years. David was married and had returned to his hometown after leaving the airforce, where he had met Jack, a man who was to become and remain his greatest friend.

Jack eventually came to live with David and his family. He had no family left of his own. His mother, now dead, was English, and although he had never visited England, he had always wanted to. Jack was a straightforward, compassionate man who, during his career in the airforce, had got something of a reputation for helping people with problems. He was a wonderful listener and very good at helping people to work things out.

Jack had been with David and his family for ten years. During that time Jack's health had been quite poor. He had never been strong physically and had suffered periodic bouts of serious illness, which left him weak and debilitated. Still, he had managed to cope with that and enjoyed life as much as he could.

Now though, Jack was beginning to feel that life was passing him by in that remote part of Canada. There were so few people nearby, and although he didn't crave for the bright lights of the city, he felt he needed more human contact. Thinking it over for a long time, he decided that he would like to visit England, and if he could find somewhere that suited him, to live there. There was a compelling reason for him to go: he had had a premonition that he would meet someone there that he could spent the rest of his life with. Jack had been married once, before his airforce days, but it had ended in divorce. He had a daughter from that marriage, but had completely lost contact with her.

When Jack told him about it, David suggested that his first port of call should be Surrey. 'I've got distant relatives there, near Guildford. Would you like me to introduce you? I could phone you know.'

'I don't want you to do anything like that. But if I did need it, I could always call or write to you from England.'

'Right, but remember if you do need a friend these people at the big house will help, I know.'

'I'm not sure where I'll settle yet, but perhaps I could go there initially and see what I make of it.'

The arrangements were made by telephone, and the time for Jack to start his journey came round so quickly. David and his family saw him off at the airport.

'We'll miss you Jack. But I'm sure you're doing the right thing.'

'I feel it,' said Jack. 'I feel – oh I don't know – ambitious, and I'm sure something good is going to come of it. I feel I'm needed there somehow. I don't know what it is, I can't pinpoint it, but I've got a strong premonition about it.'

He flew to Heathrow and travelled from there to Guildford, where he booked into a hotel. He was looking forward to making a fresh start on his own terms. He was fiercely independent. That was why he hadn't wanted to be introduced to the family at the big house. He would make contact with them when he wanted to, when he felt the time was right.

In a few days he was rested and recovered from his journey, ready to make his foray into the neighbourhood. His first thought was to get a car. That done, he decided to find the village where the big house was, which was only about eight miles away from where he was staying. He noted likely-looking properties, for it was his plan to buy himself a little cottage, quite a humble place would be suitable for his needs and he didn't have a great deal to spend on it, but there were very few properties of that description.

Suddenly he stumbled across a small house at the edge of the village, and unknown to Jack, across the woods from the big house. Even though it was somewhat bigger than what he had been looking for, he was immediately attracted to it, almost magnetically drawn to it. Feeling quite excited, he telephoned the agent, who agreed to show him round the next day.

They met there and went inside. The owners had moved away to retire to the seaside. 'It's got quite a history, actually,' said the agent, who had lived in the village for many years, and knew all the local gossip. 'There's a very large house nearby, and there's a rumour that many years ago there was a beautiful girl living here with her parents, but she was emotionally retarded. The story goes that she was out for a walk in the woods one day and met a boy from this big house. I believe it was owned by a rich American and his wife. It turned out anyway that the two young people were cousins and they both had this problem – it was inherited through the family. Well, they met in the woods and fell in love and there was a big fairy-tale wedding. Since then the descendants of that family have lived in the big house. There have been quite a few people with this condition down the years. There's one now I believe.'

'I wonder if those are the people my friend David told me about?' said Jack, and explained David's story.

'You ought to meet them, if that's the case.'

'In my own good time. I want to settle in first.'

'Do you mean you want the house?'

Jack nodded. 'It sounds as though it has a beautiful atmosphere, with a story like that behind it. I felt attracted to it straight away.' When he had looked around thoroughly, he knew he could be happy there. It was so attractive in its country setting, with the path that led from the back door down to the woods. The big lounge looked out over the woods and countryside, there was a small dining room and kitchen. Just right, he thought. Of the three bedrooms upstairs, he was drawn to one in particular. Nancy's old room. It had held its beautiful atmosphere.

'Just right for me,' he said reflectively.

'Do you mean you want it, just like that?'

'Yes. Could you get the arrangements going. I'll go back now, and we'll meet again tomorrow. I've got the money put by, but when I've bought the house, I'll be practically broke. I'll have to go on the dole or something!' he laughed.

'What do you do?' asked the agent.

'I was a mechanic in the airforce, but I'm not strong enough to do that now. I'll have to do something less strenuous. I do like talking to people though. I wish I'd been a psychologist, but I never had the education.'

'Do you know, you could be useful at Forest Dene hospital.'

'Where's that?'

'It's a psychiatric hospital very near here. In fact, one of the psychiatrists that lives at the big house works there. He used to live in a lovely house in the village, but the family up there got quite small, so he moved in with his family. The two families were very close.'

'It sounds a wonderful story,' smiled Jack.

'Why don't you try at the hospital? You could do voluntary work.'

'I couldn't afford to do that. I must earn something. Thanks though, you've been a great help.'

'See you tomorrow then.'

They started on the paperwork for the house purchase the next day. Jack thought about furniture. He furnished the house simply and cheaply, for he didn't have much money over after buying the house and the car. He already felt as if he belonged there.

It took Jack many weeks to get the house as he wanted it. Then at last came great day when he moved in. His home was furnished, pictures on the walls, everything was in order. As he left the hotel, trembling with excitement, he made up his mind to buy a dog for company. A few days later, he went to the local kennels and bought a little King Charles spaniel bitch, which he named Lassie. She soon settled in and became his faithful and constant companion.

Luckily, Jack discovered through his doctor that, due to his poor health, he could claim benefit which would be just about enough for him to manage on, even if he didn't find paid work. He was pleased about the English system, for in Canada it was a different story.

Years before, Jack had fallen severely ill while he was abroad, and he had never really recovered. His health was permanently and seriously affected, so he had to look after himself.

He was convinced as the weeks went by that the reason he had felt he had to come to England had something to do with the big house. He began to feel curious about it, and its occupants, although he had already decided that he wouldn't introduce himself straight away. Peace and quiet, and walking his dog, were uppermost in his mind. He enjoyed his solitary and tranquil life for three months.

One day Jack felt that the time had come to go to Forest Dene to see if there was anything he could do there as a volunteer. He explained to the nursing sister he saw there that he felt he had missed his vocation, that he would have liked to have been a psychologist. 'I wondered if I could come in as a volunteer, just to listen to the patients sometimes.'

'We always need people like that!' said the sister. 'I think you should meet Dr. Joe Greaves, our head of psychiatry.' She explained about Dr. Joe living at the big house, and how his mother had been the head of psychiatry before she retired. Jack told her about his friend who was related to the family at the big house. 'Well, you must meet him then,' she beamed.

Joe was pleased to meet a volunteer, as the sister introduced him.

'That's marvellous,' he said, liking the straightforward man at once. 'I think we're going to get on.'

Jack explained to him about David and his connections with the family.

'That's fantastic!' said Joe. 'You must come up to the big house one day and meet the family.'

'I'd like to, but I don't feel I'm ready yet. When I do, I'll tell you and you can invite me again. I want a little more time to settle in.'

'I understand, but you'd like to start doing something here straight away?'

'Next Monday, if that's all right. I can come in the afternoons for two or three hours, or some mornings as well, if you want me.'

'That's marvellous,' said Dr. Joe. 'So many patients have no visitors at all – they really need someone to talk to. Well, see you on Monday then.'

Jack went off whistling, feeling very pleased with himself.

He started at Forest Dene the following Monday and enjoyed being there from the beginning. After he had worked there over six months, he had still not been to the big house. Dr. Joe pestered him, but Jack was very stubborn. He wasn't ready for it yet; he just felt instinctively that it wasn't the right time.

'I'm not being unsociable. I will come when I'm ready, I promise,' he told Dr. Joe.

After a year at the hospital, Jack still hadn't visited the big house.

Dr. Joe had told everyone there about him. Tina wondered what he was like, this man at the little house. She was still the same with her anxiety state, but had managed to stay out of hospital for eighteen months. Progress was made in many small ways; like listening to her records again. The first time she listened, she felt sad, remembering how spirited she had been before she was ill. The romantic songs reminded her of how much she wanted to be loved and supported by someone special. Mr. Willis still occupied a place in her affections even though they only corresponded rarely now, with occasional talks on the phone. His parents had both died now, but he still wouldn't come to see her. He just wasn't, as he put it, 'a travelling man'.

Jane was a frequent visitor to the big house, when her husband was working away, which he did often. She wasn't afraid of Tina's illness any more, since Dr. Margaret had explained it all to her.

'Tina needs your help now, Jane. Do try and come,' she had finished, and Jane had come and found it was not as bad as she had feared. Her dear friend was, it was true, quite different now, but she still loved her. They would talk of old times together, and walk in the woods, play records, talking of love and romance as they used to. 'You're lucky,' said Tina. 'You've got a husband that you love and who adores you.'

'Well you're bound to meet your special person soon,' Jane assured her. 'Nancy wouldn't have told you that otherwise, in your vision.'

Dr. Margaret was beginning to give cause for concern at the big house. Now over eighty, she was growing quite frail. Tina suffered many anxious moments about her, but Dr. Joe knew that she would have to accept that Margaret would die one day, so he tried to prepare her for the inevitable. He also knew that Tina adored his mother, and was bound to be distraught no matter how he had prepared her. Margaret prayed constantly that she would live for many more years for Tina's sake. As it happened she did live to be very old indeed. Tina also worried about Jennifer who was in her seventies, but Jennifer was still very robust and healthy although she, as might be expected, wasn't as energetic as she used to be.

Megan at twelve had grown into a lovely girl, bright and academically inclined. Millie and Raymond had sent her to a very good school in Guildford where she was excelling in every subject. They had told her that Tina was really her mother and it had not come as much of a surprise. 'You know,' she said, 'I always felt there was something special between us. I love her.' She understood everything that Dr. Margaret and Millie explained to her. In this respect she was wise beyond her years.

Megan was fond of Richard, Joe's son, who at eighteen was about to leave school after doing extremely well in his examinations. It had been his ambition for many years to work at Forest Dene Hospital one day, and he was going off to medical school in London to begin the long years of study that would enable him to qualify as a psychiatrist.

Robert, Millie's son, was a different type of person altogether. He was utterly self-absorbed, unlike the rest of the family at the big house. He was kind to Richard, as a brother, and friendly to Megan but he had gone his own way. Robert had decided to be a solicitor and was going to do his training in a firm of solicitors in Guildford.

Each in their own way was getting on with life and doing as best they could. Even Tina, despite her illness, was making progress. Everything was running smoothly at the big house and Forest Dene Hospital. It was getting near to Tina's thirtieth birthday.

Jack was a great success at the hospital, and now that he had settled he felt ready to meet the family at the big house. He knew from Joe that they had a big celebration at Christmas and he asked him if he could go to that.

'That would be great. I'd really like you to meet Tina.' Joe had spoken of her to Jack before, in the hopes of tempting him up to the big house. He had a feeling that Jack just might be able to work with her and help her in ways that he or his mother couldn't. Jack was becoming more and more interested in her case. By this time, he really wanted to meet her.

'Well, we're having a combined party for Christmas and to celebrate Tina's thirtieth birthday. We did it once before when she was eighteen, though that seems so long ago now,' said Dr. Joe. 'Come then, to the party, won't you?'

Jack agreed and Joe was very pleased that at last Jack was coming to meet the family. He was growing quite fond of him, and respected the work he did at Forest Dene. He felt sure Jack could help Tina.

Tina was not looking forward to the party. There would be so many people there, such crowds of people – she was terrified. Joe tried to reassure her.

'Don't worry. You'll enjoy it if you can relax. And there's someone I want you to meet from Forest Dene Hospital.'

'Who's that?' her eyes betrayed a gleam of interest.

'He's called Jack, and he works at the hospital as a volunteer. Do you know, he lives in Nancy's old home?'

'I didn't know anyone had moved in there yet. It's been empty for ages.'

'He moved in some time ago now. I've invited him here before, but he wanted to settle in first. He's got a few physical health problems, but he's very happy at the hospital and he's a wonderful listener; to problems I mean.'

'Perhaps he could help me.'

'Perhaps he could, Tina. Actually I think he's quite lonely too. He's all on his own in that house, apart from his dog.'

She started to panic and become more nervous as the party approached. Despite this, however, she couldn't help a little pleasant fluttering of the heart when she thought about Jack. Although she'd never met him, she found herself wondering if he was the one Nancy had told her about in the vision.

Two days before the party, she went to bed early so that she could be alone to think. Thinking about the party, and the possibility of meeting someone as Nancy had promised, who might be Jack for all she knew, started her thinking and wondering about sexual feelings, which she hadn't had in years. Joe had described Jack to her. He was quite a bit older than she was, in his fifties. Thinking about him, for the first time in years she felt a welling up of excitement, and she felt her body all over. The thrill she felt was not so intense as before, but it was there and she enjoyed it, feeling relaxed afterwards. She went to sleep that night to dream of romance and love for the first time in years.

The next day she was quiet at breakfast, but there was a certain glow about her, the glow of anticipation despite her anxious feelings about the party itself. She decided to go for a solitary walk in the woods that afternoon, refusing gently Jennifer's offer of companionship.

'I feel I want to go on my own today,' she explained.

'That's fine,' said Jennifer. 'And it's a landmark. Do you realise this is the first time you've wanted to go on your own since your illness?' Tina hadn't thought about the years since she had ventured forth on a solitary excursion.

'I'll take Trixie,' she said.

After lunch, she wrapped up warmly in a thick sweater and anorak, and with her hair brushed and wearing a little lipstick, she looked really attractive. Dr. Margaret was in the lounge as she left, and she noted Tina's new self-confidence with delight.

'Tina, you look so pretty today!'

'Oh thank you, Dr. Margaret.'

Tina walked through the French windows and slowly across the lawn towards the woods.

She sat down by the big tree, her dog beside her. She felt better that day than she had before the breakdown. Relaxing after lunch, she leaned against the tree and dozed a while.

Jack looked out of the window on that crystal clear afternoon, and decided to take Lassie for a run instead of going to the hospital. He felt well, expectant. Down the back lane he went, into the woods, thinking and looking forward to the party the following evening at the big house. He strolled evenly about the woods until he came across a little corgi, a friendly dog which approached him and Lassie, looking for a companion. He followed the dog who seemed to be leading him somewhere. It seemed to know where it was going. Eventually Jack came upon Tina sleeping by the tree. He gazed at her for a moment, thinking how pretty she was, how sweet and helpless-looking. She was huddled up in a little ball against the cold. He took in her elfin features and the anxious furrows on her brow, even though she was asleep. Not wanting to wake her, he sat down, and looked at her.

He went on gazing at the sleeping girl for a good ten minutes, and then Tina sensed his presence. She woke up and found herself looking straight into a pair of laughing blue eyes. Her mind was in a whirl as she registered a friendly face and yet she wasn't sure if she was awake or still asleep and dreaming. Her eyes opened wide as she realised she was awake and alone with a man she had never seen before.

'Who are you?' she demanded nervously.

Jack looked her with his laughing eyes. 'I'm not going to hurt you, don't worry. I'm Jack. Our dogs made friends, so I thought I'd better make friends with you.' He was as always very jovial, and he could see that this young woman was very nervous. It crossed his mind that she might be the girl that Joe had told him about, from the big house.

'I'm afraid,' she gasped. 'I must get home – I have these panic attacks.'

'Well you must be Tina then. I've heard all about you,' said Jack. 'I know Dr. Joe Greaves. I help at the hospital, talking to people just like yourself. We must be friends – don't be afraid of me.'

At these words, her panic attack began to subside as she gradually felt more and more at ease with Jack. Remembering Nancy's words to her, she became convinced that this man was the one that had been predicted by Nancy. Her heart pounded – this time with excitement.

Jack felt the same way. He suddenly felt that this was the reason he had come to England. He had known when he left that there was a special reason. Now he felt an instantaneous attraction, but more than that, a deep intuitive bond between them. 'Oh Tina, it's lovely to meet you,' he said softly.

'You'll have to excuse my scruffiness,' she apologised, suddenly becoming aware of her dishevelled appearance. 'You see I've had this breakdown – '

'I know all about it,' Jack interrupted her laughing. 'And you look lovely to me!'

'I'm not, I know it. I wish I was beautiful like Nancy was. She had long blonde hair and big blue eyes. I look awful now. I've been so ill you see – '

'I'm sure Nancy was beautiful,' Jack said firmly. 'But everyone has their own special beauty. Everyone is beautiful to somebody. Beauty is in the eye of the beholder after all, and you are beautiful; to me. Do you see what I mean, Tina?'

'I think so and thank you for saying it.' He must be the one; she was convinced.

'Now relax and stop being so nervous,' said Jack.

She got up very gingerly.

'You won't have a heart attack, you know,' he laughed.

'I suppose Dr. Joe has told you all about me.'

'Yes he has,' admitted Jack, 'but I understand people like you.'

'You're very kind, considering you don't even know me.'

'Well, I don't feel that way. Let's make friends at once. By the way, I shouldn't have met you until tomorrow. I'm coming to the party you know.'

'I know. Dr. Joe told me. I've been looking forward to meeting you. I'm quite nervous about the party itself, though, but now I've met you, it will be easier.'

'Good. Now you ought to be getting back. It's getting dark and cold – they'll be worried about you. I'll come back with you.'

'Thanks! Then you can come in and meet everybody.'

'Yes, I'd like that. It will break the ice before the party.'

'I can't imagine that would be a problem for you. You're so friendly and relaxed,' she said. 'I wish I was like that.'

'Well, you will be in time and I'm going to help you. I feel we already have a link between us.' He took her two hands in his, and they both felt the electricity between them. They just stood there for a moment in silence, looking deep into each other's eyes. There was no need for words. Eventually Jack said, 'Be at ease with me, Tina. Everything will be fine.'

'Thank you – but I must get back now. I have to take my pill, you know.'

They walked back companionably together through the woods and across the lawns to the big house, the dogs following on behind them. The house looked beautiful, illuminated in readiness for the festivities. Tina was feeling better already as they walked in and found Dr. Margaret sitting on the settee as she did these days, looking out at the mystical woods, thinking about her life and all that had happened.

'Who, may I ask, is this?' said Margaret.

'It's Jack – he works at the hospital. Joe's told you about him,' said Tina.

'So you're the famous Jack,' she said smiling. She liked him at once. 'I think you'd better stay to supper – cheer the house up. Will you?'

'Well,' said Jack. 'I'd like that very much indeed.'

They went through to where the rest of the family was assembled at the table for supper. Joe immediately got up to greet Jack. 'Hello, Jack, what's all this?' Tina excitedly told Dr. Joe how they had met in the woods and then sat down suddenly, overcome.

'Oh my heart's banging, I feel peculiar.'

'I should think so,' Joe said mock-sternly, 'after what you've just told me. Now sit down and take that tablet.'

She swallowed it anxiously.

Millie introduced everyone to Jack, and when it was Megan's turn, Jack remarked what a pretty girl she was, which caused a scowl to cross Tina's face. She hated anyone to admire her daughter, who was indeed young and becoming very beautiful.

'Don't do that,' said Jack. 'It spoils your beautiful face.'

'Oh all right,' said Tina, smiling again. He certainly knew how to handle her. In fact his presence was like a tonic to the whole family. They all felt more cheerful in his company, and every one of them hoped secretly that this man was the one for Tina.

After supper they all sat in the lounge and talked, Tina, relaxed now, sitting next to Jack. Eventually Joe suggested that Jack should make his way home. 'You know you mustn't get over-tired.'

'What do you mean?' demanded Tina instantly. 'What's wrong with him? I don't want him to be ill.'

'It's all right,' said Dr. Margaret gently. 'Jack has got a few problems, but if he looks after himself he'll be fine for years.'

Jack laughed. 'You're quite a girl, Tina.'

They went out into the hall, and Jack stared at the portrait of Nancy. 'What a beauty,' he pronounced. Tina scowled again. 'Oh Tina, I'm only admiring the portrait. I assume it's Nancy.'

'That's right,' said Dr. Joe, joining them in the hall.

'Well, she is beautiful – no-one could deny that – but listen, Tina, don't be jealous. She's been good to you. She's really helped you through your dreams of her. Don't be silly. I've already told you, you're beautiful too, in your own way.'

'Nancy told me that as well, when I said I wished I looked like her.'

'You're yourself,' said Jack firmly.

Her jealousy faded away as she realised that Jack really did like her. Jack looked at all the portraits, so many generations of the family. 'They are wonderful,' he said. 'This is a fantastic house – and that chandelier! I've got so much to see.'

'Well you can see it all at the party tomorrow,' said Joe. 'Now I'm going to insist on driving you home.'

'Thanks. I'm grateful – I'm quite tired now. I never expected to have such an enjoyable evening. I only went out for an afternoon walk with my dog!'

He kissed Tina on the forehead and said goodnight.

'Be early tomorrow, won't you,' she said.

'I will, and I'll get you a present.'

'You are wonderful. I really like you Jack.'

'And I like you, you silly sausage.' Tina laughed. She loved his jokes – he made her feel so much better.

Joe called Jack from the car and Jack got in. During the drive to Jack's house the two men talked.

'You could do a lot of good for Tina,' said Joe.

'It's strange, but I feel that this is the reason I had to come here. It's strange I haven't met her before.'

'It probably wasn't the right time before. After what I've seen happen at the big house, through the generations, I'm beginning to think that some things are just meant to happen.'

'You're probably right.'

'See you tomorrow,' said Joe as Jack got out of the car.

Jack went up to bed reflecting on the day. The most overpowering feeling was one of physical attraction. He had not been so attracted to a woman for a long time. He had almost forgotten what it was like. And yet, he felt such compassion for her. He knew he could wait for her, however long it took. Suddenly he thought of David and decided to ring him there and then and tell him what had happened. He picked up the phone on the bedside table.

'How are you, Jack,' he asked, delighted to hear from his friend.

'Everything's fine,' Jack replied, and proceeded to tell the whole story to his astonished friend.

'It's like a fairy tale – unbelievable. Perhaps it's love at last!'

'You may be right and there may be some better news later on. If there is, you must come over.'

'It would be nice. I've never been to the big house. If you do get any good news, Jack, let us know.'

'I will. It would be great to see you again.'

They said their goodbyes and hung up.

He thought of Tina as he lay there before going off to sleep. He knew she would need a lot of help, but he felt more than sympathy for her. He was falling in love with her already.

At the big house Tina was in a state of high excitement, babbling to any of them who would listen to her about how Jack must be the one that Nancy had promised. In the midst of her exhilarated chatter, a panic attack started. Joe was not sympathetic.

'Tina, you've been warned about getting over-excited. Now go to bed and calm down. Do your breathing exercises.' They helped her to bed and Dr. Joe gave her a Valium tablet. She soon calmed down. Relaxing at last, she apologised to Joe.

'I feel so despondent, Dr. Joe. I have to go and have these attacks, even when something good happens. Jack won't like me.'

'Of course he will, but, Tina, try not to get over-excited, especially tomorrow. Now remember, Jane's coming in early in the afternoon.'

'Of course she is. I'm so looking forward to seeing her.' Tina was becoming more and more relaxed now. 'I'm tired now, Dr. Joe. I must go to sleep.'

'Goodnight, Tina.'

She fell asleep, thinking of Jack, thinking that she loved him already.

The next morning Tina woke in a panic. Jennifer came in with the tea, a reassuring presence until the tablets helped her to relax. 'Happy birthday, Tina,' said Jennifer. She felt happier then and began to look forward to the day. 'You'd better get up soon and come down to breakfast,' said Jennifer. 'We've got a lot to give you.'

'Oh?'

'Hurry up then!'

Tina couldn't hurry in the mornings. She got out of bed very slowly, fearful in case she had palpitations, but she got up, showered and got dressed in her jeans and sweater. Everyone was sitting round the breakfast table when she went downstairs, wishing her a happy birthday. The tears welled up in her eyes as she remembered her eighteenth birthday, when she had been so vivacious and in love with Dr. Margaret. She smiled as she remembered and Dr. Margaret caught her eye and smiled too.

'Come and sit by me this morning,' she said.

After breakfast Tina opened all her cards and presents. There was a video from Megan, who had gone off to school, a skirt and jumper from Jennifer, a gold necklace from Dr. Margaret, which was engraved with the inscription 'To Tina with love from Dr. Margaret', some record vouchers from Millie and Raymond. Tina was overcome by the love that had gone into all the presents. She thanked everyone and hugged them all.

Then Jennifer asked Tina to step into the lounge. They had another special present for her, from all them. It was a portrait of Dr. Margaret when she was young. 'It was done a long time ago. I had it at my home, but when we came here, it was put away. Now I want you to have it.' Tina was overcome. 'I've never had such a wonderful present. Oh thank you, Dr. Margaret, I do love you.'

'It's from all of us,' said Dr. Margaret. 'Would you like it in your room?'

'Yes, please.'

Afterwards the others disappeared and Tina was left alone with Dr. Margaret. Jennifer realised that Tina now felt the same bond with Dr. Margaret that she, Jennifer, had had with her mother Dr. Rosemary. The same deep and spiritual love.

Tina and Dr. Margaret sat on the big settee looking out at the frosty morning with the watery sun glinting on the garden and the woods. They talked awhile and then drifted off into a relaxed sleep in the sunshine, Tina's head on Dr. Margaret's shoulder.

Jennifer called them at lunch-time. They woke, surprised to find that hours had passed.

Just after lunch the bell rang and Tina ran to open the door. It was delivery of a huge bouquet of flowers. On the card it said

'With all my love to Tina, from Jack, your new friend.' Her eyes filled with tears. She sat down in the chair after she had brought them in and wept.

'Come on, darling,' said Dr. Margaret. 'Come up and lie down with me for an hour.' Tina allowed herself to be led upstairs and into Dr. Margaret's room. They lay down together on Dr. Margaret's enormous bed, which she'd had for years and used to share with her two springer spaniels.

'There's plenty of room,' said Dr. Margaret. They lay together cuddled up as Tina said 'I love you, Dr. Margaret. I always will.'

'And I love you. Happy birthday, Tina. Be happy. You'll be all right tonight. I'm willing you to be. And remember, Jack will be here.'

Tina smiled at the thought of Jack, and they fell asleep with their arms around each other. They slept soundly for over an hour. At ten to three Jennifer crept in and woke Tina, who tiptoed out so as not to disturb Dr. Margaret.

'I've put your tea in your room. Come on,' said Jennifer. Tina lay in her own room for a moment, her anxious feelings returning as they usually did when she woke up, and even more so as she thought of the big occasion before her. She felt better as always after a cup of tea and her tablet then the bell rang and Jane was brought upstairs.

'Oh it's great to see you, Tina,' said Jane, hugging her. Jane knew that Tina was a different person now to the old schoolfriend she had known. It had all been explained to her by Dr. Joe. She had been frightened of the changes in Tina and worried about the effect the drugs had on her, but not any more. She accepted Tina loyally as her best friend still.

'There's my bed! Remember when we used to sleep in here together?'

'Oh yes! I wish you could stay sometimes now.'

'I might be able to,' said Jane. 'My husband is going to be working away sometimes from now on.'

'That's brilliant. We could have a laugh again.'

'Yes, Tina, and I could help you.'

'Great. You've really cheered me up.' She started to tell Jane all about the woods and how she had met Jack.

'I'm so glad for you, Tina! I'm longing to meet him.'

They went downstairs while Tina continued to talk about Jack, laughing and giggling. Jennifer heard them and couldn't help recalling Tina's eighteenth birthday when the two girls giggled practically all the time. She realised that Jane was so good for Tina, and was glad she was there.

The two girls went into the lounge, laughing and shouting, just like the old days. Millie came in with Megan.

'We're more or less all ready for the party now,' said Millie. 'Do you want to go and have a look at everything? It's your party, after all.'

'All right, Mummy.'

'I'm glad to hear you laughing. Jane, you're very good for her.' Megan looked at Jane.

'Haven't you grown up, Megan?' said Jane. 'And you're getting very pretty!' That wasn't the most diplomatic thing to say in Tina's presence, and she could have bitten her tongue when she saw Tina glaring.

'You're pretty too,' she laughed.

Tina looked across at Megan, whose eyes were filling. She was a sensitive girl, and was keenly aware of the rift between her and her child-mother.

'I'd like to be friends, Tina,' she offered. 'We could be like sisters. I could help you.'

'I'd like that,' said Tina. 'All right, Megan. We will be friends and just like sisters.'

Megan was pleased. Life sometimes got rather lonely for her at the big house. She had friends at school, but most of them lived too far away to bring home.

Megan tagged along with Tina and Jane for the rest of the afternoon, enjoying their girlish talk and joining in with the laughter. Millie was pleased to hear them – she had been hoping for a long time that Tina would stop resenting her daughter.

They ran about the house looking at everything. There were decorations everywhere, the chandelier casting a thousand twinkling rainbows, the lights, the tree with its pile of presents. The hall had been cleared for dancing to a band, and the back hall was specially cleared for a disco for the youngsters. What a great party it was going to be.

After tea, they all got ready. It was the first time Tina had dressed up for a long time. She put on the beautiful blue dress Millie had got for her, did her hair and applied a little make-up. She looked lovely, although she couldn't help feeling still a little stab of jealousy about Megan; she was jealous of her youth and her complete health. She envied the normal life Megan would be able to lead.

Jane had a green dress, a shade that brought out her fair complexion, and the two of them made a pretty pair. They went downstairs to wait with everyone else for the guests to arrive. How handsome they all looked – Millie in red, Jennifer in palest blue, and the men looking elegant in their suits. Then Megan came down. They all looked. She looked stunning in black and red, with gold jewellery. They realised that even though she wasn't thirteen yet, she was growing up very quickly, a young woman almost, so fresh and lovely. Tina looked up in envy. Feeling shaky, she just had to get away. Running into the video room, Jane behind her, she flung herself down into a chair, gasping. 'I can't go through with it, Jane! I'm all panicky. I just can't.'

'Whatever's the matter? You looked at Megan as if you'd seen a ghost.'

'It was, a horrid ghost. She's so pretty and she's going to be a rival to me, I know it.'

'Stop being jealous! You're going to be like sisters, you said.'

'I know,' said Tina miserably, 'but Jack will prefer her to me, I know.'

'Jack wouldn't want her! She's only twelve.'

'All right. I'll try to be nice about it but I've gone all shaky. I need another Valium. Is Dr. Margaret up, or is Dr. Joe back? I'm all frightened. Get them, please, Jane!'

The door opened as Jack strode in purposefully, saying over his shoulder to Millie, 'I'll deal with this. Leave it to me.'

He greeted Jane and then turned to Tina. 'Now what's wrong with you? None of this nonsense – I've heard all about it from your mother. Now what's going on?'

'It's Megan. I'm worried, I'm all panicky. I want a tablet. Get me a cup of tea and a tablet – please Jack.'

'Don't be silly, Megan's only twelve, I'm not interested in her. Now be sensible.'

He despatched Jane to fetch a cup of tea and a tablet while he sat with Tina. Jane obeyed fearfully. She was so worried about Tina when she got like this. Jack sat with her. When she had drunk the tea and taken the Valium, they smoked a cigarette together.

'That's better,' he declared as he could see that she was calming down 'and Tina, you look wonderful tonight. Equally as lovely as Megan. She's only a kid anyway. I wouldn't be interested. Remember what I said – beauty is in the eye of the beholder.'

'I'll remember,' she said.

'Jane, come and sit with us,' Jack suddenly said, sensing that Jane was feeling left out. 'Is your husband coming?'

'He'll be here in a minute. You'll have to meet him. You're so good for Tina, and I'm really glad she has met you.'

'So am I. We're very happy together already, although we've only known each other a day. Now come on you two, all the guests are arriving, I can hear them.'

'I still feel nervous,' said Tina. 'Can we wait just another half an hour. They won't miss us yet. Please, Jack.'

'All right. Jane, you go and wait for your husband and tell Jennifer that we'll be half an hour. They'll understand.'

The party got under way. Guests came streaming through the door as the band struck up. The disco got going as four of Megan's friends from school arrived with their brothers. She put out of her mind the unpleasant scene with Tina and set out to enjoy herself with her friends. Richard had brought his girlfriend home, a fellow student at medical school in London, and she was staying for Christmas. Robert's girlfriend was there too; he had met her through his work in the solicitor's office. Some of his old school friends were there as well. The disco was thronging with youngsters, including some from the village.

Out in the main hall the band was playing and the sound wafted in to where Tina was now telling Jack her life story. 'I've never been able to talk to anyone else like this, Jack,' she said at length. 'I can talk to Dr. Margaret of course but somehow there's something between us – '

'I know. You carry on talking all you like, Tina.'

They carried on for another few minutes.

'Tina,' he said eventually. 'Something's happened to us, hasn't it? Do you know what I mean?'

She nodded, scarcely trusting herself to speak. He was the one that Nancy had predicted she would meet, who would love her for herself, the one she would be able to talk to. He was everything that she needed.

Jack slowly drew Tina into his arms. 'Something's happened to us,' he repeated.

'I know. I love you, Jack. I know I love you. Nancy predicted I would meet someone and I know it's you.'

'And I know it too. Maybe I shouldn't say it. I know you're not well.'

'I'm well enough to be loved, Jack, and it will help me to get better. I've waited so long.'

They kissed passionately, feeling the electric thrills go through them. They were deeply in love already.

Jack asked Tina then if she would get engaged to him, on Christmas day. 'If everything goes well, we could plan to marry in a year's time. Would you like that Tina?'

'It would be wonderful – and Jack I'll be able to live in your house, the little house I've always wanted. Or you could live here.'

'I think it would be better to live in my house, but let's talk about it later, much later. We've only just met. Will you marry me, Tina?'

'Yes. Later on I will.'

'And shall we get engaged on Christmas day? We could go and choose a ring in Guildford.'

She immediately looked panicky. 'Jack, I can't go shopping. I'd be terrified.'

'You silly sausage, you won't be terrified with me. You'll have your tablets, I'll drive you in and we'll park very near the jeweller's, and I'll tell you what else we'll do. We'll do some Christmas shopping. You can do yours yourself this year.'

She agreed. He had certainly taken her firmly in hand. Through Jack's help she would be able to help herself even more. They kissed once more, feeling the thrills go through their bodies. 'I love you,' said Jack breathlessly.

'And I love you. I really do, Jack.'

'Now I think we should join the party and have some of our special champagne.'

'What's that? I can't drink, Jack.'

'Well, we'll have some lemonade in champagne glasses and we'll pretend it's the real thing. Use our imagination!'

'What a wonderful idea.'

They could hear everyone moving into the lounge for the buffet. Millie opened the door and called 'Come on, Jack, Tina. We're waiting to cut the cake!'

As they went through, Jack still held Tina's hand. For them, no-one else existed. Each of them felt that they had found love for the first time.

Everyone was there in the room, but Joe noticed, observant as always, that Jack and Tina only had eyes for each other. Jack went and fetched three glasses and a bottle of lemonade. He poured the lemonade and assembled the glasses on a tray. He brought the tray over and called Jane. She came over with her husband, who had a glass of champagne.

'My wife mustn't drink because of her tablets,' said Bill.

'Well, this is champagne and it isn't,' said Jack, and whispered something to Bill, who immediately caught on. He drank his champagne with his arm round Jane, whom he appeared to adore, and Jane joined Tina and Jack in drinking the lemonade champagne.

Everyone drank a toast to Tina's birthday. She raised her glass then and said shyly, 'Thank you, everybody. It is a happy birthday.' She looked with love at Jack when she said this and then was silent.

After the cake was cut and everyone was feeling replete from eating the sumptuous buffet, they went into the hall for dancing. Even Dr. Margaret danced that night. They had a wonderful time, dancing to the old music. Tina felt so happy; she'd faced the occasion with confidence, eaten her fill from the buffet and most importantly had had no sign of an anxiety attack.

Tina and Jack danced into the night, radiating the love which they couldn't have concealed if they tried. The night was theirs; they could have been alone for all they noticed going on around them. They were only aware of one another. In just twenty-four hours they had fallen deeply in love. At last the music faded away and they had to tear themselves away from each other.

'I must go home now,' said Jack.

'I love you, Jack.'

'And I love you. I'll be with you tomorrow and every day if you'll let me.'

'Come in the morning. Come to lunch?'

He agreed and they went out on to the floodlit lawn. Standing there holding each other, not wanting to let go. Jack did eventually, and got into the car after giving Tina one last lingering kiss.

On the way home his head was filled with her. He wanted her. It was years since he had had such desire for a woman. Still, he knew he would have to wait until the right moment, when it was right for both of them.

Tina went upstairs to bed tired out, after kissing everyone goodnight.

'You're in love,' said Dr. Margaret. 'For the first time. I'm so glad but it's been so sudden.'

'I know, but it's the one Nancy predicted. I'm sure of that.'

'So am I. Be happy, Tina. You deserve it.'

Chapter 19

The next day while Jack and Tina were out walking in the woods, Jane went for a walk with Jennifer. She was feeling lonely and wanted to confide in Jennifer about her husband. 'I just don't feel he's the same person these days – he seems so distant somehow. I can't help feeling there's something really wrong,' she explained to Jennifer.

'You must be imagining it, surely?' asked Jennifer. 'He's only gone to his mother's for two days.'

'I still feel there's something wrong,' Jane persisted.

When Bill had left the big house, he'd gone to catch the bus to near Croydon, where his mother lived. There was someone waiting for him at the bus-stop. He'd met Sally at work. She had known Tina from school many years before and now was very beautiful, with something of a reputation as a man-eater. Bill loved Jane but he sometimes found her rather dull, certainly not as openly sexy as this girl was. He'd been seeing Sally for some months; she was so alluring he couldn't help himself.

At the bus-stop she was waiting for him looking as provocative as ever. They got on the bus and went to Bill's mother's. She had never liked Jane and thoroughly approved of his new liaison. They had arranged that Bill and Sally would stay there for the next few days.

'You see, Jennifer, I sense that things aren't right with Bill,' Jane continued.

'You'll just have to have it out with him when he comes back.'

'If he comes back.'

'Would you be very upset if there was another woman?' Jennifer was now alert, realising that this was no flight of fancy on Jane's part.

'I would . . . and I wouldn't. I don't feel . . . you know, that magic with Bill. I did at first but not now.'

'Well, I do hope you're imagining it,' said Jennifer at last, 'but you should tell Tina about it you know.'

'Well, I will tonight when we go to bed. I know her mind's on Jack at the moment.'

Tina and Jack were walking in the woods, towards the big tree. They kissed passionately as they sat down. The thrills went through them like electricity.

'This is love,' sighed Tina. 'At last it's happened to me!' Her face clouded over as she continued. 'Oh Jack, you know I've got this terrible anxiety problem. Will you accept me with it?'

'When you love somebody, you accept anything – you love them all the more for little imperfections. I feel that for you.'

'It's not just pity, is it?'

'Of course not. It was meant for us to meet and I just love you. Would you like to get married in June if things go well for us?'

'I'd love that. Jack, when can we get engaged?'

'I told you, on Christmas day. We'll go and choose the ring together tomorrow or the next day.'

'I can't go into town. I get frightened.'

'You will. You will, or you won't get engaged. You'll take your pill and you'll come with me in the car. You'll see.'

That night, Tina noticed that Jane had eaten very little supper before excusing herself and going straight up to bed. She asked Jennifer if there was something wrong.

'She needs to talk to you,' said Jennifer. 'Will you go up? You could do with an early night.'

Tina said a hurried goodnight to everyone and went upstairs. Jane was already in bed looking very downcast. 'What's wrong?' Tina asked her friend.

'Well, I'm worried about Bill. I'm certain he's seeing someone else. He says he's going to his mother's, but I don't think so.'

'Oh, I'm sorry, Jane. I wish I could come with you to see him and sort it all out, but I'd be so frightened. Actually I'm supposed to be going with Jack into town tomorrow to buy a ring, but I'm terrified about that.'

'How wonderful,' said Jane.

'But, that's given me an idea! Jack could do something. Let's talk to him about it tomorrow and ask him.'

'Do you think he would? Oh thank you, Tina.'

She got out of bed and went over to Tina, hugging her and shedding a few sad tears.

'If it's as you think,' said Tina. 'Remember you've always got me.'

'Thank you, Tina. I do love you.' They embraced and Jane got back into bed and fell asleep, unlike her friend who lay awake, wondering and worrying about her.

When Jack arrived the next morning to take Tina shopping, she asked him to go into the lounge for a moment. She hurriedly explained to him the situation with Jane and asked for his advice. After a moment's thought he said, 'You stay here with Jennifer today, Jane. I'll sort the problem out.'

'Thanks, Jack. I just must know something one way or the other. But what are you going to do?'

'Don't worry about that, I'll tell you later. Give me his mother's address.'

She complied doubtfully. 'You're not going there are you, Jack?'

'We'll see. Leave it to me.'

'All right,' she said gratefully.

Jack drove into town with a very nervous Tina by his side. They went straight to the jeweller's and quickly chose a simple, single diamond ring. Jack put it into his pocket. 'You'll get this on Christmas day,' he promised. 'Now what about your Christmas shopping?'

'I just don't feel up to it,' she said timidly. 'I'm so tired, Jack.'

'Well, let's just get one or two and some cards. Your mother can get the rest as agreed. It just shows you're trying, Tina. Do it for me?'

Nervously she agreed, and they went into a big department store, where she chose quite a few presents. She perked up no end, finding that it was not such an ordeal, with Jack there to hold her hand.

The shopping completed, Tina felt triumphant, if exhausted. Jack led her back to the car, and took her out of town to a little place in the country for lunch. They drove towards Croydon, and found a country pub where they ate a good lunch. Fortified by an extra Valium tablet specially given into Jack's safe-keeping by Dr. Joe that morning, Tina felt more relaxed. Once in the car again, she fell asleep almost immediately, worn out with the morning's activities, more than she had done for many months.

Jack drove on towards Croydon where he stopped to get directions to the address he had been given by Jane. When they pulled up outside the house, Tina was still asleep. Jack crept out of the car, leaving a little note on the wheel so that Tina would not panic if she woke up before he came back.

He knocked on the door and Bill's mother answered.

'Is Bill there? I'm a friend of his,' Jack lied. She took him into the lounge and called Bill who was upstairs. He appeared at last looking, as was the case, as if he had just got out of bed. 'Right,' said Jack. 'You saw me last night. I'm Tina's friend.'

'What's wrong?' Bill blanched.

'Jane's very upset. She knows something's wrong, and I think you've got another woman. Now you'd better tell me all about it.'

'It's none of your business.'

'What's going on,' said his mother, coming in.

Jack explained everything to her. 'I'm not all that keen on Jane myself,' she said.

'Yes, but that doesn't mean you have to condone this sort of behaviour. It's very wrong of you.'

'As far as I'm concerned, Bill's happiness is what matters. Jane's got her own life.'

'It's still wrong,' Jack insisted. 'They're married.'

'I don't care!' Bill came back at him. 'I want a divorce. I'm going to marry Sally. She's upstairs.'

'Call her down.'

'Why?' asked Bill in surprise.

'Just do it, and there'll be no trouble.'

Bill went upstairs and they came down together.

'Well, you look completely suited to each other,' said Jack in disgust. 'I won't make trouble for you. Now do you want Jane?' He looked at Bill.

'No.' His voice was flat as he flinched under Jack's gaze.

'Right. It's a pity; you've got your own lovely home. I'll have to tell Jane's parents and we'll go from there. Are you going to return home?'

'No. I was going to write to Jane.'

'Yes – the coward's way out. Just what I expected. I suggest you keep well away from Jane from now on.'

'I will. I just want a divorce.'

'You'll get that all right. Now, all of you, keep away from the big house. Don't ever let me see you there.'

He slammed the door as he left. He knew he'd done Jane a favour. To his amazement Tina was still asleep, and remained so all the way home. He woke her gently when they arrived back at the big house. 'Come on, Tina, let's get these presents into the house.'

Jane was out with Jennifer, doing some last minute shopping in Guildford. Jack was glad, for he knew he would have to talk to Joe and they would both have to talk to Jane.

Tina, still very tired, took her presents upstairs and lay down on the bed, exhausted. Jack had helped her so much. She hadn't been shopping since the breakdown. It was such a big step for her, more than she herself realised.

Jack, downstairs, was very concerned about Jane and phoned her parents. Her mother was upset but not particularly surprised – she had had her suspicions of Bill for some time. 'She'll have to be told,' she said.

'I know, but it would be better if you were here when we tell her. She'll need you,' said Jack.

'We'll be over shortly.'

They arrived before Jane returned with Jennifer. Jack asked Jennifer to take some tea up for Tina. She agreed, realising something was wrong, as soon as she saw Jane's parents.

'Jane, come into the lounge,' said Jack gently, his hand on her shoulder.

He saw Dr. Margaret coming downstairs and, leaving Jane in the lounge, he slipped out and told her as briefly as he could the story. 'Could you come in, for moral support?' he asked her.

They went in together to where Jane and her parents were sitting, Jane looking completely bewildered. At the same time she sensed it had to do with Bill, and that the news was not good.

'I know it's Bill,' she blurted out. 'I think he's got someone else. Just tell me if I'm right!'

'You are right,' said Dr. Margaret. 'I'm sorry, Jane.'

Jack told her the whole story of his visit to Bill's mother's, and how Sally was there. 'Oh her!' said Jane. 'I was friends with her at school for a while, but she was always after the men. Trust him to go off with her.'

'He's not coming back,' said Jack. 'I'm sorry.'

Jane was weeping softly. 'I did love him you know. But lately I've felt adrift from him. He didn't want me. I knew there was something – '

'I'm glad you've found out now,' said her mother.

'So am I. But what will happen about the house?'

'Well, that will all be seen to for you in the divorce,' Jack explained. Jane's parents tried to persuade her to go home with them but she refused, saying that she needed to be near Tina for now. 'Well if that's what you want,' said her mother, nodding.

It was arranged that Jane would stay on and her parents would return to the big house for the Christmas day festivities. They said their goodbyes, and Jane sat with Dr. Margaret, crying on her shoulder.

Tina came downstairs and Jack explained everything to her. She rushed in to comfort her friend, both of them crying. At last Jane stopped crying and began to talk of how she was looking forward to sleeping in Tina's room and what fun they would have together. They went upstairs, giggling and laughing. Jane with her easy-going ways was going to take this in her stride. She hadn't been happy herself for some time.

Christmas day was a very happy one for them all that year. There was much noise and laughter, especially on Christmas morning when they all opened their presents. To the surprise of the family, Tina wanted to go with them to church. Jack went with her and she felt on that day more blessed than she had ever felt before. Eric's sermon of hope and love seemed to be especially for her that day as he beamed down at her.

After church he came over to her. 'It's wonderful to see you here.'

'Thank you. I'm getting engaged to Jack today. You'll be marrying us in June.'

'What wonderful news, Tina!'

They went back to the big house for lunch; so many people round that huge table. Richard and Robert had brought their girlfriends, and Rene and her sister Barbara sat down with them, and of course Jack next to Tina, and Jane.

When Jack stood up and announced their engagement, the whole family glowed. They knew it was right, that Jack and Tina were meant for each other. The celebration of Christmas seemed a very appropriate time to seal their happiness together.

With so much excitement, and apprehension about the announcement of her engagement, Tina had a panic attack after lunch. She was gently tended to by Dr. Joe who put her to bed for a rest. 'You've done so much in the last few days, Tina, don't worry about this. Just try to relax.' He gave her a pill to settle her and helped her with her breathing exercises. As she gradually relaxed and the anxiety subsided she grew sleepy. Jane came in and lay beside her. They both fell fast asleep, clinging to each other for security and comfort.

When they woke up, they joined the others for the evening, feeling rested and relaxed. Late that evening, Mr. Willis telephoned.

'What a nice surprise,' said Tina. 'How are you, and how's your mother?'

'Well, she died, Tina. I didn't tell you because you were so ill. My father's dead too.'

'I'm sorry, but Mr. Willis does that mean you could come down now?'

'I can't. My wife's seriously ill and we've got a friend living with us, looking after us. But one day, perhaps.'

'Oh well, give my love to Beryl, and I hope you're happy.'

Mr. Willis noticed how different Tina sounded. Gone was the sexy voice and the teasing way she spoke. She sounded rather nervous and breathless, like a frightened child.

Tina went to bed after having kissing Jack goodnight. She was pleased that she had persuaded him to stay at the big house over the Christmas holiday. She went up to bed with Jane, talking over what a wonderful day they had all had.

Joe was still downstairs after everyone had gone to bed when the phone rang. It was Georgina. 'Dr. Joe I'm sorry I didn't ring earlier to wish you a happy Christmas – it's just that Julian's seriously ill, and I've been so worried about him. He's been ill for a month now.'

'Why didn't you let us know earlier? I'm so sorry. What's wrong with him?'

'He had a heart attack, and the doctors say he won't last very long. I can't live without him, Dr. Joe. What am I going to do?'

'You could always come back here – '

'No. I couldn't, not now. I've got friends here. I couldn't stand the upheaval.'

'Do you want someone to come down to be with you?'

'Well, I wouldn't mind.'

'I've got a few days holiday after Christmas. Vicky and I could come down. Would you like that?'

'Oh please! You're so kind, Dr. Joe.'

Dr. Joe arranged to go in a few days, and book into a hotel. Vicky was very sorry when he told her. 'I don't think he's going to make it,' said Joe. It seemed cruel that they would be parted after sharing their lives together for so long.

Three days after Christmas, Joe and Vicky travelled to Exmouth where they realised at once that Julian was very ill – it was only a matter of time. They booked into a hotel for four days, as Joe had to get back to his work. Within twenty-four hours of their arrival, Julian died in his sleep during the night, of heart failure. Georgina was devastated as they expected.

They stayed on to sort out the arrangements for the funeral, a small and cheerless affair. Julian and Georgina had so few relatives left now, apart from those at the big house, who were represented by Joe and Vicky. Georgina couldn't go to the funeral; she had gone into an immediate decline when Julian died, refusing to eat or look after herself properly. She lay on her bed in her room at the home and looked at the ceiling, wishing for all she was worth to be with her husband as soon as possible. Joe couldn't get through to her at all. When he went back two days after the funeral, he was very concerned about the deterioration that had taken place in Georgina, in front of their eyes, it seemed.

The matron of the home had seen cases like this before, where one partner of a devoted and loving couple died, only to be quickly followed by the other. She was philosophical about it. 'If they loved each other so much in life, why shouldn't they want to be together now?' she said. Joe agreed, and thought it wouldn't be long before Georgina joined her husband.

When Joe and Vicky got home they told Dr. Margaret, but decided to keep the news to themselves. A week later, there was a phone call from the matron of the home to say that Georgina had just faded away, as they had thought. 'She never ate again after Julian died. She went to bed last night perfectly normally, and she died in her sleep. It really was a happy release.'

So Vicky and Joe had to return to Exmouth for another funeral, for which the arrangements were made by the matron. It was another sad and lonely occasion. Georgina was laid to rest next to her husband in the cemetery that overlooked the seashore where they had so often walked.

The day after their return, when Joe was thinking he would have to break the news to Tina soon, she approached him. 'Joe, why did you go back to Exmouth? Is there something wrong?'

He asked her to sit down and said simply, 'Georgina and Julian have gone.'

'Gone? Gone where? What do you mean Joe?'

He took her hands. 'Julian was seriously ill over Christmas and he died; then Georgina really couldn't carry on without him. I suppose you could say she died of a broken heart. That's why we went the second time, to go to her funeral.'

Tina was very sensible about it. 'It's awful,' she said 'but what about Jennifer? Georgina was her great friend.'

'I know. I'm quite worried about her. I'll tell her tonight, but I'm going to ask my mother to be there. Now don't cry, they're happy now, together with all their loved ones.'

'I know.'

She went off to find Jack who held her and comforted her.

The next day Dr. Margaret told Jennifer the whole story of Julian and Georgina's deaths. 'It was a happy release, dear, really.' Jennifer cried bitterly. 'I'm not crying because they've gone. I expected it, they were old and tired, but it was so wonderful they went so close together, for Georgina would have been so miserable without Julian. They just had to be together.'

So saying, Jennifer was able to accept the death of these two people who had lived a happy life together.

She turned her attention to Tina and Megan, for she knew there was still friction between them, despite Megan's efforts to befriend Tina. Especially when Jack was around, Tina couldn't help feeling jealous of her daughter, though he laughingly reassured her not to be so silly.

By March things were moving apace for Tina and Jack. They were so happy together. They had made love in Jack's little home many times in Nancy's old room, although Tina found it difficult to give herself completely. Her anxiety state had caused her to be rigid and tense. She enjoyed making love with Jack, but despite Jack's gentleness it was hard for her to re-discover the old uninhibited self she had been, so she couldn't help feeling that however much she loved him there was a distance between them. Jack as always was confident and reassuring. 'It will come in time,' he promised her.

Jack was still doing his voluntary work at Forest Dene Hospital, every other day, for he knew it would not help Tina for him to be around all the time. She needed time to be alone, and to spend with Jane.

Jane had never gone home to her parents, except to pack her things. They had gratefully given their permission for her to move into the big house. They thanked Joe effusively and told him that they were retiring soon and moving away from the area. 'Where are you going?' asked Dr. Joe.

'We're moving to Devon – near Plymouth. We have some friends there.'

'Will Jane go with you?'

'I don't think she'd want to come. She'd be bored to tears – it's so quiet where we're going.'

'Well, we'd all like it if Jane made her home with us permanently. You'll be able to visit and so will she.'

'Thank you so much,' said her mother.

So Jane's childhood wish had come true. She had always wanted to live at the big house. She had started work at the nearby riding stables, where she was very happy. There was a young man there she became friendly with, but she was not prepared to think of marriage ever again. Tina often used to visit Jane at the stables, but could not be enticed to go riding; she was too fearful.

This then was the Tina they all now accepted and loved, and at last she accepted herself – no longer the fearless daredevil of her youth, but a more timid person altogether, who would always need constant love and support.

The wedding, which seemed such a long way in the future when they planned it at Christmas, was on them almost before they knew it.

A few days before saw the start of frenetic activity at the big house, caterers had to be arranged, new outfits bought, visitors were coming for the occasion. Jack was thrilled that David and his family were coming over for the wedding from Canada. 'I couldn't miss it!' said David when Jack rang to ask him.

'And, David, would you be my best man? We've been buddies for years.' David agreed immediately, and flew over two days before the great occasion.

Everyone at the big house was delighted to see David and make the acquaintance of their distant relatives, but Tina was beginning to get agitated in the presence of so many people, and with all the busy preparations there were so many strangers coming and going. To the wedding itself, Dr. Joe had only invited relations and just a few friends, but still it was a great strain for Tina.

Tina didn't want bridesmaids, just Jane as her matron of honour, but to her surprise, Megan was so upset that she had to allow her to be the single bridesmaid. It really was important to Megan to feel that she was a part of the wedding. New outfits were bought for everyone, with the exception of Tina. She was to wear Jennifer's dress – the one she had worn when she got married to Derek. Knowing that Jennifer and Derek had had such a happy and long-lasting marriage, she wanted to marry in that dress, as a symbol of the love she hoped would be hers with Jack.

Tina and Jack would live at Jack's home after their marriage, on Jack's insistence and against the wishes and better judgment of Joe. He felt that Tina should remain at the big house, but Jack felt very strongly that the move would be in Tina's interest. It would encourage her to become a little more independent. So with Jane moving in as well, to keep her company, Tina had agreed.

Just before the wedding day, Tina was feeling more and more uneasy about the prospect of moving into Jack's home. She could imagine herself feeling trapped there, and wondered if she ought to take up driving again so that she would be able to get away on her own. She wanted to speak to Dr. Margaret about her fears, but something stopped her. Knowing she should at least try it, she stayed silent.

In the days leading up to the wedding, Tina suffered many panic attacks and had to have her medication increased. Still she was determined to go through with the marriage. She wanted to marry Jack. It was her fear of change that was causing her problems.

One reason that she was prepared to marry Jack, feeling as anxious as she did, was that she was sure she could convince him, after they were married, to move back to the big house. 'I'll be able to persuade him, won't I, Jennifer,' she had said. 'You know, like we did with Dr. Margaret.'

'Well, Jack is very different,' said Jennifer. 'He's stubborn, but if you are unhappy living in Jack's house, you'll just have to come back, that's all.'

'I'm sure I can twist his arm. I can twist him round my little finger!'

The night before the wedding, Joe spoke to Tina. 'Are you sure this is what you want?'

'Yes, I just want to be married. I do love Jack, and if I'm unhappy there, or can't cope, could Jack and I live here?'

'Of course.'

'I'm sure I'll be able to persuade him,' she said happily.

Joe was not so sure.

Jack too, was having his doubts that wedding eve. He loved Tina and wanted her to be his wife, but he was still uncertain of her.

Tina sat in the lounge with Dr. Margaret and Jennifer late that night, crying bitterly. 'I don't want to leave here,' she sobbed. 'I don't want to go to that house.'

'It won't work if you're going to be like this, Tina.' Dr. Margaret was very concerned.

'It will be all right, as long as I can see you all every day. I might start driving again. Otherwise I'll just have to get a taxi.'

So Tina went to bed very troubled that night, still determined to marry Jack, but unable to get over her fear of leaving the big house.

In the morning, her wedding day, Tina did not feel elated. All the busy preparation, the beauty of the house now decorated for the occasion, the clear blue sky, none of these excited her or eased her mind about the step she was undertaking. Still there was not time to think about anything as the morning passed in a whirl of activity.

At last the cars came to take them to church. In the car, Tina's nervousness nearly got the better of her, but Joe was with her to reassure and support her. She had not seen Jack for two days before the wedding, at his insistence. He was always determined to have things the way he wanted, and this had become increasingly obvious as the wedding approached. While Joe knew that Jack's firm handling of Tina had helped her to become better and more independent, he had his doubts about how far Jack should take his firmness. When did determination become obstinacy, he wondered.

On their arrival at the church, Jack was already there, along with all their relatives and many people from the village, all crammed into the little church. Tina nervously walked up the aisle on Joe's arm, carrying her bouquet of bright summer flowers, to meet her future husband.

When they exchanged rings there was a pall of unease and dread surrounding them, unspoken but felt by everybody in the church. For all the outward beauty and happiness radiating from the two of them, there was no magic in the church that day. The tears that were wiped away by the family were not the traditional ones of pride and happiness, but of real sadness.

Tina managed to say her vows while wanting more than anything to run away; but she was rooted to the spot. There was something very wrong indeed.

As they left under a hail of confetti, Jack kissed her. She started to tell him how nervous she felt, but he stopped her with a wave of his hand. 'Now come on,' he said briskly. 'None of that today.'

Tina thought she detected a different note in his voice, a brusqueness that she hadn't noticed before.

When they arrived back at the big house the celebrations were in full swing. There was dancing, the usual speeches, people helped themselves to the feast that had been prepared for them, and the champagne flowed. Dr. Margaret and Jennifer sat back and watched all the activity. Jack and Tina were dancing, and Dr. Margaret couldn't help noticing the anxiety in Tina's face.

Much later in the evening, just as she was about to go upstairs to change, Tina succumbed to a panic attack. Dr. Joe went straight upstairs behind her, followed by Jack. 'Well,' said Joe. 'It has been a big day for you Tina – '

'Stop fussing so much,' said Jack abruptly. 'She'll be all right. I'll see to her.'

'No. I don't know what's wrong with you today, Jack. You seem different since the wedding.'

'She's my wife, and I'm going to look after her.' His tone was almost threatening.

'I will always look after her as long as I'm here,' said Joe. 'Now I think you should both stay the night in the big guest room.'

'No. We've arranged to spend our honeymoon at my home. It's all ready.'

'That doesn't matter,' said Joe. 'Tina's ill, can't you see that?'

Tina cried. 'I can't go tonight, Jack. Please understand. Stay with me here.'

'I'm sorry,' said Jack. 'I'm not going to.' With that, he walked straight out of the house, to everyone's amazement, got into his car and drove off.

Tina was hysterical by this time and had to be sedated. Dr. Margaret and Dr. Joe sat with her.

'It's broken my heart, Dr. Margaret,' she sobbed. 'But perhaps it's best to find out now.'

'Oh no,' said Joe. 'There must be something wrong for Jack to behave like that. I'm sure it can all be sorted out. I'll try and find out what's the matter in the morning. Tina, stay in your own room tonight, with Jane.'

Joe and Margaret puzzled over this inexplicable turn of events until well into the night. Joe was furious, and decided to talk to David about it, so leaving his exhausted mother to go to sleep he went down to the now quiet lounge. All the guests had long gone home and the rest of the family had gone to bed. 'Well, I don't understand it,' said David in reply to Joe's questions, 'but I warn you, he was always stubborn. Still I can't think what made him behave like that. I ought to go and see him, after all we've been good friends for years. I'll go first thing in the morning.'

David breakfasted early with Joe and set off to see Jack, who had already regretted his behaviour.

Some years ago, when Jack was abroad, he had contracted amoebic dysentery from eating a contaminated apple. He had been stubborn then, refusing to wash and peel the apple as he had been instructed to do, and as a result had suffered the debilitating illness that had dogged him ever since, recurring frequently and weakening his body. His moods were affected too and it seemed that he had grown ever more obstinate as he became weaker physically, especially in stressful situations.

He woke up the next morning feeling thoroughly ashamed of himself. David arrived and immediately asked him about the incident the previous night. 'I just felt very tired and poorly,' said Jack, 'and I didn't think it was right for them to try and keep us at the big house.'

'Why ever not? Tina was in such a state. It was only one night.'

'I can't help it. I still feel she should have come home with me.'

'But you accepted her illness when you took her as your wife. You're either going to have to accept it, or get the marriage annulled.'

'Oh no!' Jack was shocked. 'I love her. Well, perhaps she will come home today.'

'Or perhaps you could stay at the big house tonight and say you're sorry. It would be the best thing you could do, Jack.'

'All right,' said Jack at last. 'I'll come back with you.'

He packed a small case and went back with David to face Joe.

'You've got to understand Tina,' said Joe. 'It won't work otherwise.'

'All right. I'm willing to spend the night here, to try and make up for things, but I'd like us to go tomorrow for the week on our own at my home. She's got to learn to settle in there.'

'If she doesn't, you know you must move to the big house.'

'I'll never do that,' said Jack flatly.

'You are stubborn,' said David. 'It's a wonderful place to live.'

'I like the big house very much,' said Jack resolutely, 'but I never want to live here.'

Tina had woken up very upset still and cried in Jane's arms. 'I'm so afraid Jane, but I love him. What shall I do?' Jane couldn't offer her any comfort, or an answer to what seemed like an impossible situation.

Jack went upstairs and apologised to Tina. They agreed to try to make things better between them and spent a subdued day together, walking in the woods and talking quietly. That night they went together to the spare bedroom which looked over the woods. Tina felt miserable, although she loved Jack. She couldn't forget his treatment of her the previous night, and more than that, she felt a rift between them, a distance she felt she couldn't cross. They made love, but she felt tense and unsatisfied. Jack realised how she felt, but reassured her that it would be all right later on. They slept in each other's arms.

Early in the morning Tina woke and immediately had a panic attack as she looked at Jack still asleep beside her. She crept out of bed and rushed in to Jane, getting back into the security of her own familiar bed.

'I'm afraid,' she gasped. 'I feel trapped with Jack in the same room. I can't live with him, Jane, I just can't.'

Jane called Millie, who came quickly. 'Whatever's wrong, Tina?'

'I woke up feeling trapped, as if I was suffocating. I can't live with him. Help me, Mummy!'

Megan came flying in and put her arms around Tina. 'What is it?'

'I'm just so afraid, Megan!'

Millie went to fetch some tea and Tina's pills. They all fussed around her gently and she began to calm down.

Jack came striding in. 'Whatever's going on here? Why is my wife not in bed with me?' he demanded. His eyes looked steely, furiously cold.

'Well,' said Millie. 'She's a very sick girl. She can't – '

'She's spoilt. She must learn discipline. You can't give in to her all the time.'

'That's our business,' retorted Millie.

'Not now. She's my wife.'

'I'm afraid of him,' cried Tina.

Millie called Joe and David came upstairs to see what was going on. David manhandled Jack down the stairs. 'So you've started again! You are a fool, Jack. It's just not going to work. Can't you see the girl is petrified?'

'I'm going back home,' said Jack stiffly. 'I stayed the night here to please you all, but I'm going home and I shan't stay here again.'

He wouldn't discuss it any more, just got in his car and drove away.

'Well, that is it!' declared Joe.

They talked it over, reeling from the shock of this latest outrage from Jack.

Jack telephoned Joe later that morning to announce that unless Tina went to his home he would be making arrangements to have the marriage annulled.

'It's been consummated,' Joe said.

'It can be annulled on medical grounds.'

'Yes, it can be,' said Joe furiously. 'I'll see to it.' He hung up.

Joe went upstairs to ask Tina if she would be going to Jack's that day. 'I can't. I love him, but he's a different man now we're married.'

'You won't be married for long,' said Joe grimly.

Tina started to cry. 'What's going to happen, Dr. Joe?'

'It's going to be annulled. Perhaps Nancy meant that you should be friends, even lovers, but not trapped in a marriage.'

Jack didn't return to the big house, nor, the following week, did he go to Forest Dene to help the patients.

Six weeks later, the marriage was annulled. Joe had made all the arrangements with solicitors in Guildford. It was straightforward, except that Jack had to attend, cold and ominous as he answered in clipped tones the questions that were put to him. Joe was there representing Tina. It was over in no time.

As far as the law was concerned the marriage had never taken place. Tina felt nothing but relief that it was all over and she could carry on with her life at the big house as before. Thinking about her vision of Nancy, she came to the conclusion that Jack had not been the one meant for her.

Some weeks after the annulment, Jack came to the big house, his old cheerful self. Joe was shocked when he opened the door and saw him standing there. With no preliminaries, Jack said, 'I must talk to you, Joe. It's very important. Are you willing to see me after what's happened?'

'Yes, come in the lounge.'

The two men went inside and closed the door behind them. Jack began to talk to Joe. 'It's like this, Joe. First of all I want to apologise for what happened. I know it was wrong of me. But there's something else.'

'Oh?'

'When I spent that second night with Tina and she ran from

the room, I realised when I thought about it afterwards, that Tina will never be able to live with a man, or be married. That's why I knew it was the best thing for the marriage to be annulled. I've thought it all through Joe, I've thought of nothing else these last weeks. I do feel guilty about it all, but honestly I'm sure I've done her a favour. But I do love her still, I always will.'

Joe looked at Jack, into the blue eyes now softened by sadness, and he realised that Jack was sincere, and that he was right about Tina not being able to live with a man.

'Yes, I understand,' said Joe.

'I can see you've been thinking as I've been talking, Joe. You know I'm right, don't you?'

'Yes. But what do you want to do now?'

'Would it be too much to ask that Tina and I might be good friends, or even lovers if she wants to – I'd never just use her, you know that. I still love her. Perhaps we could just be friends with no strings. What do you think?'

'Well, I don't know if she or the rest of the family will forgive what you did, but I'll talk to them, and to Tina. If she's willing to be friends it's all right with me.'

'Thank you, Joe! I'll give you a ring in a day or two to see what's happened.'

Joe saw Jack out, wishing to avoid the others, and Jack drove off, hoping that the family would understand and forgive him. He would now have to leave everything in the hands of Joe Greaves.

Joe went into the big lounge to think. He felt that Jack was sincere but wondered how he would convince the others. His mother disturbed his reverie, saying as she came in 'Didn't I just hear the doorbell?'

'You did.'

'Well, Joe, what's going on? I can see you've got something on your mind.' Joe explained the whole story to her.

'I don't know what to make of that,' she said doubtfully when he had finished his tale. 'Still, if you believe him then so will I and I'm willing to forgive him. I think Tina needs a friend.'

When Jennifer, Millie and Raymond came in, Margaret and Joe told them the story of Jack's visit. They all agreed after much deliberation that it would be good for Tina to see Jack again, and told Megan about it when she came down and, seeing them all talking, knew something important was going on.

'Well, I forgive him,' she said at last. 'I trust your judgement, Joe.'

They all agreed.

That night when Tina was asleep, Nancy came to her in a dream. Tina asked her if Jack was the person she had promised, who would love her and look after her. 'Yes,' said Nancy. 'I know it's hard for you to understand, but Jack is truly sorry and he knows that you can't be trapped. That's why I said little about marriage. You must never marry him or anyone else. Jack will come back, wanting to be friends and to help you. Take his friendship and love, be lovers even, but never marry.'

'Oh Nancy,' said Tina. 'That's what I would like, for us to be friends.'

'Well, he is the one.'

'Will he come back soon, Nancy? I do miss him.'

'He has been back and talked to Dr. Joe. Now it's up to you. Dr. Joe will tell you in the morning.'

'He'll be surprised, won't he? I'm so happy. I'll forgive Jack and ask him to forgive me. We'll put the past behind us and start again. I'll take your advice.'

'There's something else I must tell you. Jack is a sick man and has only a few years left but do not be sad, for when that time comes, you will be stronger and able to cope, and there will be something else for you to do. So for now, love him and enjoy him while you can. Never tell him what I've said.'

'How long has he got, Nancy?'

'I can't tell you, but I promise you it is more than five years. Now go and make the best of your life with him.'

'Thank you, Nancy.'

Nancy vanished into the mist and Tina slept on in a peaceful dreamless sleep until the morning.

After breakfast, Joe asked Tina to go into the big lounge for a talk.

'Tina,' he began. 'Somebody came to see me yesterday night.'

She regarded him, smiling. 'I know, and the answer is yes. I still love him.'

'How do you know? Surely Jennifer hasn't told you?'

Tina told him all about Nancy's appearance and her advice. 'So you see, Dr. Joe,' she finished, 'I've got to see him as quickly as possible, I've got to make the best of the time he has left.'

Joe's experiences at the big house over the years had led him to trust these appearances of Nancy, and he now told Tina that she must follow the advice that Nancy had given her.

'Now why don't you go with Megan and Jane this morning for a walk in the woods?' he suggested.

'Yes, I really feel like that today. We'll take Trixie and the other dogs.'

'And if you'd like me to, I'll arrange for you to see Jack tomorrow.'

'Oh, can't it be tonight? Remember we've got to make the best of the time we have.'

'All right. Oh, and by the way, everyone knows about him coming back, and they've all forgiven him. Nothing will ever be said. As far as we're all concerned the marriage never took place. Jack won't mention it either.'

'And nor will I.'

Joe went to phone Jack. 'All's well, Jack! And do you know, I didn't have to ask Tina. She already knew.'

'How's that?'

Joe told him all about the vision of Nancy, except for the part about Jack's health. 'Now come and see her tonight. Come for supper. She's going out in the woods today.'

'I will. I'm so happy, Joe. We can start all over.'

The two men hung up, each for his own reasons delighted with this outcome. All would be well.

Tina, Jane and Megan enjoyed their walk in the woods. They were all in good spirits that morning, laughing and chattering. The nightmare of Tina's marriage was behind them now and would never be mentioned again. Just before lunch, Tina started to flag and Megan suggested that it was time they went back. 'You'll need to rest after lunch before you see Jack this evening.'

'Yes,' Tina admitted. 'I'm beginning to feel a bit nervous.' She was breathless and Megan had to help her to relax and do the breathing exercises that helped Tina's anxiety state. Joe had taught Megan, and she was pleased that she could help prevent a panic attack. 'Come on now, Tina. Breathe in and out easily, and you'll soon feel better.'

'Oh thank you, Megan. I am beginning to feel better. You're so good to me. I do love you.' That was the first time Tina had been able to tell her daughter that she loved her.

'And I love you,' said Megan, big teardrops falling down her cheeks. She was so happy. She held Tina's hand as she and Jane helped her back to the big house.

They sat down together at the table, a bright and loving trio. Everyone caught this new mood of closeness between Megan and Tina and were pleased about it, for both of them.

At suppertime, the doorbell rang. Tina and Jane rushed to the door in great excitement, and there, grinning, was Jack. 'Well, my old sausage, how are you?' he said, as if nothing had happened. 'It's a fresh start, isn't it?'

'It's fresh start,' said Tina. 'Shake on it.'

They shook hands. 'Well, Jack,' she said mock-politely. 'Do come in!' They roared with laughter as he came into the lounge. Tina started to talk to him, and didn't stop. She was so excited.

Each of them felt that there was nothing at all to worry about now.

When they went into supper Jack took Tina lovingly by the arm, and she looked into his laughing blue eyes. Their hearts turned over as they knew this was a new start for them. 'I love you,' Jack whispered.

In the weeks that followed there evolved a new routine. Jack worked less hours at Forest Dene Hospital, seeing just a few patients in the mornings. Tina was glad to spend time with Dr. Margaret and Jennifer then, especially Jennifer, who seemed to be ageing fast. The afternoons and evenings Tina spent with Jack, one day at the big house, the next day at Jack's little house. With the knowledge that she would always be able to sleep in her own bed at the big house, Tina no longer felt trapped with Jack. They became lovers again; always on the days she spent at Jack's they made love.

A few weeks after Jack and Tina's new start, when life at the big house seemed perfect once more, Jane's father rang with the news that Jane's mother was seriously ill. 'I need your help here, Jane,' he said. 'We can't afford to pay for help. You'll have to come. I know it's a long way.'

'Have I got to come?'

'I'm sorry but you must, Jane.'

'All right.'

Jane stood by the phone sobbing when she had hung up. She loved her mother and knew how ill she was, but she didn't want to leave the big house. She talked to Dr. Joe about it and explained that she would have to leave the next day. 'I'll have to go,' she said.

'Well remember that when your parents are gone, your home is here.'

'Thank you, Dr. Joe.' He embraced her.

Tina cried when she was told, for she did not know how long it would be before she would see her best friend again. Joe drove the two girls to the station. They cried pathetically at having to be parted. Jane called from the train as it left, 'I'll be back when I can!'

'I'll write!' cried Tina as the train disappeared from sight.

Jane's departure upset Tina a great deal, and even though Megan moved in to share her bedroom, she could never replace the dear friend that Jane was. Still Tina was glad of the company and the two of them grew very close.

A few weeks later Jane phoned with the very sad news that her mother had died. She had had a stroke which would have left her paralysed had she lived. 'I've got to stay and look after Dad now,' explained Jane.

'I know,' said Joe, 'but you'll be back one day.'

'I know, but I'm so unhappy. I miss you all so.'

Joe knew that she was a dutiful girl who would feel she had to look after her father for the rest of his life, and that's exactly what she did.

Tina was sad, but she had other things to occupy her. Her relationship with Jack was going really well.

Six months after Jane's phone call, Jennifer was taken ill. She had become frail and senile, and her illness was not entirely unexpected. She hadn't left her room for weeks.

A specialist was called who diagnosed that she had suffered a heart attack. He told Joe that she should stay in bed, for she could go at any time. Jennifer did not seem fearful for she was ready to go, to Derek and all her loved ones.

Tina went in to see Jennifer. She was heartbroken herself, for they had been so close. Not so much in recent months because of her relationship with Jack. Joe felt that this was probably a good thing and would enable Tina to say goodbye more easily.

Jennifer told Tina how much she loved her. 'And you'll be looked after and helped by Jack and the others. You know I have to go, don't you? I'm going to Derek and Gordon and Nancy and everyone we have loved. Now, Tina, get on with your life and all will be well for you. I feel that.'

Tina burst into tears and fled from the room. In her own room, Megan comforted her.

Two days later, Jennifer was still very weak, and while she was sleeping Nancy appeared to her. 'Oh, you've come!'

'Yes. You're coming to join us now. Tina will be able to manage. She can cope now.'

'Will Dr. Margaret be all right for a while? Just a little while?'

'Yes, she's been given extra time for Tina's sake. She has a little while longer. Aren't you happy to be joining all your loved ones, Jennifer?'

'Yes, I'm happy and I'm ready.'

'I came because you were a little fearful. There is nothing to be afraid of. We live on.'

Jennifer slept on for about half an hour and when she woke Joe and Dr. Margaret were by her bedside with the doctor. She knew the end was near. She told them about her vision of Nancy.

The whole family was called in and they all said their goodbyes to Jennifer – really it was au revoir, for they knew they would see her again when their time came.

Tina was very upset and still crying. 'Don't cry, Tina,' said Jennifer weakly. 'I'll be with Nancy and I'll be looking after you too. Who knows, I may even appear to you in a dream. I can promise you one thing though: one day Jane will come back, and she will stay for always.'

Jennifer died peacefully two hours later with Dr. Joe and Millie at the bed. Eric came over soon afterwards and said a blessing for Jennifer. He talked to Tina, explaining that she too would join Jennifer one day, but for now, Tina should be glad that Jennifer was happy with Dr. Rosemary and Derek, and all the rest of them.

Jennifer's funeral took place at the village church a few days later. Eric Brown spoke of her life, and they all agreed that it was very poignant. Tina attended the funeral, but had to leave early in distress. Jack took her outside and drove her home. He encouraged her to talk about her feelings for Jennifer, which she did for hours. Like everybody at the big house, Tina would miss Jennifer a great deal. For a long time afterwards they felt her loss keenly in so many ways every day.

Megan was a great support to Tina during this time and they continued to share a room. They grew closer than ever.

Chapter 20

Megan was now sixteen. The three years since Jennifer's death had flown by. Megan was still determined to be a doctor, and was encouraged by Joe and Dr. Margaret, who were also thrilled that Richard was coming up to finishing his medical degree. Robert was living in Guildford and making a great success of his job in the solicitors' practice there. He would often come home to the big house on a Sunday afternoon, with his girlfriend.

Tina and Jack's relationship went from strength to strength, and as it progressed, so Tina was so much better.

A year later, Megan left school and went to college in Bristol, leaving Tina alone in her room at the big house, but she promised to come home when she could at weekends. Dr. Joe realised that Megan would have to make a life for herself in Bristol. She could not be expected to give up her young life completely for Tina, although Tina, still so self-centred, thought otherwise.

Joe was still watching Tina's progress and hoping that he could find a drug to eliminate the anxiety attacks. So far though, he hadn't come up with anything. He was concerned that when Dr. Margaret died, as they had to expect almost any time now, Tina might have another breakdown. Margaret was now extremely frail and tired. For himself as well, Joe was dreading that time. He adored his mother. She had been such a wonderful example to them all.

One day in the spring after Tina's thirty-fifth birthday, Jack reminded Tina that it was her turn to go to his house that evening. 'I know. But I feel I must stay at home tonight, Jack. Do say you understand.'

'But why, Tina?'

'I don't know. I can't pin-point it. I want to be near Dr. Margaret tonight.'

Jack went home in his car, alerted by what Tina had said, for he knew how intuitive she was, especially where Dr. Margaret was concerned. She had loved the old lady for years and now she felt uneasy about her.

That day Dr. Margaret had felt stronger. She had come downstairs and sat in the big lounge, looking out at the mystical woods feeling somehow detached and distant from her surroundings; thinking back on her life, her mother, her grandfather, and all the stories she had heard about the big house. She belonged there, she felt.

Tina come into the lounge and found her lost in reminiscence, gazing out over the woods. She sat down next to the old lady and held her hand. Dr. Margaret fell asleep as they sat there quietly. Millie came in and suggested that she get Dr. Margaret to bed. 'You can go and see her later if you like.'

'All right.' Tina went up to her room, and lay on her bed thinking about Dr. Margaret, unable to shake off the melancholy mood that surrounded her.

Margaret was helped to her room. Millie could see that she was failing fast, and seemed very weak. In Joe's absence, she told Vicky that she was worried about her. 'It's funny as well, Tina hasn't gone to Jack's today.'

'Perhaps she can sense something. Margaret isn't going to last long, I'm sure,' said Vicky.

They made Dr. Margaret comfortable and she drifted in and out of sleep. Millie called the doctor and Vicky called Joe at the hospital. They both said they would come at once.

Dr. Margaret knew that she only had a little time left. As she slept on, she saw her mother. 'You're coming to us soon,' said Dr. Rosemary.

'I'm so tired, I just want to be with you all. But I'm worried about Tina.'

'I know you've been worried about her for a long time. She is a little better, but not making the improvement you would like. I want to tell you now the name of the drug that will help her. She'll never be perfect as you know, but she can be helped, and she'll be able to do her painting again.'

Dr. Rosemary told Dr. Margaret the name of the drug. Margaret was surprised as it was something she had already considered and dismissed. Still Rosemary was very insistent. 'You must see that she is given those tablets. Tell Joe before you join us. Your work is done now and you will joining us soon.'

'I love you, Mum, and I am tired. Will they be all right here? Will Tina be all right?'

'She will be much better on this new medication.'

'Thank you.'

Dr. Rosemary disappeared and Margaret opened her eyes, looking round her, thinking what a wonderful thing had happened. 'I want Joe,' she managed to whisper.

'I'm here, Mum.'

'Joe. I've seen mother.'

'You've been dreaming, Mum.'

'No,' said Dr. Margaret urgently. 'I did see her. She gave me a message for you about Tina. She gave me the name of a drug that would make Tina a lot better, and she said that she would be able to do her painting again.' She told him the name of the drug.

'Well, it's one we've talked about in the past, isn't it? Did she really say that, Mum?'

'I promise you. I'm telling you the truth, Joe.'

'That's wonderful, Mum. I'll start her on that at once.'

'Now let me see her.'

Joe went to Tina's room where she was lying on the bed, distraught. 'I think she's going to go, Joe. Oh what am I going to do?'

'She's very old now, Tina, and tired. Come and see her now, to say goodbye. Be strong now, for her sake.'

He led her by the arm to Dr. Margaret's bedside. Tina took her hand. It was so cold. 'I love you. I'm going to miss you, Dr. Margaret,' she faltered.

'You've been very brave and I admire you, but things will get better. My mother Rosemary has come to me and told me of some new medication that will help you. Please say you will try it and not be afraid.'

'I love you, Dr. Margaret,' said Tina. 'I wish you could be here to see me get better.'

'You won't be perfect,' warned Dr. Margaret, 'but you will be better on the new drugs and I will see you – as Nancy does and all the rest of the family who love you. We'll all be looking upon you with love. Now don't be sad for me. I'm tired; I need to go. I want to be with my mother, Dr. Rosemary, and Jennifer. I miss them but I'll be looking after you.'

'All right.' Tina's voice was shaking. 'Oh Dr. Margaret, I love you so much!'

'You must leave her now,' said Dr. Williams. He could see that she was going and he wanted Tina out of the way. She burst into tears and fled from the room.

Dr. Margaret said goodbye to the rest of the family, and to her son Joe whom she loved so much, then Megan arrived to say her goodbyes and ran from the room in tears. She heard Tina still sobbing and went to comfort her.

'Now remember, Joe,' Dr. Margaret said urgently. 'Start the new medication with Tina as soon as possible.'

'I promise,' said Dr. Joe in his choking voice. 'Thank you for everything you've done for me. I love you, Mum.'

Dr. Margaret closed her eyes. Joe sat with her until the end. Dr. Margaret died a few minutes later, peacefully.

Dr. Margaret's death affected Tina very badly. She continued to cry constantly, and have panic attacks. Megan looked after Tina through this time. She was extremely capable and managed to get through her own grief at the same time.

When Jack came to the big house, Joe begged him to stay a little while to comfort Tina. 'I'm nearly out of my mind with grief myself, Jack. I know it's for the best, and she was old and all that, but I miss her so, more than I could have believed possible.'

Jack agreed at once and went home to fetch some clothes, offering to stay until after the funeral. He was to have a room next to Tina's. She was delighted that he would be there; a comforting presence.

A few days later Eric Brown took the funeral service in the village church, which was full to overflowing. There were colleagues from Forest Dene, the family from the big house, ex-patients and people from the village. Eric spoke of how Margaret had been living on borrowed time for years, and how he believed she'd been given that time by God to continue her work with those who needed her so much. Everyone nodded in agreement, their eyes shining with tears. It was the most moving service he had ever taken. Tina had to be taken out of the church by Jack before the end of the service; she was overcome with grief and crying hysterically.

They went back to the big house together and sat in the lounge looking out towards the mystical woods. Tina poured out her feelings for hours and Jack listened patiently.

Meanwhile Dr. Margaret was laid to rest near her loved ones in the graveyard, a peaceful and tranquil resting place. The assembled company made their way back to the big house for a quiet reflective reception, talking about Dr. Margaret and the enormous amount of good she had done in her life. Tina went up to bed; she couldn't face the thought of appearing at the reception. Jack spoke to everyone and was a great comfort to the family.

In the quiet after everyone had gone, Dr. Joe went to Tina, and found her and Megan curled up in each other's arms, asleep.

'I bet she's still keeping watch over them,' said Joe in a quivering voice.

'She was a wonderful person, Joe!' said Millie, still crying.

Then another disaster happened for Tina. Her little dog, the faithful companion, died. She was very old and they had all expected it, but this on top of losing Dr. Margaret was a fresh blow for Tina, reminding her once again of the loss of her dear friend.

Life had to go on for all of them, though, and Joe threw himself into his work with renewed vigour, inspired by the example of his mother before him. Two days later, he brought home the new tablets for Tina. He sat with Tina and Jack in the big lounge, and told her about this new drug which would, they hoped, make such a difference to her life. 'I want you to start taking them while Jack is still here. He is staying until the weekend, and then he must go back to his own home.'

She agreed to start taking the new medication the next morning.

Megan was such a support to Tina; without her best friend Jane, she had become reliant on Megan for support. They were closer than ever now, like a pair of young sisters. Jane had been unable even to come to Dr. Margaret's funeral. In the beautiful card she had sent there was news of her own father's illness, and how he needed her full-time attention now.

The next morning, Millie came with tea and the first of the new tablets. Megan woke up at once. 'I'll come and sit with her while she takes it; she's bound to be a bit nervous.'

'Thank you, Megan. Jack's coming in a minute. He's just getting up now.' They woke Tina gently and gave her the tea. She had had a bad night. The prospect of change always frightened her, and it had become worse since she had her anxiety state.

'I'm afraid, Mummy,' she said, wide-eyed and frightened. 'I can't take it.'

Despite the best efforts of Millie, Megan and Jack, she persistently refused. She went into a severe panic attack. They called Joe and he advised them to leave it for the time being. 'It's no good, we'll have to give the Valium today, and I'll talk to her tonight.'

Tina was distraught. 'I'm sorry, Dr. Joe, I'm just so frightened. I feel guilty, I know you're doing your best for me.'

'Don't feel guilty, Tina. Rest now and we'll talk tonight.'

This was the second time that Tina had refused to follow the guidance she had been given. First, from Nancy about the drugs, which she had not given up, and now, she was refusing to follow the instructions for her treatment that Dr. Rosemary had given to Dr. Margaret. Because she hadn't done what Nancy had asked, she had brought about the severe anxiety state by which she would be dogged for the rest of her life, and now, if she didn't take the new medication that was offered, she would have to go on suffering.

That night, Dr. Joe had a long talk with her, but she was adamant. 'I just can't take them. Please, Dr. Joe, let me stick to the Valium.'

He sighed. 'Very well. But I'm only going to give you another month, and then I'm going to make you take them.'

'I'll try then. Just give me a little while longer. You see Megan's going back, and Jack's got to go home.'

'I understand. Let's leave it a while then. It is very soon after Dr. Margaret's death.'

Even after a month, Tina wasn't ready to take the new drugs, and wouldn't, until she had suffered even more.

Chapter 21

It was two years later. Tina was now thirty-seven. She was still seeing Jack, making love with him, talking psychology. They still had their arguments, but they always made it up, for deep down their relationship was solid and loving. It was a strange kind of love they had, but Jack thought enough of her to put up with that odd kind of relationship. It was either that or nothing.

Jack, Dr. Joe and Richard, who was about to start work at Forest Dene Hospital, all tried to talk to Tina and persuade her take the new drugs, but she wouldn't listen to anyone. She had come to rely on the Valium and was afraid to try anything new.

Megan had now made up her mind that she wanted to study medicine, and possibly psychiatry after that. She had grown so fond of Tina, and understood her, that she wanted to help others as well. The family were delighted when she was accepted at medical school in Bristol. Her course started a month later.

Tina was becoming very run down. Through not eating and looking after herself properly, she had a stream of colds and viral infections. Dr. Donald Williams had advised her to take vitamin supplements, but she complained that they made her heart race. Due to her own self-neglect, her health was deteriorating.

She became very ill. The doctor was sent for, and he advised that Tina should have some blood tests. A week later, Dr. Williams came to see Dr. Joe with the news that Tina had glandular fever, an illness which would confine her to bed for a long time. 'When she gets over this, I strongly advise you to change her medication, as her depression is what is making her neglect herself.'

Tina was acutely ill for three months and had to stay in bed.

Physical illness always terrified her and she was convinced she was dying. She was depressed and lethargic. In Megan's absence everyone else rallied round to support and look after Tina. In Bristol, at medical school, Megan wondered whether she had made the right decision to leave her mother in that state, but she couldn't give up the opportunity for which she had worked so hard.

Slowly, with rest and the love that surrounded her, Tina began to recover. Dr. Joe insisted that she ate properly and took her vitamin supplements.

'I'm going to watch you take them,' he said sternly. 'It's for your own good you know.' He also cut the dose of Valium. The panic attacks began to subside – she almost didn't have the energy for it. Dr. Williams explained to Joe that the aftermath of the illness could sometimes continue for years.

Tina recovered to the extent that she could be out of bed each day, and had been advised to take short walks in the fresh air. She was still weak though, and had to go to bed after lunch, exhausted.

Six months after the onset of the illness, when Tina was obviously making progress, Dr. Williams told Joe that she should change her medication. He felt that the Valium was keeping her down, and that she would begin to make a more complete recovery only when she changed. Joe talked to her. 'We feel that you won't recover properly unless you do change the pills, Tina. In fact, Dr. Williams thinks that if you had taken them when we first talked about it, you might have avoided this illness altogether.'

'This is the second time then that I haven't taken advice and had to suffer for it,' said Tina bitterly, the tears coursing down her face. 'I'm sorry, Dr. Joe, I'm such a nuisance. I'm no good.'

'Don't ever say that. You're just a silly, stupid immature girl, but I love you, we all do, and we just want you to get better.'

'I know. I'll take the tablets. I'll start in the morning.'

That night, she took her last Valium. The next morning, Dr. Joe came in with Millie, with tea and the new pill, which she took willingly, if fearfully. She had suffered enough.

Over the next few weeks, as she felt better and did not have the heart attack she had been frightened of, she came to realise that there was nothing to fear from the new medication. 'I thought they might harm me, Dr. Joe, but now I don't mind them.'

He laughed. 'Well, you haven't had any panic attacks either, have you? We're really pleased with your progress in every way. You look better, and I can tell you're feeling better.'

'Yes,' she said simply. 'I am.'

After three months, Tina was so much improved. Following the advice of Dr. Joe, taking her tablets, looking after herself, she was like a new person. There had been one or two anxiety attacks, but these were minimal compared to before. She still got tired easily, because the debilitating disease would take time to pass.

Jack was thrilled with her progress. She was going out more, asking him to take her into town. Generally she was beginning to enjoy life again.

Just before Christmas, she asked Jack to go with her to Guildford to do her Christmas shopping. That completed, they had lunch in a restaurant and went for a drive in the country. Life felt good.

'Do you know, Jack, I think I'd like another dog, but this time a little boy.'

'If you really think you can take him out and look after him, I'll get you one for Christmas. It would be good to have one a little older, I think, because you still get tired, and it wouldn't be so much trouble.'

'All right, but I want a corgi.'

'You leave it to me.'

Christmas came and everybody congregated at the big house for the party to celebrate Tina's birthday. Although she enjoyed the party, she had lost interest in dancing. She seemed to have changed a lot since taking the new pills. The family had noticed that her personality was changing completely. She was more confident and outgoing, wanting to do things, worrying less about her appearance. Although she had put on weight since her new medication was introduced, she said to Jack, 'You'll have to take me as I am,' – a completely new departure for the girl who had always worried so much about what she looked like. She could even accept that she was getting older.

Megan, home for the holidays, was growing into a beautiful young woman. Even that didn't threaten Tina; she could rejoice in her daughter's looks. Megan noticed the change in her mother – she thought and talked about things these days that had never concerned her before. Keen now on discovering the countryside, she wanted to venture further and find out more. She even spoke to Megan about going back to work at the riding stables.

On Christmas day the whole family went to church. Tina found the service especially moving that year, with its associations of new beginnings and a new life. Church was followed by Christmas lunch and then the ritual of opening the presents round the tree. Jack was absent from the lunch-table – he had taken it into his head to have lunch alone that day. Joe knew the reason – he just wasn't up to it. Tina hadn't noticed, but Joe had, that Jack wasn't very well.

In the midst of the present-opening the bell rang. Tina went to answer it, and there was Jack as expected, but with him was a beautiful little corgi dog, obediently sitting by Jack's side.

'He's gorgeous, Jack!' She flung herself at him in delight.

'Well,' explained Jack. 'I couldn't find one at the kennels, but I saw this one advertised in the paper. His owners are moving and they can't take him. He's three years old, they said, and very well behaved.'

'He's gorgeous,' said Tina again, and the dog jumped up and licked her nose affectionately. 'Has he got a name?'

'Well yes, he's called Marcus – it's a funny name for a dog.'

'Oh, I don't like that. Do you think he could get used to a new name?'

'He's quite young; I expect so.'

'I'd like to call him. . . .' She thought for a moment. 'Barney!' she pronounced triumphantly. 'Dr. Margaret once had a springer called that. I like it.'

'Come on then, Barney,' said Jack. 'Come in and meet the others.' He was a friendly dog and made a great fuss of everyone, rushing around, licking them all. Millie brought the other dogs in to meet him and they all got on famously. 'I want him to sleep in my room,' Tina requested of Millie. 'There's the armchair he can sleep on.'

'Yes, but you'll have to put a rug on it,' said her mother. 'That's a good chair!'

'I'll cover it over,' Tina promised.

They continued the festivities with great enjoyment, only momentarily clouded by the remembrance of Dr. Margaret. Tina also thought of Jane with regret, wishing she could be there to share the wonderful day. She decided to ring her that evening.

'Dad's been very ill,' her friend told her sadly, 'I've had an awful Christmas, but you remember Bill my brother? Well he and his wife are going to have Dad in March for a fortnight, so I'll be able to come then.'

'That's wonderful.'

'Well I'm trying to persuade them to look after him for a month – I've had him all this time.'

'So they should.'

'You sound so much better, Tina – different somehow.'

'Well I am, and I've put on a lot of weight. You know I had that awful glandular fever. It still recurs and makes me tired sometimes, but I'm taking my vitamin pills and eating well, and my new pills have helped my anxiety state. The doctors say I should get over it completely, eventually.'

'I'm glad, but you must still look after yourself – and just think, in three months we can share a room again.'

'Oh, I'm longing to see you, Jane. Happy Christmas.'

'I'll be happier when I'm with you. I really miss you.'

Tina hung up, feeling sorry for Jane, who sounded so miserable. Then she phoned Mr. Willis, who told her that his wife had died some time ago. He hadn't written to let her know. 'Tina, you sound so much stronger. I can hear it even in your voice!'

'I'm sorry about your wife.' She then told Mr. Willis the story of the new tablets and her illness, and he explained that he was still living with the friend who had shared a home with him and his wife, Kathleen.

'Why don't you both come down for a visit?' she suggested.

'No, we can't,' he said hurriedly.

'I thought you'd say that!' she laughed.

'No, we just like to lead a quiet life.'

'OK, Mr. Willis. Thanks for the card and the money. I'll buy something for my dog.'

'You've got a dog? Of your own?'

'Yes – Jack bought it for me for Christmas.'

'That's wonderful. Now look after him won't you?'

'He is to be my dog, and he'll sleep in my room, and I'll be looking after him and taking him out every day,' she stated.

'You are better. Carry on with the good work. I'll go on praying for you.'

'I'll talk to you again soon.' She hung up.

Jack stayed until the new year. Tina noticed that he really wasn't very well, and was able to support him, knowing she had the others around her. He went back after his week at the big house. He had accepted Tina's new personality with a smile.

Jane came as promised in March. What a shock she had when she saw Tina. 'You look so different, Tina!'

'I know.'

'And your hair looks so lovely cut short like that.'

Jane liked the new Tina – she was cheerful, bright and more outgoing. Jane was a country girl too, and they spent a wonderful fortnight in the open air. Jane even persuaded Tina to go for a ride at the stables, which amazed Dr. Joe. They walked the dogs for miles. Tina still needed her rest each afternoon, but she would liven up again in the evening and come down and watch videos with Jane. The sound of their laughter could be heard all over the house.

When it was time for Jane to leave, the two women cried in each other's arms.

'You'll be back again soon,' said Dr. Joe. 'For good next time.'

'I know.'

Dr. Joe and Tina drove Jane to the station. 'You will be back, Jane, won't you?' Tina pleaded. 'Ask your brother if he could have your father more, please.'

'He said he would in the summer. I'll phone you.'

Jane was sorely missed by Tina, but she had other things on her mind. Jack wasn't well at all. Dr. Joe had been worried about him for some time. Now that Tina had noticed it, he explained it all to her. 'Jack's had to give up his work at the hospital – he just can't do it any more.'

'What's wrong with him, Joe? Please tell me. I can take it now.'

'All right. It's best for you to know the truth.'

'I'm not surprised. You see it's over five years that I've been with Jack.'

'What do you mean?'

'Nancy told me that I wouldn't have him too much longer after five years had gone by. That it would be true love, but only for a short time.'

'I see. So you already knew that something was wrong.'

'Well, when I saw he wasn't well, I thought, this is it.'

'Do you know, you would never have been able to talk to me rationally like this when you were on the Valium,' said Dr. Joe in amazement.

'I'm just different now. It's changed my personality, hasn't it?'

'Yes. You look really good now, you're dressing differently, you're leading a much healthier life, eating properly and getting plenty of fresh air.'

'I just don't want to be bothered with dressing up all the time. I like to be comfortable now. I like it here at the big house. Sometimes, I still wish I could have a small house of my very own, that I could go to. You see in that vision Nancy said about doing my painting and I'm beginning to feel that the time's coming soon when I could do it.'

'That's wonderful. You've got a great gift, Tina. Nancy had as well, though she never used it. But your talent is even greater than Nancy's.'

'Will you show me some of her work one day? If it's still around.'

'It is. It was put away with all the old things that belonged to the people of long ago.'

'How romantic! I'd love to see them.'

'I will show you later on, but you've got quite a lot to think about with Jack so poorly.'

'Now tell me about him.'

'You know Jack ate that apple abroad, what we call the forbidden fruit? Well he has repeated occurrences of the illness caused by that, amoebic dysentery, and he has treatment for it, but he was stubborn, and in the first place didn't go for treatment for years, until the disease had got a real hold on him. Now it's affecting his lungs. It's possible that he has an abscess there, but there's nothing that can be done about it – his lungs are already too damaged. They say it's only a matter of time. I'm so sorry. It's now affecting his heart. That's why he gets so tired.'

'That's why he's so irritable, isn't it?'

'Yes, but be patient with him.'

'Actually, he does have wonderful days, you know, when he's really well, and then another day he's so terribly niggly and irritable.'

'Well, it's also affected the back of his neck, so that he would be in constant pain without very strong medication and the painkillers affect his moods. Tina, you're taking this all very calmly. You've really grown up.'

'I try,' said Tina, 'but I'm really going to miss Jack when he does go, and that dear little house. Life will be empty without him. I wish Nancy would come back and tell me what's going to happen next!'

'Well, go and see Jack this afternoon, and see if you can cheer him up.'

'Yes. Could you give me a lift?'

'Yes, of course. Actually, now that you're so much better and you do still get tired if you have to walk a long way, would you like your own car again?'

She grinned. 'I was going to ask if there was a chance of that. If I could have the money from my trust.'

The trust had been set up generations ago, by Bert, the American millionaire whose son Gordon was the first young one at the big house, to look after the young ones in the future and see that they did not go short of anything. Of course there were trustees who looked after the fund and made sure it was not spent frivolously. Dr. Joe and Millie were the current trustees.

'I'll talk to your mother about it. In the meantime you could get back into practice in mine, just round the drive.'

'Oh thank you. I couldn't borrow it this afternoon, could I?' She was at her most persuasive now.

'Well, I'll come with you to make sure your driving's up to scratch, and then I'll walk back. I could use a walk. We'll take the dogs and I'll walk them back. You go and have a rest and we'll go after that.'

After her rest, Tina had some tea and got ready. Joe was downstairs waiting for her. They put all the dogs in the back of the car, and Tina took the wheel. Joe got in beside her. She drove as if she had never stopped. Joe was amazed at her confidence and felt perfectly at ease at the thought of her driving back unaccompanied.

When they arrived with Barney, Jack was sitting in his lounge, looking rested but still far from well. He cheered up at the sight of them. 'Would you make some tea, Tina?' he asked her.

She disappeared into the kitchen to make it. Joe sat down and talked to Jack. 'I've put Tina in the picture about you. She knows everything.'

'Is that wise?' Jack was alarmed for Tina's sake.

'Well, you remember that Nancy told her in a vision about you? She was told something else as well. I won't say any more about that. I'll leave it to her.'

After Joe had drunk his tea, he went off with the dogs to stroll back to the big house, through the woods, the way Nancy used to go.

Jack and Tina had one of their 'psychology' talks that afternoon. 'I must prepare you,' said Jack.

'You know then?'

'Yes, I've known for a long time.'

Tina felt the tears welling up as she listened to him. 'Tina, remember we've had our eight years together.'

'Well, we'll probably have some more.'

'I hope so,' said Jack.

They talked until late and then Jack realised it was ten-thirty. 'You must go, or you'll be exhausted tomorrow, and I'll see you the day after tomorrow.'

'Jack, shouldn't I see you every day now you're sick?'

'No, I just get so tired. I can't manage it.'

'All right, but if you want me, let me know, won't you?'

She got in the car and drove back, confident, even in the dark. She felt proud that Joe had let her use the car. Sitting at the wheel with Barney next to her, she felt so pleased with herself.

Back home, she went straight to bed, thinking deeply about Jack, knowing how much she would miss him. She cried herself to sleep that night, knowing that soon Jack would not be with her. It had to be faced. She knew she was being given the strength to do so.

Some months later, when things were still the same, Tina was seeing Jack every other day and looking after him as much as she could, Eric Brown telephoned. 'Tina, I'd like to see you. I've got a surprise for you.'

'What's that? What is it?' she said urgently.

'I want you to come and have a cup of tea with me tomorrow.'

'I can't tomorrow. You know Jack's very ill, and it's one of my days with him tomorrow. Could I come the day after?'

'All right. Come to tea at three.'

'Can I come on my own, or do you want me to bring someone?'

'Come with your dog.'

'All right,' she agreed. 'I'll try and borrow a car. Dr. Joe will be using his, but it's possible Raymond's will be free. I'm getting a car of my own you know.'

'You lucky girl. I'm glad you're driving again.'

'I feel even more confident now.'

'See you the day after tomorrow then.'

She went into the lounge where Millie and Raymond were sitting facing the woods, talking to Dr. Joe. 'Hello, Mum, Eric's just invited me to tea at the vicarage the day after tomorrow. He says he's got a surprise for me and he wants me to go on my own.'

'Wait and see,' said Dr. Joe, his eyes sparkling.

Millie rounded on him. 'You know something, don't you?'

'I'm saying nothing,' he said firmly. 'I'm the only one apart from Eric who knows the secret.'

'I'll wait then,' said Tina.

'Well you go on to bed now,' said Joe. 'You look tired.'

She went up, consumed with curiosity, racking her brains to think what it could be. That night, she was also consumed with sexual desire, as she thought of the time she had last made love with Jack, a month ago now. She had to relieve her sexual feelings on her own.

The following afternoon, Dr. Joe called Tina to the front door. 'Come here, Tina, Millie. There's a surprise for Tina.' She looked outside and there standing in the driveway was a little Ford Fiesta. She was almost overcome with joy.

'Oh thank you, Dr. Joe. Can I drive it today? Oh please?'

'You can drive it to Jack's,' said Joe smiling. He handed her the keys.

'Can we come with you to Jack's, just for the ride?' asked Millie.

'Of course,' Tina said proudly. So the three of them went, with Barney, and when they got to Jack's, Tina called to him to come and see her little car. Jack looked terrible. 'I've had a bad day today. Tina can stay a couple of hours, but that's all I can manage. I'm sorry.'

'It's all right,' said Joe. 'Why don't you come and stay with us, and be looked after properly?'

'No, I'd rather be on my own.' Jack was still proud and obstinate.

'Please yourself, but remember it's an open invitation.'

'I like the car, Tina,' he said. He looked at it, but wasn't well enough to be as enthusiastic as he once would have been. They all went inside, where Millie made tea for them all. After tea, Joe and Millie took their leave and walked back through the woods. They talked about Jack. 'He looks awful – grey!' said Millie.

'I know. I don't think he's got too much longer. I'll have to warn Tina.'

'I don't think you should. Let things take their course. She's had so many upsets.'

'Well let's hope the surprise at the vicarage will take her mind off Jack.'

Tina helped Jack that day. His housekeeper had stayed on and prepared tea for both of them. After they had eaten, Jack looked crumpled. 'You're so tired,' Tina said to him tenderly. 'Can I help you to bed?'

'I would be grateful. Tina, you could never have coped with this before. You are marvellous.'

'Thank you. I don't like you being here alone, Jack.'

'Come and talk to me for a little while before I go to sleep. I'll be all right.'

'Now, you will call if you need anything, won't you? The phone is right by the bed.'

She sat beside the bed, sad to see him look so poorly. He fell asleep holding her hand. She stroked his head, looking round to make sure that everything was there that he might need.

Tina put an electric kettle by the bed for Jack, so that he could make tea without stirring from the bed. He hadn't far to go to the toilet, and she made sure the phone was close by. Covering him up, she made him comfortable, aware of all the rows of medication surrounding him. She looked down at him, asleep now, so white, and she had a strong feeling that disaster was looming. Beginning to feel quite trembly, she decided she ought to get back home, and said a silent prayer for Jack's safe-keeping, a far cry now from the days when she only thought of herself.

She drove herself home in the new car with Barney, having left Lassie, Jack's old faithful dog, lying beside him, as if she knew he needed her. Dr. Joe was in the lounge with Millie when she arrived back. Raymond had gone to bed. 'Even Raymond's ill,' blurted out Tina. 'It's horrible – everything's horrible again!'

'I'm sorry,' said Dr. Joe. 'Your mother's so worried about Raymond.'

'What's wrong with him?'

'We don't really know – but he has got high blood pressure,' explained Millie. 'He just has to take it easy.'

'Jack's so ill – I'm so worried about him. I don't like him being in the house alone, but he wouldn't let me stay.'

'He's very stubborn,' said Dr. Joe, 'but it's up to him – if he wants help he'll have to ring us.'

'I've put a tray of tea and everything ready for him,' said Tina. 'He has the phone and the kettle right by the bed, and I've left his tablets ready, and let the dog out and put her to bed with him. I left him asleep.'

'Do you mean you put him to bed?' Millie was astounded. 'You did all that? You're doing marvels! We're so pleased with you.'

'And proud!' chimed in Joe.

'That's all right. I'm so tired now, do you mind if I go to bed?'

'Have some supper,' said Millie, 'or you'll feel weak.'

'I'll try a little, but I'm so worried about Jack, I don't know if I can. I do love him.' The tears welled up in her eyes.

'Come on,' said Joe. 'I'll come and have a bit of supper with you. The others have had theirs.' So had he, but he wanted an excuse to be with Tina for a while. He knew if she was alone she probably wouldn't eat anything.

Tina relaxed a little with Dr. Joe, and ate a little while they talked. Then she went to bed. 'I wonder what the surprise is at Eric's tomorrow?' said Joe as he said goodnight. 'Cheer up, Tina. Think of that – it may be something really nice.'

'Maybe it will.' She brightened momentarily at the prospect, but then felt desperate again as she thought of Jack, ill and in pain. Once again she prayed that Jack would get better and that God would not let him suffer. With that prayer on her lips she fell asleep.

The next morning Joe phoned Jack to see how he was. He was aware of just how ill Jack was, with his medical knowledge, and knew he had cause for great concern. Jack was still in bed. 'It was good of her, Joe, to leave the tea all ready for me. I'm so grateful to her, she's been an angel, but would you ask the doctor to call on me today? I feel so awful. These terrible pains in my chest. I was going to call you.'

'I'll call him at once, and I'll be over myself as soon as I can.'

'What about Tina?' asked Jack.

'Perhaps she'd better just go to the vicarage today and if you feel up to it she can call on you tonight.'

'Don't worry her now, please Joe.'

'All right,' said Dr. Joe. 'I'll see you soon.'

Joe didn't mention his conversation with Jack to Tina at breakfast. She was a bit down still. 'Can I see Jack today? Have you heard from him, Joe?'

'He's not feeling too well, but I'm going to call in on him later. You go to tea at the vicarage, and perhaps I can take you up to see Jack tonight. I think it's best if I come with you, as he's so poorly.'

'Right. I'll take myself off to the woods for a think. I'm going to take Barney.' Tina often walked in the woods when she was worried about something, although these days she was much more calm and self-confident. The panic attacks were mainly a thing of the past – she could cope with everything so much better, although she would always need help in a crisis.

Off she went with Barney, to sit by the big tree where all the love and romances had taken place through the generations, remembering how she had met Jack there, and thinking that even though she couldn't cope with marriage, what a wonderful relationship they had. She knew she had to be brave, for she had a clear and powerful intuition that something was going to happen to Jack.

Tina walked sadly back to the house in time for lunch. Dr. Joe had been to see Jack, and had met Dr. Donald Williams there, who had told Jack that he should not be left alone. 'Either you'll have to come into hospital or stay at the big house to be looked after.'

'But I love my little home . . .'

'I'm sorry. You're just not fit to be alone. After all, you've had heart problems and you could have an attack. You know that. Really you should come into hospital for a week. Will you?'

'I don't want to. I'll go to the big house. Dr. Joe, is it all right?'

'Of course. You're welcome. Sylvia can look after you, and Tina will help. I'll be there if you need me.'

'Thank you. The daily woman's in now – she's downstairs; I'll get her to pack my things and she'll be here all day. Could you pick me up this evening, Joe? I'd like to be alone here today.'

'All right, as she's here,' Dr. Williams agreed. 'I'll visit you at the big house tomorrow.'

Jack had a feeling, after they left, that he would not be coming home again. He was right as it turned out.

Joe arrived back at the big house, late for lunch, to tell Tina about Jack before she left for the vicarage.

'Have you seen him?' she asked anxiously.

'Yes, I have. He's very sick. He's not going to be able to stay at home, Tina. He's going to have to go into hospital or come here. But we feel he might be all right here for a while.'

'However did he accept that? He loves his little house.'

'It's sad, but I think he realises that he won't be able to stay there alone.'

'What's going to happen?'

'Well, he's coming over here just after tea. We'll put him in the big spare room. He'll be all right there, and there's plenty of people here to look after him.'

'Including me,' said Tina. 'I'll look after Jack. He's done a lot for me.' She thought how nice it would be to have Jack at the big house, especially as she now knew that he didn't have long to live. At least she would be able to see more of him.

'It's a good thing you're going to the vicarage this afternoon,' said Millie. 'We've got to get ready for Jack, and he'll be here when you get back.'

'All right. I'd better go and have my rest now, and then I'll drive to the vicarage.'

Millie woke her after the rest with a cup of tea, and then Tina dressed in a smart pair of black trousers and a black sweater. With her denim jacket over, she looked quite attractive.

'Do I look all right, Mummy?' She did, with her hair brushed and a little lipstick. Millie liked the way Tina dressed these days, still youthful, but casual and fresh-looking. She drove off with Barney, and Millie, watching her go, realised how much better she was.

Eric greeted Tina with a smile when she arrived at the vicarage. 'I'm glad you've come – I've got a great surprise for you.' She walked into the lounge, wondering what the surprise was. As Eric opened the door for her, there standing in front of her was Mr. Willis.

'Good heavens, Mr. Willis! I never thought you'd travel down here but what are you doing at the vicarage? Why didn't you come to the big house?' She was flabbergasted.

'It's a long story. Sit down and I'll tell you.'

Tina listened eagerly as Mr. Willis looked at her, noticing the changes in her physical appearance. He was most surprised to see how plump she had become, he thought she looked better – better too for not wearing all the make-up and tight clothes of old. He explained what had happened. 'It was all very sudden and quick, Tina. You know that my wife died and I was left with a friend at Exmouth?'

'Yes.'

'Well, she died. I didn't let you know. It was some months ago – she was taken ill suddenly and died very soon afterwards. It was a great shock to me, and I felt so alone. I wanted something to do. I know I'm getting old, but I wanted to do something useful with the rest of my life and I've been so tied to my mother. I always wanted to go into the church, you see, but mother and father would never help me when I was a young man. I've always regretted that. Anyway, I saw an advertisement in the *Church Times* that a vicar needed some help. He didn't necessarily want a curate, just somebody to help in the parish, a sort of lay reader. There was a flat in the vicarage which went with the job, so I got the job and I live here now. I moved out of my home, sold up practically all my things and brought the rest with me. I didn't realise at first it was so close to you. Anyway, once I'd moved in, Eric and I got talking, and he was telling me all about the big house and I realised it was your family. Now that I'm here, after all this time, I really want to help you. Eric has told me about Jack and how ill he is.'

Tina's face clouded over. 'Mr. Willis, I love Jack so much, and he's so ill – will you help?'

'Of course, in any way I can. I'll have a lot to do here, helping Eric, but I'll make time to see you. You can come here whenever you like.'

'Thank you.'

'Now,' said Eric. 'Here's the tea. Tuck in, Tina.'

They enjoyed their tea together, and Mr. Willis entertained Eric and his wife with stories of Tina's antics when she was young. Tina roared with laughter, and Eric realised how much she must have changed. She stood up at last. 'I must go now, Jack's being moved into the room upstairs at the big house. He can't be alone in his house any more.'

'We'll pray for him,' said Eric.

'Would you like me to come back with you?' asked Mr. Willis.

'It would be nice, just for an hour, to meet the family. I'd love it. I'm so pleased to see you.'

Tina drove Mr. Willis back to the big house, thrilled to pieces about the surprise the family would get when they saw him. When they arrived, Jack was already installed. He had been helped to bed straight away, on doctor's orders. 'Come in, Mr. Willis, come and meet the family.' They were all sitting at the supper table. Tina called to Sylvia, 'Lay another place – I've got a guest!'

They went into the dining room and Tina proudly introduced everybody. 'This is Mr. Willis!'

'Good God!' exclaimed Millie. 'The Mr. Willis that doesn't travel. How did you get here? What on earth's happened, Tina?'

Tina explained how Mr. Willis had come to the vicarage and was now living there.

'What a coincidence!' said Millie. 'This house seems full of them.' Joe hoped that Mr. Willis would be able to help and support Tina, for he knew that Jack would not be alive too much longer. Mr. Willis had come at just the right time.

They enjoyed the supper-party, and everyone took to Mr. Willis. The feeling was mutual He told them all the story about the advertisement in the *Church Times*. 'You see I didn't realise it was so near you, until I got here. I've got such a poor sense of direction,' he laughed.

'Welcome to the family,' said Dr. Joe. 'Another friend. We could use you now, Mr. Willis.'

After supper they all went into the big lounge, and Tina excitedly told Mr. Willis about the mystical woods. 'What a wonderful view!' he said. They sat drinking coffee for a while and Tina took Mr. Willis up to meet Jack. When she opened the door of his room, Jack was sitting up in bed, looking very frail. He had picked at his supper but that was all. 'Well, Jack, it's lovely to see you. I'm glad you're here. We'll look after you.' She kissed him. Mr. Willis could see how much love there was between them. 'Jack, this is Mr. Willis.'

'How do you do?' said Jack. 'I'm sorry you've got to see me in a state like this.' He put on as a cheerful a voice as he could, but his blue eyes looked hollow, above his thin frail body. There was no hiding that Jack was very sick. His illness had caught up with him at last.

'You take it easy,' said Mr. Willis. 'We'll be praying for you, Eric and I.'

'Thank you. I'm glad you're here – company for Tina now and again.'

They chatted for a little longer, and Tina took Mr. Willis downstairs where Joe took him to the car and drove him back to the vicarage. Tina went back upstairs to Jack. They sat quietly together, Tina holding his hand. When he needed to rest, Tina went to bed as well. 'Now remember, the intercom's here. The buzzer's in Joe's room if you want him in the night.' She left the room, feeling worried and concerned.

Over the next few days, Jack showed no improvement. Dr. Donald Williams came in daily, but it was clear that he was not going to rally. Eric and Mr. Willis came and spent hours talking to him, for he knew that he was going to die. Eric helped him to overcome his fears of dying, explaining the spiritual life to him. It was a great help to Jack, for he knew that he would be all right, but he didn't want to leave Tina and made Mr. Willis promise to keep an eye on her. 'She told me that there would be someone else, after me – perhaps it's you,' he said to Mr. Willis.

'I'm an old man now, I could only be a friend to her,' Mr. Willis replied.

'Well you could help her psychologically, perhaps. That's what she needs,' said Jack. 'Will you promise?'

'Yes.'

During the month that followed, Tina tried to be brave, but she was becoming more and more depressed. Even though she saw Mr. Willis a few times, and he was a great comfort to her, she felt the weight of Jack's illness.

One night, Jack buzzed Dr. Joe on the intercom. 'I think I'm having a heart attack,' said Jack. He was in a cold sweat, with severe chest pains.

Joe examined him swiftly. 'I'm afraid you'll have to go into hospital, Jack.' He rang the ambulance immediately, and they arrived and quietly took Jack to the hospital, accompanied by Joe. He was rushed straight into intensive care, but had another heart attack as he arrived, His heart stopped, but the medical staff were there and quickly resuscitated him, using electric shocks to his heart. When Jack regained consciousness, he knew that he had been 'dead' and they had brought him back to life. He had been sitting on the railings, and saw himself on the bed.

After two days in intensive care, Jack was moved out to a large ward, as he was much improved. Although he was still too weak to get out of bed, he made friends with the man next door, who would come and sit in the chair next to Jack's bed and talk for hours. Jack told him about his death experience and how he had seen himself being brought back to life. Sitting there on the railings, observing himself, he had felt so well, like he had as a young man. He really wanted to stay there, and then suddenly he was back, in his body and in the bed. 'That happens quite a lot when someone is near death,' said his new friend. It's an out-of-body experience. There have been lots of cases recorded.'

Jack believed him – it was logical when he thought about it. 'It's taken away a lot of my fears,' he said. 'Fears of dying, I mean.'

'It would. It happened to my wife. She nearly died several years ago in an accident. She felt as if she was going through a tunnel and saw a beautiful bright light at the end of it, but then she had to go back.'

Jack pondered about his experience, wondering why he had had it, and what it meant. He eventually came to the conclusion that he needed to come back so that he could tell Tina about it, and prepare her for his death. He started to make good progress, and was soon feeling much better. Eric and Mr. Willis came to see him, and he told them about his experience. 'It's a great comfort to me,' said Jack.

'I'm glad it happened,' said Eric. 'You won't be so worried now, and we can help you spiritually; we're praying to give you strength.'

'Thank you. Tina's coming later. I'm so looking forward to seeing her.'

She came that afternoon with Millie, and she and Jack talked about many things. She couldn't stay very long, but was amazed when he told her what had happened to him. He told her the whole story.

'It's wonderful!' said Tina. 'I bet you'll live for ages now, Jack.'

'I do feel much better.'

Jack would never be completely well, but he was well enough to go back to the big house a fortnight later. He stayed there, as his doctors had advised him that he couldn't live alone again. For the next nine months his condition was up and down, and he went back into hospital a few times.

Just before Christmas, around the time of Tina's fortieth birthday, David came over from Canada to see Jack and to spend Christmas with the family. Jack was overjoyed to see him, and the family just had a small, quiet party that year. No dancing and music, just a dinner party which they all enjoyed.

Although Tina had a wonderful birthday and was thrilled that Jack was there, after all his illness, she was dreadfully disappointed that Jane couldn't be there. The children came though, and they all seemed happy. Megan was now set on the path to be a psychiatrist, working very hard at her exams, and Robert, now a solicitor living in Guildford, was getting married. He announced it at the party, and asked if he and his future bride, Joanne, could come and live at the big house. Millie and Raymond were so glad to have Robert at home again. Richard was at the party too, with his new girlfriend. It was such a happy time. The atmosphere was lightened by the arrival of all the young people; even Jack felt it and cheered up no end.

Tina had a wonderful time on her birthday, in spite of the gloom of the previous months. She enjoyed young company, and felt revitalised.

At Christmas, everything was as they usually had it – the tree in the hall, the presents, the floodlights outside. Tina had done her Christmas shopping with Megan for company, and everything was now ready. Christmas itself was good fun for everyone, but in the midst of the good cheer, Tina suddenly had the strong feeling that this would be Jack's last Christmas. She did her utmost to ensure that he had a marvellous time, and he did. He came down to lunch, and then again in the evening, when Mr. Willis came for supper. Mr. Willis gave him a lot of spiritual guidance, and Jack requested that Mr. Willis would talk to Tina, help her and guide her when he was gone, and felt more at ease knowing that this would be so.

In the evening after supper, everybody sat in the lounge, looking out at the mystical woods. With the grounds floodlit, the trees were illuminated and looked beautiful. They all agreed that it was one of the best Christmas days they had spent for a long time.

After Christmas, they all got on with their lives. Megan went back to college, Richard went back to Forest Dene Hospital and Robert returned to his office to work in Guildford. Jack continued on an even keel, and the family started to make arrangements for Robert's wedding.

What concerned Tina most about the wedding day was what she would wear. Eventually she chose a silk suit with voluminous trousers, which Millie did not approve of at all. 'Really Tina, you look awful in that thing!'

'I don't care!' said Tina confidently. 'I'll wear what I like.'

In the event, Tina wore the suit, a dark blue silk, and looked fine. With it she wore her boots, much to everyone's amazement, and gold jewellery – a pair of earrings that Dr. Margaret had given her long ago, and a necklace and bracelet. She was still a law unto herself.

The bride looked beautiful in white, a creation of lace, which went with her delicate looks. She came downstairs, wearing her veil which set off her pale gold hair and blue eyes. Many of her relatives had come down for the wedding, and they were joined by Megan, looking darkly attractive as always, Millie, Sylvia, Robert and Richard, all dressed up for the occasion. The only sad thing was that Jack couldn't go to the wedding, and Mr. Willis kindly came up to sit with him, so that he wasn't left alone.

The church was packed, with all the relatives from the big house, and many of the people from the village came to look at the spectacle. It was indeed a moving and magical wedding. Those two were so much in love. After the service, there was a reception at the big house. There was music and dancing, a wonderful buffet in the reception hall, champagne flowing, a wonderful atmosphere. The young couple gave speeches, as did Raymond and Millie, and Joe. Everybody felt the magic of the occasion.

Joanne went to change into her going away outfit, in the large room that would be theirs when they returned from their honeymoon to live permanently at the big house. The two were seen off on their honeymoon to Italy, and the rest of the revellers continued with the party.

Chapter 22

About a month after the wedding, Jack frantically rang the buzzer in Joe's room in the middle of the night. Joe knew something serious was wrong, and went rushing in to him. 'Jack, what's wrong? Oh my God!' He stood transfixed as he saw Jack coughing up blood. He knew this was the beginning of the end and, collecting himself, he rang the ambulance immediately. Once in hospital Jack seemed to pick up a little. The next day he was sitting up in bed in the ward, and to everyone's amazement, he looked quite well, almost his old self. Tina came in to see him.

'Do you know, I'm going to be all right this time!' he greeted her.

'You've said that a lot of times,' she said quietly. 'You must be like the cat with nine lives.'

'I must be, I feel really well again today. I'm sure I'll be home again soon.'

They talked quietly for a while, then she kissed him and left. He waved to her as she was leaving, and she turned around and looked at him. She waved back and continued on, until she felt, as she got to the end of the corridor, that she wanted to go back and kiss him once more. Panic set in as she turned and rushed back into the ward.

'Jack! she said urgently. 'I love you so much.'

'And I love you, you silly sausage! Don't worry, I'll be all right.'

'I know.'

She came back again and again to wave to him, and Jack was getting quite worried about her. There must be something wrong. He knew how sensitive she could be. She dragged herself away at long last, and Jack lay there, thinking. He didn't want to eat, since he'd been in hospital; he just felt very thirsty. For the rest of the day he was fine.

That evening Joe came in on his way home from work. 'I'm sure I'll be all right this time, Joe, but Tina seemed so worried when she left.' Joe passed it off with a reference to how Tina got agitated sometimes over nothing. But Joe did wonder; Jack seemed too well somehow. Joe left with the promise that he would call in the next day. 'I'm sure Tina will be in as well.'

That night Jack was in such good spirits, laughing and joking with the nurses until the small hours. Eventually the night nurse had to call a halt.

'For heavens sake, settle down Jack – you're keeping everyone awake!'

'I feel so much better.'

Eventually just after half-past three Jack called out – he was coughing up blood. The nurse rang the buzzer for the emergency doctor, but by the time he got there Jack was gone. He had died instantly from a haemorrhage in the lung.

The doctor rang Joe. 'It was so sudden,' said the doctor. 'I'm sorry.'

Joe was philosophical. 'He seemed too well when I visited him. I know that can happen sometimes. I'll make all the arrangements. He hasn't got any one over here.'

Joe explained it to Tina the next morning. She was beside herself with grief, sobbing uncontrollably. Even though she had had nine good years with Jack, and this last Christmas, and she knew she ought to be grateful for that, she was absolutely devastated. She had known. Now she was bereft of her counsellor, lover and friend in one stroke.

Dr. Joe made all the funeral arrangements. Tina just couldn't make herself go, although she wanted to. Millie stayed at home with her, but Tina became very withdrawn and insisted on being alone. She lay on her bed, thinking of Jack and the past, and then the empty bleak future without him. 'I hope I see my lady again soon. She said there'd be something else.' She felt completely alone. Megan was away, Jane was away. Millie came in and tried to comfort her, but she cried inconsolably.

The funeral was attended by everyone else at the big house. Reverend Eric Brown spoke some very kind words about Jack's life, how he had helped at the hospital, how he felt he had been guided to come to England to help Tina.

Chapter 23

After Jack's death, Tina could not adjust. She took it very badly, worse than anyone had thought she would. It had hit her so hard. She couldn't truly believe that it could happen to her beloved Jack. He had been the love she had waited for – the only love she would ever have, she thought. Her heart was broken.

After a month, Tina still stayed in her room most of the time, wondering why Jack had been taken from her. Mr. Willis and Eric tried to talk to her, to comfort her, but she was so depressed. She just didn't know what to do with herself. Her mother and Dr. Joe tried their best to help her, but she was beyond their reach.

Jack had only had a little money when he died, but he had made a will and put his affairs in order. He felt that the house should go to Tina, especially as it used to be Nancy's house. Somehow he felt it belonged in the family. Tina had always said to him that she would love a little house of her own, where perhaps she could live with a companion, and Jack had also instinctively felt that in the future Tina would use her talent as an artist. With this in mind, he left the house and contents to her. There was no one else to leave it to. The car, he left to Megan in memory of her kindness and goodness to Tina. There was a little money in his savings account, and he left that to Dr. Joe to help those at Forest Dene Hospital.

When Joe heard the will, he was very touched. He went straight home to tell Tina. 'Where is she?' he asked Millie when he got home.

'She's moping in her room again,' said Millie matter-of-factly.

'Come up with me, Millie. I've got some good news for Tina,

and I'd like you hear it; and Megan's home this weekend, isn't she? I want her to be there as well.'

'It must be good news,' said Millie. 'We all need some cheering up at the moment.'

He went up to Tina's room. 'I want to talk to you, Tina.'

'I don't feel like it!' snapped Tina.

'I must talk to you. Please come down,' he said firmly. 'Millie and Megan and I will be waiting in the lounge. I've some good news for you.'

'I don't want to!'

'Please yourself.' He knew that curiosity would get the better of her. He was right. Ten minutes later, Tina came down the stairs and dragged herself into the lounge, sitting down on the settee facing the mystical woods. Megan took Tina's hand. Joe sat opposite.

'I've got some good news for you,' Joe began. 'Jack made a will, and I heard it today at the solicitor's. He's left you his house, Tina, for your future.'

'What would I want with the house?'

'Jack thought you might be glad of it in the future, for your painting, and when Jane comes back. You might like to stay there sometimes. Jack felt that when the big house gets crowded with all the youngsters and their families, you won't like the noise and fuss. He thought you'd be glad of the chance for some quiet sometimes.'

Tina was looking animated, for the first time since Jack had died. 'I see what you mean.'

'The house and contents are yours.' He handed her an envelope. 'There's a letter for you from Jack, about the house, and the keys.

'Isn't it wonderful, Dr. Joe – that house was once Nancy's and now it's really in the family. I'm so grateful to Jack; he must have really loved me.' The tears welled up in her eyes.

She read the letter, as her tears overflowed. It explained everything. The house was to remember him by, in the hopes that she would do her painting there, and it would stay in her family for the future. She brightened up considerably after she had read Jack's poignant letter. 'Oh Dr. Joe, I'm going to have my own furniture. Mum, you're one of the trustees – may I sell the furniture that's there and buy what I want? Something light and cheerful. I loved Jack, but his furniture was so dowdy. I could sell it and use some money from my trust to add and buy some new stuff.'

'Oh, could you?' said Millie doubtfully.

'Yes, I could, it's my money.'

'She's right,' said Joe, winking at Millie. 'She ought to have some cheerful furniture.' Joe was delighted that she was taking an interest in the house.

It was agreed and Tina was glad, as she knew she needed something to occupy her mind. Apart from seeing Mr. Willis, mooching around at the riding stables and watching videos, she had very little to occupy her at all. The idea of making that house her own, and doing her painting there, was suddenly very attractive.

Then there was the car.

'Megan, you need a car, don't you?' said Dr. Joe.

'Yes, I'm saving up for one.'

'Well Jack left his car to you. He knew you were saving for one, and how much you loved that car of his.'

Megan flushed with excitement and disbelief. 'The car's mine?'

'It's outside now, and here are the keys.'

Megan cried for joy.

'I'm so glad,' said Tina. 'We'll have lots of fun. Will you help me get the house ready?'

'I will at weekends, and I've got my holidays next month. It'll be great – we'll have such a good time.'

They flew upstairs to the bedroom and starting making plans.

'What a relief!' said Millie. 'It looks as if she is going to be all right now. This couldn't have happened at a better time.'

'Jack thought she would be like this, and that the house would give her an interest. She needs something of her own, and somewhere of her own, now she's getting older. She won't like the children when they start coming along – I'm sure there are going to be lots of children later on.'

'You're right,' sighed Millie. 'I suppose we're all getting older. I'm quite worried about Raymond actually, his blood pressure is very high. He's not going to like a lot of noise either. There's something I've got to tell you Joe, and it might as well be now. Raymond and I have decided to move away, somewhere quiet.'

'Well, where would you go?' Joe was shocked. 'It's quiet enough here.'

'Well I know it won't be in the future,' said Millie firmly. 'A little bird told me of a plan that you might have for the big house in the future.'

'I know, but that doesn't mean you have to move away.'

'We've made our decision, Joe. We just want to be on our own.'

'Where are you going? Have you planned anything?'

'We've decided to go to Cornwall. Raymond loves it there as you know, and I love the rugged scenery, so different to here. Our plan is to take a holiday there next month, find somewhere to buy and then go there from time to time to get it ready. When it's exactly as we want it, we'll retire there.'

'That's wonderful! I'll be really sorry to see you go, and the house will be empty without you, but the future of the big house is going to be with young people. I'll be the old one then, and Vicky.'

'Well, we don't want to move for a year, because of Jack's death – we don't want to give Tina another shock. By then, you never know, Jane might be back.'

'Yes. I've heard her father is very sick.'

'It's all settled then,' said Millie. 'We'll forget about it for now. It'll be interesting to see how Tina manages with the house.'

'Well, I don't think it will be much of a problem. Listen to that!'

They could hear Tina and Megan upstairs, shrieking with excitement and laughter.

Megan took Tina out for a spin in her new car that evening. After an exhilarating drive around the country lanes, they went to Jack's house, which was to be Tina's new home. For a few moments she felt very sad, and the tears brimmed over, but Megan comforted her, reminding her that Jack was no longer suffering. He was at peace.

'I know,' said Tina.

They went round the house thinking about what Tina would keep and what she would dispose of. She especially wanted to keep the desk, which would always remind her of Jack, and she decided that she would have Jack's old room as her bedroom. It had been Nancy's old room too, and she loved the atmosphere. At last she owned a little house, just as she had wished for when she was a young girl at school.

Tina threw herself into organising the house, helped by Megan at weekends, when she proudly drove herself from college in her new car. Tina had acquired a new self-confidence. The panic attacks were almost a thing of the past.

All the furniture, apart from Jack's desk, some chairs and the television, was sold at an auction, even the pictures. Then Tina went to Guildford, accompanied by Megan, Millie and Dr. Joe and chose everything she wanted to furnish the house to her taste.

During the week before it was delivered, she had fresh paint put everywhere in the house, in bright cheerful colours. That newly-furnished, light and pretty house would be the symbol of the start of a new life for Tina.

She was ready to start her painting again, as Jack had wanted her to do, and she had one of the upstairs rooms as a studio. 'As Nancy said to me in the vision, I would start painting again when the time was right – and I think this is the time she meant. Now I've got my own little home and peace and quiet to do it. I'm going to buy the paints and things next week.'

That night, Dr. Joe took Tina in to a big old room at the back of the big house and they looked through what seemed like an Aladdin's cave of old treasures. There were old ornaments which used to belong to Nancy, which Dr. Joe said Tina could have, then they looked at Nancy's old paintings, some from when she was very young. The two that Tina noticed especially were stunning – a picture of the woods, with a young couple illuminated from above, and one of the two dogs playing on the front lawn. She asked Joe if there was enough money left in her trust fund to have them framed, for she had spent such a lot on furnishings and equipping her home.

Joe, to Tina's delight, offered to buy them for her for her birthday and Christmas. She decided to have some gold-coloured ones and pine ones. 'They won't be too expensive, Dr. Joe, and thank you!'

Nancy had done many imaginative paintings, of imaginary worlds with fairies, imps and elves. The beautiful and delicate colours led Tina to think that Nancy must indeed have had a great gift, and a beautiful mind, to have expressed herself in this way.

By the following weekend everything was in place – all Tina's painting equipment in her studio, and many of Nancy's paintings adorned the walls. Tina was so proud of her little house as she looked around and she dearly hoped that one day her large bedroom, which had been Nancy's, would be shared by her and Jane, for she still missed her dear friend. The room was dominated by a huge king-sized bed for, as she explained to Dr. Joe and Millie, she would want to share it with Jane when she came back.

'Don't get the wrong idea, Mummy, we just like to be close. We're not gay or anything.'

'I know,' said her mother, laughing.

'Anyway, it will be warmer in the winter.'

The colour scheme was a pretty pale green, with curtains and bed-linen to match, the green echoing the deeper green of the woods outside the window. Tina was thrilled with it, and with the smaller guest room, decorated in blue with co-ordinating fittings – all ready to receive a guest, especially, Tina hoped, Megan if she wanted to stay when she was home from college.

So Tina evolved a new routine. She didn't live at the little house, but spent most of her days there, accompanied by Megan at the weekends, enjoying the tranquil atmosphere and looking forward to when she would start her painting.

Chapter 24

Joanne gave birth to a son a few months later, much to Robert's delight. They named him Julian Paul. Tina was pleased for them and went to the christening, although she wasn't really interested in babies. She treated her dog like a child and preferred it that way. Of course the family watched anxiously for any signs that baby Julian had inherited Nancy's condition but they wouldn't be able to tell for a while.

Richard and Ruth had some good news as well – they were getting married very soon. The wedding took place just before Christmas, and Tina was reflecting on the year just past, as she realised what a lot had happened in those twelve months. Jack had died, Julian had been born, Tina had a new house and now there was to be another wedding in the family. Richard and Ruth would be living at the big house after they were married. So much had changed.

Tina didn't yet know that Millie and Raymond would be moving away. They had been to Cornwall, as planned, for a holiday, and bought a cottage, just big enough for the two of them and a housekeeper.

Christmas that year was loud and crowded with so many new occupants at the big house. Megan came home just before Tina's birthday, with an important announcement to make. She was in love. She had met a boy in Bristol, and they were very happy together. Megan was nervous about telling Tina, for she knew it might upset her, especially as they were to get engaged. She had had many love affairs in the past which she didn't take seriously, but this boy was important to her. She explained to Paul, her fiancé, about Tina her child-mother, and asked him just to accept Tina as she was. 'I will, of course,' he replied.

'She's going to be upset, so be prepared,' warned Megan. She had told him everything, and about the possibility of having a child like Tina. He loved her enough, he said, to accept that risk, and was willing to live at the big house as Megan had asked him to. She would soon be qualified as a doctor and psychiatrist and hoped to work at Forest Dene. Paul was an accountant and knew that he would be able to get work in Guildford.

On Tina's birthday, her forty-first, she couldn't help remembering the previous year when Jack was alive. But she also remembered how ill he had been and how he had suffered. Still there was plenty going on to keep her cheerful. Megan was expected, Jane would be phoning her with news of a possible visit after Christmas.

Just before Megan was due to arrive, Dr. Joe called Tina in to the big lounge. He knew that Megan was bringing Paul with her, and he felt he had to give Tina some warning. 'I've something to tell you, Tina. Megan's coming home, as you know.'

'I know,' said Tina happily. 'She'll be able to sleep in with me.'

'I know. But there'll be a guest in the next room.'

'Who's that? Is she bringing a friend?'

'Not exactly. She's bringing a boyfriend and they're getting engaged and they're getting married very quickly.'

'That's not fair!' cried Tina. 'Megan promised to always look after me, and love me!' She was furious with jealousy. She stamped her foot, and ran up to her room crying.

Dr. Joe ran after her. 'Oh Tina, try to accept it.'

'It's my birthday and she's spoilt it. I hate her!' she raged.

Tina refused to get ready for her party; she just lay on the bed, sobbing. Dr. Joe had to leave her in the end, for Megan had arrived with Paul. She could see by Dr. Joe's face what had happened. She introduced Paul to Dr. Joe, who didn't take to the young man, and Millie felt uneasy about him when she was introduced. Still, it was Megan's choice and they decided to accept him.

'Go and see Tina,' Joe urged her. 'Please try and persuade her to come down.'

Megan went upstairs to where Tina was lying on the bed in her old jeans and sweater, staring out of the window. As soon Megan came into the room she said furiously through gritted teeth, 'I hate you, Megan. I don't want anything more to do with you. Don't sleep with me. Go and sleep with him!'

'I know you must be jealous, Tina, but I'm young and I'm in love, and I'm qualifying soon. Then we're getting married and coming to live here.'

'Well, I shan't stay here then. I shall go to my place and live.'

'You can't go there on your own. You'll have to wait until you get a housekeeper or something. I don't want to be the cause of you going. We'll find somewhere else to live if it's going to upset you.'

'You'll do nothing of the sort,' said Millie, walking in. 'This is your home too, and Tina's just got to accept it.'

They eventually persuaded Tina to go downstairs, still in her old clothes, by which time the party was nearly over. Dr. Joe felt he had to explain to the guests that Tina was upset. Mr. Willis was there and came to try to talk it over with her. 'I don't like Paul,' she said petulantly. Having met the young man, she had taken an instant dislike to him. He had thought she was behaving like a spoilt child, and had no patience with her at all. Megan wondered, then, if she had done the right thing in agreeing to marry him. They had just announced their engagement.

Tina went back upstairs and Millie helped her to bed, where she drifted into a restless sleep. When Megan came up to say goodnight, Tina was already fast asleep, curled up into a little ball, just like a child.

Nancy appeared to Tina that night. 'Tina, you've spoilt your birthday. I know you don't like Paul, but I've come to tell you to be nice to everybody. Don't spoil Christmas for Megan. She's terribly fond of you. I have something else to tell you, which you must promise not to tell anyone. Megan will not marry her young man. He will let her down. I can tell you no more now. Now be nice to her. As for you, Jane will come back and you will spend the rest of your days together. I promise that.'

'Thank you, Nancy.'

'But you must try to be unselfish about Megan, and not ruin Christmas for everyone. They don't deserve it. You've been so blessed, and Tina, try to start your painting soon. Now remember you're not to tell anyone of what I have told you.'

'I promise, Nancy.'

With that Nancy disappeared, and Tina slept peacefully for the rest of the night. The next morning she remembered the vision vividly. She got up as if nothing had happened; she was her happy self again, much to everyone's amazement. She was even polite to Paul.

Everyone then got busy preparing for Christmas. It was a traditional big house Christmas, with an enormous tree, with decorations sparkling in the light from the crystal chandelier, surrounded by piles of presents. The garden was lit up like a fairy tale. Christmas was lively that year, with the now extended family in residence – almost too lively for Millie and Raymond.

'I'll be glad when we're in our own little place,' whispered Raymond to Millie in the middle of the festivities. Tina's day was made when Mr. Willis came to spend Christmas day with the family. Everybody sat round the tree replete after lunch and exchanged their presents. What a wonderful time they all had, although the day was tinged with a little sorrow at the thought of Jack, who was missing.

After Christmas, Megan tried to spend as much time with Tina as she could, but Paul was very possessive of her and didn't like it at all. He had no understanding of Tina and her condition. Megan began to feel uncomfortable, and couldn't wait to leave. They went back to Bristol after a fortnight.

Tina started to paint after Megan left. She wasn't herself though, and Dr. Joe wondered if the medication she was on was affecting her. She seemed permanently tired. It seemed as if her metabolism had slowed right down – she was gaining weight and seemed very sluggish, as well having problems with her menstrual cycle. Dr. Joe reduced the dose of the drugs to see if that would help her, and she did improve.

In the summer it was time for Raymond and Millie to move to Cornwall. Tina had to be told, but she handled the news with great calm.

'I doubt we'll ever come back here,' said Millie. 'We just want to be quiet now. But you can come down and see us, and we can keep in touch by phone.'

Tina accepted the move completely – there had never been much love lost between Millie and her daughter. They had grown closer over the years, but Tina had matured too, so she could cope with change more readily.

When Millie and Raymond drove off the day after a removal van had gone down with their things, Tina cried. She said 'Good luck to you both. Be happy,' as she kissed them goodbye.

'Come and stay as soon as we're settled in.'

'I will when Jane comes back,' promised Tina.

They looked back at the big house as they left, but felt no

regrets. They were looking forward to living in their cottage near Penzance. Peace and quiet at last, thought Millie.

Tina missed her mother for a while after she moved, but she soon got over it.

Chapter 25

When Julian was three years old, he was tested for signs of the inherited condition that ran in the family. To everyone's relief he was found to be normal, and Joanne was expecting another child. Richard and Ruth had had a son, Joe, and were looking forward to having more. Ruth stayed at home to look after little Joe.

Tina sometimes found the children a bit much and wished she could go to her own little house to live, but she wasn't very well – still she had side-effects from her medication and her metabolism was very slow. At forty-five too, she was having the beginnings of the menopause proper. She had seen a gynaecologist, who had wanted to operate, but she was too run-down to undergo the operation. Tina was not fit physically, but also she had been found psychologically unfit to have a hysterectomy. The hormones she had been prescribed did not help; they caused headaches. She was becoming more and more sensitive to all sorts of medication. She just had to put up with the troublesome symptoms, but it made her very angry. All she could do was wait.

Megan, now qualified, was working in a hospital in Bristol, still engaged to Paul.

By the summer of the following year, with Megan still away, and no sign that Jane was coming back, Tina became very restless and unsettled. With two more additions to the young families, Geoffrey and Susan, the big house was not a tranquil place to be. Tina realised why Millie had gone away. She wanted to go to stay with her parents, but couldn't go alone and no-one had time to go with her. She was beginning to feel pushed out. Vicky, the proud grandmother spent more and more time with the children, and Dr. Joe and Richard had their work to do as well.

She felt isolated. The only person she felt close to was Sylvia the housekeeper. She prayed every night for Jane to return. Mr. Willis was a faithful friend and she saw him most days at her own little house. 'I'd go mad if it wasn't for you,' she confided in him one day.

'Well I've always liked you, Tina, and it's nice for me to spend time with someone younger!'

I'm so miserable at the big house now. I feel as if it belongs to a new generation.'

'Well, it does in a way.'

'Dr. Joe and Vicky don't seem to mind.'

'Well they wouldn't. They're the head of the house now that your mother's gone. And Megan's all but gone.'

'I know – it's awful.'

'I feel that something's very wrong with Megan. I feel very concerned.'

'So do I,' said Tina. 'I've tried to get in touch with her with no luck. Dr. Joe has asked her to come back and apply for a job at Forest Dene. She hasn't married Paul. Something's gone wrong.'

'I think we'll find out soon,' said Mr. Willis. 'I've got a feeling about it.'

After Megan and Paul had got engaged, they went back to Bristol. They lived together for a while and she adored her fiancé, but Paul did not understand about the young ones at the big house, the interests Megan had, and he refused point-blank to consider living at the big house when they were married. 'We'll live here, near my family.' He was adamant.

'Well, I shan't marry you then,' retorted Megan. 'If I marry anyone, we'll have to live at the big house.'

'Well, I'll think it over.'

So they had carried on at Bristol as they were. Megan qualified and continued to work in the hospital there. They carried on living together, but soon they were leading quite separate lives. Paul went out a lot without Megan. She suspected that he was seeing someone else. She knew too after living with him that he was not a sincere person and that the relationship would have to end, even though they were still physically attracted to each other. Having decided to confront Paul about everything, she missed a period. She went for a pregnancy test which proved to be positive. Now she was in a quandary. She wondered briefly if she could make it work with Paul, but the thought of being married to him was repugnant to her, knowing that even now he was out with other girls. Knowing that the situation was impossible, she decided to have it out with Paul that night. She went home to their miserable little flat, devoid now of the loving atmosphere that had been so magical when they were first together. Paul had just come home, and announced, as soon as he saw Megan, that he had to work that evening. 'I don't believe you!' She faced him head-on. 'You were seen out with somebody else last night.'

'Well, I wasn't doing any harm – it was just a work colleague.'

'You shouldn't do that if you're living with me.'

'If you don't want me any more, Megan, just say so.'

'I'm having a baby,' she stated flatly. 'Your child.'

Paul didn't seem thrilled at all – he suddenly looked crumpled and depressed.

'It's not going to work,' said Megan.

'Well, get rid of it then,' he said in a hard voice.

For the first time she saw him in his true colours, and she knew it would never work. He didn't want her or the baby. Somehow she felt relieved. Her mind was made up. She would take the job she had been offered at Forest Dene and finish with Paul. She would have the baby at the big house and bring it up herself. Paul broke into her thoughts. 'Well? Are you going to get rid of it?'

'No, I'm not,' she snapped.

'Well, don't expect me to stand by you. I've got someone else. I'm going!'

'Good riddance!'

'Well what about support for the baby? I'm honourable enough to help you there.'

'I don't want a penny of your money. Just leave me. Now!' She walked out of the flat, unable to stand the sight of him any longer. She was glad to be rid of him. As she walked down the road, she felt light, liberated. Seeing a little café, she stopped for something to eat, realising that now she was having a child, she would have to look after herself.

She went back to the little flat. Paul was gone, bags and baggage. He hadn't wasted a minute. Megan was relieved. She sat down and rang faithful Dr. Joe.

'I've got some news for you, but I'm not going to tell you on the phone. I'm coming home and I'll accept that job they offered me at Forest Dene if it's still vacant.'

'I'm so pleased to hear from you – and yes the job's still vacant. But what's wrong?'

'I've let you all down, I know it, especially Tina.'

'Yes, you have,' said Joe. 'She's very upset – and she's sick of all the children at the big house, sick of the lot of us I think. She's missing her mother, missing all the old times with Dr. Margaret and Jennifer. She's not happy but she likes the little house and wishes you and Jane were back. I think she'd move in there if Jane was there, or you.'

'I've thought of that,' said Megan. 'You see . . . Oh, I'll tell you all about it. I'll be there tomorrow night.'

'All right. See you then.'

Megan went into her workplace the next day and explained that she had finished with Paul and needed to make a complete break and go home. She was allowed to leave without notice and almost sang as she went back to the flat in her car. She couldn't wait to get home and set about packing her things in a hurry. As quickly as she could she got everything packed and got into the car, feeling lighter by the minute. Off she drove, back to Surrey and the big house.

Arriving just before tea-time, she found that Dr. Joe was still at work and Tina was at her own house, painting that afternoon and was expecting Mr. Willis for tea there. Vicky greeted her with a smile. 'How lovely to see you, Megan! Joe told me you were coming home.'

'Well, I've got something to discuss with everybody tonight, but I don't want to tell Tina yet.'

'We'll all congregate in the big lounge after supper, and you can tell us then. Tina might not even be here – she might stay on at the little house with Mr. Willis.'

Megan went up to her room, while Vicky thought how good it would be to have Megan back. She had missed her.

Megan unpacked in her room and then went to prepare Tina's room so that she could sleep there that night with Tina, thinking how pleased Tina would be to see her. Then she lay down and dozed off.

Waking refreshed, she changed into her jeans and went downstairs to lie on the settee in the lounge, looking out at the mystical woods. Just before supper, Joe and Vicky and all the families came in to greet and embrace her.

'How are you all?' she asked. 'I've missed you. Please forgive me for being a blind fool. I really thought I loved Paul, but I've got something to tell you all about that after supper.'

'I've phoned Tina,' said Joe. 'I've told her there's a surprise for her at home, but she must stay there for supper. Mr. Willis said he'd stay and keep her company. So we can have that talk before she comes back, she won't be in until ten.'

After supper, the children were put to bed, and then, as many times before, they all gathered together in the lounge which faced the mystical woods.

'Now,' said Megan, her eyes filling. 'I told you I've been a fool. I know you didn't like Paul, Joe, and now I've got myself pregnant.'

'It seems that history has a habit of repeating itself in this house,' said Joe.

'I'm keeping it! I couldn't get rid of it. I'm sick of men now. If I meet the right one later on, all well and good, but I want to concentrate on my work, and Tina and my baby from now on.'

'Now there's something I've got to tell you. It's something Dr. Margaret and I discussed a long time ago.' No-one knew Dr. Joe's secret. 'Are you all ears everybody?'

'We are!' they all chanted.

'It's like this. Margaret and I wondered what it would be like when the big house was rather more empty, as it is now, with all the space here, all the spare rooms that are empty. What we want to do is to open a home for the young ones. Retarded children of any age. Dr. Margaret left a substantial amount of money in trust for this purpose. What do you think of the idea?'

'I think it's a wonderful idea,' said Megan. They all agreed and began to talk excitedly about what each of them could do to help.

'They'd come here up to any age,' said Joe. 'Now hands up, all of you who agree.' Every hand went up. They were all thrilled at the idea.

'I'll set the wheels in motion then,' said Joe, 'but, Megan, tell me truthfully how you feel about it, and Tina will have to be told.'

'Well,' said Megan. 'I think it's a wonderful idea and I want to help. I shall work here when it's all set up. When I have the baby, I may get someone to look after it – I must work you know. I feel that Tina will want to live in her own little house, for you'll have a lot of work to do in converting the place won't you?'

'Yes, I've already got the plans drawn up.'

'Well, I would like to live at the little house with Tina, and if Jane comes back she could be there too. I'd like to bring up my little son or daughter there. I feel drawn to it. I'd like to live there as soon as possible, if Tina agrees.'

'Of course she will. She won't want to be here with all the children around, and she'll need someone to be with her there.'

'That's all agreed then,' said Joe with great satisfaction. 'It's nearly ten o'clock, everybody!'

Suddenly the door burst open. 'What's going on?' demanded Tina. 'Why are you having a meeting without me?'

So they all sat down again and told Tina the whole story. When they had finished, she said, 'A long time ago, I would have hated the idea, but I feel absolutely marvellous about it. Megan, thank you for saying you'll live with me, for I've been yearning to live at my own little house for a long long time. Oh, when can we move in?'

'Let's do it straight away in a few days – then Joe can get on with his plans,' said Megan.

'That will be great! I've started my paintings. You wait until you see them!' Tina was beside herself with excitement.

Eventually they all trooped off to bed, tired out. Tina and Megan slept in the room together – 'Like old times!' said Tina. 'There's only Jane to come back now and everything will be complete.'

Megan and Tina moved into the little house, with all their things, during the fortnight's holiday that Megan had before she started work at Forest Dene.

'There's something I need to ask you,' said Megan to Tina. 'When Jane comes back, she'll share your room, but my little bedroom won't do for me and the baby. He or she will need a room – '

'I've thought of that,' said Tina. 'I'm having a summerhouse built outside that I can use as a studio. I'll prefer it, being outside – it's more inspirational somehow being in the open air. I'll have electricity put in so I can heat it in the winter. So you can have the other room for the baby.'

'Oh thank you, Tina!' Megan could hardly believe her good luck. How kind Tina was.

The two women were very happy indeed, and a few days later they spent their first night at the little house. They were well looked after by the lady that had worked for Jack. She cleaned and did the chores, and cooked them a meal once a day. Megan was now quite busy, having started her job at Forest Dene, and Tina went on with her painting.

Up at the big house, the work on the conversion was started.

By the time Megan came to have her baby, the work on the big house was almost complete. Already people were writing to ask if their children could come to the big house when it was finally opened. It was to be a boarding school as well, like Greenacres, but children would be taken from an early age, and would be able to remain there as long as they wished.

One night Dr. Joe answered a ring on the doorbell at the big house, and standing there, as large as life, was Jane. 'I've come back at last, Dr. Joe! I know Tina's at the little house, but I don't know where it is.'

'Come in! It's great to see you.'

'Gosh, isn't the place different?' she said as she walked through the door. Joe told her the whole story. 'How wonderful! I'd love to help.'

'I think you'll be needed to help Megan with the baby. She's going to live at the little house with you and Tina.'

'I'd like that. I always wanted a baby, but you know I had to be sterilised. Mummy didn't think I was fit to have one of my own.'

'Well, I think you'd be good with the baby now,' said Dr. Joe.

'Now, Jane, as it's so late, you'd better sleep here tonight.'

'Great,' said Jane. 'I won't be so tired in the morning, and I'll surprise them.'

Jane had had a terrible time. Her father had died a few weeks before and her brother had seen to everything. He'd insisted on moving in to his father's house, Jane's home, with his wife and family. To compensate for the loss of her home he had just given her some money in lieu of her half of the house, which their father had left between them, and had promised more later on. Jane wasn't worried about the money, for she knew she would be going to the big house, to Tina. She was just glad to get away.

Loving her father dearly, she had nevertheless been relieved when he died, not just for herself, but for his sake; he had been old and had suffered a great deal. Paralysed for years by a stroke, he had been so miserable.

She went to bed in Tina's old room that night, very happy, planning the next day when she would be able to see Tina and move herself into the little house.

The next morning Dr. Joe offered to drive her to Tina's. They put everything into Joe's car and set off, Jane on the edge of her seat with excitement. They drew up outside the little house and put the cases outside the door. Jane rang the bell and Megan answered, stunned to see her standing there.

'Hello, Jane! Are you here on holiday?'

'I'm here for good. Home at last. Oh Megan, I'm so happy. Where's Tina?'

'She's just getting up.'

Megan and Dr. Joe went into the sitting room and Megan made some tea, while Jane went up to see Tina. The next thing they knew there was a scream from upstairs and peals of laughter. Jane had crept up on Tina and leaped out at her. Tina's scream of shock had quickly turned to a squeal of delight, and then into laughing and crying at the same time.

'You wouldn't think, said Megan primly, 'that they'd grown up at all. They sound like a pair of schoolgirls.'

'They always will be young ones,' said Joe, smiling.

'Dr. Joe, do you think my baby will inherit from Tina?'

'Well you must be prepared for that, Megan.'

'I know.'

At that moment, a tornado came flying downstairs. First there was Barney, barking with delight, followed by Jane and Tina hurtling down behind him.

'At last, our lives are complete with Jane here,' said Tina delightedly. 'Everything will be all right now.'

The four of them started to chat, nineteen to the dozen. There was so much to catch up on, Jane's story of how she came to be there, Megan's baby, the conversion of the big house, Tina's painting and moving in to the little house. Eventually Joe had to leave. 'Well I must be going. I'll leave you to it. Don't forget, Tina, that you have an appointment with the optician tomorrow.'

Although Tina wore glasses for reading, she'd recently been having problems with her eyes at other times, with flashing lights and blurred vision. Dr. Joe knew that it was a side-effect from the drugs she had to take. The three women decided to all go and make a day of it. Megan offered to drive them.

After Dr. Joe had gone, Tina took Jane up to her studio and showed her some of the paintings. 'They're beautiful!' Jane was very impressed. 'Have you sold any yet?'

'No but I'm going to try soon. It's a surprise for the family.'

'That one of the woods is gorgeous! It's something like that one you showed me of Nancy's. Have you never thought of doing portraits?'

'Yes, but I don't feel it's the right time yet, and I can't see very well at the moment, with the flashing lights and the headaches. I'll have to wait a while. Anyway, we're going to be busy for a few days, aren't we?'

Chapter 26

That night Dr. Joe had a call from David in Canada. 'How nice to hear from you!'

'Hello, Joe, how is Tina? Has she got over Jack's death? I don't suppose she has yet, it will probably take a long time.'

'Well, surprisingly, she is a lot better,' said Dr. Joe. 'She has a great deal to occupy her these days. Jane's back, and Megan's come home, expecting a baby, but parted from her fiancé. She's going to live in Jack's little house with Jane and Tina.'

'Is everything ready at the big house? I mean for the home for the young ones.'

'Yes,' said Dr. Joe. 'There are some children arriving next week actually.'

'That's marvellous!'

'Well, everything's complete now – we've got staff arriving this weekend. It's been such hard work. I'm completely exhausted. I shall probably have a week's holiday soon when everything is going, but why did you ring, David?'

'There is a reason. I've been talking to my son Michael who lives on a farm in a very remote part. His son as you know has always been a bit retarded emotionally, and a little bit backward mentally. His parents feel that he's not going to get a chance in life on a farm in the wilds of Canada, where there's only a normal school within reach. Michael did try him at the local nursery school, but he had such a hard time, and was teased so dreadfully. There's no-one else like him. Anyway I told Michael, when he visited last week, all about the home you're opening. Now we all feel that he would be better off in a place like yours. The family doesn't want to leave Canada, but we'd like to send Gordon over to you.'

'Good God!' said Dr. Joe. 'Do you mean they would give him up?'

'Yes, for his own sake. He's so lonely, it's a dreadful life for him, and remember, Michael has four other children who are completely normal. Gordon can't relate to them at all. They feel if he was with children more like himself, he'd be a lot happier, in spite of not being with his own family. We've really talked it through and we've made up our minds. If you agree, I am to bring him over in a fortnight's time. Now, have you got room for him?'

'We can always find a space for a relative,' said Dr. Joe, 'but are you sure that's what you all want?'

'Yes.'

'Gordon, did you say his name was?'

'Yes.'

'That's amazing, for it was Gordon who was the first young one at the big house so many generations ago. He was a distant relative of yours a long way back. He met Nancy in the woods and there was a big romance – you remember the story.'

'Oh yes,' laughed David.

'Anyway,' said Dr. Joe, 'We'll have him and I promise you we'll look after him well.'

'Right, I'll see you in a fortnight.'

'That's settled then,' said Dr. Joe.

The next day Megan drove Tina and Jane into Guildford where Tina had to see the eye specialist at the hospital. After a battery of tests the doctor told her that her eyes were very weak. 'And you can't see properly to drive, unless you wear glasses. You should wear them all the time. If you go on not wearing them, you'll not only be unable to paint, but you could go blind through eye strain. You must wear them. I insist on it.'

'Well, I am supposed to be starting hormone replacement therapy, next week, I think,' said Tina, nearly in tears. 'Could that improve my eyes?'

'It might, but I don't think you'll ever be able to stop wearing glasses. I'll give you the prescription, and you must get it made up straight away.'

'All right.' She said no more to the specialist; she didn't want to humiliate herself in front of him, but once outside, she burst into tears.

'Everything's gone wrong again, Jane, Megan, I'm going to be so ugly if I've got to wear glasses all the time.'

'There are lots of really attractive frames around these days. Lots of young people wear them. Don't be upset,' said Megan.

'Nancy and Jennifer never had to,' she cried bitterly. 'Oh why couldn't I have looked like Nancy – she was so beautiful.'

'I thought you'd stopped worrying about those sort of things,' said Jane.

'Well I have. I suppose it doesn't matter. He was right. After all, some people are blind. I haven't really got anything to complain about.'

'Good girl,' said Megan. 'Now come on, let's get the choosing over with, and you'll have them soon and you can get painting again.

They went to the optician's and Tina chose some ordinary frames for her reading glasses, and then looked for something special for the ones she would wear all the time. She chose two frames obviously designed for young wearers, a pair in bright blue and one in ivory. Once she had them on, she was quite taken with them.

'They really suit you,' said Megan, encouraging her.

'They'll be ready in a few days,' the assistant told her, 'and we'll let you know when you can collect them.'

After all the fuss she made at the beginning, Tina was quite happy with the idea of wearing her glasses all the time. She felt they gave her a nice new personality.

They went home and then to the big house for supper. Tina told them all about her glasses and they reassured her that she was bound to look nice in them. 'It did bother me at first,' she said, 'but not now – I quite like myself in them.'

'Anyway, at least you'll be able to get on with your work again,' said Dr. Joe.

'As soon as I get them, I'm going to start something really good,' she promised.

When the glasses were ready, Tina was so pleased to find how much her sight improved. She felt she looked good in them as well, and everybody admired her.

The following week, Tina went, with Dr. Joe for moral support, to see the gynaecologist and explained that her periods were still giving her trouble and making her feel drained.

'Well, you're at the change of life, and it will get better. When I have the blood results, I'll be able to let you know about hormone replacement,' the doctor, a Miss James, explained. 'We have to be careful what we give you, due to your mental condition and your drugs.'

'You do understand, don't you, Tina?' Dr. Joe asked.

'Yes, I do,' said Tina, feeling glad that her doctor was a woman. She would have felt embarrassed in front of a man.

The following day, Tina went with Jane to see Mr. Willis and Eric at the vicarage for tea. Mr. Willis was amused and delighted to see Tina so childlike and fun-loving with Jane.

'You look very nice in your glasses, Tina,' said Eric. 'I expect you'll be getting back to your painting soon. When are you going to paint a portrait?'

'I don't know. I've got something in mind, but I'm not telling a soul.'

During the afternoon, Tina said to Mr. Willis how much she thought of him as an uncle, and Jane immediately asked if he would be her uncle too. Mr. Willis laughed and agreed, so the two girls would call him Uncle Stan from then on. 'I'd be honoured,' he said. 'I never had any nieces or nephews of my own.'

They left the vicarage that afternoon with a feeling that all was well with the world.

The following week Tina went again with Dr. Joe to see Miss James.

'Your blood-tests show that your hormone balance is all wrong, due to your medication and your illnesses, and you are approaching the menopause. You can't have an operation – it's out of the question – and really you don't need surgery so much as hormone treatment.' Miss James and Dr. Joe discussed it very carefully. Tina smoked; she took certain medication; had mental problems and brain damage. They would have to be very careful what she was given, as she was hyper-sensitive to all medication.

Miss James gave her the prescription and told her to report back if there were any problems. 'And see me in three months.'

When the trio went to the big house for supper that night, there was great excitement afoot. The children would begin to arrive the following week and David was coming with little Gordon the week after that. Fancy, another Gordon. Will there ever be another Nancy? thought Tina.

That night, back at the little house and in bed next to Jane, Tina lay and thought about her painting. She knew there was something she should paint now, but she wasn't sure what it was. She prayed for guidance that night, so that she could fulfil her cherished wish to produce at least one really great painting.

As often happened when she had a lot of excitement, Tina had strange and vivid dreams, and in the midst of them she saw her lady, Nancy, with the big blue eyes and the long blonde hair. It had been a long time since she had seen her. 'I promise you that you will soon feel stronger, Tina,' she said, 'and I want you to go on with your painting. I know you want to paint a portrait next, and I want you to paint one of me, not like the one hanging in the hall at the big house, but as I am now – as I appear to you. You will remember in the morning and be able to do a sketch and work from that. Look at pictures of me around the age of twenty.'

'Can I really do it? Will I be able to?'

'I promise you it will be the most wonderful painting and there's something else. It's going to start all over again.'

'What is? What do you mean, Nancy?'

'Us.' And with that, Nancy disappeared.

Tina remembered the vision when she woke up in the morning and puzzled over it. Jane noticed that she seemed preoccupied. After breakfast, she wandered into the studio and sketched the vision, complying with Nancy's wishes.

Megan could sense that Tina was worried or anxious about something. 'What is it, Tina? Something's on your mind,' she said.

'Oh Megan, I saw my lady, Nancy, last night and she said such strange things.'

'What happened?' Jane was curious.

'I can't keep it to myself. She told me she wanted me to do a portrait of her at the age of twenty.'

'But you won't know what she was like.' Megan, as practical and sensible as ever.

'She said she was appearing to me as she was when she was twenty, she looked beautiful, but she said there are pictures of her at the big house somewhere that I could use for reference. I sketched what I remembered.'

'That's wonderful!' said Megan. 'It could be a great success, but it will take a lot of hard work. Don't try to rush it. You must only do it when you feel inspired.'

'I'll remember that. There's so much going on at the moment, with your baby due, and Gordon arriving next week. Oh, and that reminds me, I must tell you this – it's so strange. Before she disappeared into the mist so suddenly this time, she said something about it starting all over again. When I asked her what she meant, she just said "us".'

'Well, I don't understand that,' declared Megan.

'It's a mystery,' said Jane.

'Well, we'll have to think that one out,' said Tina. 'Don't let's worry about it now.'

That night they all went to supper at the big house and Tina told everyone there about her vision. Dr. Joe thought long and hard about it when they had gone. Still, he had other things on his mind, and he knew that they would know when the time was right.

The following week went by in a whirl at the big house. They could accommodate fifty children at the big house. Geoffrey was the youngest, and Gordon coming from Canada the next week, would be company for him. The rest were older, from eight years old to thirty. They had all arrived by the end of that week. It was Dr. Margaret's wish that the house would be called simply the 'Home for the Young Ones', and Dr. Joe saw to it.

It took them a week to get the children settled in, but they were happy within days, for the place was so homely. In a day or two, the house was full of noise and cheerful high spirits. Tina came over to see it in full swing, and she loved to see everyone so happy. The inside of the building had been completely altered. There were dormitories with eight beds, two four-bedded rooms, and two single rooms. The attic, which had been unused for years, had been opened up and converted. Downstairs, the great hall, that had been used as a dance hall in Bert and Mabel's time, was used as a games hall. There were gardens and playing fields and soon there would be a swimming pool in the grounds. Joe was looking forward to that. The big lounge that looked over the mystical woods was now part of Dr. Joe's quarters. Tina was glad though to get back to the tranquillity of her little house.

Joe and Richard went to Heathrow to meet David and Gordon off the plane. Gordon was a very distant relative of those at the big house. He looked frightened, but Dr. Joe was struck by his likeness to pictures of Gordon, the young one who had started the story at the big house – he had the same wavy dark hair and dark eyes. He spoke his thoughts to Richard and David.

'I'll have to look at pictures,' said David. 'It's uncanny if it's true.'

Joe sat that night deep in thought after Gordon was settled in with Geoffrey. The two of them would be with the other young ones during the day, but Gordon was to live as part of the family, a companion for Geoffrey.

Tina, Megan and Jane came up that evening to see David and meet Gordon. Tina with her observant eyes, after having looked through so many pictures of Gordon and Nancy, immediately noticed the family resemblance. Tina looked out at the mystical woods and thought about the vision she had had. 'Us.' Gordon and Nancy, she thought. Gordon's here; perhaps there'll be a Nancy.

Tina went to the vicarage for tea the next day. She hadn't told anyone how she had connected the vision with the little boy who had arrived the day before. She explained it to Mr. Willis and Eric. 'It was strange for her to say "Us" and then this little boy arriving, looking exactly like Gordon, even called Gordon . . .'

'You're thinking of Megan's baby, aren't you?'

'Well, I can't help wondering.'

'Well, it's all in God's hands,' said Mr. Willis.

'You're right – anyway, I'll let you know what the child is like when I come next week. It should be born at any time.'

'Fine, but you are coming to tea on Sunday, like you promised aren't you?'

'Yes.'

She went home happy that night, and went straight to sleep next to Jane, thinking about the baby, and whether it would inherit the family condition. Megan was just looking forward to the birth of her child and had given no thought to that.

The following week, there was a special opening ceremony for the Home for the Young Ones. Megan still hadn't had her child and she was able to be there. Tina went, dressed up in her silk trouser suit, no longer worried what people thought, stronger and more self-assured than ever. Jane went with her, and Tina really felt that everything was right with the world at last. Dr. Joe was proudly there with Richard and their families, all the staff, people from Forest Dene. It was a huge party, with a buffet in the halls, cleared specially for the occasion, and outside, on that July day blessed with beautiful sunny weather. All the young ones were playing happily outside. It was a perfect day for the opening.

Tina was struck even more by Gordon's likeness to the other Gordon of long ago.

Eric came and declared the home open. 'And may there be more homes in the future,' he added. 'God bless you all, for what you've done here.' He called upon all the ones from the past who'd been associated with the big house, Dr. Rosemary, Dr. Margaret, Gordon and Nancy, Jennifer and everyone else and felt sure they were looking down at this present endeavour and blessing it. 'Be happy everyone, for you deserve to be.'

Dr. Joe and Dr. Richard stood up and replied to him, and Megan said a few words, then, the formalities over, everyone enjoyed the party, the music, the dancing, the laughter.

When it was all over and the children were tucked up in bed, Dr. Joe sat looking out at the mystical woods. Tina, Jane and Megan were still there, as was Dr. Richard. They were so happy that the home was open – it was the fulfilment of a dream.

While they were sitting there, Megan's labour pains started. 'I think you'd better get me to the hospital, Joe,' she said.

'Can I come with you?' asked Tina.

'No, dear, it's so late at night and you'll get over-tired.'

'I'll be all right, I promise. I'm much stronger on these tablets. Please, Dr. Joe?' she begged.

Dr. Joe agreed, and he drove the three of them, for Jane insisted on going with Tina, to the hospital.

Megan was settled into the ward and Tina and Jane sat with her through her labour, which lasted many hours. Tina and Jane began to get very tired as time went on and still the birth was some time away. Dr. Joe sent them both off into the waiting room for a nap and promised to call them as soon as there was any news.

They were given a cup of tea, and very quickly the two of them were fast asleep, exhausted after their long and exciting day.

While Tina was sleeping, a wonderful thing happened. Nancy and Jennifer appeared to her together.

'Nancy has something to tell you,' said Jennifer.

'The child that will be born to Megan will be like me. She will look like me.'

'Do you mean like reincarnation? I've heard about that,' said Tina.

'No. She's an individual soul but she will be like me. This child will want love, just like I did. Never be jealous of her, Tina. Help Megan with her, and let her always live in that little house. She won't want to mix with the others. She'll be a quiet reserved girl like I was. There's something else I want you to do for me. Finish my portrait. As soon as the baby is settled in at home, start the work. Use the photographs. Look at the ones of me as a baby, and when you see Megan's baby you will see the likeness.'

Jennifer said, 'Tina, we're so proud of you. You're doing very well. You'll get through the change of life and be much better.'

'Thank you. I'm so pleased you came, Jennifer. I've missed you so much at the big house. It's all different now.'

'I want you to tell the others how pleased we all are about what they've done at the big house,' said Nancy. 'Please tell them.'

'I will, and thank you both. I love you,' said Tina.

'And we love you,' they said, disappearing into the mist.

Tina awoke sometime later, remembering the vision and told Jane quickly. She was thrilled to be able to talk about it. 'Jane, it's so wonderful, isn't it?' Just then the nurse came in to tell them that Megan had given birth to a daughter. 'Come in and see her now.' They saw Megan looking exhausted, but so happy after the hard work of her labour. Tina looked at the baby girl, and saw a beautiful child, who looked completely normal, with blonde hair and big blue eyes, just like Nancy's.

'She's identical,' Tina said out loud.

'I know,' said Megan quietly. 'She's going to inherit, I just know it. She's beautiful, and whatever she's like I shall love her.'

'And so will we,' chanted Tina and Jane.

Megan had to sleep then and the baby was laid in a cot and cared for by the nurses. Dr. Joe went home, for a sleep, and Jane and Tina went with him.

'But we must see Megan tomorrow,' said Tina. 'It's important.'

'I know,' said Joe. 'I've seen it too.'

On the way home, Tina told him about the vision of Nancy and Jennifer.

'You're very blessed,' he commented. 'I'm amazed. Oh well, it's almost sure that she will be one of the young ones.'

'Yes, and she's to live at the little house,' said Tina. 'She won't want to live with so many children.'

'It'll do you both good. You'll take on a little more responsibility now.'

'Perhaps we can accept it now,' said Jane.

'I guess so,' Tina said doubtfully. Like Jennifer and Nancy, she never wanted to feel grown-up.

They got back home and fell into bed. Dr. Joe drove home and told everyone the news, including what Tina had seen and heard from Nancy and Jennifer. They all sat up, discussing it into the small hours.

Tina and Jane slept in late, and after lunch, Tina drove Jane to the hospital to see Megan. Dr. Joe was already there.

'I feel fine now,' said Megan. 'I've had a good sleep.'

Megan's little daughter was brought in and laid into her arms.

'What shall I call her?' she asked, looking round.

'You've to name her Nancy,' said Tina, without a second's hesitation. Then she told her all about the vision she'd had. Megan's eyes filled with tears; they all felt misty-eyed at the thought of another child like Nancy.

'Well, I shall love her all the more for that,' said Megan at last. 'She's beautiful.'

A few days later, Megan came home with her baby daughter, home to the little house. They had made the bedroom so sweet for the new baby, with a blue carpet, pretty, animal wallpaper and a dear little cot. There were toys everywhere, for when she could play with them. The baby was named Nancy Mary, exactly as Nancy had been called.

Tina saw Mr. Willis a little while afterwards and told him the whole story. He was amazed. 'It's uncanny! Eric and I would like to see little Nancy soon, we'll come round and have a cup of tea with you all, for we'll want to arrange the christening, won't we?'

'Yes. That would be great.'

'Isn't she beautiful?' said Eric when he saw baby Nancy, 'and just like the portrait! Even now you can see the likeness.'

The family at the big house thought the same when Megan took Nancy up for the first visit.

Tina felt her life was really complete at last. She was getting on with her painting, preparing to paint the portrait of Nancy. The rest of her work she had put away; she wanted to show it later on when she had finished the portrait.

Nancy was christened soon afterwards in the church in the village, another happy occasion for everyone at the two houses. Millie and Raymond were there and Millie was so proud to be at the christening of her great-grandchild, yet her feelings were mingled with regret that Nancy would have problems in her life, like all the young ones.

Tina and Jane were godmothers to the little girl, and Dr. Richard was the godfather. Megan was astonished and delighted that Tina volunteered for this duty. It was such a lovely occasion, and everyone saw how beautiful she was. 'Little angel' was on many people's lips when they saw her.

Life established a new routine at the little house. Tina carried on painting and Jane helped Megan with baby Nancy while she went back to work. From the start Nancy was a sweet-natured child, and everyone loved her.

The home for the young ones went from success to success. Christmas that year, shared with all of them, was a joyous occasion. There was a party, and dancing, as of old, and the house resounded with the sound of warmth and laughter. When it came to opening the presents on Christmas day, there were so many of them, they sat all along the hall, up the stairs – the place was filled to overflowing.

Chapter 27

It was Tina's fiftieth birthday and she was having a party to celebrate being 'half a century old' as she put it. She was much better. The hormone treatment had really helped, and she was nearly through the menopause now. Her moods had improved, and she was no longer so irritable, and she adored little Nancy. Now three and a half, it had been verified that Nancy had inherited the condition that ran in the family. She was one of the young ones – emotionally immature. She definitely had Nancy's looks, her blonde curly hair and beautiful big blue eyes. Everyone loved her, for she was such a sweet-natured girl.

Megan planned that Nancy would go to school at the big house when she was older, but she did not want her to stay there. She knew intuitively that Nancy would need the peace and quiet of their little home for a long time yet.

Tina had been painting various things during the last three years, but secretly she had been working on the portrait, using her big new studio, out in the garden. She had planned to have it ready to show on her fiftieth birthday. It was going up to the big house.

They all trooped up to the big house for the occasion.

'Well, I may be fifty today, but I still feel young,' announced Tina. They had a wonderful time on Tina's birthday, followed by Christmas celebrations. There were two more additions to the family – Joanne had had another daughter, Sheila, and a son had been born to Ruth, William Richard. The future of the big house seemed pretty secure now. The home for the young ones was successful, as Nancy had predicted.

Tina dressed up for the party, and she looked beautiful that day – hardly more than about thirty-five years old. There was a radiance about her as she appeared downstairs in her long blue dress. Drinking lemonade from a champagne glass with Jane, Tina felt so happy with all the family around her, as they all toasted her. Even Mr. Willis was there, still sprightly at just turned eighty, to wish her well. Eric and his wife joined them, and Millie and Raymond had been brought by a friend for Christmas. The house was full up; with people and with happiness.

'Will you all come with me?' she asked, in the midst of the toasting. Curiously they followed her to a little room just inside the hall which was used as an office and waiting room. There was the portrait of Nancy that Tina had been working on for the last three years. She was so gifted, and had caught Nancy's expression of innocence to perfection. The beauty of it took everyone's breath away. They all gasped.

'Tina, you've shown us your true gift at last,' said Dr. Joe. 'You are an artist, my girl.'

'I'm a real artist!'

'You could sell it for such a lot of money,' said Millie.

'Sell it? I don't know.'

'Prints could be made of it,' said Dr. Joe, 'but this portrait will never be sold. It's Tina's work. Look at all the others as well! There's so many of them, and, Tina, you've framed them all.'

'I shall perhaps sell some of those,' said Tina, 'and I'll probably hang up one or two of my favourites. Those two little fairy ones are for little Nancy.'

'Well, you've really achieved something!' said Millie. 'I'm so proud of you.' Millie burst into tears and hugged her daughter.

At last, after all these years, Millie and Tina felt close to one another. Tina's eyes filled with tears. She felt so emotional suddenly, as she looked round at all those faces she knew so well and loved.

'You've amazed me – all of us,' said Dr. Joe. 'I'm proud of you, really proud of you.'

'Thank you.' Tina choked on the words, she was so happy.

'If we make prints of the portrait and sell them, you might become well-known. Do you think you could stand it?'

'I don't know.'

'Where will you hang the portrait, Tina?' asked Joe.

'I'd like to hang it here, for it is of Nancy as I see her in the visions. It's my gift to you all – you've done so much for me over the years.'

The love Tina had put into the portrait showed and it was this that made it so attractive. Tina was so glad she had achieved something and given her family a reason to be proud of her.

That was the happiest birthday ever for Tina, and Christmas was just as joyful. 'Happy Christmas to you all,' said Dr. Joe, when everyone was seated around the trees.

They all exchanged Christmas greetings and then a little voice piped out: 'Happy Christmas, everyone, Happy Christmas, Mummy, and Tina and everyone. I love you all.' It was little Nancy.

'Happy Christmas to you and everyone,' replied Tina. 'And may the big house go on and on, for it was planned this way. We all know that.'

On that Christmas day, each person in the big house felt that their lives couldn't get any better. They were bound to have their ups and downs in the future, they knew that, but they were conscious of a new beginning for all of them.

Later, prints were made from the portrait of Nancy and offered for sale. They sold in great quantities and she became well-known as an artist. What an achievement! Tina had found her vocation at last. All was well at the big house and the little house.

Epilogue

Twenty years later a beautiful young girl walked out of the little house with her little corgi dog, Trixie, for a walk in the woods. She carried a bottle of lemonade with her and went down the lane at the side of the house towards the woods. Nancy, with her long blonde hair and big blue eyes, strolled around in the woods until she found a tree to lean against. She sat down, day-dreaming, remembering a dream she had about a young boy with dark hair and brown eyes, wishing she could meet a boy like that.

Feeling warm and drowsy on that summer's day with the sun speckling the trees in the mystical woods, she leant her head against the tree, and fell asleep, her little dog beside her.

At the big house a young boy walked through the French windows and across the lawn with his dog. The warm balmy weather had beckoned him out for a walk. He was drawn as if by magic to the woods; he didn't know why, he just knew he had to go there.

Once there, he wandered around, enjoying the atmosphere, until Toby his dog started to bark. A little corgi ran up to him. The two dogs made friends at once, playing in and out of the trees. Gordon looked around for the owner of the dog. He had dreamed many times of a beautiful girl, with long blonde hair and beautiful big blue eyes. He walked through the trees, and then following the corgi, who seemed to want to show him something, he came upon Nancy, fast asleep by the big tree, her blonde hair gleaming palely in the sunlight. He looked down at her, astounded. It was the girl in his dreams, surely. For a time he could do nothing but gaze at her sleeping form.

Nancy stirred, vaguely aware of someone's presence. She opened her eyes, looking wide-eyed and frightened. He smiled at her and introduced himself.

'I'm Gordon. What's your name?'
'My name's Nancy,' she said slowly.
'You're just like the girl in my dreams, I can't believe it.'
'And you're just like the boy in my dreams,' said Nancy.
'How wonderful! Let's be friends at once, shall we?'
'Yes.'
Gordon took her hand and helped her up.
They walked in the woods for a while, and then they sat, drinking lemonade, talking, as if they'd known each other for years.
'I've never been so happy in my life,' said Nancy.
'Nor have I. I'm sure I'm going to fall in love with you.'
'And I feel the same,' said Nancy shyly. 'Oh Gordon, it's wonderful that we've met here. I've seen you before at the big house, but I didn't realise who you were.'
'I felt I had to come here today. I couldn't help myself.'
'So did I.'
They looked into each other's eyes and each knew that they had met the one they loved.
It had started all over again. Gordon and Nancy had met and fallen in love under the big tree in the mystical woods.